A Stone of the Heart

"Towers above the mystery category as AN ELOQUENT, COMPELLING NOVEL . . . a tragic drama involving many characters, each so skillfully realized that one virtually sees and hears them in this extraordinary novel . . ." – PUBLISHERS WEEKLY

"A MASTERFULLY CRAFTED WORK of plot, atmosphere and especially characterization . . . Minogue, thoughtful, clear-eyed and perhaps too sensitive . . . is a full-blooded character built for the long haul of a series . . ." – MACLEAN'S

Unholy Ground

"RIVETING . . . The suspense builds to barely bearable intensity . . . crackles with pungent Irish idiom and its vignettes of the country's everyday life." – TORONTO STAR

"Excellent Sergeant Matt Minogue . . . MARVELLOUS DIALOGUE, as nearly surreal as a Magritte postcard the sergeant likes, and a twisting treacherous tale." – SUNDAY TIMES

Kaddish in Dublin

"MATT MINOGUE, THE MAGNETIC CENTRE OF THIS SUPERB SERIES . . . and Brady's tone of battered lyricism are the music which keep drawing us back to this haunting series." – NEW YORK TIMES

"Culchie Colombo with a liberal and urbane heart . . . like all the best detective stories it casts its net widely over its setting . . . [Minogue is] a character who should run and run." – IRISH TIMES

All Souls

"As lyrical and elegantly styled as the last three . . . A FIRST-RATE STORY WITH MARVELLOUS CHARACTERS." – GLOBE AND MAIL

"Nothing gets in the way of pace, narrative thrust or intricate story-telling." – IRISH TIMES

"A KNOCKOUT." – KIRKUS REVIEWS

A Carra King GLOBE AND MAIL TOP 100

"DENSE AND MULTILAYERED . . . a treasure of a crime novel." – TORONTO STAR

"Brady has a great eye for the telling detail . . . and a lovely slow pace of storytelling. There's much talk and thought . . . you can't read this book at warp speed. Instead, save it to savour." – GLOBE AND MAIL

Wonderland GLOBE AND MAIL TOP 100

"IF THERE ARE AUTHORS BETTER THAN JOHN BRADY at chronicling the events of modern Ireland, I HAVEN'T YET READ THEM . . . Brady's best so far." – GLOBE AND MAIL

"ANOTHER SUPERB NOVEL BY A WRITER OF INTERNATIONAL STATURE." – TORONTO STAR

"BRADY'S BEST: informed, subtle and intelligent, with Minogue revealing a hitherto unseen depth of soul, humour and emotion." – THE TIMES UK

Islandbridge GLOBE AND MAIL TOP 100

"PARTICULARLY POWERFUL STUFF . . . GENIUS." – TORONTO STAR

"Sheer poetry to the ear." – NEW BRUNSWICK TELEGRAPH JOURNAL

"BRADY TAKES HIS TALENT TO NEW HEIGHTS . . . MUST READING." – GLOBE AND MAIL

POACHER'S ROAD

AN INSPEKTOR KIMMEL NOVEL

JOHN BRADY

POACHER'S ROAD

AN INSPEKTOR KIMMEL NOVEL

McArthur & Company
Toronto

First published in Canada in 2006 by
McArthur & Company
322 King St., West, Suite 402
Toronto, Ontario
M5V 1J2
www.mcarthur-co.com

Copyright © 2006 John Brady

Library and Archives Canada Cataloguing in Publication

Brady, John, 1955-
Poacher's Road : an Inspector Kimmel novel / John Brady.

ISBN 1-55278-565-3

I. Title.

PS8553.R245P63 2006   C813'.54   C2005-907851-0

Design and composition by *Mad Dog Design Connection Inc.*
Printed in Canada by *Webcom*

The publisher would like to acknowledge the financial support of the
Government of Canada through the Book Publishing Development Program,
The Canada Council for the Arts, and the Ontario Government of Ontario
through the Ontario Media Development Corporation Ontario Book
Initiative.

10 9 8 7 6 5 4 3 2 1

For Hanna, with love

And in memory of Chris and Mary Brady,
Josef Zniva,
and Michael Crowe.

What thou lovest well remains
The rest is dross
What thou lovest well shall not be reft from thee
What thou lovest best is thy true heritage.

Canto 81
EZRA POUND

DER WILDERER

(The Poacher)

Peter Rossegger, from unpublished journal entries for
Geschichten aus der Steiermark (Tales from Styria), 1871

St. Kristoff is approached by minor roads. It was on one of
those roads little wider than a cow-path, one of the many byroads
known locally as a Wildererweg or poacher's path, that I came
down off the mountains one evening many years ago. It being late,
I beheld the last remnants of the dying sunset over the crags and
forests above the village as the darkness descended, but not
before I perceived the splendid views of an innumerable multitude
of hills to the southeast.

It is a farming village and its people retire early. But as I
plodded up one of the narrow lanes that leads to its church, I heard
voices within, and soon the tones of an organ. The sound of that
instrument has from childhood filled me with a strange mixture of
mirth and foreboding, and that night this sensation descended
upon me again as though the decades of living in our cities had
vanished, and I was a child again, listening.

It was expertly played, and the old hymns that had sounded
here for centuries floated out on the night air to me. Soon they
were joined by voices, both men's and women's, and I passed a
strange and not unhappy half-hour. Around me was the sweet

scent of woodsmoke from houses unseen, and the smell of the earth with its autumnal exhalations. I fell into a reverie, where the events of the long day arranged themselves alongside tender thoughts of my wife and little ones awaiting me back in Vienna. Such were the exertions of the day in these mountains as wild and remote as any on the continent, that in a matter of minutes I passed from reverie to sleep there on the grassy bank below the church.

It was with a violent fright that I awoke not long after, and in the manner of a primitive ancestor awakening in terror at the cave-mouth where he stood guard over his clan, I was on my feet before being quite awake. I was not alone, and for several of the longest moments of my life I remained in that world of the Grimms where the woods are ever deep, and they harbour fantastic beings. In front of me was a monster, I thought, with huge shoulders and horns askew. Is this even the great Wotan, I wondered, that ravening god that has been with us Germanic folk since we became a people.

The monster spoke.

"Good night," it said, in an accent that would be studied amongst my colleagues at the University as though its owner had descended from another planet.

"Good night," I believe I replied.

The dark shape of the monster began to yield some form. Soon I saw that this was one of my own, a human, a hunter, who had brought in a young deer on his shoulders. But it came to me that he was in all likelihood less a hunter than he was a poacher. It is long a custom here for those facing hardship to enter the forest and take a deer without the permit of any of the local nobility or the rich who own the rights here. This, along with the custom of mountain treks that last for days and even weeks by men who must feed their families, walks that neither know nor respect the lines drawn on the bright maps our little ones learn in their schoolrooms.

"You are a hunter," I offered then.

To this he made no reply or gesture.

"I was passing the church and heard the music," I said. "I must have dozed off."

At this, the monster nodded and shifted his load. I saw that he had a rifle on his back. I began to wonder, and then to marvel, at how this man could have hefted this not inconsiderable load home from the forest.

"You are a traveller," he said.

"That I am."

"Everyone is a traveller," he said. "On God's earth."

I thought to ask him what he might mean by this but something in this man's demeanour, or perhaps his way of speaking, told me that would be an impertinence.

"You are late in from the woods," I said instead.

"That's how it is," he said. "One must wait for the right time."

Seeing that the monster was but a man, and that he was in all likelihood a villager here, I was emboldened to try a little mischief.

"You are not afraid of the spirits in the forest?"

"The spirits?" he said after several moments. "Which would they be?"

"The ones we hear of, ones in the old tales. Perhaps you don't believe in them then?"

"That hardly matters," he said after a moment. "They are there all the same."

This silenced me, and to this day, I do not know why his

sparing words should have had such an effect. I knew immediately that he was not being mischievous with his words, and it galled me that I had no words to address him further on this, so strange was his pronouncement.

Perhaps it was the air of the mountains, or the long day's hiking in the woods and over moors and valleys, but the words did not come. He then asked me if I were looking for a place that I might have an evening meal. I was indeed, I told him, and a simple Gasthaus where I could spend the night. He directed me to one, and we then parted.

I retired that evening after a hearty meal, full sure that my sleep that evening would be the soundest sleep possible, and perhaps the only dreams would be those of the skies and trees, and the bright sun that had guided me all day. Instead I passed several hours pondering our meeting, this hunter and I, and I resolved to tell my colleagues of this man who seemed to live a life no different than one of centuries past. How is it possible, I wondered, that a man in the age of telegraphs and trains can believe as he did?

We all have our trove of stories, do we not, of bijou events and 'characters' that we collect and later relate, to show the rich variety of our world and society? The retelling so often makes our pleasure keener, we believe, especially if they raise a smile or a laugh, and such tales as we collect and retail serve to make us more sociable and to enhance our own public selves while they make those occasions more entertaining.

But now, all these years later, I cannot conceal from others how I have tired of those coffeehouses and dinners, those lectures and conferences. For all the learning of my colleagues and friends,

I find my thoughts returning to that small village of St. Kristoff, high up on that hill, with the forest around it, so remote from the bustle of life here. I returned to the village several times over the years, and it had altered not a whit. Yet I have never been visited by any desire to inquire for my hunter there. For a time, I half-believed that I had not met him at all, but that he had come out of my dream. I still remain undecided on the matter.

I told no one of my meeting that evening so long ago, but committed it here to this journal instead, to consider its meaning yet again.

ONE

THE DAY BEFORE THE TWO BODIES TURNED UP IN THE WOODS, Felix Kimmel was staring at the grasses by the side of a road. This klamm, as Styrians call these narrow mountain roads, had all the steep grades and sharp turns that visitors remember long after their travels in this southern province of Austria. Even sophisticates from Vienna who come for the Apfelfest and its potent ciders soon stop comparing the endless rows of hills and green mountains here to the Alps, or to their own summer escape of Semmering, with its picturesque views and cool heights, and its sudden, but few, green valleys.

Felix had spotted a bird hopping about amongst the spring growth. It had had a worm in its beak, and he was waiting for it to hop into view again. Even thinking about this bird was better than listening to his sister Lisi, in whose car he sat now, hungover and listless. Too many of her stray, random thoughts had been spoken aloud. She'd been nervous, he understood, and sad. Talk was her way of dealing with it. But there was nothing to be done about the day really, just to get it over with.

He looked up again at the lumber truck that had blocked the road ahead. It was reversing laboriously from a muddy road that led into the woods. The driver had misjudged a metre of ground by one of the wheels. The soil here was still saturated, and for several minutes now he had been gingerly edging the vehicle out onto the roadway. He'd let the truck back a few metres in a controlled roll, and try to coax it back up again. His eyes stayed locked on the rim of mud that was pushed up higher by the rear wheel.

"You'd think the idiot would know," Lisi said.

"I suppose."

"You suppose? Didn't you recognize him right away?"

"He looked familiar."

"Really," she said. "Did you just wash everything out of your head last night, or have you really forgotten the people here? So soon?"

He said nothing.

"Bad enough that they are going to destroy the forest, but it has to be that idiot Maier doing it. Manfred . . . ?"

"Ah, him. Freddie."

"It's not his fault he's got that face. But he was dumb. Now he drives a Beemer, a new one. Maybe you'll catch him speeding in it. Wouldn't that be funny?"

"Natürlich."

"Well," Lisi said after several moments, "I'm not superstitious. But you'd wonder. Wouldn't you?"

Felix nodded.

He let his gaze up the hill. Screened by the growth of conifers above the grassy verge was the hilltop village of St. Kristoff am Offenegg. It was well above them yet, with its ancient, baroque church and graveyard perched tightly on the hilltop, and a clutch of houses huddled just below. There were long views from the steps of the church, Felix knew, across the valleys and hills to the south, toward Slovenia. He and Lisi had 20 minutes to reach the village, and that church, where the anniversary service for Felix's father, also a Gendarme in the Austrian police, was due to begin.

Maybe that bird knew something, Felix thought. But it had gone, with its prize. He had listed bird watching on his application to join the Gendarmerie. It had been his own joke, the only sly response he could come up with that particular day to his mother's gentle, persistent nagging. She had brought the application form to him one evening a few weeks after he had come back from his trip. She had photocopies ready: birth, driver's licence, and, of course, the sorry record of his undergraduate academics up until he had elected not to continue after second year.

His mother had also prepared the ground, using the contacts she had kept up with the friends and colleagues of her late husband in the Gendarmerie. That was her way, and it worked. Today it would work again, of course. For the second year, it was now the expected duty of Felix Kimmel Junior – Felix the Second – to take care of his grandfather Kimmel for the memorial service, and to manage the old goat. It meant sitting next to him at the service without appearing too solicitous. It also meant that Felix should be a buffer between his mother's family and what was left of his father's.

"Is Opa Kimmel . . . ?" he began, but soon lost the thread of how he could phrase his question.

Lisi gave him a knowing look.

"Is he coming to the restaurant afterwards?" she asked. "Is that it?"

"Exactly."

"Relax," she said. "You know how he is. That'll never change."

It took the lumber truck another minute to make it out onto the road and to begin its trip down to the mill in Weiz. Through the open window of his sister's Opel, Felix heard the crunch and the hiss of brakes as Maier prepared for the trip down. He gave a big wave as he passed. All of that family had that same lantern jaw, Felix remembered now, the jutting chin of the underbiter.

Lisi said something under her breath, but she managed a smile and a half-hearted wave to Maier. She let go of the handbrake, revved as she let the clutch in, and resumed the slow, winding climb up toward the village. There awaiting them would be their extended family, neighbours from the old house, and friends of their father.

Felix kept his window open. His eyes still hurt when he moved them. He rubbed at them but stopped when he heard a strange ticking from them.

"Ironic anyway," Lisi said.

He looked over at her. She was seven years older, but to Felix she seemed middle-aged already, this 29-year-old teacher. The famous 29.

"The lumber truck," he repeated. "I get it. Ironic, yes."

Could she just not talk, for a minute anyway? He turned back toward the patches of view across the valley that were beginning to appear more and more between the trees. He wanted to believe it was the altitude making this hangover worse. He stared at a gap, and hoped that would beat back the images that were now coming to his mind.

It was the second year now since Felix Kimmel Senior had been killed in a collision with a lumber truck on the Weizklamm. His duties had been those of Abteilungsinspektor, department chief inspector, in the Judenburg district. In the tribute speech at his funeral it was pointed out that he had been looking in on his aged father, Peter, a widower who lived alone up here. Speed had been a factor, as the phrase went.

But Felix had had a glimpse of a Scene photo of his father's Audi. It had been during a class exercise at the Gendarmerieschule on how to use EKIS, the police database. Felix Senior's car had been accordioned and pulverized by its long fall down off the road. Felix had also learned about the booze in the car.

His mother had been angry when he'd told her about it, a rare thing indeed between them. Why was it necessary to dig into that? Whom would it help, to know this? Her anger quickly had turned on what worried her now – her very own son. Could he not just give this a try? A couple of years only? Couldn't he see that joining up now was perfect timing? The Interior Ministry was sticking to its plan to do the unthinkable, to amalgamate the Gendarmerie and the Polizei. Things would really be opening up. They would be looking for people who had a few years of Uni. The old days were gone, forever. He could even finish his degree at night, yes!

Guilt works, mother guilt best of all. Felix had finished his course, passed his Dienstprüfung exam, and received his posting. He did not ask how or why he got a posting to Stefansdorf, a sleepy village near enough to Graz that he could hold on to his social life.

But his friendships from Uni had become awkward acquaintances, and rare phone calls. Seven months travelling from beaches in Spain to a squat in Copenhagen had not really settled him much. Giuliana had remained constant, however, but lately there had been something in the air there too. He did not want to think about that.

The woods ended. Ahead of them the narrow, winding ribbon of road twisted around another hairpin before its final run into the village.

"You won't want to hear this," said Lisi, "but I'll say it anyway. You look good in that uniform."

She glanced over after he made no reply.

"You lost your brain in some pub, some stübe, the night before Dad's memorial?"

"It wasn't that much," he said. "Maybe it was an unconscious thing anyway."

"Don't try that Freudian crap on me. I've read it, you know."

She left the car in second now. He began to think, dimly, if anyone had studied the effects of high mountain air on a hangover. Frische luft, his oma – his mother's mother – called it. Frische luft macht frisches herz! Fresh air makes the heart anew!

"Well, how's Giuli then."

This was conciliatory, he knew, but still he felt like asking her how her boyfriend Karl was, or Superbore, as he called him. Still as exciting as cold Baïschel? The thought of that sliced meat lying cold in its greasy sauce made his mouth taste chalky and sour.

"She's fine."

A lie, he wondered: a white lie? Maybe it was a hope, more than a statement of fact. No: she was fine. Truly. She'd get over it. "It" was this thing that neither of them wanted to put a name on. If it had a name, it might be "commitment" or something like that. "The future," maybe – "our future," to be precise.

"It was nice of her to come to the blessing."

For a moment, Felix did not understand.

"She knows a lot about that stuff," said Lisi. "I didn't realize."

"Religion?"

"Not religion exactly: taferls and things."

Felix got it now. His sister meant the roadside monument to his father. It was a hand-carved one of Jesus on the cross, paid for by the Association. A local carpenter had made it, not "an artist." As with so many other of these traditional shrines and statues, it stood by the roadside where the accident had happened.

"So tell me about your boys' night out. Where do cops go to unwind?"

"There's no one at the post I want to unwind with. It was Viktor and a few guys."

She grasped the wheel with both hands and turned to him.

"Watch the road, will you," he said.

"'Viktor and a few guys'? Jesus, Felix."

"I don't see them that often anymore."

He steeled himself for her to say: since you dropped out, and they didn't.

"We all know the Gendarmerie are more 'relaxed' than the Polizei."

She had spoken in the slow tone of a teacher delivering a gem of wisdom. "But associating with Viktor and those other profession-al students? Really."

"Who says I can't?"

She laughed a teacher's laugh.

"Oh I get it," she said. "You're undercover – infiltrating them now. Good work."

He glanced over and saw that her mouth was set to fire anoth-er comment his way. Instead, her attention was taken by an older man standing next to a Skoda parked half in the ditch. He was unloading fence wire from a trailer.

She waved and he smiled.

"You know everybody still," said Felix.

"He was a friend of Dad's."

Who wasn't, Felix almost said. Even the poor truck driver that Felix Senior had clipped, sending himself down the gorge in the Weizklamm, battering and flattening it with every crunching slam, end over end, until it stopped a hundred-odd metres . . .

"Are you going to throw up?"

"It's okay," he said.

He could feel her disapproval like a mantle of cold air over him. He tried harder to keep the images from returning. The driver, yes: a hulking, big, wall-eyed guy, full of regret and awkwardness and apology, had come to the funeral, Felix remembered, and had shed tears. Apparently he'd met Felix Senior before, and this had made him feel even worse.

"Anyway," she said, and gave his uniform a quick once-over. "You'll make a fine impression at the service. Really. I'm not being sarcastic. I mean it."

He followed the line of the wall that enclosed the church and graveyard. The grounds within had risen over the centuries, and the wall had been raised to match it as though it were a dam, or a dike, in rising waters. When Giuliana had visited the village first and walked down the lane here, it had freaked her out to be walking at the same height as the coffins on the far side of the wall.

"I think I see Mom's car," Lisi said.

Felix spotted the yellow Polo parked near Gasthaus Ederer. There were a half-dozen others there too. He didn't see any Gendarmerie patrol cars. This was good.

Lisi looked at her watch, and she let the car down the narrow gasse, the lane that led to the side of the church. She turned the wheel sharply for an unexpected space next to a Nissan. Felix tried to ignore the sudden listing in his intestines. To distract himself while she straightened the car out, he looked out at a slice of view by the end of the wall. It was one of so many walls, and lanes, and views of distant mountains and valleys, that he'd known so well in this village where he'd grown up. It had also been a place he could-n't wait to get out of, and go to the city.

"Damn," she said, and rolled her eyes. "Look: it's Opa's car, I think. We're late."

"He still drives?"

"It looks like his ancient heap," she said.

They stepped out. Felix tugged at his uniform and looked at the cars jammed into the confines of the lanes.

"No tellerkappe, Inspektor?"

Felix knew earlier on that he had left the traditional Gendarmerie duty cap in his own car, his mother's old Polo, that was going to be fixed by this evening. The getaway car: it had to be ready and reliable for his and Giuliana's week down in Italy – the big escape, they'd taken to calling it.

As for the Inspektor bit, he let himself believe that Lisi hadn't meant it sarcastically. It was the correct term, of course, but he'd never get used to it. It just sounded too self-important. He preferred the old names: Gendarme, or Grenzgendarme, the term for a probationary policeman in this old rural Austrian police.

And then Felix felt the first relief from his crushing hangover – at the thought of their week ahead. It would be his first break for nearly a year. He still wasn't sure how he had managed to stick it out in Gendarmerieschule.

"No," he said. He even managed a smile for his elder sister. "Forgot it."

Somebody was playing the church organ, quiet and slow. It was likely his mother would cry. A dignified crier, he would have to say of her. If he had to sing, he'd need a week to get over what it'd do to the tender remainders of his brain not ruined with the hangover.

He took a deep breath and looked over the valley below. Some of the early-morning haze still clung to the deeper valleys far off. It was probably a 50-kilometre view he had to the south. How come he didn't know exactly, and he a native son? And there were more still behind that light, faded horizon. Das grune Herz von Öesterreich: The Green Heart of Austria.

Something moved around in his guts again. He should try to walk off a bit before going in the churchyard gates. Down by the war memorials with their ever fresh bouquets and meticulous plantings, where there always seemed to be at least one candle lit, his child's eyes had run along the names, the families of the soldiers, ever since he could remember.

Could he? Yes: Seiser family, six men, or boys, in two wars. Oberhummers, five, two in WWI. The Seidls, his father's neighbours when he was growing up, were next. They had two sons killed. One had not returned from the Eastern Front. He tried to figure out how old one would be were he alive today.

"Come on," Lisi called out.

He let his gaze run up the road, saw the beginning of the track where Maier had nearly mired his truck. The put-put of a tractor brought him back. Coming down the laneway toward him was a Kubota, driven by an old man. The face was ruddy, nearly leather, and the battered-looking traditional green jacket, the lodenjanker.

"Grüss Gött!"

"Servus," Felix called after him. In from the high meadows near the village, he guessed.

Lisi held out peppermints.

"Believe me," she said. "You need these. Take a lot."

His heart suddenly ached.

"You're bothered," she said. "That's why you were out last night. I know."

He wanted to argue but it would be useless. He wondered if it would always be this way. She didn't mean to smother, anymore than their mother did. It just ran in the family. Like wooden legs, his Opa Nagl might say.

The thought of his irreverent grandfather brought him some relief from the gloom now pressing down on him. The same Opa Nagl had a saying for everything, from genetics to stupidity. He held the farm still, even though it was only admitted recently that Theo, the eldest, would not return to farm at all. Opa Nagl had been philosophical: well, why would a tool-and-die man want to come back to farming? It had been leased out the next year.

Felix took two mints and walked with Lisi to the gate, his mind still on his grandfather. A short man, was Opa Nagl, and a huber bauer through and through, a real farmer, a countryman forever. Too young himself to be directly mauled by the war, he was almost proud to still remember some Russian curse-words he had picked up from playing with the occupiers who'd taken over here. Opa Nagl had farmed ambitiously, got drunk several times a year, and voted Sozi. This was even if he despised a leader of the same Social Democratic Party. He had a saying to paper over any inconsistency. How many times had Felix heard over the years from Opa Nagl that he'd prefer to be wrong with the Sozis than right with the brown-shirt bastards in the Freedom Party?

As funny as his opa could be, he was no pushover, however. Felix still remembered how Opa Nagl got his message across years ago. It had been when Felix had snuck through the yard and then up the pastures to throw clods of earth at the cows. The bells had been heard back at the farm. When he returned, there was Opa holding out a brush. It had been a monstrous brush, twice the size of the nine-year-old hellion Felix. Cleaning the farmyard – something Felix had never seen done before, and never again – had taken until abendessen.

"Der kleine Kimmel nicht aus Himmel," Opa had muttered later, with a hint of a mischief flickering around his mouth. The Kimmels didn't arrive from the heavens.

"I miss Dad," Lisi said, and she dabbed at her eyes. "I have to say it."

Felix put his arm around her shoulder.

"Me too," he said, and wondered.

She blew her nose and composed herself. Then she took an envelope from her pocket. She handed it to Felix.

"I want them back," she said. "Scan them, if you want. They're from Uncle Leo. He found them."

Felix took out a few. Here was Dad hoisting him into the air by the water in Stubensee. A big hairy chest – a Turk, Felix's mother used to joke. There might have been some truth to it, due to a half-acknowledged illegitimacy back a hundred years or so. And there was the chain he always wore, that chain from his army days. His dad's get-togethers with his former comrades from the battalion used to be riotous, but they'd toned down in recent years. Felix's mother had been able to prevail on him to take her to a hotel on one of those weekends.

One year it had been just outside Klagenfurt, in the adjoining province, up in the mountains where his battalion had done many of its exercises. Dodl Korps, he called it – the idiot corps, after some of the scrapes and blundering that several well-liked thick heads had led them into. There had been huntin' and shootin' reunions on the high plateaus over Sommersalm. One, a decade or more ago, result-ed in three of the Dodl Korps, podgy middle-aged characters now to a man, being brought to hospital after the VW jeep one of them had painstakingly rebuilt had flipped. "On manoeuvres" his father had called it. Felix remembered him laughing every day for a week at the snapshots.

"Aber scheisse," said Lisi, slowing. "Look who."

Sure enough, here was Edelbacher. A tall man whose nickname had been Elli, for Elephant, Gendarmerie Major Richard Edelbacher always had some of the ungulate about him. This was a semi-cruel fate for a man who took good care of himself. He was an assiduous, if slowing, sportsman still. He managed a kid's soccer team in Voitsberg, the town where he worked. He was clearly a man born to be a caretaker. Edelbacher waved, yanked open his door of the unmarked police VW, and flung himself out from behind the wheel in one fluid motion. He even had his hat, Felix saw.

"No need, Felix," Edelbacher called out. "No rank today, uni-form or not. Oh no."

Felix wondered yet again how, or when, he would ever tell Edelbacher that he never felt obliged or inclined to salute him.

Unlike the anal Bundespolizei who would soon be the equally unwilling partner in this shotgun wedding that the Interior Ministry had decided just had to happen, Gendarmes had always been first-name people. That was all the way up the ranks. Why would a veteran Gendarme like Edelbacher suggest otherwise?

Well, it was simple enough, Felix had glumly concluded long ago. It was not so much that Edelbacher was just a moron who pushed his rank, his office, his uniform a bit too much. It was that Edelbacher was trying to insinuate some authority over Felix Kimmel, or subtly insist on some respect from him, this son of the attractive, and well-provided-for, widow of his boyhood friend.

In an emotional speech after the funeral, Edelbacher had pledged to take care of the bereaved Kimmels. It had been so out there that Felix could remember what he'd said almost word-for-word for days afterwards:

"Felix told me, if anything ever happened, to take care of you and, by God, I will do my duty, and my privilege, yes I will!"

And now he was upon them, all big teeth and high forehead, towering.

"You look good, Felix," Edelbacher said. "So good."

This much cologne would have appalled Felix, hangover or not. He held his breath while his foggy brain, still crippled from the drinking that he hadn't planned last night, curdled again at the sight of Edelbacher's expression: this idiot thinks that one day soon their mother will marry him. It didn't improve his mood much to see then that he'd gotten off easy here, when he saw Lisi accept an air-kiss from Edelbacher.

God knows, Felix thought as the Major rolled out every platitude available, Edelbacher was a trier. But he just didn't get it. He probably considered himself a gently persistent and undemanding suitor, well versed in the needs of a working woman of a certain age. A modern – no, a contemporary – woman, he'd say. Their mother, however, had been hinting more and more to Edelbacher that he had a misplaced sympathy for her. There were moments when Felix felt almost sorry for Edelbacher. He'd never understand that Greti Kimmel didn't want to be protected, or taken care of, or that she would not remarry. She did not want to let him down hard, but neither could she get through to him.

Had some part of Edelbacher's brain picked up on this, and this only magnified her attractiveness even more? Or was it, as Opa Nagl had muttered, that he simply saw a woman not yet 50, a fine woman with a paid-up house, an insurance windfall, a good pension, and a job? Smitten, huh? How about a gold digger? There was nothing funny about it at all. In his cynical moments, Felix had thought it might make a good reality TV show, like the Lugners and their idiotic lives.

But like the church door ahead of him, and this day itself, here he was, in front of Felix, this gormless bachelor, as sincere as he was possibly calculating too, but also a superior officer. Felix tried to look alert.

"Thank you, Major," he said.

For which observance, Felix received Edelbacher's signature greeting, a sizeable knuckle on his upper arm.

Then he leaned forward toward Lisi again.

"Dad would be proud of his boy today, right, Lisi?"

He raised his eyes quickly to the sky and nodded.

"Wouldn't he just," he added. "Felix's boy has found his own path."

Felix boy's stomach lurched. He concentrated on his own steps leading him to the doors of the church. An hour, he thought, and both his mind and guts seem to reel in unison when Edelbacher gave him a manly clap on the shoulder. The longest hour he could imagine.

TWO

FELIX AND HIS MOTHER STROLLED DOWN THE LANE ARM-IN-ARM afterwards. There was relief amongst them, and it was awkwardly concealed. It was a memorial service after all, but now that Opa Kimmel was gone home, the meal promised to be something they could actually enjoy. There would be a few more smiles and tears over the stories that would come out again, of course.

Oma Nagl walked beside him. Opa Nagl walked beside Felix's mother on the valley side, explaining something about turnips. Lisi was stuck with Edelbacher behind. Felix was pleased by that.

Well, he had made it. There had been tears and some his own because he hated to see his mother sad. As expected, he had sat beside his Opa Kimmel and two aunts of his father's. He had been attentive to his grandfather's rising and sitting, to his finding the hymn, and to guiding him down the steps afterwards, walking stick and all. Naturally, he made sure to not let it look like he was helping.

Felix had felt eyes on him during the service. He had concluded that they had been his mother's. It was as though by staring at his back she could encourage him, or maybe to remind him that it would be over soon, this task of being his grandfather's male heir here beside him for this hour.

From time to time during the service, he'd managed to steal glances at his grandfather's profile. Now in old age his white hair seemed to make him look almost benign, sometimes even fragile. The lines on his face, by his eyes especially, did not look like perpetual frowns so much. There was the meticulously shaved face, the closely cut hair little more than bristles, halfway toward his scalp as it had been for 60, or even 70 years, and the bushy eyebrows jutting out, all accompanied by the faint smell of shaving soap Felix always remembered. He'd heard the soft sighs as he'd sat and stood, the firm but flat way he had of saying the prayers. But none of these signs allowed Felix to relax around him, or even to feel much pity for this old man, his own grandfather, who had lived long enough to bury his own son.

Outside the church later his grandfather Kimmel had stood next to his in-laws, a little distracted looking, nodding at times. The small talk was painful. Felix saw that the look on his face was still there. It was that look of restrained politeness, and a distant interest, as though other matters awaited his thoughts and he wished to be away. In bygone years it had been closer to impatience, or even disdain.

Felix had walked him back to his car. He had even asked his grandfather if he would change his mind and come to the restaurant. He wondered how good an act that had been, and if his grandfather had not seen through it. With a mixture of relief and guilt, he'd watched the old man drive off, returning the wave that the smaller group now made. Come by when you're not busy, the old man had said, and given him a dry, firm handshake. There were things of his father's that Opa Kimmel wanted to give him.

The group walked down the lane in a ragged, talkative clump. From behind, Felix heard snatches of Edelbacher's enthusiasm for strudel, some of his scorn for how the amalgamation of the police forces was proceeding, and the beginnings of a rant about how people took too much for granted these days. Opa Nagl had moved on from turnips to organic crops, and then somehow made it to the topic of topless beaches in Italy. For a moment, Felix's addled brain tried to trace back how this had happened: was it a remark someone had said, his mother perhaps, about him finally getting time off, and heading for Italy with Giuliana?

Felix glanced over his shoulder. Behind Lisi and the towering Edelbacher were a few more than a dozen people. The others, the 30 or 40 more he was surprised to see in the pews, had gone off to their jobs, or home.

But there was Aunt Gusti, the Ancient One, a widow for many years, from the dorf up near Knipplfeld. She was walking sideways, like a horse, next to Willi Hartmann, another neighbour from the old days. Willi – Berger Willi was his local name – had returned from the war an amputee and unable to reclaim his passion for climbing these mountains. Somehow he had returned to farming, and even now, in his eighties, was robust. Opa Nagl had passed on some wag's story that Berger Willi was determined to get to at least 88. The joke was that Berger Willi had been an artilleryman, his expertise the fearsome 88.

Felix heard a comment from Opa Nagl, something about topless men at the beaches in Italy, drift over. Such lardy men could only be Germans, of course, not the adaptable and courteous Austrians. The smiles passed down through the group in a ripple. Having a colourful local character for a grandfather growing up had to count for something, Lisi had said many times before. Felix had sometimes wondered how a man like his Opa Nagl, a man who spoke out, and mocked things that nobody wanted to talk about, in public at least, how it was that he could be so well liked, and his company sought after in the village, for being so . . .

"Colourful," he thought again. Was there no other word? No doubt Lisi had also heard the same stories Felix had: of how Opa Nagl had been outspoken, of how he had even lost a tooth in a scrap over politics. It was well after the war had ended, and it was because he had been serious about his politics then. Being so clearly left at that time was an improbable thing. That was even more so for a farmer up here, in a village where the Soviets had squatted for long after the war. Opa Nagl had been more than willing to concede that Stalin was a lunatic – certainly he was! – and the Russians could be barbarians – undoubtedly so! – but a few times he had used his fists to defend his claim that none of these meant socialism wasn't good, that socialism wasn't Austria's future.

So well liked by almost everybody, Lisi had reminded him. She didn't need to say the name, of course. They hadn't talked about the enmity between the two sides of the family since then. It had been one evening not long after their father's funeral, one of those strangely giddy times, days when nobody had slept, when nights and days seemed little different. There had been a surreal look to everything, Felix recalled, a dreamy quality to the talk and the faces. It was a time when grief and laughter collided, and memories cratered into loss so sharp it stabbed, and odd things were dredged up, even odder conversations.

Opa Nagl didn't hate Opa Kimmel – he had just given up on him years ago. He had mocked him, or to be accurate, people like him who believed in that stuff. No doubt it had turned sour and bitter by times. It hadn't helped, of course, that Opa Nagl could come up with barbs: "That housepainter arshloch with the moustache, the one who just about burned the world to the ground for some stupid Reich dream!" So savage as to be memorable, word for word. But the little pantomimes he did, with his forefinger for a moustache, and his arse in the air goose-step – one had surely been performed sometime in the past for the benefit of Opa Kimmel. How else to explain the loathing, the silences, one about the other, over the years? Felix's mind went back to the goose-stepping troublemaker.

"What are you smiling about?" his mother asked. "The good memories?"

He saw her eyes were less red now. She had that half-smile back.

"Those too," he managed. He glanced over at Opa Nagl.

"Actually, I was just thinking about Opa here, listening to him. The things he comes up with."

"Unique," she murmured, with a look in her eye that bespoke long practice at summing up her father. "There's no doubt."

"How different," Felix said, without thinking.

She gave him an inquisitive look.

"From the other one, I meant."

His mother looked away, and he could not see if she had kept her smile. Laughter broke out behind now, and he turned. Now, somehow, Opa Nagl had brought up the topic of teeth, or horses, or something.

"Of course, I'm right," said Opa Nagl. "You want to know a good husband, a good wife, before you go to the church to marry? Look at their teeth. It's like a horse."

The manager was waiting for them by the restaurant door of the gasthaus.

"Grüss Gött, Inspektor."

Felix returned the greeting, and shook hands. He was sure he'd hidden his irritation at the title.

He and Oma Nagl turned, waiting for the stragglers. Aunt Gusti hobbled in last. Berger Willi Hartmann was almost licking his chops in anticipation of a meal. A true pro, Felix had heard before, attending many funerals and memorials, praying devoutly whether Catholic or Protestant. It was as though those indiscriminate prayers along with his energetic stumping along at such an epic age were a way to firmly declare that he had many more years of his own to complete.

Felix began to believe that some soup and sausage would be manageable now. Then he'd have a grossen braunen to perk him up, its milder mixture of espresso coffee and cream firing up at least some part of his brain. He might make it after all.

Felix realized his mother was eyeing him. Of course – he was supposed to lead, he was the man now.

"Mutti," he said to her. She nodded and smiled again.

"Geh' ma jetzt? Will we go in?"

THREE

GIULIANA WENT BACK TO SLEEP, OF COURSE.

Felix, the new and improved Felix Kimmel, who had manfully made it through the purgatory of yesterday's hangover and service – and afternoon shift – was back on the planet Normal. As such. He wondered if it was the prospect of a week away that had lifted him, or more the relief at getting through yesterday. Did it matter which?

Gendarme Felix Kimmel's optimism crested at the same time that a man on a remote farm in the hills outside Graz finally decided to make a phone call. Though he was sure in some way that it was necessary to get help, he felt like a clown. He did not know who to phone. So he sat in his kitchen, all the while watching his son fiddling with wooden blocks as he had for days now, refusing to leave the house. Should he phone the gemeinde, to ask if they knew about anything going on around here, up in the woods? But how or why would the local authority know anything about this? They were busy enough now with the spring, fixing the roads.

He had considered the support group where he drove his son every week for two afternoons with others like him. They did shopping, and some games, and even some cooking. His son liked it well enough, especially if one of the minders was the girl he liked. But even this he didn't want to do now. The man worried that this was a sign of something he hadn't been told about. It might be a change, that that no one really knew about yet, even the doctors, a deterioration or some kind. After all, didn't kids like his age faster?

His son began murmuring, but he couldn't make out the words. He was talking to the blocks. He wouldn't play with any of the stuffed animals or the toys he had made for him. Could it be dreams the boy was getting? Maybe something had turned itself over in his mind until it became frightening. It didn't take much. Worse, it was never predictable. Lieber Gött, he almost muttered aloud, it could even be that Petzi the bear from the children's television show: wasn't that bear always playing in the woods? That might explain it all right. His son looked over at him, and he saw again the dark patches under his eyes, the stubble. The electric razor frightened him now.

"Make me a tractor," he said to him. "A nice big one, Hansi."

He went back to trying to figure out who to phone, how to do something about this. How many days had it been? Something had to give.

His son began murmuring, but he couldn't make out the

Felix had coffee first. He took it to the bathroom, and finished it as he shaved. Then he picked at buns over a second coffee, at the table. At ten to the hour, he put on his tie and his belt. He lifted his uniform off the hanger by the door to the apartment without making a sound.

"Don't forget," she said from the bedroom doorway.

"Did I wake you?"

"I'm always awake."

She yawned and pulled the housecoat tighter. The lust ran up his body in a wave and settled in his groin.

"Two more," she murmured. "Then – to a beach."

It was that bedwarmth smell, he believed. Or her perfume, even yesterday's worn-out scent hanging in the apartment, or the morning breath on her lips, even. She leaned her head against the doorjamb and finished her yawn with that cat-stretch movement of her arms straight out, in fists, not paws.

"What," she said, suddenly still and wide-eyed. "What's that look?"

He slipped his hand in the fold.

"There's time," he said. She let him work on the knot there and then glanced down.

"Well, I can see what's on your mind."

"Mind?"

Her stillness made him pause.

"Tell you what," she said. "I'll wait right here, right here until you get home. I won't move. I'll be your little hausfrau. Okay?"

"Come on," he said. "It's evolution. Why argue?"

"Do you think five minutes is too long?"

"Well, you got out of the wrong side of the bed."

"Lose the belt at least when you get home, okay? Sorry, it's just, you know."

"'It's different for women.' Did I say it right?"

Giuli had the best range of pout. He offered a smile.

"The uniform still gives me the creeps," she murmured. "I hate to say it."

"I like it when you're so frank," he said.

"You should change at the station."

Felix took two apples from the bowl and rubbed them. The apartment was all her, really. He would have had a bookshelf, a stereo, something to keep his laptop off the floor and near a phone jack, and some hooks. Oh, a place to stack empty bottles, of course. And yes, since he'd gotten kicked out of the place he'd shared with Viktor and a rotating series of friends – overnighters, hazy friends of friends – it still struck him sometimes that he was living in a sort of art gallery. Or perhaps an artist studio. The afternoon light in from the platz reminded him of something from a Dutch Master. How could he possibly complain, living in an apartment in the centre of town, which for years now, Giuliana had added and decorated and transformed?

"You had a busy evening yesterday too," she said. "And night."

"What? I crashed out the minute I hit the pillow. What was it, one? Is that what you mean 'busy'?"

"I meant dreams. You dreamed, didn't you?"

"I think I must have," he said. "I dreamed that one where you and I were like we used to be when we started out. Not this hausfrau and mann routine."

"Get lost," she said. "I'm not the one who puts on a uniform to go to work."

"Maybe it's time to try teaching your students how to make them?"

"Art," she said in a monotone. "Uniforms don't come into it."

His thumb had found a soft spot on an apple. He looked down at it.

"Nine hours," he said. "And we're free. Movie tonight, right?"

She pushed her hair behind her ear to one side. It was the Berlin art student cut, he'd joked at first. When would the severe glasses show up?

"You talked," she said. "All night, it felt like."

"I don't remember," he said.

Her eyes had lost that glaze now.

"What," he said. "A lot went on yesterday. So, sorry."

"Your father. You were talking to him."

"More than I did in the past, I suppose," he said.

He gave her a chaste buss, a kiss, on the forehead. She grabbed him.

"Oh, it's okay if you do it, is it," he said.

"Be quiet," she said.

She brought his head down and kissed his eyes, one by one, slowly. Then she stepped back, her arms at full length on his shoulders.

"You Italians," he said. "I don't stand much of a chance with you, do I? Tease, lecture. Tease, nag, fly off the handle. Hey, instead of a movie, do you want to–"

"The movie," she said. "I've been looking forward to it."

Just as he had not. Some documentary thing made by an Italian about Tibet.

"What a strange and complicated little boy you are," she said.

FOUR

Work gave Felix a break from trying to figure out what had made Giuliana moody. Sepp Gebhart glanced up from his keyboard as he came into the duty room.

"Grüss, Gebi."

He glanced toward the Bezirkinspektor's office. Schroek's desk lamp, one that he put on no matter the time of day, was not lighted. The same Dieter Schroek commanded this post in Stefansdorf by remote control some days. It suited everyone. Felix had heard solid rumours that Stefansdorf would be closed as soon as the amalgamation happened. That was all to the good, in Felix's mind. More than a few months here would drive him up the walls, he had decided. It had been a soft number for many years now, the "landing strip" it had been called, where they eased in new Gendarmes while they eased out the veterans. Nothing happened in Stefansdorf, a half-hour outside Graz, this village that had stayed small. By way of introduction to the area, Gebi had passed on a clue to Felix shortly after he'd arrived: Why do all the dogs in Stefansdorf have flat noses? went the joke. It was because they were always chasing parked cars.

Felix put his hat on the shelf and unlocked his drawer. Gebhart sat back.

"Greetings yourself, Professor. A spring in your step today."

Felix winked at him.

"I'll think of you while I am away."

"Italy, you said?"

"I want to make a good impression on her family. Natürlich."

"On a topless beach."

"Funny you mention that."

Felix nodded toward the closed door to the Bezirkinspektor's office.

"Dieter is consulting," said Gebhart in the same dry tone. "In regards to the investigation of the thefts of those containers up from outside the warehouses last week. The cigarette case."

Gebhart had hinted that when Korschak, the other member of the post, went off on the training course to Vienna, they'd expect Felix to be Korschak's replacement "temporarily." Big changes on the horizon or not, Felix did not like the sound of that.

Korschak, the third member of the post, arrived with the huge bag that he used for his sports paraphernalia.

"Grüss, Gebi. Felix. Wie gehts?"

"So far so good, Manfred," said Gebhart. "But you know Stefansdorf. All hell could break loose. You're duty officer today, right?"

Korschak nodded and dumped the bag on the floor.

"What in the name of Christ and His Mother Mary is in the bag today?"

"Soccer," Korschak said. "Pylons and things."

"You'll get that burglaries report done before you go? The one on Tirolergasse, last week?"

"For sure," he said, and headed – wisely, Felix believed – to the klo.

"As for you, Felix," said Gebhart, pushing back in the chair. "You come with me."

"Traffic detail?"

"Genau. What else? Today we make the highways safe. The spring has all our Schumacher wannabes out on the roads. We're getting calls, and calls. Get the cases and gear, will you? I have to wrap up a thing from last night, the busted windows and puke over in Kleindorf, by the autobahn."

"Again?"

"Yes, again. Soccer fans were from Carinthia. Wolfsberg. Barbarians, of course."

Felix knew that Gebi's wife was from Wolfsberg.

"Coming home from a riot – sorry, a soccer match – in Hungary. The cops in Hungary don't put up with crap so these guys were fairly itching to do something."

"Wolfsberg? A long way from home, isn't it?"

"Precisely. There is a lesson in everything, I tell you. You didn't believe me at first, did you."

"What's the lesson here, Seppi?"

"The lesson, my young friend, is this: shit lands on our path, unpredictably. So be flexible."

"Thank you."

"If you ask me, it's the bus driver should go up in the dock. He's the idiot got off the autobahn, so as the real idiots could start the trouble. 'But they were going to go in the bus!' he says."

"Go, like, pee?"

"Oh it gets better. 'It's Number Two,' says one fellow. 'I can't just go in the woods!' Would this have anything to do with eating salami from the side of a road in Hungary, then unknown litres of beer? Rauschkugal: a proper bunch of drunkards."

Gebhart left any further lament for the stupidity of the general soccer-going, beer-swilling, bus-taking hooligans unsaid. He returned to the computer, where he pecked out a few words with that tentative, check-every-word style of one who distrusts the device. He saved with a flourish of the mouse and logged off.

Then he scanned what looked like court deposition forms, yanked open the drawer and slid them in, but not before checking something there already. Satisfied, he slammed the drawer shut and laid his meaty hands on his blotter. He watched Korschak head down the hallway to the kitchen, and then turned to Felix again.

"Is that too loud for you today?"

"No. I'm fine."

"A change from yesterday, then. Let's get ready."

Gebhart took keys out of his pocket, fingered his way to the one for the armory, and then squinted up at Felix.

"Remember," he said. "I really don't want to hear about it if you're not one hundred percent because of your, extracurricular, is that the word? This is a paramilitary service you're in. That's page two of the manual. Memorize it. You know where the Gendarmerie is from, right? When we had the Turks thinking they'd plunder our green valleys here?"

Felix nodded.

"Pack the gear. Make sure you get the proper tripod, that new one."

Felix signed out his Glock first. He laid it on the cloth and then replaced each of the cartridges in the clip in turn, feeling the slightly oily smoothness of their tips as each clicked home. He checked the pistol's action for the regulation six times. Then he inserted the clip, and safetied the pistol. He'd make sure that Gebi would see him loading the pistol later.

Next he replaced the cartridges in the spare, and slid the holster on his belt to just in front of his hip bone. The leather was still stiff and the button clasp on the cover took work to get thumbed down. The Kripo had had the American quick release for years now. Banditti, Gebi called them.

"Load," he said to Gebhart.

Gebi nodded and watched him draw one into the chamber, and put the safety back on.

He fastened his belt then, made sure the plastic restraints weren't dangling at his back, and replaced the signing folder back on the shelf. He looked at the machine pistol locked behind the steel mesh to the side of the armoury safe. It had never been used, Gebi told him, in the seven years since he started here. The station had been staffed for five then. Gebi did the monthly commissioning, removing the gun's movements from the other safe and inserting them.

Gebhart stepped out and around the corner, and rapped on the kitchen door.

"Fred, sign up," he called out. "We're going any minute."

Felix headed for the equipment room, noted that it was only a minute off six o'clock now. He passed Korschak coming out. He took down the vests first, and then made sure he had the tripod that Gebi was so particular about. The laserpistole – the radar gun – was a pig on batteries. He took the second pack from the charger and slipped it into the bag that held the odds and ends.

He closed the case again, and parked it, along with the tripod and vests, by the door. Then he returned to the duty room.

"Rush hour until nine," he heard Gebi say, to Korschak, he presumed. "We'll probably do three spots, to keep ahead of the snitches."

Gebhart took two hand sets from the charger.

The dawn was milky, with parchment and orange streaks still. Gebi helped load the gear into the boot of the Opel, the second of the two patrol cars at the post. Felix had noticed the care Gebi showed in how he warmed the engine, and how he coaxed it up to 100 before backing off and muttering about "strain" and "transmission" and "clear the injectors."

"Start over by Semmarach," he said to Felix. "There's a spot near a farmhouse there. You know it? You get the real headers tearing up there. They know they're close to the autobahn."

Felix checked the car radio with Korschak and gave him their destination.

"That Korschak," said Gebhart, straining to look back at a bread van unloading.

"What about him?"

"I used to think he was one of those. You know? Don't tell him."

"Playing for the other team?"

"Yeah. Your bunch knows all about that, of course. Who am I to talk?"

"Do you mean people who live in Graz? People my age, or other gay men like me?"

"Very funny, Professor. I meant your generation. As if I cared whether a man is gay or not. Macht nichst."

"It makes no odds to you at all?"

"You seem surprised. My generation is not allowed to be tolerant?"

The sky behind the hills was still glowing now, but a tiny sliver of moon remained over the last of the lights on the houses. It might be shirtsleeves by midday today yet.

"Morning drivers are quite polite when you nail them," said Gebhart then. "Did you know that?"

"I've only done one trap. It was in the afternoon."

"You're going to track a couple of real fliers at least, though."

Now wasn't the time to tell the same Gebhart that last October he'd gotten to Vienna in 90 minutes on the autobahn. There was a separate corps in the Gendarmerie for the autobahn patrols and traffic. Quite a serious bunch too. They could take your car for that kind of a stunt.

"The real damage gets done on the local roads, doesn't it," he said to Gebhart.

"Stimmt. Those are stats you can't argue with. They're speeding just to get to the autobahn, just to save what, two minutes? What does that say about human nature?"

"That people are predictable, maybe?"

"Did you make that up just now? Or is it some fancy logic thing, some philosophy thing?"

"Who says people aren't cranky this time of day?"

Gebhart gave him a considered look. Felix had learned to grade them. This one was minor – not quite glare, more curiosity and skepticism together.

"I was trying to make a point. So do we need the irony crap? I say no. What, you thought I didn't know irony? I respect the book stuff. I respect your, uh, poetic leanings. Just don't be a pain in the arsch."

"Thanks. Nothing personal. Right, Gebi?"

"Absolutely. You know that."

"'Nothing personal, Felix, but you're an idiot'?"

Gebhart chortled.

"You're good," he said. "When you're not being a dummy. Come on now. We have a job here."

There was a line of six cars behind the Opel already. None dared pass, of course. Felix began to wonder what some of them were thinking, especially the guy in the Mercedes two back. Swearing probably.

He liked the way this was turning out.

FIVE

By nine, Gendarmes Kimmel and Gebhart had amassed a reasonable sum for the coffers of the Austrian state. Gebi had even nailed two drivers for flashing the oncoming traffic too. One of the flashers had played it right, however, saying he hadn't realized it was an offence. He spoke in a respectful, resigned tone about how he had been merely hoping to slow down a couple of crazy ones; that he thought it might lower the danger, blah blah. But Gebi had shown no mercy to an elegant woman in a 7 Series BMW. Felix heard him mutter something about a boy-toy coming too early, as she accelerated away, expressionless. She had been unperturbed by the fine.

The one to remember was a large, morose man in an old Kadett. Felix had written him up. For a while he couldn't concentrate on the form. His mind was full of the man's sullen menace. It was as if it was being pumped across the air between them in a relentless cloud. He became preoccupied almost immediately with re-enacting the drills in his mind, the ones for pacifying a guy who had an obvious size advantage. The man hadn't said more than two words in total. Felix wondered if the guy would do more than keep up that baleful, blank stare at him.

Gebi was good, better than he let on, at picking up on things like this. He must have noticed the guy's expression. When Felix looked up from the clipboard again, Gebhart had left the lazerpistole and taken up a position behind the driver's side of the Kadett, his hand in his belt. The move wasn't lost on the driver. His eye strayed from Felix to his mirror more often. Gebi shifted to see better when Felix handed the driver the ticket. After a count of 10 he barked at the driver.

"Get moving there, Citizen. You're a hazard here. Read your ticket at home."

The sun broke through the mist at last, and the greens and blues took on depth. They moved three klicks down to the next exit and set up on the Birkfeld Road. Gebhart hung back awhile in the Opel listening to the traffic on the radio. There had been an accident near Birkfeld.

Felix set up and checked the charge in the laserpistole. He half enjoyed the effect their car was having on the traffic, the glances, the brake lights, the frequent embarrassed smiles. Prevention was part of the job too. The sun grew warmer on the back of his neck and he heard a tractor's diesel clanking from somewhere. Behind the hill the constant hush of the autobahn spread across the fields and hedges.

Gebi closed the door and made his way over.

"We'll get a few of the grocery and school mob now," he said. "Some of those characters you pinch on their way to the autobahn, boy, they give me the creeps. Like that gypsy in the crapmobile, that Kadett."

"How do you know gypsy? 'Strozek.' That's Hungarian back somewhere."

"You think I turn my safety off and loosen the button on my shooter for a guy just because he has a Hungarian-sounding family name? Grow up."

"Fake papers? Wouldn't that have popped up when I radioed in the licence?"

"Gypsy. Albanian. Chechen? Who knows. Who knows where the Balkan Route begins or where it ends. These days."

Felix looked at his partner, and for the first time that he could remember, he couldn't tell if Gebi was putting out some sly humour, or not. At least he hadn't come up with the real slur, Die Tschuchen. If "nigger" was brought to Europe, and slapped on any-one from the Balkans, this would be it.

"Maybe I should have done him an emissions test?" Felix tried. "See the smoke when he took off?"

"Now there's a thought," Gebhart murmured.

He turned to let his glare stay on a Mercedes that had braked hard. The radio came to life.

"Zentrale to Stefansdorf Ein."

Korschak. By the book, always: never just Car One. Stefansdorf One, never Stefansdorf Two. It didn't matter there was only one patrol car out at a time from the post, ever.

"Go ahead Zentrale."

"Telephone call for you Gebi, you might want to consider it after your assignment. Local, not urgent. You want it, over?"

Gebhart frowned.

"Might as well, Zentrale. Over – wait, give me a name first, and I'll know."

"Family Himmelfarb?"

"What about them? Over."

"Will you be up his way today, he wants to know. Over."

"What does that mean? A police matter?"

"He didn't say. But you know him, his son, he said. Over."

Gebhart hesitated.

"Look," he said then. "I'll phone him when we get back. Over?"

He shook his head as though bewildered, and replaced the mouthpiece. He sagged lower into the seat and looked out the side window. Felix stole a glance over. To see if there was any clue about what the message meant. There was none.

He drew into the lay-by that was in sight of a small scatter of older houses.

"Okay," said Gebhart. He seemed to rouse himself from what-ever had made him turn in on himself. He checked the laserpistole he had been holding and tugged the side of his green vest tighter.

"Let's pinch a few hausfraus," he said. "The little ones are in the school now, and the hubbie's gone to work. This is the hour the entertaining starts."

The raised eyebrow and the refusal to smile left Felix baffled. "Entertainment?"

"And they'll be speeding, let me tell you."

Gebi – Josef, or Seppi – Gebhart wasn't a cynic, Felix had come to conclude. He had wondered at first how a 41-year-old Gendarme had not moved up in all those years of service. He rarely mentioned his family, and it seemed that he kept work and home very distinct. Felix had found out from Korschak who had muttered something about having smart daughters who gave him grief, a son who had some issues. "Issues?"

Out on the road now, he took up position beside Gebi, who had the pistole mounted and scanning quickly. He watched Gebi's impassive face as the cars came by. None tripped the pistole limit. There weren't even any dives, those half-funny giveaways that showed the driver had been speeding. They must have been spotted.

"Don't give up yet," said Gebhart. "A few more minutes. You'll see."

Felix looked across the wet fields, his mind drifting. It was seldom lately that he'd found himself wondering whether some cynic, or maybe some old enemy of his father, had put him here in Stephansdorf, with Gebhart, as a joke. Maybe it was a test: prove you can work with anyone, Kimmel: we've been saving this one for you. Survive this, and you'll do fine. Or had it been a kindly gesture in disguise, from someone in Postings who had read something into Felix's CV, and his temperament, and engineered his posting here as a warning: this is what a stale cop looks like. Do you want to grow to be like this cop?

Then he heard the alarm go from the laserpistole.

"What did I tell you," said Gebhart, and he raised his arm. "Blonde, of course."

Felix thought of the rasp of Giuliana's skin on his knee, the way she pushed and arched, the way she muttered and even grunted at him when she was close to losing it. Parsley, he thought suddenly, and realized that he must have been thinking about this somewhere. That was it: the scent of her was parsley.

SIX

FELIX DROVE THE PATROL CAR BACK. HE TURNED BY THE PLATZ, and into the station yard.

It took time to get the gear out and tame the paperwork. Gebhart had Nescafé and a bun with salami for his brotzeit, his morning break. He stood chewing and nodding slowly while he took a phone call. After it was over, Korschak talked to him about how if it wasn't floods in some of the fields again this year, it'd be drought by July.

Felix thought about a sandwich but fell instead for something sweet. He took some lebkuchen from a package by the kettle. Gebhart came over and poured a half cup of leftover water from the kettle into his mug, smelled it, and then drank it.

"Come with me," he said. "A minor job. Let Manfred get the glory here."

"Out to . . . ?"

"Die bauern," said Gebhart. "Maybe you'll learn something from it."

Felix waved his hand over the forms he had been collating and checking.

"They'll keep. Geh'ma jetzt – off we go."

Gebhart drove. Felix could afford to enjoy this unexpected escape from an afternoon of paper, phones, and a small pile of inquiries for licences, criminal checks, and court preparation requests. He totted up the hours remaining before he had his freedom. It would be five hours to the beach, and as little time as possible with Giuliana's relatives.

Gebhart coaxed the Opel over through hairpins with the gears more than brakes. They passed waterlogged ditches and bottle-green fields exploding with growth. Soon they were in the hills, and there was no let-up. Still the road climbed, up beyond the last of the trees, until it slowly descended a little to patchy scrubland where the conifers took over again, hesitating it seemed many of them, in small, scruffy plantations on this high plateau.

"You know this area?"

Felix shook his head. Gebhart squinted up out of the windshield at the heights that came slowly closer as they wove through the curves.

"They're a bit cracked up at these altitudes," Gebhart said. "Spinnt, as they say. You think it's true?"

"'Nothing personal' here, right?"

He was glad to see a small grin eke out over Gebhart's features. The air was cool, with an edge to it. There were few cars. Gebhart slowed and stopped by the entrance to a mildly rutted road. He scrutinized the roof of the house that nestled behind a brake of trees there.

"A red roof on one of the barns" he muttered, and moved on

"I thought . . . ," Felix began, but stopped awkwardly.

"That I know this area, or where we're supposed to be going? Well I don't."

"But a rough idea? Isn't the person a, well someone you know?"

"I only met him a few times. In a place in town. He has a kid, I have a kid."

Something in Gebhart's tone drew a curtain down over further questions.

A half-dozen Simmentals clustered around a feeding cage at the corner of a half-hectare patch to the right.

"There's a red roof," said Felix.

"That's the one," said Gebhart, "I'll bet. The big wooden gate too."

There were pools on the laneway. It was hard to tell how deep they might be. Felix rolled down the window. The sun had gone in behind a fairly solid mass of clouds not long before. He heard water swish at the floor pan as Gebhart let the Opel down the lane.

"You said this was a bit out of the ordinary," Felix tried.

Gebhart's tongue had been flicking from side to side as the car wallowed gently and then rose out of the puddles.

"God's country," he said. "Die Heimat. Can you imagine Polizei coming up here? They'd be wiping their shoes every ten metres. Phoning for a translator."

"Is it a criminal matter here, Gebi?"

Gebhart flicked him a glance, and made himself unnecessarily busy with the gears. The Opel bottomed out and shook itself up from a puddle.

There were reeds growing in the damp spots all about. A lone, thin wire that brought hydro from the road. Someone had taken great care with putting together stone walls near where the lane approached the farmyard. His mind rebelled at thinking how long it had taken to gather these rocks from the fields. By hand? And what could you grow up here anyway? A couple of the cattle looked up and toward the gently bouncing and now muddy police car. A sheepdog came trotting out to the laneway.

"Here's the story," Gebhart said. "Listen."

Felix looked over.

"There's a kid. But he's not a kid, that's the first thing. Just pretend he is."

"Do you mean handicapped?"

The farmhouse came in sight beyond one of the walls. The wood had weathered into a grey but the whitewash on the bumpy stone walls was fresh. A collection of smaller buildings, some with fresh wooden shingles, took up a different side of the near rectangle that was the yard proper.

"Our job here is to humour this boy," said Gebhart then. "Got that?"

A woman was walking slowly from the door of the farmhouse, her headscarf and floral housecoat reminding Felix of somewhere in Yugoslavia, or somewhere east.

"So he's not going to make a ton of sense, this boy."

"You want to interview him?"

"Interview? I want you to just, what do your bunch say now? 'Hang with him'? Just listen. Let him relax."

"Should I give him a massage maybe?"

"That's good, Professor. Now: you've had your fun."

"But what's he got for us?"

The distaste had returned to Gebhart's voice now.

"Are you listening to me at all? Don't they teach listening at Gendarmerieschule anymore?"

"Gebi, you're not telling me things. That's why I'm asking you."

"What do you think police work is? You ask, they answer, everybody goes home?"

Felix's reply was interrupted by the car's lurch deeper into a puddle. The Opel's shocks bottomed out on it, and the car rolled back a little.

"Jesus and Mary," said Gebhart, and quickly put it into first. Felix heard the water move under the car. He looked down to see if any had come in.

A Mitsubishi four-wheeler was parked near a tractor. Gebi parked near what looked like a storehouse and yanked up the handbrake. The woman had already called the dog and was holding its collar as she led it away.

"Put on your hat," said Gebhart. "And spare me the look, will you? Remember. Number one: your job is to listen. Number two: everything goes slow up here. Slow and polite and serious. People like this don't call the Gendarmerie just for the heck of it."

The woman pulled the door of a shed behind her, and tied it up with a loop of rope. Felix still saw the snout in a gap at the bottom. She folded her arms, and returned Gebhart's quiet greeting.

"Grüss Gött."

Felix noted the high-pitched accent. He did not want to stare at her lined face. She waited for Felix to come around from his side of the Opel. There was stiff leathery feel to her hand.

"You are close to heaven here, Frau Himmelfarb" said Gebhart. "Thank God."

She nodded, but did not smile. Felix wondered if she even got the lousy pun: Himmelfarb – the colour of heaven. She was probably shy more than slow-witted, he decided. Who wouldn't be, living up here. Except for the four-wheel pickup, this was a place out of time. He adjusted his beret and took in a narrow piece of a view that had not been visible from the laneway in. To the side of a barn, there was a prospect clear over the hills toward Carinthia.

Frau Himmelfarb had high cheekbones and the ruddy face he'd seen in travel books, belonging to peasants in Andalusia and Bavaria and Holland and the Crimea – and pretty well anywhere else east of China. Her husband appeared from a shed then. Stocky with hooded eyes that suggested Hungarian or peoples farther east in the family tree somewhere. He was a little shorter than the missus. He took off his hat, with its depleted feather and one small metal pin, and scratched at his forehead as he came over.

Gebhart was right, Felix had to admit. These people wanted their police to be people they took their hats off to. And this bandy-legged farmer who had the same rolling walk as Opa Nagl, the same deep-set eyes topped by wiry, grey eyebrows he didn't trim. The same delta of minute veins on his cheeks, more so on his nose, from a life in the open. All the bone buttons were intact on the faded green lapels of his lodenjanker, the traditional Styrian jacket that stubbornly found its way into each generation's wardrobe. A hand like a swollen ham hock extended to shake Gebhart's, and then Felix's hand.

Introductions made, Gebhart fell easily into a slow and polite parade of pleasantries and chitchat. Wild mushrooms, a passion of many yet, were first.

"They'll be whoppers," said Gebhart. "The snow stayed so late."

Himmelfarb did a lot of nodding and made gentle, noncommittal flicks of his head, but said very little. Wild mushrooms were not to be discussed with those who might come back later looking for such delicacies. Felix and Frau Himmelfarb waited. The talk came to cattle, and mad cows.

Finally, in a lull after a comment about dangers to the hoofs for cattle up here, Frau Himmelfarb came to life: would the gentlemen like coffee? Gebhart said he did not wish to put her to any trouble. It was none, according to her, of course.

"Then most certainly, gnädige frau," said Gebhart. "A kindness indeed."

Felix followed them into the kitchen. The scent of ashes and a fainter scent of the ham, or sausage, that hung somewhere being cured, came to him as he reached the door. Felix began to recall pieces of something his father had related a long time back, about when he was a small kid visiting relatives. Yes: they actually had spoons and knives tied to the table, these ancient relatives, in the old style, where you wiped them with a fetzen, a rag, when you were finished.

Surprise: the kitchen was all modern convenience. There were even IKEA-ish–looking blue and yellow napkins covering plates of something on the table. But the old tiled kachelofen had been kept, and still used, along with the wood panelling on the walls and door frames.

"Now," said Herr Himmelfarb.

For the first time Felix believed he saw some expression on the weather-tightened face – a little pride at this modern surprise, he suspected. He tugged at and wiped his nose in one clutch of finger and thumb. Then he sat heavily down at the head of the table.

"Hansi won't talk."

Behind him a feral-looking cat lay against the kachelofen staring at Felix. Herr Himmelfarb took the napkins off and began folding them. There was strudel, another pie with red berries, a jug of cream. Felix eyed the big eyebrows moving around as Herr

Himmelfarb seemed to be looking for a way to say something further.

"We get that too," said Gebhart. "Days, even."

It was several long moments before Himmelfarb spoke.

"Yours is, what, fifteen?"

Gebhart nodded. Felix found that he was staring at Gebhart. He suddenly seemed very different. Even his voice had changed. And in the back of Felix's mind something had burst – remorse, some anger too, spiralling into itself. How had he not known? Why had Gebhart not told him?

The only sounds now were Frau Himmelfarb's careful arranging of things over near the sink.

"Is he not able?" Felix asked.

Himmelfarb exchanged a quick look with Gebhart before turning to him.

"Oh he's able, all right. We can't shut him up some nights. Isn't that so, Mutti? The junge, how he'll talk?"

"He likes to talk, it's true," Frau Himmelfarb said.

"He talks to himself," she went on. "He talks to the dog. He talks to the cows."

"That's often a wise move," said Gebhart.

Frau Himmelfarb's face seemed to ease a little. You take your humour as you find it up here, Felix thought. The Himmelfarbs had an accent stronger than any he could remember in a long time. The half-finished words, some of them fired out and others barely audible, were even beyond the baying, "bellen" tones of most Styrians.

"But he won't even talk to you, I'm afraid. I told him, and, well, you don't see him here, do you?"

With that, Himmelfarb leaned forward and narrowed his eyes. He nodded toward a door that led into the rest of the house, and he winked. Gebhart raised his eyebrows and nodded at Felix too.

"Schade," said Gebhart. "That's a great pity. I do like to talk with Hansi."

Himmelfarb cocked his head and kept his eyes on the door.

Gebhart waited, and then spoke in the same clear, slow tone, addressing the door.

"We have the patrol car outside, of course. There are quite a number of toys in that, you know."

Frau Himmelfarb undid her scarf then. Felix imagined her careful braids golden yellow again, a younger Mrs. Himmelfarb dancing, laughing. It would have been centuries before she became mother to a retarded kid way up here in the middle of nowhere.

"Well," said Gebi. "Fair enough. But I wish Hansi were here. We could show him our toys. It's too bad."

The door handle went down and Hansi Himmelfarb stood in the doorway. He was holding a kitten. Felix thought he heard Gebi sigh.

"Well, Hansi," he said in a voice Felix hadn't heard before. "May we meet your kitten?"

Felix didn't want to stare. He'd seen Down's people before. Who hadn't? But there was the look of a deer or something to him. Maybe it was the stubble hair or freckles. He could be 20, or 40.

Gebhart was on his feet now. He was allowed to scratch the kitten's belly and have his fingers chewed a little in return.

Hansi was suddenly unsure of something. He walked away, and stopped by the sink. He closed his eyes as he stroked the kitten. Gebhart sat down again and looked at Himmelfarb.

"The boy is up at night," said Himmelfarb. "He is afraid to sleep, he says."

"Regressing," said Frau Himmelfarb, and glanced at her son, who seemed oblivious to their words. She began pouring hot water from the kettle into a jug. Instant coffee, Felix believed. It was better than nothing: a little.

"Well what has he told you? You said 'puppets,' was it?"

Himmelfarb hesitated.

"'Puppets.' Mostly that. Puppets, forest."

Hansi opened his eyes and looked at his father, before turning his eyes toward Felix.

"The woods? He likes to go in there, you told me before."

"He's regressing," said Mrs. Himmelfarb again. "Something bothers him."

Felix spooned out some cream. When he stole a look back at Hansi, the eyes were closed again. Frau Himmelfarb carried over the tray. The Thermos jug had that scorched smell of instant coffee, all right.

"That's too bad," Gebhart said. "It must be hard on you."

"All he says is 'sleep' when I ask him. "'Sleep' or 'sleeping.'"

"Do you need a sleep, Hansi?" Gebhart called out. "A nice sleep?"

Hansi shook his head several times. He did not open his eyes, but held the kitten up closer to his face. Frau Himmelfarb sighed.

"He won't leave the house," she said. "Coffee for you both?"

"Three days now," she went on, as she poured the coffee.

"I haven't seen him at the club," said Gebhart.

"Won't leave the house," said Himmelfarb.

"And he cries," Frau Himmelfarb added. "He never cries. He is as happy as the day is long. Even when he is ein bisschen krank – even when he's a bit sick."

Nobody seemed to want to say anything then. Felix blew on his coffee, and took sly looks around the huge kitchen. The walls were nearly a half-metre thick by the windows. Hansi stood by the sink caressing the kitten. He was looking out the window now.

"It's been a long winter," Gebhart said quietly.

"It's always long," said Himmelfarb.

"Hansi is always out," his wife said. "We blow a whistle, he comes back."

"We wonder," said Himmelfarb. "Did he meet someone out there? You never know these days, the terrible things. People they take advantage of kids – it's happened, I know it. It's on the news, nicht war, Mutti?"

She nodded.

"Oh, the crimes these days," Himmelfarb went on. "People behave worse than animals. You see it every night."

Felix hadn't noticed a satellite dish on their way in. He'd remember to look when they left. What sense could an older couple like the Himmelfarbs make of all the crap pouring down from satellite channels now?

Gebhart turned in his chair.

"You're a good boy Hansi, aren't you? I'll bet you are. Everybody knows that."

Felix became aware of Frau Himmelfarb's gaze on him. When he turned toward her, a smile ready, she quickly looked away.

"Hansi," said Gebhart. "Do you like the police? Wah wah, the siren?"

Hansi met his eyes for several moments. Then he nodded.

"I thought you did, yes. Well, will you meet my friend? I have a new friend, yes."

Hansi glanced over at him. Felix noticed that Hansi's eyes were mostly directed toward his beret. He began to believe that Gebhart could well have predicted, and even planned, every move here. Somehow he worked up a smile for Hansi.

"Come over here, Felix," said Gebhart. "Felix likes kittens. Don't you, Felix?"

Felix reached out and got a gnaw from the kitten on his knuckles.

"Felix will do the wah wah for you, Hansi. Go with Felix."

Felix tried a hard stare and his best ESP with Gebhart. There was no go there. What if this boy/man throws a fit with the siren?

"Go with Felix, Hansi. Felix is a good boy, just like you. But he doesn't know anything about farming. Or the woods, either. Do you Felix?"

"No," said Felix. "I know nothing."

Gebi gave him a measured look before turning back to Hansi.

"See, Hansi? But I hear you know all about the farm. Show poor Felix. Felix lives in town. He's kind of lost, you know."

A look of concentration crossed Hansi's face. Then he walked to the door, and put the kitten in a basket there. He looked at his father, to Gebhart, and then to Felix. With a sinking feeling, one made up of pity and annoyance, and now a clear desire for some sort of revenge on Gebhart, Felix saw that Hansi was keen now.

"Wah wah?" said Hansi.

"Atta boy," said Gebhart.

Hansi held out his hand.

"He does that when he's bothered," said Himmelfarb.

Felix fixed Gebhart with a glare. Gebhart knew better than to look over. He had already begun to compliment Frau Himmelfarb on the strudel.

Hansi grasped Felix's hand and tugged on it. Felix opened the door out onto the cement step under the wooden balcony where the window boxes had already swollen with blooms. He heard a cow-bell, then others. He heard the talk about the strudel stop, the quiet, before he closed the door.

Hansi had the huge hands of his old man but they were soft. Felix tried to take his hand back, or at least switch to his left, so he'd be unable to get at his restraints or his pistol even, if this Hansi made a grab for it. Hansi grabbed tighter.

What if he screamed, or threw a fit, Felix wondered. Or crapped his pants or something?

"Wah wah."

"Oh, I'll give you wah wah, all right, Hansi. Is that what Gebi does for you?"

Hansi frowned and nodded, and pulled harder.

"Easy, Hansi. I need my arm for later, okay?"

Felix let himself be towed toward the patrol car. He looked over his shoulder, but saw no faces in the window. They could still be watching from somewhere. For a moment he wondered again if this was some joke of Gebhart's. Had Gebhart or some others at the post come up with this initiation rite, a way to show the new recruit up?

He tugged back a little. Hansi slowed, and looked at him with a blank expression.

He had frightened this big lug? For the first time, he stared into

Hansi's face. He couldn't read it at all. He became suddenly ashamed at the thoughts that had come tumbling into his mind along with the resentment and the low burning desire to get back at Gebhart for this – crazy things like a cannibal family luring people here, like some dark Grimm tale. If he'd heard right at all, Gebhart had a kid with Down's, and he and Himmelfarb seemed to know one another because of that. And that was why he'd come all the way up here. Just to help, a bit.

"Wah wah, wah wah."

They stopped at the car.

"Hansi? I need my hand back so I can get into the car okay? For the wah wah?"

That worked. He sat on the edge of the seat.

"It's loud, you know? Are you ready? Loud, okay?"

He held his hands over his ears. It took a few tries for Hansi to get the idea.

Felix held his finger over the switch and checked to see if Hansi was ready. So this was part of Gendarme Josef Gebhart's policing duties, he thought, after a fleeting image of Hansi freaking out with the racket that was coming up when he hit the switch: a Gendarme's day included an escape from the post, getting up in the mountains, tucking into home cooking, chatting about cattle or weather . . .

Hansi jumped when the siren went off. Felix changed it into highway mode, then to traffic-park. Hansi's eyes were as big as saucers, but he was smiling. Christmas and birthday rolled into one for this boy, Felix thought. The annoyance had gone now.

"This is to tell someone to stop."

Hansi let his hands down and began rubbing them together. Then be began to lift one leg, then the other. Marching?

"This is for when you have to clear traffic, Hansi."

He didn't want to say accident.

"You stop and you keep people away. If there is, you know, a problem."

Hansi didn't like the slow one. He blinked at the lights as they cycled through. Felix wondered if the geeks who programmed these ever considered they might set off an epileptic fit? He turned it back. Hansi began to jump now.

"Okay Hansi. Genug – enough."

A cruel thought came to Felix: maybe it was like being stoned all the time?

"Wah wah."

"No more wah wah, Hansi. I'm getting a headache."

"Wah wah."

Felix looked toward the windows of the farmhouse. He saw no faces.

"Look, Hansi, don't be a scheisskopf. You're not dealing with just a common idiot cop here."

"Wah wah."

"I'm going on holidays tomorrow. Did you know? Let's go back to the house."

The confused look returned to Hansi's face. He was getting agitated.

"Wah wah."

"Uh uh. Go on home, Hansi. Go home to the kitten."

For a moment Hansi's frown had Felix thinking there'd be trouble.

"Get some of your mutti's strudel, okay? Yum yum?"

How could he not take the big lug's hand again. He wondered if Gebi had a digital camera he hadn't let on about.

"Sleep."

"Right, Hansi. A nice nap. Wouldn't that be good?"

But Hansi had stopped and he wasn't going to budge. His grip had grown tighter. Felix looked over. Hansi was half turned toward the woods and the boggy uplands behind the barn. The look of concentration on his face could mean anything. Felix glanced down for any signs of a diaper.

"Sleepy."

"Let's go, Hansi. Your mother wants you."

"Komm."

The tug was more a yank. Felix pulled back. For a moment he saw Giuliana's face: how she'd throw her head back and do that laugh that came from the back of her throat. The Italian Witch Laugh.

"Hansi, you are getting annoying. You know? Now let's get out of here. You've been cured, okay? Here you are, outdoors. I've done my duty. Everyone's had a good laugh, okay?"

"Sleep."

What it was exactly that made Felix Kimmel give in was something he would think about a great deal later that day, and into the evening after the detectives had arrived from the Kriminaldiest in Graz. He let himself be led on a 10-minute walk that began almost as a trot, and left him winded. Hansi had been babbling, or intoning, words that Felix could not understand, but he stopped abruptly near a clump of pines that edged out toward a path leading through the woods.

SEVEN

THE WAY BACK DOWN FELT LIKE IT TOOK BUT MOMENTS. Felix's throat and his chest hurt from the spasms that had had him almost doubled up. There was still vomit on parts of his shoes. It was he who had grabbed Hansi by the hand hard to get him to return to the house. On the way up here, his annoyance had vanity for company. He had been proud to have gotten Hansi's trust, even to cure him in some way. Hadn't he won him over, when even his own parents hadn't?

Things skittered through his mind, and fear made him glance over his shoulder many times as he hurried down.

What he said later, much later, to Gebhart was this:

"I don't know. I really don't. I guess I felt sorry for him. Or maybe his parents, Christ, Gebi, they look so worn out. I don't know. Maybe the air up here got to my brain."

Gebhart had made the call, and was soon a panting, red-faced, out-of-shape policeman with a bauch full of strudel and coffee, his chest going in and out as he stood there after the climb.

Himmelfarb, hardly noticing the steep climb, was standing there too, with a face full of alarm and bewilderment.

"The boy wanted to go for a walk," Felix said, uselessly.

"A walk," said Gebhart, his breath whistling. "And look what you got. Holy shit."

Gebhart took only a few steps, with his hand on his pistol, standing on tiptoe to get another look at the bodies. Felix watched the vein throbbing along his neck.

"This is a crime scene," he muttered more than once, his voice barely above a whisper. "Be careful."

"Jesus and Mary," Himmelfarb said, many times. He had blessed himself a half-dozen times. "Are there more, farther in?"

The blood on their faces was black and brown. One of the men's heads was swollen at the forehead, and though Felix didn't' want to look, there was that slight grin, and a tiny parting between the eyelids.

"When's the last time you came by here, Karl?" said Gebhart. Felix had his notebook out. He felt stupid with it hanging there, so he wrote down the time. Then he wrote that Karl Himmelfarb didn't give a direct answer but merely shook his head.

"Ausländers," said Himmelfarb. "Look. The shoes. And the schwarzkopfs on them, the black hair? The jackets? Where do you see these in Styria, or anywhere else? Foreigners, for sure."

"Time enough to find that out, Karl. I said: when were you last up here?"

"Why would I come here? I'm a farmer. There's damn-all to farm here, can't you see? Nix."

Gebhart raised his eyebrows at Felix. Himmelfarb bent slightly and leaned to peer into the depths of the woods.

"This is what we get," he muttered. "This is what we get in the EU? The end of the borders down there?"

Gebhart leaned over to whisper to Felix.

"Where did you, you know . . . ? I'll need to tell the KD when they show up."

Felix searched about, and nodded toward a tree.

"I'm not totally sure, Gebi. Sorry."

Gebhart backed them out of the woods the way they'd come in. Their handsets had been fading in and out.

Gebhart grunted and looked at his watch.

"The one day I don't bring my damned Handi."

"Handy what?" said Himmelfarb.

"Cell phone – my Handi."

"Hah," said Himmelfarb. "Those things don't work up here. You might as well use a hunting horn."

Gebi had phoned the post 20 minutes ago, and they had made the climb back up right after.

"Inside the hour, I'm guessing," he said to Felix. "The whole bit. A site crew, a truck no doubt. Forensics later. You're one lucky fellow, Professor."

Before Felix could say anything, Gebhart turned to Himmelfarb.

"Karl, best you wait down at the house. Nothing should be disturbed, you see."

"It's my land, you know."

"Stimmt, Karl," said Gebhart, and laid a hand on the farmer's shoulder. "Just so."

"Cars come over the alm at night here this past while, you know."

"We'll talk about that, Karl. That's important."

"What are we going to do?"

"Everything will be taken care of, Karl. There are procedures."

Felix watched Gebhart get Karl Himmelfarb started on his walk back. He waited then, and when Himmelfarb turned after a few metres, Gebi had some words for him. There was a lot of head nodding and a bunch of soothing gestures with his hands.

"I'm lucky, am I?" said Felix when Gebhart made his way back up.

"Are you okay? Do you need to, well, you know?"

"Nothing left. Empty."

"Ah you poor kid. No, I don't mean lucky like horseshoes in your arsch. I mean experience. You'll learn a lot from this."

"Whether I like it or not."

"Natürlich. It's the way of the world. They don't teach that at the Uni?"

Felix too began to look around at the trees and hills.

"What do we do now?" he asked after a while.

"Damned if I know. Never did a murder before."

"There must be something."

Gebhart turned back and gave him a quizzical, almost pitying look.

"We just secure the site. The Kripo can do the rest."

"Like CSI?"

"You watch that crap too?"

"Only when it's on."

Gebhart eked out a thin smile.

"See? You're beginning to get it. You'll make it. Maybe you'll bring me luck. I should blow my beer money on the Lotto soon as I get back to town."

"That's the kind of luck I prefer."

Gebhart sighed.

"You have a boy like Hansi?"

Gebhart nodded.

"You know Himmelfarb from that place?"

"It's more that he knows me. Like a dummy I went there in uniform once after work. Well, straightaway I was a movie star. There's something about a uniform."

"That's why he phoned?"

"He didn't know who to phone."

"Social work, they call that, don't they?"

"Call it what you want. Up here the Gendarmerie do a bit of everything."

Felix shook his head. Gebhart said nothing further. He seemed to be listening for some sounds from far off. Then he took out his cigarettes, the Milde Sorte that everyone said they bought to try to cut down. He didn't offer one to Felix. He needed only one flick of his lighter to get the cigarette going.

"So here we are," Gebhart murmured after several moments. "Up here in the arschloch of Styria. Excuse me – the picturesque centre of Styria. And you're on the job, what three months? You go for a walk with this fellow. Then, Jesus, you come back down to the farmhouse, with your face as white as a sheet with your news."

"With puke on my shoes, don't forget."

Gebhart let his eyes wander to the hills behind Felix.

"Who cares," he murmured.

"Can I ask you something?"

Gebhart blew out smoke and nodded.

"Did you set me up with that big lug, going for walkies, holding hands? So you could get a laugh?"

"You think I would do that to you?"

"I'm asking you. I heard stuff like that in training."

"You want to know? I looked out the window and I thought: there's a good day's work being done. It was kind of nice, actually."

"Nice?"

"You were trying to get the kid out and about again. That's good."

The voice on the walkie-talkie was very clear now.

"Whoa," said Gebhart. "That was fast. They're close."

He waved Felix off using his walkie-talkie and began to give sparing directions.

Felix didn't want to look back to where the bodies lay. The woods seemed to be blanketed with an extra quiet now. He heard birds only occasionally, and far off. The clouds must have come lower. Sure enough, the crest of one mountain to the south was cut off. That sick feeling had left him, as had the swarming thoughts, but he could hear his own pulse. He realized he was glad of the cigarette smoke around him. Maybe there was a smell coming from the bodies that he hadn't noticed himself, but Gebi had. He watched as Gebhart smoked, and nodded, and said "yes" almost too often, his thumb stroking near the button on his walkie-talkie.

EIGHT

WHEN FELIX AWOKE, HE HEARD GIULIANA'S BREATHING. THERE was a faint lisp at the beginning of each breath in, and now he felt it on his shoulder. The room came out of the darkness, and brought the shapes he knew and expected, the corners and bulks, the lines, light and dark. Felix let his eyes run along them many times and he listened to her breathing. Well, he had slept awhile anyway.

He had to think a minute to remember – the big-shot detective's name from the Kriminaldienst: S– not Schmidt. It had two syllables. It was a real Austrian name: Speckbauer. Horst? Yes Horst. How hard could it be to come up with a normal Austrian name like this, he wondered. It wouldn't be that hard, unless your brain was scrambled by hours of interviewing, plodding, talking, writing, remembering, sorting out.

Speckbauer was a heavily moustached Oberstleutnant with hair running to grey. The rest of him was running to fat under the expensive suit that Gebi whispered they liked to wear. "They": Speckbauer and others, one a detective Engel who stood around a lot of the time, saying little, taking lots of digital shots and using a minicam.

Gebi had said he'd seen Speckbauer before somewhere, but he couldn't remember where. It certainly wasn't on a visit to HQ down in Strassgangerstrasse, in a western suburb of Graz. It might have been a piece in the *Gazette*. He looked like a proper Bananenbiegers, Gebi had muttered. When Felix asked him later what exactly a banana bender was, or did, Gebhart only waved the question away.

Speckbauer had a quiet tone like he was attending a funeral. Was there a weariness there, Felix had wondered, because he knew from long practice there were procedural questions he had to go through, but expected little from them? There were odd ones that Felix thought about afterwards: Did Hansi use any word except sleep? Can Hansi tell time? Did he make any other gestures? Did he point at places?

Felix had counted five police cars at one time, along with the wagon, and a big Mercedes commercial van that had two windows high up on one side. It was like a survey crew, with the markings and the tape and the screen they put up around the bodies. A generator had been started and flood lamps brought into the woods. Flashes went off every now and then. A movie set? A lot of guys in suits standing around, three – one woman included – in the white jumpsuits and hats, who later shed them (including, to Gebhart's keen interest, the woman technician) like chrysalises at the back of the van.

Of course there had to be royalty from the Gendarmerie showing up. By two o'clock, it was Pommer, the Gendarmerie kommandant for the district, and his 2-I-C. He had called Gebhart Sepp and he had told Felix that he had done good work. The pat on the shoulder, the direct look, and tight smile had confused Felix. Gebi saved him with a cough: this was one of those rare times when a Gendarminspektor should salute, and do it parade-ground style. Gendarmerie Kommandant Pommer returned the salute, much pleased, and perhaps even a bit surprised.

"Your father would be proud of you, Inspektor Kimmel."

"He knows everyone, does Pommer," he remembered Gebi telling him as the Gendarmerie Kommandant moved off.

"He knew my dad?"

"Everyone, I said. Now Pommer knows you. I'd better keep my eye on this Kimmel kid, I'll bet he's thinking. He's no depp, is Professor Kimmel. At this rate, he'll be Commissioner soon."

He and Gebi had stayed until 5:30. He remembered being given soup, and bread, by Frau Himmelfarb, and eyeing Hansi holding hands with his father at the door out to the yard. Felix had stayed at the post to get his notes word-processed and filed into the database. Had to be done, Gebi had said, not without sighing a few curses. It was all too likely one or more of those detectives would go straight to GENDIS this evening for some detail or other. They worked whatever hours they had to, he'd explained.

Then Felix thought again about Speckbauer, and the slow lumbering way he moved about. His handshake, the "We'll be in touch, Inspektor Kimmel" that had no real irony he could be sure of, had been delivered under his still, flat eyes. Kuhaugen, Felix's Oma Nagl might call that look, cow's eyes, resting on his for longer than felt normal.

He had phoned the garage and gotten his car back finally late in the evening, with a call to the guy's home to get the key. His head was still spinning when he got to the apartment finally, and he felt some vague cloud of something had followed him in. At first he did not intend to tell Giuliana, but it didn't take long. He remembered her not-impressed face as he downed three Gösser from the fridge as he talked.

Later he had wanted her ferociously. She was puzzled and slow and quiet, and he said he was sorry later, but she shushed him. He remembered her drowsy later on, her skin hot and damp everywhere and his own body dissolving into the sheets.

He rested his eyes on the drapes that mostly had the yellow glow from the platz below. A car – no, a small truck or van to judge by how its diesel clattered – went by. In a few hours he'd be sitting into his car and heading over to the post. They had to get the traffic safety thing started at the schools this week. It was to be his pleasure alone, Gebi had told him.

"Are you okay?"

She had been so quiet.

"Yes. Sorry. Go back to sleep."

He pulled the sheet over her shoulder and he kissed her neck. There was that scent again, of vanilla and parsley carried to him from the bedwarmth that wafted up over him. She muttered something. He waited for her breathing to lapse into that steady measured sigh that would mean she was asleep again.

Sometimes he teased her when she couldn't remember waking up in the night to go to the klo. The sight of her hips swaying and the swell of her bottom as she stumbled out, more sleepwalking than anything else, was more than he could bear by times. He stirred and the ache settled and grew. He glanced down at her. No, it wasn't fair: tomorrow was a workday for her too.

He lay very still and tried staring at the patterns on the wallpaper. That trick had often worked when he was a kid. Giuliana was way off on that stuff, he decided. If they ever could decide where they were going to move, there'd be no wallpaper, retro chic or not.

He pretended to be drowsy then, but still his thoughts played on, roaming farther, sharpening, and leading him back again to the woods above that farm. No longer were those meadows and trees just a background, like a mental postcard, typical sights you knew as far back as you could remember and just took for granted. Was it the shock of coming on those two, or did everything change when you were a cop? Nothing could go back to the way it was.

He wondered about the Himmelfarbs. The boy – the giant, he should start calling him – might not leave the house for weeks now. He remembered Himmelfarb muttering, and Gebhart's ways of trying to calm him. Ausländers, he had said, with some vehemence that Gebi had taken to be panic. Had he said something about gypsies too, or was Felix imagining that? But many people that age, especially the likes of the Himmelfarbs who'd lived up in God's country all their lives, would have mental furniture like that. It was no secret.

Felix moved his gaze to the ceiling. That didn't help. The grey there became a screen for the images that swirled into his mind. He saw again the forensic team stooping, with those funny-looking white suits that almost glowed white against the trees, the camera flashes, the detective talking into a recorder of some kind. The big move had happened very late in the afternoon, getting the bodies into bags and carrying them to the wagon. They had not been asked to help. He had looked away. Gebhart, he knew, had not.

So why, Felix wondered, was he thinking of his own father now? Maybe it had been the memorial yesterday, or the photo of the roadside taferl the Association had built for their fellow officer. As his eyes moved about the ceiling, he remembered this man who was his father coming into the kitchen after his shift, proud to wear his uniform home, and smelling a little of what he'd later know was a liqueur brandy. He'd tickle and then grab him, and soon he'd have Felix doing "the plane," spinning at arm's-length, the big hands on his ankles like a vice. Laughing, but being a bit scared too, the room flying by him.

NINE

"YOU SLEPT AT ALL?"

Felix wondered if he should surprise Gebi by telling him that young guys always slept well because they got laid.

"Medium," he said.

Gebhart came over with a sheaf of papers. He separated them, and laid them out on the counter next to the armoury safe.

"Come here. You're involved here, okay."

Felix saw the first was a print out of the statements he'd filed on the computer last night. Another was a list of the changes for the court appearance of the burglary gang they'd caught up to back after Christmas. There were lists of the grundschules for the public safety visits.

Gebhart tapped his finger on the list of schools.

"This will be a decent change today. You'll get a giggle out of this anyway," he said. "The small kids actually will put up their hands to ask your permission to go ludeln. You better be wide awake for that. Actually, I learned you should ask the teacher if the kids have been to the klo first."

"What, they get agitated or something?"

"Too true they do. They get scared some of them. They'll stare at you. You'll be taking reflective armbands or something, but they'll be staring at you like you're God, not hearing a word you say."

"As if they ever do," said Korschak from the far side of the cabinets.

"Fred," Gebhart called out. "You have the biggest ears. I'm going to miss them."

Felix looked down the list. He didn't recognize any of the teachers' names.

"The rumours will be flying today, I tell you," Gebhart said, and nodded toward Schroek's office. Felix looked up from the list. Gebhart had a printout of notes from yesterday.

"You heard Himmelfarb?" Gebhart went on, scanning the paragraphs. "He went though the whole list, I think. Did he actually say Russians at one point, even?"

"I don't think so. If he did, I didn't hear him. Did you?"

Gebhart stared at some point beyond Felix's head.

"Huh," he said. "I wonder if there was any sleep at Himmelfarbs' last night."

He looked to Felix then for corroboration, but his eye was taken by whatever he saw through the blinds on the glass that opened out to the public office. A short man with Gandhi glasses and a Gandhi hairdo had stepped in.

"Shit," said Gebhart. "Already."

He walked to the doorway.

"The Kontrolinspektor is on the phone," he called out.

Felix watched the man's reaction. A smile, a glance at his wristwatch, a hand holding a small device.

"Keep him waiting," said Gebhart when he came back. "Do him good."

"Who is he?"

"A scribbler, from the *Kleine*."

"A reporter? The *Kleine* . . . ?"

"Correct. What, you don't read the *Kleine Zeitung*? Everyone else in the province does. But this one has got the foreign angle already, no doubt. Now you forget about that side of things, okay? That was yesterday. You've done your paperwork, and it's moved on. And remember: don't talk to any reporter or media type. Schroek does that stuff."

Felix nodded.

"You're set up for the morning anyway, okay?"

"I think so."

"Bike safety video? Armbands?"

"Got it, and the posters."

"Those new bookmarks with the 'cool' website? The T-shirt prize?"

Felix almost grinned at how Gebhart did the air quotes for "cool." Again, Felix nodded.

"Well, bugger off then."

Gebhart yawned and sighed.

"Didn't you sleep?"

"I slept like a Christian, in case you need to know. But in the Coliseum."

Felix waited until Gebhart looked up from the paper.

"What is it? You have a question?"

"Have you done stuff like that before? Yesterday, I mean."

"No."

"Nothing like this? Never?"

Gebhart seemed to gather his thoughts by staring at his desk.

"You mean scare-the-hell-out-of-yourself stuff, or just things you see? Car accidents? Factory accidents?"

"I suppose."

"There was one thing comparable maybe," Gebhart said. "But I was in the army. Yes, I was keen, after National Service even. I took five years in it. You'd learn things, you know? Straightened me out actually. The service, it bred fellowship, you know? No, I don't mean mountain rescue camp or the trekking or the rest of it. Maybe we knew who the enemy was, then."

Felix zipped up the bag.

"Ach, you wouldn't want to hear it."

"What enemy, the Russians?"

A look of irritation crossed Gebhart's face.

"What's with all the Q & A today? Go do your duties."

"My dad said it was partly the whole Eastern Bloc thing, to be ready at least, if they came in. But that's been gone for years."

"Oh, I get it. The sun rises in the west now? The official line is we need Uni boys, more computer jockeys, more foreign languages. Well let me tell you something. Maybe we were a bit rough around the edges, or we didn't use the dictionary much, but, boy, you knew where you stood. Yes, we got things done. And no, that wasn't ancient times."

"Was it in the army, or in the Gendarmerie?"

"The thing that happened? It was the army. It was a winter exercise. Winterwerk, we used to call it. They gave us a lot of gear, and we had a hell of a lot of lugging to do. It was up high, you know, with a load of heavy snow. Anyway. A heavy machine gun went off on a guy. Seven or eight rounds, just like that. Everyone was bone tired, see? Sleeping in the goddamned snow. It was careless. But it was bad, I tell you."

He looked down at the nylon carry-all that they called the School Bag.

"Four hit him. And that's the nearest I've been in my life. It's not like TV."

He stretched again.

"I had nightmares, for a while, then."

Then Gebhart jerked his head up.

"No more yammering," he declared. "Scram, will you? You've got stuff to do."

Leaving, Felix caught a glimpse of Schroek's stone face as he listened to the reporter ask some questions. It was a look that he had seen on other cops too, part of the buttoned-up look that cops seemed to pick up with their uniforms and wore when they were not amongst their own.

But it was Giuliana's face that rose up in his mind again as he crossed the yard. This time tomorrow they'd be leaving, maybe on the road already. He'd be practising his Italian, but it wouldn't be serious for long. It was almost a year since that Night They'd Never

Forget, a terrible evening of arguing and shouting and tears that had quickly become The Night They Never Mentioned Since. The closest they had come was "that other time . . . " or "we don't want to go there again . . . "

It had been a stressful time for her, with evaluations and things. Felix himself had been grouchy, full of doubts and aversions to the training at the Gendarmerieschule, and the future he could imagine in the job. The bottles of wine hadn't helped. Maybe he'd brought it on unconsciously. Maybe she had?

He winced as he sat into the patrol car, remembering.

"Can you commit to anything?" she had yelled. "Anyone?"

Commitment: did the word haunt everyone these days?

It was true: he had been whining, and he had been whining because he was covering up something, even from himself. She sure had hit a nerve when she yelled that he was faking it.

Faking? All his moaning: how this had all been rigged by his mother, and that he should have known it; how he'd signed up at a time of guilt and bad judgment, when he was broke and unsure, and the dates had gone by for readmission to repeat the year; that many others in his class were stand-offish because he'd gone beyond a Matura. Others in the class hadn't even finished that far in school.

Felix had never found out, and never tried to find out, for sure if some of the trainees had heard about his father. And he had to admit that he too would have wondered about this Kimmel guy and if someone hadn't greased the way for the poor widow Kimmel's young lad to join up the Gendarmerie.

Faking, most definitely. The simple fact was that he didn't mind the training at all. The complex fact however was something that Giuliana had latched onto right away in that rousing, bitter fight. It was that he complained because he was beginning to enjoy the demands made of him, its impositions and schedules, its rules and habits. He just couldn't admit it to himself.

He checked his walkie-talkie and then the car radio. Korschak okayed him and reminded him to speak slowly. Ha ha. He pulled out of the yard, mentally plotting his way to the school again, and scanned the platz and the corner by Gasthaus Weber as he coasted by. He returned a small wave from the geezer who usually hung around on the bench there.

That was the thing with Giuliana, he'd understood: she said it right out. Always.

It was as if she could reach right in and say exactly the thing he couldn't, or didn't want to, put into words. She had learned that growing up, he was sure. Her father had walked out when she was four. Her mom had been a waitress, a cleaner, and some kind of higher up at the old folks place in Weiz. Too proud to go back to some place near Milan, the mom had stayed and made a new life, that of a single mom, with an Italian accent that could only remind all she met in the small town where they had been stranded that she was from an inferior society. You didn't get many chances with a background like that.

Felix got by the lights near the schule and was soon in sight of the huge chestnut trees that hid much of the library across from the school. He began to add up the years people spent in schools of one kind or another. He thought of Vikki, a perpetual student in the making. If he was up at all, he was maybe in some café in Graz. He was probably chatting up a girl. Now that the spring was here, he might even be up on the Schlossberg at that café near the top, looking for unattached female tourists of a certain age.

It would be only later in the day that his friend would be arguing in that mocking way he had about how people were addicted to work, or how Austrians were boring, dutiful. Cowed – that was his word. That required beer, probably at the Parkhaus in the evening, the restaurant in the city park that had just been rebuilt and had returned to popularity, pretty well instantly, with the mélange of bohemians, disguised civil servants, artsies that Graz brought together with ease. As long as someone was paying for the beer, of course.

Felix found himself smiling at the thought as he drove along. Vikki would always be okay for a night on the town, even if Felix had paid for most of the beer again. Would he ever tell Vikki how he had hiked up a half a kilometre hand in hand with a retarded kid? That he counted that as part of his day's work, the "Nice job" that Gebhart had called it? Probably not.

He parked near the library and took the carry-all and the case with the projector out of the back of the patrol car. Already there were faces in one of the windows upstairs.

☩

It went well at the start. The little ones were suitably awed. Most got passionately involved with the welfare of Helpless Hans, the cartoon character. Hans was thoughtless near traffic, stupidly did what his sneaky peers wanted of him. There he was drinking from bottles whose contents he did not know. Next he was distracting a shop-keeper while his so-called mates rifled chocolate from a shelf. He was then telling whoppers at home to cover for himself and others. The false friends all had eyebrows that arched, Felix noticed.

Felix himself had done pretty well all these things in varying degrees. Now his work was to urge others not to follow in the mis-creant's way. The colouring sheet and word puzzles were a hit. There were no men teachers at these ages apparently, and, so busy and keen were the little ones, that he had time to chat with a few teachers about the Internet, about burglaries, about a first cousin stationed in Judenburg name of Rudi, and about other matters. He had a little time to stroll the hallway. It wasn't Helpless Hans he was thinking of then for a moment, but a different Hans, the unshaven Hansi Himmelfarb. He distracted himself by paying attention to the wild improbability of the art on the walls. He liked the serious intent on the kids' faces, and the cheerful teachers. The tiny chairs, and the huge toys made him smile. Some kids picked their noses fearlessly. He heard at least one fart.

Fortified by not-bad coffee in the staffroom where he saw but two men amongst a dozen teachers, he had forgotten what the older kids could be like. His guide was a talkative, bespectacled nerd in the senior class. He kept asking Felix how fast he had ever driven "chasing the bad guys" while he unhelpfully guided the trolley with the TV and video, and Felix's charts and handouts, down the terrazzo hallways.

They had congregated two classes for the presentation. The teacher who remained was a defeated-looking guy with a finely trimmed beard. He expected to be left to mark things and after a few perfunctory remarks, retired to a desk and began writing things. The kids had that X-ray vision and a feral instinct for new teachers, visiting teachers, and it transferred well to the probationary Gendarme.

Questions started early. Felix heard himself say "Good question" too many times and for a while he was unable to stop. He managed to improvise, however: "Let's take that after you see the video." One dickschädel, a short fellow with a smile that was more of a leer, a ringleader no doubt, kept going, of course. He wanted to know about drugs, parties, and if you had to say even one word to a policeman who wanted to talk to you. And had he ever shot someone, by the way? And why? And had he been shot?

By the end of the hour Felix was close to the edge. He wanted to walk over to Teacher Man and tap him on the head so he'd look up. Then he wanted to tell Junior Lawyer of the Year that a little pisser like him would last about a nanosecond on the street with a mouth like that.

It was recess when he left the room. A smartass followed him down the hall and told him about Rohypnol, MSN house party lists, and how a kid he knew had to go to the hospital last Christmas with alcohol poisoning.

"Thanks," said Felix. "I think it's recess, isn't it?"

"They know so much," said the useless Teacher Man, safely behind his glasses and with a vacant look to him. "But they understood so little."

Felix, who had badly wanted overpaid Teacher Man to wade in a half-dozen times so the big mouths could be shut up, nodded. He even offered a sympathetic shrug when Teacher Man droned on about the perils of unsupervised Internet access at home and the American video games that were so violent. And the movies and TV, Mein Gött!

But as he passed by the doorway, Felix heard the shouts from the schoolyard. Recess was definitely his best subject at that age. It was a breezy, sunny day now. Kids were on swings, playing soccer. The winter was gone. This wasn't the time or place for thoughts of two dead men in the woods. He and Giuliana would be making their escape tomorrow, and they'd head down to the beaches on the Adriatic side. Soon, there'd be time to bum around the Hofgasse to take a day at the hot springs in Waltersdorf.

He caught sight of the kid who'd been the pain in the ass in the senior class – Mr. Rohypnol, he would call him – calling out something that his friends laughed at. Felix didn't see the victim of his wit, but Mr. Rohypnol caught his eye. Felix nodded. Mr. Rohypnol mimed smoking a joint to his friends.

Felix turned away and strolled down the hallway. He rehearsed a conversation with Gebhart, one he would never have, while he waited for recess to end:

Felix: Gebi, this is going to be hard on you. It's about our work. Prepare yourself.

Gebhart: You're a Gendarme for five months and suddenly you're a genius?

Felix: Listen, it came to me today, in school. I was actually conflicted.

Gebhart: Get married. That fixes all that psychological stuff.

Felix: Here it is: we're actually inciting kids to do things that we warn them against. It's the old forbidden fruit thing!

Gebhart: That's you. I wish I could forbid you from talking.

Felix: Kids want to be trouble; they want to do the naughty stuff.

Gebhart: What a colossal idiot you are. Unbelievable.

Felix: It's evolution, Gebi. There's nothing we can do.

Gebhart: Absolute shit. That's nihilism, and nothing but. And you learned that at the Uni? Sue them for your fees back. You were robbed, I say.

Felix: You're in denial. That's how I know I'm right, my friend.

Gebhart: I'm not your friend. I don't make friends with bull-shitters.

Felix: They want danger. They want to trespass. It's arousing.

Gebhart: Are you on medication? Too much? Too little?

Felix: The uniform, the school, the rules and signs – they cannot stamp out human nature. If we only took a look down through the levels of consciousness more, instead of lectures and rules–

Gebhart: I know it's a democracy. But maybe it's time for laws against blöde talk like this. Especially from a cop.

Felix: Did you ever wonder if, maybe some cops are people without the courage to be criminal?

Gebhart: Really? Your dad would be delighted to hear you talk this way. I don't think.

Felix: One must suffer sometimes for the truth, Gebi–

The door to the office opened. It was the secretary he had been introduced to first thing this morning. Her glasses hung almost on her nostrils.

"Grüss Gött, Inspektor– can you take a telephone?"

"For me?"

Then he remembered: he had switched off the walkie-talkie. Gebi had reminded him to do it.

He pulled his trolley back to the door of the office.

"Kimmel, Felix?" the secretary asked, eyeing him over the rim of her glasses.

"Yes."

"Well, I went to school with your father," she said. "God rest his soul. Felix."

"He had many friends."

"'Ein bisschen Kümmel,'" she said. "'A little caraway goes with everything.'"

Felix did not tell her he had never heard that one before. He smiled and he followed her through to a small room with a table and a phone, and a small window that looked out over the schoolyard.

It was Gebhart.

"You're just about finished your arduous duties there?"

"I am."

"Okay. Me I'm going to lunch but I wanted to get in touch with you before I left. It's so as you can prepare yourself. A two o'clock meeting, with you involved."

"Just me? What for?"

"It's the KD from Graz, some of the ones who came out to the site yesterday."

"Himmelfarbs?"

"You remember them?"

"A weird-looking guy with shades, who said nothing. A big guy, moustache, Speckbauer?"

"Well, maybe you can be a real cop, with recall like that. They– he, Speckbauer– wants to talk to you. So the minute you get back, get your notes, get a printout and get ready. I say you should buy a sandwich and do your reading over lunch. You don't want to look stupid, okay?"

Felix thought about the big mittagessen that Gebi favoured, his favourite soup and pork and potatoes in a small stübe at the back of the butcher's. It was always full of farmers and older men.

"What about you?"

"What about me? I told you, I'm hungry."

"No. I meant the interview."

"Oh, I talked to them already. No big deal. But they didn't want to take you away from the school thing."

"On my own, these two guys?"

"Was gibt? What's the issue here? You think they're going to beat you up, Mr. Prime Suspect?"

"But I didn't do much, Gebi. Nor did you. And we talked to them yesterday up at Himmelfarbs', didn't we?"

"Well, burli, you may be a bit puzzled. So am I. They seem quite keen to talk to you. Don't forget– you and Hansi were together. This Speckbauer, he's quite the character. I checked him out. He's no joker, this guy."

"Okay. Thanks. Maybe."

"Don't let any of that smartass sarcastic stuff leak out of you, didn't I tell you? That's if you want to keep this job. 'Felix the Second.'"

"What's this about, this 'Felix the Second' crap?"

"It was Speckbauer said that: 'Felix the Second.' You've got to be double careful, I tell you. Bad enough he's a big wheel from Zentrale, but he's like the Holy Spirit or something. Knows everything. I've got to go – I've got leberknödel suppe getting cold."

Felix adjusted the volume on the mouthpiece of his walkie-talkie and told Korschak he was back on the road. He put Helpless Hans, the whole two hours of his stupid but instructive antics, and the posters, in the car. Scheisse: the box of bookmarks was full – he'd forgotten to hand them out.

TEN

"THEY WANT TO MEET OVER COFFEE," FELIX SAID TO GEBHART.
"But somewhere else."

"You're not making sense," said Gebhart. "Did they knock you
around in there or something? What's going on?"

Speckbauer came out of the klo. He had combed his hair.

"Can we borrow the kid here, Sepp?"

"A duty call, you want him for?"

"Natürlich. It's a few details concerning the business yesterday.
You're senior here at the moment?"

Gebhart hesitated. Korschak pretended to be studying court
documents. Even he wasn't that dumb that he wouldn't have picked
up the tone in Speckbauer's question.

"No reason why not," he said. "But not for too long."

He looked at Felix.

"Give me a minute with him; see what he needs to hand off."

"Absolutely," said Speckbauer, and stepped aside. "Half an
hour?"

Gebhart motioned Felix over to his desk.

"What have you done, kid?"

"Nothing. I don't know. They're yapping and then pitching in
a weird question every now and then."

"That guy with the shades, you know about him yet?"

Felix nodded.

"He went through the wars, I tell you. I phoned a guy I joined with, in Strassgangerstrasse. He knew this guy right away. Nearly got toasted. Wife left him; about a hundred operations. They called him the Mummy, I hear. Speckbauer is a bigwig of some kind. They give him offices, a budget, a bunch of gadgets. He has lines to important people, so off he goes and does his own thing. Has he . . . ?"

Felix shook his head.

"My friend thinks that Speckbauer is part of a group. They work with the guys in the BP or the James Bonds out of the C.I.S. They sit down with suits from Interpol every month, in Munich mostly, or Brussels, and they talk about satellites and syndicates and poppies and prostitutes. Are you getting any of this?"

"Bits. But what does this have to do with yesterday?"

"Well, ask him," said Gebhart. "I'd be interested to see how he handles that one. All I'm saying is, these two are not Peter and Paul cops. Watch what you say. Come straight to me or Schroek when you get back so we can figure out what the hell to do about them."

Felix glanced over at Speckbauer and Franz. Speckbauer leaned against an opposite wall of the hallway, apparently examining his shoes and murmuring to the other. Speckbauer held a large envelope under his armpit.

"Okay, Felix," said Gebhart, replacing papers with others and closing a folder. "But you have to be there for the two o'clock. You're the officer issuing, so it's in person or the guy can ask for a walk from the judge."

"Thank you, Bezirkinspektor Gebhart."

"Don't be an arschloch," he heard Gebi whisper as he passed.

ELEVEN

THE THREE POLICEMEN STOOD IN THE GASSE, THE LANEWAY, outside the post for a moment.

"There's a konditorei next to the SPAR," said Felix. "That's pretty well it for restaurants here."

"An excellent choice, then," said Speckbauer.

There were a few German plates on the cars parked around the platz. Felix returned a greeting from the jaded-looking woman who ran a small blumen shop. She was still a practising hippie according to Gebi, big into flower-power.

"Charming little place," said Speckbauer. "But kind of compact, isn't it?"

"Pretty much so."

"It has to be the smallest Gendarmerie post in the province," added Speckbauer.

Speckbauer looked up and down the street.

"There's a rumour it'll be closed up when we amalgamate with the Polizei."

Speckbauer's smile lingered.

"Ach," he said. "I have the feeling you're ready for bigger things. But wait– your timing in joining up was good. The new police service will open things up."

"So I have been told."

"And you know this area? The people, hereabouts?"

"Sort of," said Felix. "More each day."

"But the general area," Speckbauer went on. "Up the mountains, like yesterday?"

Felix remembered Gebi's caution. He tried to calibrate his answer.

"Well, some, I suppose."

"You grew up there though."

"You mean right here? No."

"St. Kristoff."

"Yes. That's where."

"You knew the Himmelfarbs before yesterday?"

"No. Not personally."

"But you know your way around, all up there?"

Felix met his gaze.

"It's been a few years," he said. "The university thing, and so forth, in Graz."

Speckbauer nodded at this, the air of kindly interest and the smile undiminished.

Felix held the door of the konditorei for them. He caught a glimpse of graft scars up close as Franz passed. A faint scent of medicine or some hospital smell was left in the air after he passed.

Konditorei Fischbach had made itself over last year, Gebhart had told him. Apparently it had been a dark kitcheny place that hadn't changed since the Archduke had gotten in the way of a bullet. Now it had gone almost techno.

"Lieber Gött," said Speckbauer. "A space station?"

The woman behind the counter was the daughter, and she was the brainchild of the reno, Felix had heard. She went with the belief that the new parts factories would be bringing people to the area, even to this sleepy corner.

There were two thirtyish women at a table near the far end. The smell of baking was strong.

"Grüss," said the woman and nodded at Felix. She pushed back a strand of gelled hair that fell over her eyes like a batwing.

"Servus," said Speckbauer, brightly. "Coffee I think: a grossen braunen, if you please, gnädige frau."

She glanced at Felix to see if the old-fashioned courtesy was genuine.

"Melange for me," he said.

"Mineral water also," Speckbauer added. "For my associate here."

Franz moved into the booth slowly. Felix thought he heard him sigh once.

"Watch and make sure that she doesn't spike the coffees," said Speckbauer. "Right Franzi?"

Franz nodded.

"Ah, but why complicate matters?" said Speckbauer then, and turned to watch a van negotiating the lane to the side.

The music was techno, a continuous tattoo with heavy backing. It sounded like an electronic string section made of tired banshees. Speckbauer began to hum something, tapping his finger rhythmically on the envelope. Felix still couldn't see Franzi's eyes behind the sunglasses. Still he felt sure he was eyeing the two women across from them.

"So," said Speckbauer, and drew his elbows up on the table. "How'd you like it so far?"

Felix didn't know what to say.

"My duties?"

"Yes, your duties."

"Well, there's a variety of them I hadn't expected, Herr Oberstleutnant."

"Oberstleutnant?" said Speckbauer. "You know the rank? It didn't come up in yesterday's chat, at the farm. Yesterday I was Horst and you were Felix."

"Correct, er."

"Let's go back to that. No rigmarole, please. Even in suits we're still Gendarmes."

"I understand."

"Good. We have enough things to make us unbehaglich, don't we? And stress can kill. Isn't that so, Franz? The stress?"

"Terrible harm," said Franz, tonelessly.

The waitress/owner was prompt with the coffees. She laid napkins and a plate of wafer biscuits.

"Mannerschnitte, how could I forget," said Speckbauer.

"They are complimentary," she said.

Speckbauer told her she was very kind, and that he would be telling everyone he knew to go to this restaurant. Felix stirred his sugar in and wondered if she were trying to make up for something earlier. Maybe she hadn't taken the two for cops when they came in.

Speckbauer tore open his sachet of brown sugar.

"Did you know Franz is also a Leutnant?" he asked. "No? But he wears it lightly. He's the deep thinker. I am the talker. And the sunglasses? You were too polite to ask, I think. So, I will tell you. Franz' favourite movie is *The Matrix*. So there. The American dreck wins, all the time. You like that new Clint Eastwood one, the girl boxer . . . ?"

"I haven't seen it."

"Before your time, maybe. Franz? Clint Eastwood. Yes, or no?"

"No. I told you before. I suspect he is a latent homosexual."

"Franz is well educated. Night school. I made him go. Isn't that funny? I mean funny peculiar, of course."

Felix made a noncommittal gesture.

"Damn but that is a fine coffee," said Speckbauer, and sucked at the ends of his moustache.

"Franz was feeling sorry for himself, you see," he went on. "So I kicked his arsch around the room quite a number of times. Right, Franzi?"

"Just so. Many times."

"I had rank on him then. But now he caught up. You can see how outspoken he is. Tactless – insolent, actually. Some days he is unbearable. Yesterday, for example. See, did you hear him say a word yesterday? All those hours up at that delightful farm five million kilometres from dreary city civilization as we know it?"

"No, actually."

"Do you speak Italian, Felix?"

Felix tried not to react to the sudden shift.

"No."

"Not even a bit? *Mi amore*, that sort of endearment?"

Felix shrugged.

"*Cappuccino*," Speckbauer said. "*Ciao, bambino. Carabinieri,* maybe?"

"They are police, that I know."

"Indeed they are. Franz, how do you rate our friends in the Carabinieri? Give us out of five – only the last couple of years, with our team, our side."

Franz held up three fingers.

"They are only good when we can see what the hell they're doing. If you go to, I don't know, Sicily or Calabria, well all bets are off. Where is Giuliana from?"

"Giuliana who?"

And Speckbauer exploded into laughter.

Felix was surprised to realize that his own anger soon disappeared. He looked over to Franz who was wiping the corners of his mouth with a paper napkin. His mouth was like a slash, thin-lipped. There was something of the alien look to him.

"Keep going," Franz murmured. "He likes it when you kick back."

Speckbauer's laughter subsided and he stopped shaking. He rubbed at the corners of his eyes with his knuckles.

"Good," he said, and lifted his cup again. "It's been a while since we had that. Did Gebhart warn you?"

"He said to smarten up and mind my manners."

"Lovely. Solid advice indeed. Been to Zagreb, have you?"

"No."

"Why not?"

"Because in Zagreb I heard there were problems, gangsters probably."

"Okay," said Speckbauer. "But that has changed – for tourists anyway. I forgot, sorry. You'd have been a kid when the crap hit the fan there. Been to Sarajevo?"

"Same, no."

"Slovenia? Laibach, Lyubanya they call it there?"

"Sure. Maybe a dozen times since I was a kid."

"Family trips? Dad driving, like?"

"Most of them."

"You went on a bash or two though, surely. Come on – the student drinking weekends? Really, now."

"I don't get this," said Felix. "Is this some kind of a test?"

"No, no. Why, do you have a problem chatting with colleagues?"

Felix said nothing.

"Sure we're from the big Zentrale and all that. But we're on the same team. You remember provincial headquarters?"

"Of course," said Felix.

"Ah, those were the days, for me too. Soccer, training, the firing range. All that."

Felix nodded.

"But what a day yesterday, no? I don't remember getting any training for that. Do you?"

"No. It was bad, all right."

Speckbauer nodded sympathetically.

"Bet you never saw things like that before. Upsetting, no?"

Felix nodded. He wondered if it was a hint about him puking.

Speckbauer got up.

"So tell me, Felix. Are you good on faces?"

"It's hard to say. We did the points of comparison training and things of that nature. But it takes practice, I would think. Or experience."

"Indeed. And how well you put it."

Speckbauer stretched.

"Okay then," he said. "Franzi? Exhibit A?"

Franz made a final few slow dabs at his lips with the napkin.

"Remember I said that Franzi here is the thinker, Felix? And I am the talker? Franz doesn't like to talk much. He likes to save his energy. Weird, uh?"

Felix watched Franzi drink more mineral water. He heard noisy gulps.

"He is not really the guy in *The Matrix*, Felix, I must confess. It's a story, a little spielerei we have. The shades are quite necessary. Franz and daylight are not compatible. But he is not a vampire. Are you Franzi?"

Franz shook his head. His baby finger worked at a piece of food lodged in his front teeth. His other hand came up and pushed his sunglasses up off his nose. Felix took in the shiny white skin, the wandering lines that sometimes had pink edges. The eyes were from science fiction, but Franz let the glasses down again.

"Franz doesn't cry. I suppose part of his job is to make others cry. But he cannot produce tears, or to be more accurate 'express' them. Is 'express' a doctor word, Franzi?"

"I believe it is."

"Ah, so indeed. There was damage done there. The grafts cannot fix that apparently. And Franz has troubles putting out enough fluids there. Am I saying it right, Franzi?"

"Most. Enough."

"I should practice more maybe. But the winter is hard on him, and the wind too. There are little bottles he applies quite often. I tell you all this Felix, so . . . ?"

"So you can tell me something else, or ask me, afterwards?"

Speckbauer made a gentle smile.

"Sehr gut. Anyway. When they set Franz on fire they were hoping that that was the last of him. But they did not know our Franz. What's the name of that fountain again, Franz?"

"Mandusevac."

"And a filthy fountain it was. But right in a square, a main one too: they don't care, you see. Jelacica, that's the place, the square. We had a meeting there, didn't we?"

Franz nodded.

"Well, Franz was out of the car and into that cesspool as fast as, well, as fast as Hermann Maier down that slalom. A hell of an achievement, I tell you. Better than any gold medal Klammer or any of those ski genius boys can pull off in Kitzbühel. The prize? Way better. Right, Franz?"

Again Franz nodded.

"He got to keep his eyesight. Well most of it."

"Which I guess makes it maybe a little ironic here," Speckbauer went on. "He gets to see the face of the guy who did it to him."

"You mean yesterday?"

"Franzi, you still think, you know?"

"Hard to be sure," said Franz. "Like the Chinaman said. You know?"

"I don't get it," said Felix.

"Right. It's an old joke. A Chinese guy flies to Vienna. It's his first time out of China, no? An ORF guy is there to interview him, you know: millions of tourists from China, billions of shillings – what am I saying, Euro – dancing in the brains of the Tourism Department. Are you with me?"

"Sort of."

"Good enough. So the interviewer gets the camera on the Chinaman. He sticks a microphone under his nose – oh, I didn't tell you this Chinaman has been studying German since birth, did I? – and asks the fateful question: 'What are your first impressions of us Austrians?' What do you think he said?"

"I don't know."

"You're thinking dirndl? Cowbells? Sacher torte, decent coffee? Strauss, maybe. Skiing? None of that Hitler crap, obviously. What do you think the guy said?"

"I haven't a clue."

"Really?"

"Really."

"Well, this is what he said: 'These Austrians, they all look the same to me.'"

Speckbauer didn't laugh. Nor did he smile. He remained intensely interested, it seemed to Felix, in a passing tractor that did not slow as it wheeled by the konditorei.

After seconds passed with no response from Felix, Speckbauer leaned in.

"What this means is that these two characters up in the woods could be any of them. 'Them'? Well, we don't really know 'them.' 'Them' seems to start just southeast of here. Remember, before the Slovenes got into the EU club, when they had the border post? You rolled up to the border post and seeing all that Russian-looking alphabet starting just the far side of the barrier? The Cyrillic words . . . ?"

He sat back and eyed Franz a moment.

"But this much I do know. I want Franzi here to be able to use those eyes of his to see the face, or the faces of the men who sprayed the gasoline in the car and threw a match in on him. Verstehst? Got that?"

"I think so."

"Good. And I don't much care how we find them."

Speckbauer looked around the restaurant again, and stretched. Felix caught a glimpse of the pistol in its holster under Speckbauer's arm as he arched.

"More coffee?" he asked Felix.

TWELVE

GIULIANA WAS MARKING SOMETHING WHEN HE GOT IN. FELIX
had driven back to the apartment by one of those freak journeys, a
miracle where he couldn't actually remember long stretches of the
road. Nor could he remember what he had been thinking about. It
unnerved him. It also made him aroused.

"What the hell," she said as his arms went around her.

"Is it a bad time?"

"It's not that."

He heard her voice change and she was pushing the papers and
her empty cup away. He slid his hands under her T-shirt, and felt the
dampness by her armpits.

"Jesus," she murmured. "You're hardly in the door."

"Pretty close. Come on."

He covered her mouth with his, and felt her rising from the
chair. Her breasts flattened against him and his hand traced her
spine up and back to her hips, straining now against her track pants.

"You want me so badly," he whispered. "I just know it."

"You goof," she said.

His hand slid around her and pulled her into him. He felt her
hips push back and she settled her crotch with a small movement
against him. He thought of her ass, of how she was embarrassed in
the beginning always but then gave way and stretched, with that cat
smile, her eyes almost closed.

She gave a little sigh and he felt her breath puff onto his ear.

His fingers sought the parted flesh and slid over the hairs there, finding their way to her bone and the soft folds he sought.

"You're terrible," she whispered. "What's gotten into you?"

"It's called 'We're on holiday.' And you made me do it."

"Me?"

He raised his arms under the T-shirt and did too as he pulled it over her head.

"No staring," she whispered, but her eyes were almost closed already.

"Will if I want."

His breath was coming out in short deep gusts now. She held her arms behind her head and opened her eyes.

"Not fair," she said. "You, you first."

He tried to keep his eyes on hers while he got his clothes off. He almost lost his balance with the first leg of his pants.

"How long have you been walking around with that?"

"With what?"

She threw her arms down and lifted the band of his underpants. Then she dropped to one knee to draw them down. Before she had reached his knee, she had grabbed at him.

"No," he said, lying. "No."

He felt her teeth settle in, leave and settle in again.

"No, Giuliana?"

She lifted her head, and she slid back on the carpet and kicked off her pants. Her scent reached him and seemed to envelop him, and he stared at her bush as her legs went up, until the cleft appeared. She pulled the last leg off her foot and her hand reached for her crotch.

"Is that what's on your mind?"

He tried to nod but the muscles in his neck were so tight that he shuddered instead. She was staring at him and the smile was gone. Her hips made a small, sliding movement.

"Let me," he said. It came out as a croak.

"Let you what?" she whispered. "What should I let you do?"

"Let me do it for you. Come on."

Her eyelids almost closed.

"Tell me what you want to do."

He stepped out of his underpants, his penis giving a spasm. His belly contracted in a shiver. Her forefinger had disappeared, he saw. There was a roaring in his ears, like he was underwater.

He got down on his knees. She reached a leg around him.

"Let me."

"I haven't had my shower," she said.

It was the old fake, and he'd guessed from the start that she'd say it. It was the same way she said her ass was too big, or that her boobs wouldn't ever go out on a topless beach. It was to dare herself, and him.

He stilled her hand, drew it away. Her hair was like breath on his face, and the soft tissue that met his mouth seemed to dissolve.

She sighed, and seemed to want to draw back. He pulled her more to him until at last he felt her hips begin to move, and to push gently against him.

"You," she said in a clear voice. "I want to."

He slowed, and raised his head. Her face was flushed and strange.

"Lie," she said, turning, and drew up her leg.

"I don't," he tried.

"I know I know," she said, and she pushed against his chest.

She was not tender now. She moved around a lot, tugging and releasing, only to use her tongue in the intervals.

"You should stop," he said again.

When he felt it, he tried to pull her up.

"Giuliana!"

She pushed at him and then he was lost to the brushing of her hair on his belly. She worked harder, even when he cried out. He tried to sit up again, but then he let go and her mouth clasped around him, and he went still.

Things cascaded through him, an avalanche, as the last tics got weaker. Guilt, some frantic wish he couldn't pin down, and his senses exploding as everything raced through him, fled, and then crashed over him again.

"Not fair," he said weakly. "Not fair."

Then her face was over his. He felt her breasts drag across his chest. She looked at him with an expression that was almost a smile.

"Let me," he said.

But as he reached for her, she was up.

"We're not finished," he called out.

He heard a tap running.

"Be quiet," she said. "I know. I can't just get off like that. Not now."

He listened to the tap water, heard it divert and splash.

When she came back there were water drops on her breasts. She knelt on the bed and sat back on her legs.

"Let me," he said. "I want to."

She smiled now, and it reminded him of how he'd seen a blind-man smile.

"I know," she murmured and let herself be pushed back. "You are so spoiled, kiddie, so spoiled."

THIRTEEN

IT TOOK UNTIL FOUR TO GET TO KITZBÜHEL PROPER. FELIX didn't want to flog the Polo to death to get there a half an hour early, especially with the rack and bike frame on top. It would be light until nine anyway, now.

Giuliana had dozed on and off for an hour after they'd hit the M1. He'd stopped to fill the tank just before Spittal, right off the autobahn. They had semmels and wurst – not-bad cured ham and the buns were still warm – and a few slices of Havarti in a bakery next to the Fina. They sat at a bench to eat them, just as the sun came out. He bought beer before they left.

They were soon amid thickening traffic that he guessed was Salzburg-bound, and he was glad to get off again at Bischofshofen. He stayed on the main road after, rather than the slower and more scenic route that would have led them by St. Johann.

Giuliana put down a guidebook on Thailand. She looked at the sharp edges on the crests of the Kitzbüheler Alpen that had risen up steadily to their right.

"I can't stop thinking about that," she said. "What you did up there. It would give me nightmares for sure. The two, you know . . . ?"

"Who knows," he said. "You do what you have to. Mom will tell you how squeamish I was when I was a kid."

Kitzbühel was fairly cluttered already, with more tour buses than Felix expected. He let the Polo through the outer streets toward the zentrum, eyeing the Beemers and Audis and SUVs. A tour bus with a lot of Asians was jammed at the curve that led to the train station. Giuliana giggled as they inched by and looked up at the faces.

"Banzai!"

"How do you know they're Japanese?"

"They look like rabbits."

"Are you one of those racist cops who picks on Albanians and Nigerians, huh?"

"Ouch. Are you Red Brigades? Humour, please, liebchen."

"Don't 'liebchen' me. I'm not one of your Alpine maidens."

He turned down the lane he had found the first year he'd come with the ski club in hochschule. They'd gotten drunk before going on the lift and nearly fell off.

He pulled in beside a cream Fiat with a German plate and a Munich crest on the window.

"That might be one of our guys," he said. "See the rack?"

He looked over at Giuliana and looked around her face, at the faint glow of perspiration high on her forehead. The air conditioning in the Polo had failed a couple of years ago now. It wasn't worth fixing.

He liked how her hair rattled out into a loose bundle as the breeze had tugged at it, mile after mile. She gave him a skeptical stare.

"What?"

He raised an eyebrow.

"I know that look."

"You do, uh?"

"What are you thinking about?"

"Last night."

"Oh," she said and batted at him. He laid his hand on her leg.

"I have X-ray vision," he said. "They teach it at the Gendarmerie school."

She smacked his hand and then opened the door.

"Stop it. Come on. Get the stuff."

He took the bike frame down and laid it on the grass margin

that ran along the front of the car park. He took out the wheels then, and the Velcroed pouch that held the tools.

Giuliana still kept her first rucksack from when she was a kid. She had filled it with books and paper and fruit and nuts and God knows what else. He began strapping the wheels to the frame, paying a lot of care to where the spokes rested. Then he tested the weight of the package.

Giuliana chewed on an apple, looking off over the roofs toward the cable car lines that rose from the town up the slopes of the Hochkitzbühel. A cable car was moving slowly at one of the steepest sections, a 70-degree length close to the top of the Streif. It was that sheer drop where skiers made their bones, where they could declare they had skied the Hahnenkamm, complete with the Mousetrap, the section that had ended so many Olympic hopes. Felix thought about the trail up beyond the hotel there, the Ehrenbachhöhe, over the ridges that led to Penglestein summit and on to Blaue Lacke.

He checked the glove compartment before settling the parking permit better on the dashboard. Giuliana checked the doors a second time while he loaded up his pack.

The streets were busy, with people standing around, moving in groups slowly down the sidewalks, pausing to look at the souvenirs and clothes. There were plenty milling about the steps to the Andreaskirche too. The cafés on Klostergasse were close to full. A deeply tanned man with designer stubble and unnaturally white teeth he liked to display, along with his bare feet in those American-style moccasins, gave Felix the thumbs-up from behind a glass of beer.

"Sehr gut, mann!"

Felix sniffed the air for signs of chemical happiness. He couldn't manage even a fake smile.

"Have a nice day, man," he replied.

A cluster of Asians with silly hats stood listening intently to a woman dressed up in a flowery Tyrolean dirndl, with the endless

pigtails and the stout shoes. To round things out, a youth in leder-
hosen was explaining something in fluent Italian to two heavy-set,
sweating women that Felix decided could only be nuns in civvies up
from Rome. They listened, nodding gravely, and looked up the path
of the cable cars above.

He bought the three-day pass and let the ticket seller eye how
he had kitted up the bike. It was a slack time for ascents, apparently. They walked through the empty passageway toward the ramp.

"Well, now you have company," Giuliana said. "Your play-
mate."

Peter was the real mountain man. He had been loud and
clomping from birth, Felix had concluded early on after their first
meeting at the Gendarmerie intake in Graz. Schwartz Peter, they
called him soon enough – the joker of the pack. Felix had soon
learned there was something behind the pose, however. The same
Peter very ably rested a keen brain, and big ambitions behind the
goofy pose. The same Peter Moser had already impressed the CO at
his post in Graz that he should be training at the central
Gendarmerie college in Mödling.

"My God, Giuliana," he called out in that deep Styrian voice,
the bellen that Schwarzenegger had exported to the world. "I was
hoping you'd bring someone decent this time."

Peter gave Giuliana his trademark sweaty bear hug. Felix eyed
the newish bike that Peter had brought with him.

"Scheisse der auf," he said to Felix then. "You're expecting this
bunch of cheap metal of yours to keep you going across to Blauesee
even?"

"I don't need designer bikes, you big oaf."

"Don't you save any money down there in where-the-hell,
Schweinwein?"

"Stefansdorf."

"Or does this nice lady here take it from you?"

"He's predictable," said Giuliana. "If nothing else."

"Damned right. We're hitting the paths the minute we get out of this coffin on strings, huh? You too, Giuliana, has he converted you?"

"No heroics," she said. "It's just a recreation for me, not a way of life."

"Some of my best friends are bookworms. Hey, what are you reading this time?"

They got the Kanada car on the gondola. They had to wait for a grizzled old man in traditional mountaineering gear complete with a new feather in his hat and a walking stick, and a woman Felix hoped was his daughter, to alight first.

Peter unburdened himself of a longish joke about a German and a Swiss and a Swede who got drunk in a stübe in the nowhere end of Burgenland one dark winter night. Felix pretended to listen, all the while watching Giuliana trying not to freak, even a little, as the gondola began its traverse of the meadow and sheds below, the gentle glide that would become something altogether different after the next few pylons.

The joke over, Felix allowed a chuckle. Peter looked around the car, taking in the view of the clusters of houses and streets, the Pfarrkirche that made up Kitzbühel. Across the town Kitzbühelhorn, all two thousand metres of it, stood sharp against a deep blue sky. Up the valley beyond Aurach, the Höhe Tauern, the Alps proper, began. There were serious pockets of snow even midway up there yet. They joined, most of them, into solid caps clear against a lighter blue sky to the north.

Felix let himself sag into the seat more. He rested his eyes for several moments on the almost luminous greens of the nearby valleys, those exuberant bursts of growth that sprang up at the end of the long winters here, not 50 kilometres from the Bavarian border. The air growing cooler already. He found himself slipping into a mental rehearsal of what he would do with Giuliana out there in a sheltered spot. It'd be a grassy patch well in from the trails, and plenty of sun, and a breeze.

Peter shifted in his seat.

"What's the news in Sleepyville," he asked. "Your exciting gendarmerie post, with, what's his name again, your guy?"

"Gebhart."

Felix didn't want to mention the bodies up near the Himmelfarb place.

"The usual," he said.

"Well I tell you, up my way we're action central since Easter."

"All of a sudden?"

"Genau. I thought it was just spring madness, or something. But the old guys in the post say there's something different this year."

Felix was still irritated at how Peter had landed a post in a big place like Liezen, while he had ended up in one-horse Stefansdorf.

"Like?"

Peter rested his elbows on his knees and nodded at Giuliana.

"You're not hearing any of this, Giuliana, right?"

She glanced up from her intent study of her rucksack and shook her head.

"Drugs. Big time – in a garage there. And what a set up! The Nobel Prize, I tell you. Did you hear about it? And the shoot-out?"

"I think so."

"One guy dead, two in hospital. Seven arrests, and we almost got a big one. Guess what language these guys don't speak so well – except one local, who used to do paperwork and meet landlords and that. Guess."

"Nicht sprach gut Deutsch?"

"Wow. You're going to end up in the KD yet, Felix. Guess the home countries now. Go on."

"Afghanistan?"

"Not the drugs, man. The big shot. The one that got away."

"Local guy?"

"Hell, Christ no. An ausländer. Why do you think I'm asking you? He's a brute too by the way. You should hear some of the things they say about him."

Felix gave him the eye: maybe not.

"He was one of those paratroopers from Bosnia. Just about the cream of the crop. No doubt he's sitting pretty at some café back there now, planning his next effort."

"Well, does he mountain bike?"

Peter looked over at Giuliana too. She had a pasty look now, Felix saw.

"Hey, Giuliana. All this fresh mountain air?"

A look of panic flickered on her face as the gondola car clattered through a pylon. The steeper parts of the run were below them now. Felix watched the mountains rise up again through the roof windows as the car was drawn out of the pylon again.

Peter began to hum and stroke his sideburns. Felix stayed still, only turning his head once to catch a glimpse of the tiny houses clustered around the Liebfrauenkirche far back in the town. For him, the sway and resonance of the car brought a kind of comfort. His father had been a hiker, and a vigorous one at that, striding ahead even when he and Lisi were small, pointing out everything with a stick. There must be things the body remembers, he thought, his eyes on Giuliana's tight form perched on the edge of her seat, eyes determinedly locked on some part of the bike there. Yes, the coming down, leaning against his father, almost sleeping, proud of his day's hiking, a kid and as close as they ever would be.

His eyes left Giuliana then and rested several moments on Peter. The guy trained at something all year. If it wasn't Nordic skiing, it was kayaking in someplace in the Czech Republic, and if it wasn't mountain biking, it was taking a run at some Iron Man thing. He even skied in shorts here sometimes: "the ladies love it." Weights, football, water polo, city marathons. Peter was going to leave nothing to chance in his campaign to get into the Alpini. From there, he assured Felix, it would be a hell of a lot easier to have a serious chance at his final goal: Kobra Squad. Even a provincial command Kobra, he claimed, because that was good enough.

Felix eyed the tanned tree-trunk legs on his friend. He imagined their owner rappelling down from a helicopter in an avalanche, or pushing on through a blizzard towing a ridiculously huge sled of gear toward a plane crash. Or his blackened face peering down over the sights on one of the Uzis they were issued, and then leaping off a roof in those boots you could walk across a ceiling upside down with.

So, was it envy, Felix still asked himself, that made him return to wondering if Peter really was fooling himself about his Kommando prospects? Maybe no one had told him. Or maybe he was in denial, as they say: he was just too damned big. A giant really, more like the great export Arnold than the trim endurance-built acrobat types that Gebhart had heard were sought for specialist squads in the Gendarmerie.

Another pylon arrived, with the few seconds slowing, followed by the rumbling and the sharp tug as it was pulled through. He heard Giuliana catch her breath. Almost there, he wanted to say to her, but knew she wouldn't like his pity, especially in front of Peter.

He sat forward slowly to look to the wood cut far below. He felt something move along his calf then, half guessed what it was – his damned Handi – and made a grab for it. It hit the floor of the gondola with a dull hollow thump.

Even Peter started.

"Jesus," said Giuliana and flinched as the car swayed a little from her jump.

Felix picked up the phone. It was still on. There was a text message waiting.

"You are a very religious woman," said Peter. "I like that. Is it just around Felix here?"

Giuliana did a first-class eyeball roll and returned to studying her knapsack on the floor in front of her. Felix thumbed through the menu and watched the text appear.

In a moment his mind was on a slalom, with everything almost over the edge, rushing at him. Why had he turned off the ringer? Hansi Himmelfarb holding the kitten in the farmhouse kitchen. The way Speckbauer's comments always had a ring of not quite sarcasm.

Sitting with those two detectives in the restaurant yesterday in a weird conversation.

He sent the message scrolling again. Something fastened and closed tighter in his chest and he gasped. He had to think, but he couldn't. He saw his own hands turn the phone over. He stared at it, and read the logos and indentations on the back. Battery, he thought, his mind skittering, serial number. Had he snapped?

"Busted?"

It was Peter. Felix looked up at him. The light, the views over the valleys and mountains, even Peter's face – all seemed to have changed.

"Is it broken?"

"No."

Peter shrugged and half smiled. Felix looked out the window at the clearing below where they creaked and swung upwards. There were no maniacs hiking it up today, straining and sweating every step to the top of the mountain.

He looked at his feet. He didn't know what to do.

"What's going on in there?"

It was Giuliana. The strain on her face was easing. He was suddenly overwhelmed by gratitude that she was there, present, alive, and still trying to beat her nerves about heights and cable cars, just to humour him.

"Something's wrong?"

Peter would find out eventually, one way or another, he decided.

"Gebi texted me," he said and cleared his throat. "Remember the incident up at the farm, the Himmelfarb family?"

"How could I forget?" Giuliana said.

Felix saw that Peter wasn't even pretending that he was not all ears.

"Gebi said, well, he texted that . . . something happened. A fire. They're dead."

Volkswagen Polos – Felix's mother's seven-year-old model Polo – will top out at 180. On a good day, as Gebi might say. With the föhn behind you, that warm winter breeze, or a tornado maybe, going down the side of a wall.

Felix wavered at 150, imagining a cloud of black smoke, a serious clank and grind and one good big metallic bang, and then only the decision of what scrap yard he'd send it to.

Still he pushed it. He wanted something, anything, to seize his attention and hold it, so he could not think. He got the eye several times from drivers rolling along nicely at 130, in cars that could do twice that. He came through Schladming after he got off the A10, and he was barrelling down the A9 an hour later. The lights were on a half-hour before he got to the outskirts of Graz.

He phoned Giuliana after he got off the autobahn. She had settled into the hotel. No, she hadn't been "checking out" the other guys, the dozen or so off-duty Gendarmerie guys who had shown up for the trekking. And no, she wasn't really fooled by this lame humour. Peter wouldn't put the moves, sober or wipsi, she told him. She had her books, they had their bikes and, later, their beer. And yes, she had a lift down to the bahn tomorrow and a ticket, if she changed her mind. And no, it was no problem. She wanted at least one night up on the mountain, with Felix or without.

He picked up some buns and milk before he let himself into the apartment. He waited until he had eaten half of the buns and cheese before phoning the post. Korschak told him Gebhart had left a message at the end of his shift. Korschak's tone conveyed something to Felix as he recited Gebhart's home phone number. It was not resentment, Felix decided, or annoyance that Gebhart had conceded a valuable invitation to the new recruit, but perhaps the smallest trace of awe.

"So Felix," said Korschak. "Look at you. You are hardly in the door here but you get to talk to Gebi – and at the Gebhart residence too, I might add."

"Is it really that big a deal?"

"Is the Pope Catholic? Gebi never mixes home with work. Never. Even Dieter is scared to phone him at home. You, my friend, are special."

Felix couldn't remember hearing that tone of sly humour from the friendly enough but starchy, by-the-book careerist Korschak before. He had recited the phone number in a slow, portentous tone.

"So phone him," Korschak added, "Something on account of a boy? You'll know, he said."

Felix put down the phone, and sat back. He decided again that he didn't know what the hell he was doing, or should do.

He examined his hands. He had walked hand in hand with Hansi Himmelfarb, gotten the butt of half-serious jokes about it. What would the fire that killed the Himmelfarbs have done to that hand?

FOURTEEN

GEBHART ANSWERED THE DOOR HIMSELF.

Felix had been around the area before, up and down the myriad roads and lanes that functioned as roads in this hinterland area just outside Graz. Trust Gebhart, he thought, to live on a road that still looked out over farms and woods and held the pungent scent of manure in the air. The nearest neighbour was 200 metres away. A new Skoda was parked next to Gebi's down-at-heel Fiat.

"Pretty heroic driving," said Gebhart. "What are you looking at?"

"Sorry."

"You think I sleep in my uniform, do you?"

A face, a woman's, appeared from a doorway behind.

"My wife."

"Delighted," said Felix.

"Don't be too delighted," said Gebhart. "She's a nurse in the emerg."

"How do you work with this crusty old krot?" Mrs. Gebhart asked.

Gebi led him into a parlour. A very tall girl with her father's nose, and a book, and rimless glasses stirred under a cupola of light and slowly stood.

"Claudia, this is Felix. He is a Gendarme."

The kid was a gangly 12 or 13 Felix saw, with that mix of open curiosity and reserve peculiar to the age.

"He's just like daddy. More of an action man you might think, my dear bookworm."

"De– I'm happy to meet you, Fraulein."

"He bikes around goat tracks in the mountains near Kitzbühel for recreation," said Gebhardt. "Something you might consider, my dear?"

She rolled her eyes and held her book to her chest and walked out. Gebi held the door before closing it.

"Beer? Coffee?"

"No. No thanks."

"Well I'm going to have a Puntigamer. You should. It's the only beer, really."

Gebi gave him a considered look.

"Look. Don't be a clown. Have one. Nobody comes to my house from work. Consider yourself a movie star or something."

Felix looked around the pictures while he waited for Gebhart to return. There was one from the 1980s, it looked like, to go by the cars, with a young, trim Josef Gebhart. Yes; minus 10 or 15 kilo, that was him standing with fellow officers against a Gendarmerie car high up somewhere, with snow in the background. There was a snapshot from long before that, a man standing in the open door of a VW Beetle. He looked like Gebhart. Men, unshaven, in white camouflage gear, eyes squinting in the blazing sun, again up in the snow somewhere.

Gebhart brought only the bottles. He sat in an old armchair. Felix took a longer swig of the bottle than he had planned. Gebhart kept up his baleful gaze.

"You drove like a goddamned madman back here, anyway," he said.

"I felt I should come back. Now, I don't know."

"That's okay. But coming right off your precious week's leave, that is something. That pushed my buttons enough to actually allow you to enter . . ." Gebhart made a desultory wave of his arm around the room, "the Gebhart sanctuary."

"Pretty exclusive, I hear."

"Damn right it is. You're going to have to come up with something good to justify me giving in to my kleine herz over this."

Felix gave him the eye.

"Well? You broke up with your girl?"

"No."

"Okay. Let me make a guess. But before I do, let me tell you something. I could kick myself for telling you about that phone call, you know. I wasn't thinking."

"It's okay," said Felix. "I'd have found out anyway. And I would have been annoyed you hadn't told me."

Gebhart gave a small nod. He took a swig of beer and held it in his mouth before swallowing it.

"Well yes," he said. "It was a message for you after all. But if I'd known you'd be flying down at top speed from the far side of the country, well I'd have waited."

"Wah wah," Felix murmured, and shook his head.

"Don't start that what-if stuff, you hear?"

"I can't help it. Maybe he would have told me then, if I'd not been so—"

"Stop that, I said. Are you listening to me at all?"

Felix nodded.

"How can you know?" Gebhart said. "And even still, what's 'a secret' for the likes of him? It could be anything. You don't know. Nobody knows."

Felix thought again about asking Gebhart his son's name. If his Down's was severe. If Gebhart knew a lot about that sort of thing. Of course he must, he upbraided himself. He looked up from the bottle he had been cradling in his hands.

"But why would he not tell his own parents? That doesn't make sense."

"Tell me about it," said Gebhart. "Isn't that what I'm saying to you here? Whatever he wanted to tell you, this 'secret,' well they're wily enough, those Down's kids. They want what they want. So it was nothing really, believe me."

"But," Felix said. "It's just so . . . what happened. It's so . . . I can't say what."

"Hard, isn't it?"

"That kid, I mean, the son. An only child. And now this?"

Felix's gaze drifted over the photos again. Gebhart said nothing.

"You said 'suspicious,'" said Felix. "Did you mean it?"

"Yes, I meant it. The word I got from the fire brigade guy up there, old hand, Dorner's his name, yes – said something started it. I think he even said he thought paraffin. That's just blather for now, until we hear from their experts. And show me a farm where they don't keep paraffin or gasoline, anyway."

"How come no one got out, or woke up?"

Something changed in Gebhart's expression.

"You're asking the wrong cop there, kid. Me and Korschak got there pretty damned quick, just the same time the feuerwehr were coming in. The place was an inferno. That I know. The arson guys showed up after a couple of hours, along with some forensics. They went through what they could."

Gebhart shrugged.

"I don't know. I did perimeter for a while, talked to a few neighbours. Then a car with two uniforms came from Graz to take over the site. They, er, got them out, the remains, before I left. So they're getting the P.M. done."

"How did it happen?"

"The fire? I don't know."

He held up his bottle to study the label.

"But I think your mind is working overtime here."

"You think it was deliberate?"

Gebhart put down the bottle.

"I try not to think about it."

Felix watched him turn the bottle slowly on the surface of the table. Then he looked at the pictures on the wall. A minute passed. He noticed skis, mountain rescue gear, a helicopter in the background in one of the pictures now.

Again he thought back to what Gebhart had told him.

"Look," Felix said, and prepared to get up. "I'll go."

"Finish your beer. Don't waste it."

"Why am I here? I just feel bad about it. Maybe I'm going nuts?" Gebhart nodded.

"Could be," he said. "Do you want some advice?"

"Can I try a sample first?"

"Sure. It's not hard. A) Don't drive that scheisse of a car you have at supersonic speed anymore."

"B?"

"There isn't a B. But if there was, it'd be this: go back to your holiday. Don't heat up your brain over this stuff. You're shocked. That's a nice, normal human reaction. But your best place is – you know. Just for the record, did anyone ask you to drive all the way back here, without your girl too?"

"She's taking the train down tomorrow," said Felix. "It's just not the same; I don't want to go back now."

"So what are you going to do?"

"Well, the trekking thing was only for the weekend. Italy, still. I hope."

They fell silent again. Felix heard the TV through the walls.

"Paraffin," he said after a while.

"Gossip. I heard one of them say it, but that's all."

Felix took another mouthful of beer.

"Why are you avoiding this, Gebi?"

"Avoiding what? Avoiding making a depp out of myself, jumping to conclusions?"

"You're not suspicious, not even a bisschen, the tiniest bit?"

"Look," said Gebhart. "Give them a day or two. What if it's just an accident? There's the father, Himmelfarb, and he's not sleeping because the kid is up all night. There's a word for that, I think."

"'Sleep deprived.'"

"Right. So wait for a preliminary, I think they call it. Nothing's instant in the job, even for the PlayStation generation."

"I feel a lecture coming on."

Gebhart took a long drink and sighed.

"It's like your mutti always told you: Morgen kommt besser."

"'It'll be better in the morning?' My mom never said that."

"Listen to you. You are like our resident bookworm in there. Whatever I say, she is always 'But,' or 'No,' or 'You haven't a clue.'"

"Did I say those things?"

"You don't have to. What's behind the look, or the words is: 'You're a dummy. No, you know zip because you're not online or glued to your mobile. Geezer.'"

"What century were you born in, Gebi?"

"This is how you repay hospitality? Beer?"

Felix was sure he saw a flicker of humour on Gebhart's face.

"What century? Well I sometimes wonder. Come now, you don't want to hear my philosophy, if you can call it that."

"'Go home, get some sleep and tomorrow we'll see.'"

"Exactly."

Felix's gaze strayed to the photos again, and his mind wandered to questions he'd someday ask Gebhart.

"A fine bunch, huh?"

Felix broke his gaze on the pictures.

"Guys you worked with?"

"Genau. Some times we had, I tell you. By God they could enjoy themselves, these fellows."

"Not you?"

Gebhart hesitated before replying.

"Things you do," he said, and shrugged. "At certain times in your life."

FIFTEEN

GIULIANA HAD A SLEEPY VOICE. HER REPLIES WERE SLOW AND YAWNY.
"You're reading, aren't you," he said.

"How do you know that?"

"Because I know you. Because you get into something and you don't stop until it's finished. What is it, are you back to those old bores like Hesse?"

"He's not an old bore. Everyone should read him again."

"I'd rather be tearing your clothes off and reading your skin, and watching your face as you come."

"My my," she said, and he knew she was smiling. "You'll have to tie your hands behind your back when you go to sleep tonight."

He slouched back further in the sofa.

He felt himself putting the conversation on automatic while his thoughts wandered.

"You went out for a walk at least?"

"Yes, the guilt got to me. I met up with a wife of one of your mountain guys. She's not into the crazy biking and . . ."

He listened, but he was thinking about what fire would do to an old house like the Himmelfarbs'. It would have been an inferno in minutes. But Gebi was right: what farmer wouldn't keep paraffin around for getting a blaze going on a heap of weeds or rubbish, or even running a heater to keep the chill off newborns in the shed.

". . . she's nice. She says it's an addiction though, but she laughs. For now."

"Addiction?"

"The whole business: the fitness thing, that's okay, but twelve-hour bike marathons up in the Alps?"

"Right. Is Peter hitting on you?"

"What? I'm in my room, looking out over the valley, reading."

Speckbauer and his weirdo skin-graft sidekick 'Franz' returned to the forefront of Felix's thoughts.

"And drinking wine."

" . . . and thinking of . . . ?"

"Of how much a genius Hesse really was."

"That's it? That's all you're thinking?"

"Basta – it's enough, isn't it?"

Speckbauer had given him a mobile number. Maybe he'd go to a call box, phone him and hang up, just to annoy him. Herr Supercop Speckbauer, coming out from city to the lame-head trottels in Stefansdorf because, as everyone knew, the three Gendarmerie there couldn't put their heads together enough to make heat.

"Listen, Felix. Go to bed."

"I'm in the wrong part of Austria."

"Go out and buy a teddy bear or something then."

"You make sure you get on that train tomorrow, okay? I'll pick you up in Graz and we'll carry on our weekend. I'm sorry it screwed up."

"Don't be."

"I thought it was over, that business."

"I wish I were there, you know. But . . . "

"If," he began, and then let it go.

"If what?"

"It's nothing."

She waited

"Tell me," she said then.

"If he hadn't have been, well, you know."

"The boy you . . . ?"

"'Boy,'" said Felix. "Everyone calls him that. That was funny, sort of. But not anymore."

"Felix, you're upset. I'm worried about you."

Stubbled faces, the blood gone black as the men's hair, and the glitter from dead eyes visible where the eyelids were slightly parted.

"Go to your mom's tonight, or Lisi, maybe?"

He returned to her.

"The cure would be worse than the problem," he said.

He found a filler to wind up, and finished the conversation with a small private joke they had about how Giuliana lay when she slept. Was he sure he didn't want to come back up for the Saturday night, she asked. It wouldn't be the same, he told her. Then he made sure he had the arrival time of the train back to Graz Hauptbanhof.

He shifted noodles from the freezer to the microwave. He ate them while he finished two cans of cheap lager in front of the TV. Then he lay back on the couch and, rather than compose his thoughts as he'd hoped he'd know how, he conked out.

✠

Felix's furry mouth had been improved considerably by 10 minutes in the shower the next day at seven o'clock. He had had none of the ghastly dreams he'd expected. He put on a T-shirt and jeans; he did-n't bother shaving. Then he put away the debris from last night, and decided he'd get a croissant and a coffee at the Anker near the bridge. His mood had lifted, he was beginning to believe: there was a holiday to resume, for God's sake.

He was pulling the door of the apartment shut when the phone went. He dithered for two rings and answered it.

"Well, I am glad to hear your voice," said the caller.

"You are?"

"I am Horst Speckbauer. You may remember me from the other day?"

"Oberstleutnant Speckbauer."

"You are not on duty I know, but I'd be much obliged if you could give me a bit of your time."

"Well, is this really necessary? I'm supposed to be on holiday."

Felix winced at the limp "supposed to be."

"It is a matter of some importance. I think you will find it interesting, what I will tell you."

"You will tell me?"

"I know you are concerned, and I wish to assist you. It is a tough thing that has happened, a very tough thing."

Felix looked down at the notepad by the phone. A "tough thing" indeed: he was ready to yell that he never wanted to hear either Speckbauer or Gebi or any other cop calling something like this "tough" or "hard." Cruel, was what it should be, and outrageous.

"You returned," said Speckbauer. "Last night, was it?"

"A temporary visit, I am hoping, Oberstleutnant."

"Please. I will come over to your place. Ten minutes?"

In the few moments before he replied, Felix understood that he'd made up his mind a long time ago: there'd never be another cop talking business where he and Giuliana lived. Gebhart had it right: you keep your family life private, shielded from this. He wouldn't give Speckbauer the satisfaction of asking him how he'd gotten his home number, or how he'd known his movements.

"I'm going out for breakfast."

"Great. Tell me where."

"Keplerstrasse. There's an Anker there."

"Anker?"

"You know the bakery and restaurant chain? Just across the bridge."

Felix looked out to the bike rack to make sure his city bike was still locked there. He checked he had his keys and his mobile. He considered taking a couple of aspirin. His headache was coming back, and he felt a tension starting in his shoulders and neck.

He took his time on the way to the bridge, trying with little success to relish how sprightly the people were in this green city now booming in late spring. What was wrong? There were even halter tops out, and few enough tourists. He had nothing against tourists, even though the European City of Culture Award a few years back had blown the place wide open.

It was more than just the tarted-up museums and galleries and exhibits and sandblasted façades, more even than the gigantic Art Island in the Mur that he'd watched going up, along with the enormous building on the bank beside it. Something had changed in this city, but he couldn't say what. Maybe, as Giuliana had half joked last year at a party where everyone had shown up and drank far too much into the early hours, maybe Graz had been moved close to Berlin, and away from the East. Just the green mound at the heart of this old city, the Schlossberg, remained. Most times they forgot the "cave" beneath that they'd drilled out for the same City of Culture year, and installed computers and holograms and the like.

Felix still liked to walk up the steep paths of the Schlossberg. If nothing else, it was a workout of sorts. Once, just after he had started Uni, he had tried to run to the top, with some loony idea that he would race a group whom he had passed on their way to the funicular. He had had to walk about three-quarters of the way up – near the beer garden – with spots exploding before his eyes and his heart hammering. The last of his ascent had been strange, and unexpected. Maybe it had been his exhaustion, or the sharp, clear October sky, or more likely the absence of anyone else at such an hour, but he had felt he was far from the city then. It had felt like he was actually approaching the summit of some remote peak. The red roof tiles and the gentle curve of the River Mur that held in the old city centre so far below seemed new and unknown.

But what right did he think to imagine that it was "his" city at all, he thought, as he eyed the traffic on his way to turn up Wickenburg Gasse and head for the Kepler Bridge. It was Giuliana, daughter of an immigrant, who had struggled and succeeded, and had secured herself an enviable place right in the heart of the old city here, something he couldn't have begun to imagine he'd have found. "Stowaway," Giuliana had called him several times right after he had moved into her place. A joke, of course, and it had gone on for a while, part of the private language of sorts they came up with. Bedroom talk, silly anywhere else.

He locked his bike and got his order in before he turned at the creaky door's opening and the surge of traffic noise.

"Double that, gnädige frau," Speckbauer called out as he crossed the floor. "I'll pay also."

Felix waited. Speckbauer was humming. Then he engaged the woman preparing the tray in a short one-sided banter about spring, holidays, and the need to know when it was necessary to simply stop working and enjoy life.

Felix took in the studied breeziness. Speckbauer was quite the performer. As though aware of Felix's thoughts, Speckbauer turned to him.

"If you're wondering about Franzi, he is otherwise engaged. Saturdays he relaxes in his own way."

"Is this a workday for you?"

Speckbauer seemed to consider the question.

"It is," he said and made a smile. "I do believe it is."

Then he stretched, and he turned to the windows. Something seemed to please him: the blossoming trees along by the river, the air of purposive, pleasant shopping and Saturday café hopping, perhaps, Felix guessed.

"Ah," said Speckbauer, and rubbed his hands together briskly. "To have all of this. Life is good, huh? For those who can live it."

He paid and left a tip, and carried the tray to a table against the back wall.

"Don't worry," he said, tearing up one of the croissants. "So eat up."

Felix dipped his and watched a couple disentangle themselves from their embrace near the bridge.

"I will talk then, if that's okay with you?"

Felix looked for any giveaway signs of sarcasm.

"Go ahead."

Speckbauer took a considered sip of his coffee, and dabbed and wiped his moustache with a napkin.

"Chronologically: your good police work, and the good instincts of our supervisory officer Gebhart, have led to the discovery of a double murder. This is in a remote area, relative to our cities and towns. It is in the forest beside a farm. On a little weg that goes along by the land of the Himmelfarb family. Known locally as Wildererweg. The poacher's path, or road."

At this he paused, stared for a moment at the pieces of croissant still uneaten.

"The matter is being investigated," he went on then. "By expert police and police specialists here in Graz, to determine how, when, and ideally why these men were there. And who they are, natürlich. So far, by the book, okay?"

An Asian couple passed outside, one holding a bag tightly to her side, the other a high-end digital camera at the ready.

"You, a probationary officer, under the guidance of the experienced Bezirkinspektor Josef Gebhart, are now considered officer ancillary to this investigation."

"What does that mean?"

"It means you are part of a team. It will be noted to your credit how you helped initiate this investigation. It will be a valuable experience for you in particular. When the Gendarmerie and the Bundespolizei are finally amalgamated, well . . . "

Speckbauer left the sentence unfinished, but gave Felix a knowing glance to indicate the golden future awaiting. Then he pushed his chair back. He took out a starched, cloth handkerchief and blew his nose.

"Well, may I ask a question?"

"Absolutely," replied Speckbauer.

"Why are you phoning me at my apartment?"

"Isn't that your home?"

"Of course it is. But is there something irregular?"

Speckbauer eyed him with a glazed look while he blew his nose again. What housewife had starched her man's handkerchief, Felix wondered. Did anybody else in the 21st century use a cloth hand-kerchief?

"Ah. Before I answer this, let me make a guess at something. I think that you wish that you could address me as a person you met on the street, let's say. As if there were no rank or hierarchy to confuse matters. Is that so?"

"Isn't that human nature?"

"You perhaps want to say, who knows – 'Pas auf? Get lost?' Or, something like: 'Who the hell are you to annoy me like this, Kripo guy, with my week's leave I've been dreaming of since I got out of Gendarmerie school?' Or at the very least, 'Do I have to put up with you so as not to jeopardize my employment? My chance to be in the Alpini maybe?'"

"I don't know about that."

"Sure about that? That you didn't wish you could speak more, er, directly?"

"It's possible, I suppose."

"Go ahead then."

Felix gave him a dubious glance, but Speckbauer waved his hands.

"Okay then," said Felix. "First is, how do you know all these things? My phone number, what I might want to work at? My girl-friend's name?"

"When you enter the Gendarmerie, you allow information such as this to be open for inspection by certain branches of our service."

"I don't understand how anyone could just access those files."

"I am not just anyone. What were your other observations?"

"Am I suspected of doing something wrong?"

Speckbauer gave a short, sudden guffaw.

"No. But did you wish to volunteer information perhaps?"

Felix shook his head.

"You are too polite to put other questions, perhaps."

"I am here talking with you. That means something."

With a slight nod, Speckbauer seemed to flick away a retort unspoken.

"Indeed," he said instead. "On your first 'normal' weekend since you started. Wait until you have a family."

"Really?"

"Oh sure. You'll move up the ladder if you have kids. You'll be awarded the sacred weekend more often. You'll do great, I'm sure. Education and all that."

"Well, I suppose I'll bear that in mind, Herr Oberstleutnant."

"'Herr Oberstleutnant?' Are we back to that?"

Felix gave Speckbauer a skeptical look.

"I think it might be preferable, under the circumstances."

"What, are you suspicious of compliments?"

"But how can you make that observation?"

Speckbauer's eyes narrowed, but not unkindly.

"For example, you held the hand of this unfortunate boy, Himmelfarb, when it was necessary. You won his confidence, didn't you?"

"I–"

But then Felix stopped. He wouldn't let Gebhart look bad in front of this cop.

"I know," said Speckbauer. "You were 'encouraged to.' I know. But look at what happened. He fell for you. He wanted to tell you things, and you only."

Felix watched an old woman enter the shop.

"Hansi Himmelfarb had found a friend in you. So you have a gift, I say. People trust you, you see."

Something sagged inside Felix. He thought of Frau Himmelfarb, her leathery face already ruddy from the wind and sun of the spring and her outdoor life, the headscarf she would have put on each morning and left on until going to bed. All the Himmelfarbs had wanted, or expected, was to continue their simple life there on a mountain farm that had probably been in their family for centuries, to carry on the routines, to improve things a little, to hand it on.

Speckbauer's scrutiny of him was not the cynical survey he had expected.

"You are agitated," he said. "Don't be suspicious. It's to your credit."

"What?"

"Agitation suggests you have morals. You are not 'cool.' All to the good."

"I don't know where this is going."

Speckbauer rested one leg over the other, ankle over knee, and studied the side of his shoe. A woman with deep olive skin and a hijab entered the bakery.

"You drove down here because you believe you need to be involved," Speckbauer murmured then. "That's not irrational. Guilt too, perhaps? Were you trying to think of what you might have overlooked on that visit to the Himmelfarbs', when you had that pedal ground into the floor on the autobahn, putting the Mercs and the Porsches in your rearview mirror?"

"Some of the time, yes."

"What did you remember then? From when the boy was talking."

"That's the trouble," Felix said. "Nothing."

"The kid said 'sleep.' 'They're sleeping.'"

"Yes."

"But he wouldn't go up there. He wouldn't go out of the house, basically. Don't you think he knew they were dead?"

"Who knows what goes on in a mind such as that," said Felix.

"The shrinks call it 'averse.' Are you sure the boy didn't mention days, or time?" "No."

Speckbauer put his leg back down and he studied the tabletop. Then he narrowed his eyes.

"Well, you were out of town," he said. "So you didn't do it, did you?"

"That's not funny, if you'll allow me to say so, Herr Oberstleutnant."

POACHER'S ROAD

"I will. I certainly will. But you've surely copped on to why I'm talking to you here. You know, I'm sure of it. I saw it on your face."

When Felix didn't speak, Speckbauer leaned in over the table.

"Okay, then, I'll say it. There is something wrong when a citizen phones his Gendarmerie post with a request to talk to them – to a certain officer Kimmel – and he and his family burn to death in a house fire not long after. Are you hearing me?" Felix nodded.

"Now you need to know this as well. I– we– are checking each and every part of the goings on concerning this, including calls and records from the post that day. Even gossip. Things overheard, and passed on. Rumours. Notes left lying around. Remarks passed to spouses. Fiancées, even."

Speckbauer's gaze was not unfriendly.

"Everyone," Speckbauer added. "Without exception."

The Muslim woman at the counter was not quick with her change. Felix eyed the carefully neutral expression of the clerk waiting. It was the Austrian way in action all right, Giuliana had said many times: whatever you say, say nothing.

"You have an opportunity now, Felix," said Speckbauer. "Or Inspektor, if you prefer. Your opportunity is to assist in this case. Your expertise is being requested from your post Kontrolinspektor at the moment. Schroek? So it is a semi-big deal."

"Expertise? I don't have any. I'm a probationary Gendarme."

"Ah, but you have a friendly face. And you are a local boy."

"But my duties at the post?"

"Duties? Permit me to say this: those duties can be assumed by other staff there. Doing talks to pimply teens who are going out to piss cheap beer into your garden that night anyway, just to show you what they think of your presentation, well that's a duty – fair enough. But it's one that can wait. You know the area up there, don't you?"

"The mountains? A bit, I suppose."

"Of course you do. Your grandparents are seven kilometres

across the mountain. Your father spent half his youth up there, didn't he? Didn't you go with him at all? Of course you did. All those wee roads and tracks? The passes? The Wildererweg?"

"It was some time back."

"Really, now I doubt you'll be so modest in your experience profile when you make a serious try for the Alpini. Stop back pedalling, okay? You can drive, can't you?"

"Of course."

"And, equally important, is your interest in night life?"

"Pardon?"

"Come on now. Clubs? You have mates that can still ring the bell late into the night, don't you?"

In Speckbauer's gaze Felix now read a sly dare to bite back.

"You could go into a club or a cool-guy bar, and you wouldn't look like me – or, Gött sei dank, our dear Franzi. What I mean is, you won't look like a cop. Got it?"

"No, actually, Herr Oberstleutnant."

"'All will be revealed,' as the good book says. 'In the fullness of time.' For now, take my word on it. Have I come to the problem side yet? The negatives?"

"It sounds like it's been done."

"Ah. Funny fellow. Listen to me. This part is not so funny."

Speckbauer waited for a couple to go by.

"It is now beginning to dawn on you that this is a serious affair, I hope. When we find out who those two dead men are, then I'll be telling you what that means. But right now, I think that there are people who may be curious about what you know."

"But I don't know anything, beyond what I've told you."

"Sure. But who's to say someone doesn't think that the Himmelfarb boy, or his family, told you something? And that you know something important that they'd prefer you didn't know . . . ?"

"Who?"

Speckbauer's eyes went flat, as though they had slipped out of focus.

"Who could that be," Felix repeated. "Who are you talking about?"

"Ah. I see I have your attention here."

"I don't think you should play games like this, Herr Oberstleutnant, with respect."

"Really," said Speckbauer. "You can shove your respect and your Herr Oberstleutnant up your arsch, Gendarme. You're mad and I know it. That's good. You should be."

"This is some kind of a threat you are suggesting?"

"If I knew who 'they' were, I'd tell you. I don't put people's safety at risk. Especially not a fellow officer."

Speckbauer sat back and studied the intricacies of the fittings that held the shelves and counters. Felix wondered if the faint low tone he was hearing was Speckbauer humming again. He was about to push back his chair when the sunglasses appeared in the window. It took Felix a moment to realize that the pale face and the glasses belonged to Speckbauer's sidekick.

He tried not to study the strange small jerks that Franzi made as he entered the restaurant. Speckbauer did nothing to indicate he had even noticed his partner enter.

"Zero," said Franz.

"Aber gut," Speckbauer grunted. "Good enough."

Felix nodded as the glasses swivelled his way, but he couldn't see the eyes. The glasses went back toward Speckbauer.

"Well?" he said.

"I don't know," said Speckbauer. "I don't think he gets it yet."

Franzi turned to Felix again.

"I thought you were smart. Let's not waste any more time."

Felix sensed that Franz would not be sitting down, no matter how much longer they'd stay. It'd be too much for him getting up again, maybe. He heard Franzi breathe out impatiently.

"Damn it, Franzi, I hear you thinking, even."

Speckbauer turned to Felix.

"Now we must close this information session. The 'zero' you

heard is good news. It means that Franz and two other fine veteran plainclothes officers can report that no one is in your apartment."

"What?" Felix managed.

"Why didn't you hit him with this earlier?"

Speckbauer waved away Franzi's question.

"You haven't come to the correct conclusion, kid," Franzi went on. "Drop it on him, Horst, for Christ's sake."

Speckbauer spoke in a quiet tone now.

"Are you getting it yet?"

Felix was thinking of a farmhouse ablaze, and a dark purple hole in a man's forehead.

"I think so," he was able to say. "I think I am."

SIXTEEN

GIULIANA WAS TRYING HARD TO SOUND LIKE SHE WASN'T FREAKING.

"I can't tell you any more at the moment," Felix said, gently.

"It's to do with that family, those two men they found?"

"It's a precaution," he said. "There's probably nothing to it. I have to be careful."

He told her he'd be on the platform waiting. That seemed to awaken something in her. He heard her breathing in short gasps then.

"What am I going to do, to take, though," she said. "God, I can't think. Where am I going to start? Jesus!"

"We'll go to the apartment right away," he said. "There'll be somebody with us. We get your stuff and we go to your mom's."

"She'll freak if she knows."

"Well, don't tell her, okay?"

"Where will you go? Your mom's?"

"No. I'll tell you later."

The detective who had come up with Speckbauer was hanging around by the door, drinking one of Giuliana's fruit drinks.

"Nice," he said to Felix. "Nice place. Very artistic. You?"

"No."

Felix went to the living room. Speckbauer was eyeing the goings on in the small sliver of Kurosistrassse that could be glimpsed between the poplars in front of the apartment block.

"Well," he said. "How'd it go?"

"You can imagine."

Felix looked around the living room. The laptop, he'd take for sure, right now. Giuliana could figure out what she'd want when she made it in this evening.

"Is Gebi getting the same attention?"

"No. Why, should he?"

"Well, he was at the farm too."

Speckbauer seemed to ponder this information. From the kitchen, Felix heard the soft sigh of the fridge door opening.

"You want a Gösser, take one," he called out.

"Good," said Speckbauer. "If you're not being sarcastic, that is. Surveillance is no picnic. Christ, but you can get hemorrhoids like nobody's business."

Felix headed for the bedroom to pack some things.

"What did you discuss with Gebhart anyway?"

"When?"

"Last night. At his place."

"Ask him, I should think."

"I did."

Felix stopped in the doorway and turned. Speckbauer turned away.

"Get some stuff," he called out. "You've got five or six hours to kill before your girl shows up. After that, you and me are going spatzieren – yes, taking to the hills."

True to his word, Speckbauer got into a police Passat and took out two maps from a folder under the seat. There was a stale smell of peppermints in the car, but Felix had spotted the top of a small magenbitter bottle in the trunk as Speckbauer had cleaned space there for his bag. The hint of gastric trouble for Speckbauer pleased Felix a little.

"Am I at work now?"

"Work? Do you see a desk here?"

"Well, I think I should know the conditions here."

"Okay. Yes you are on the job 'ancillary officer.'"

"You guarantee I get back here, to the bahnhof, I mean, by seven?"

"I guarantee that. And you will guarantee that you will show me the ins and outs of the high country."

"The maps?"

"But I want to follow your way too," said Speckbauer. He tapped a forefinger on his forehead several times. "What way would a guy like yourself go, one who knows a bit about the area?"

"Take the Lendkai down and come back over the Schönaügurtel," said Felix. "It's not bad. Then there's the A2. Get off at Gleisdorf. We'll go by Weiz, and then up."

Speckbauer nodded at the mass of the Schlossberg between the buildings.

"Is going that way worth it?"

"It looks long," Felix replied. "But it's quicker."

Speckbauer nodded.

"Okay," he said. "A good start. See, I knew you had it in you."

When Felix finished his phone call, Speckbauer was already passing the station at Münzgrabenstrasse and accelerating down the link to the Graz Ost ramp onto the A2.

"That's a little awkward," said Speckbauer, himself thumbing his Handi.

SEVENTEEN

"You'll pardon me, being so outspoken. But I couldn't help but hear."

"It's my grandparents' place," said Felix. "It'll be fine."

"You know it well?"

"A fair bit."

"Servus, Franzi," said Speckbauer then. He held the phone tighter to his ear. "Yes. We are prospecting. The name of the woman who runs that pub again? The one in that hole in the hedge up by the Himmelfarbs?"

Felix began rummaging in his mind which place Speckbauer could mean.

Speckbauer finished the call with a grunt. How long had these two policemen known one another, he began to wonder.

Speckbauer didn't signal when he changed traffic lanes. The needle ran quickly enough to 200 but he eased off. Through the blur of hedges and barriers that raced past, Felix spotted tractors at work often, their passage semaphored by circling gulls. Speckbauer hummed intermittently. It was a strange waltzy melody that stopped and started, and kept no proper time.

"Your colleague works 24/7 also?"

"Franzi? Christ, no. He is the laziest. Well, maybe I should not say that. When he is doing something that interests him, he is a goer. It's not like he doesn't have the time."

"Like yourself, perhaps?"

"How nicely you put your questions. You were well reared. Well,

126

let me put it to you this way: Franzi and I are veterans of the same campaigns."

Felix didn't want to sound too inquisitive.

"But his wife is a bitch," said Speckbauer. "But mine is, was, always sweet."

He glanced over toward Felix.

"I've made many mistakes, let me tell you. But isn't that how we have progress?"

The Gleisdorf junction was soon upon them. Speckbauer seemed to enjoy leaning hard into the curve, using the gears.

"Smaller screw-ups," said Speckbauer. "That's how we know we're winning."

"Winning?"

"Christ, this is an interview?"

He snorted once. They skirted Gleisdorf, and Speckbauer soon had them on the road up to Weiz, rocketing past a laggard lorry before a succession of blind bends.

"She couldn't take the changes," said Speckbauer.

"Your wife?"

"Franzi's wife. To be fair, it wasn't the injuries, the physical deformities, totally. No. But Franzi is hard to live with. Take my word for it. He always was. Me, I fell into my job. It went to my head. I fell in, and I couldn't get out. The current took me. But my former wife is a wonderful woman."

"I'm sorry to hear of that."

"That she is wonderful?"

"You know what I mean. Perhaps I should not have said anything."

"'Herr Obersleutnant,'" said Speckbauer. "You forgot, that time."

"Well, what am I supposed to call you? Are you my C.O. or not? I have never done this kind of work."

"Yes, yes, yes. Call me the devil if you wish. And no – I'm not your C.O. You are seconded temporarily. Do you know what that means, seconded?"

"I think so."

"Being as you are Felix the Second . . . ?"

Felix kept his eyes on the hedgerows.

"You're not offended, I hope. Your father's good name travelled on down to you, I understand?"

Felix shrugged. He wondered if it had been Gebhart's doing, letting slip the nickname that was so rarely used now.

"Well, what was I saying . . . We try to stay flexible. It is no use dropping some big shots on something like this. We need locals, locals' knowledge. Wissenschaft is what it is, yes: the lessons of ecology need to be applied to Euro-crime."

Felix looked over.

"You like that Euro-crime bit?" Speckbauer asked.

"Is that what's going on?"

"You may get to see a bit of the inside of a very frigging big, complicated, messy federal investigation. What am I saying 'Federal'? I should be precise: transnational. You may be the only probationary cop in our country so privileged. There's destiny for you. You are working with the Vatican."

"The Vatican?"

"It's an expression. No, it's not about fellows rappelling from helicopters. In our world we adapt. We go small and quiet. Think small mammals in the dinosaur world. Who survived?"

"And who are the dinosaurs?"

"I will tell you who they are not: Serbian gangsters are not. Albanian Mafia are not either. They are the rodents. Rodents are smart."

"But . . . the agencies that are trying to . . . "

"Yes? You are getting warm."

"I think I get it."

"Ach so. I don't wish to be disloyal. But the good guys are never going to get anywhere unless we size down and let people use initiative."

They crossed the first of the series of smaller hills on the route to Weiz, descending through broad curves to fields that had already gone green with the starting corn. The steeple of St. Ruprecht am Raab appeared over the flat farmland that ran to the base of the hills.

"Christ on his cross with the thieves," whispered Speckbauer, jerking the wheel and correcting it an instant later. Felix looked behind at the farm lorry still reversing onto the road. A smell of manure entered the car and stayed.

"Fewer errors," Speckbauer murmured. "That's how it works. Did I say that?"

He glanced over at Felix and then beyond him to the farm-houses.

"Even Franzi is beginning to be a believer."

"Was he . . . ?"

Speckbauer smiled and shook his head once.

"Ah, what a good choice I have made here. Permit me a little crowing now, as it reflects as well on you. You don't see it? It's that finesse you have, that way of insinuating yourself. 'Getting under the radar' my Yankee friends call it."

"I don't mean to pry."

"Of course you don't. But you're a born diplomat. Very discreet. The ladies love it, I imagine. You will do well up in the hills for sure. Tell me, is it something you were taught, this diplomatic way? Your mother, let me guess? Stop me if that is an impertinence."

It was a dare Felix could not resist.

"My mother is quiet, they say."

"'They say.' I like this. It is like you tell a story. 'They say.'"

Felix said nothing.

"Have I offended you?"

"No."

"Merely confused things? My apologies."

Felix believed him. It took him aback to know it.

"I spend so much time with certain types of people, that, well you can see the results. Hell, have they moved Weiz, or what?"

"St. Ruprecht, then Weiz. Maybe four kilometres."

"They say that spouses grow to resemble one another. Their clothes, their manner of speech. Have you noticed?"

"I suppose," said Felix.

"Well, there's Franz and me, a case in point."

"Spouses?"

"Might as well be," said Speckbauer. He moved his head from side to side, gazing into the distance. "We're making a stop in Weiz before going up to hillbilly territory. G'scherter, isn't that what the city people call mountain people, huh?"

"I've heard it used."

"Ach, you surely have. You have a foot in both places. But what was I saying?"

"Spouse, you said."

"Right. So, are you confused when I say spouse? No, I'm not gay. Franzi isn't either, but we might as well be sometimes, I wonder. It's funny. We share a place."

"Live together, you mean?"

"A generational term – hah. Yes and no. Franzi was unmanageable when he came home from the hospital. Very badly behaved indeed. I don't think he'll mind me telling you. Ach, I don't care if he does. There, that proves it – we are sort of married when we talk about one another like that."

Across the fields, the higher hills and mountains began over the town's red-tiled roofs. Forested slopes shifted and slid with the twists in the road, as the yellow walls and dome of the big church, the Weizberg, came into view. They passed a suburb, Preding.

"The wife left. I moved in. Franzi was a bear. I never left. I suppose I should," he smiled slightly as he went on.

"But who could turn down a location like that place I ask you. Know anyone else who has a parking garage, a roof garden, and a three-bedroom place on the Hofgasse, right in the middle of Graz?"

"That's where you live?"

"Temporarily – for three years temporarily. Movie stars would want it, uh? Franz inherited it, lucky bastard. That's the way. The destiny thing, maybe."

Speckbauer looked over until Felix met his eye.

"You believe in that, the destiny stuff?"

"No."

Speckbauer smiled and tapped his fingers twice on the wheel.

"Good. Me neither. Arsch mit ohren, as they say. 'An arse with ears.' That's destiny."

Speckbauer showed no mercy at the roundabout in Neustadt coming into Weiz. He only slowed seriously when Gleisdorferstrasse – where the B64 pinched small as it reached this thousand-year-old city – closed on the Weiz Zentrum proper. He turned down a lane at Europa Allee and let the Passat coast in second over the cobbled surface to a small platz where there were a dozen diagonal spaces.

"We're stopping here in Weiz?"

"Stimmt."

Felix had been to and through Weiz many times, but since his teens, less and less. His father knew everyone there, as in other towns and dorfs all around, it had seemed. He remembered his father stopping the car once and parking it by the chemist's just to walk back to the benches close to the rathaus at the top of the platz. There he had talked and laughed with the elderly man he had spotted, for hours it had seemed.

It had only been a half-hour probably, but Felix remembered being summoned from the car by a wave from his father. His mother, ever the diplomat, usually bribed them with a few schillings for ice cream. She knew to expect these impromptu meetings. Often the older ones would do the ritual cheek pinching and hand squeezing. Often he remembered listening to accents so thick he had barely understood more than "family" or "healthy," or "weather."

"You seem to know your way around here," Felix said.

Speckbauer's eyebrows went up and down in lieu of a remark. The Passat's tires made a soft kiss and rebound off the edge of the footbath. He turned off the engine.

"Down that way," he said.

He nodded toward a cobbled lane curling down between an old house and some newer buildings to the other side.

Felix closed the door behind him, and stretched.

Speckbauer took his time with something in the car. The trunk lid clicked and swung a little before settling again. Felix noted how Speckbauer was out of the seat, the door closing behind him, and at the back of the car in one easy, sort of curving motion.

"There's a plan?"

"There's always a plan."

Speckbauer opened the trunk and cast about for something. Felix saw plastic-wrapped files, a grey metal box in the centre of the trunk. Speckbauer picked up a newspaper and tucked it under his arm.

He looked over Felix's chest.

"A T-shirt. What use is this? Next time, then."

"Next time what?"

"Next time get a shirt you can put something on, or in. I can clip it or you can just drop it in a pocket. A kleine transmitter."

He opened his hand to show something with a single earpiece and a slim cord attached.

"I like to listen in."

"I don't get this."

"You are making a rest stop, on our little jaunt. Down that lane there is a place I want you to buy yourself a beer, or something. I will be at a café a bit down toward the zentrum."

"Why am I doing this?"

"It's your new job."

"Just a beer?"

"Just one beer. It's Saturday, remember? You can do these things. See, everyone's out shopping today. You're thirsty. You're not so happy. Your wiebi, your annoying wife, has gone shopping and you know she'll overspend. So . . . "

"Why don't you go in?"

"Because I am not stupid, that is why. They are not stupid either. Me, I look like a cop. I probably smell like a cop? You though, you're nobody. Verstehst? Got that?"

"What am I supposed to see there?"

"Whatever you like. Go in, enjoy the beer. Grumble a little, if you like. But know the layout before you leave. You might be going back under different circumstances, and it should not be the first time. Ready?"

"Ten, fifteen minutes?"

"Sounds okay. Now put on your pissed-off face. You're a hard-working guy over at, I don't know, the Magna plant in Gleisdorf. Okay? You do car assembly or panels or something. You're hungover. Swear if you must. Do you know how?"

"I can manage that."

"Well, things are looking up, then. Look, I'll leave and wander about a bit. Wait a minute and then go yourself. And don't get lost."

Felix watched Speckbauer stroll down the lane. A Fiat Uno delivery van went by, then a two-stroke whiner 50cc Puch. He counted to 60, and studied the buildings around this small platz. Ahead of him was the only hof that had not been given plate-glass windows and chintzy cobbled treatment. Above the recessed arch, the row of old tall windows had been flung open. Some kind of operatic singing came from them. It seemed to stir the curtains a little as though one should see just how thick the old walls actually were.

He made his way down the lane then, Karl Rennergasse, filing along with an irregular line of shoppers with kids and a pram. Built for older times and the passage of but one wagon, the lane filled up with sounds, echoing them. After 50 metres, he heard the bass thumping of a system further down the lane, where it opened out a little for proper sidewalks and a clutch of shops.

It was the English group, Fleetwood Mac, an oldie remixed, and it was just plain loud. It was coming from a place called Zero Point Joe's. Two umbrellas took up the small slice of pavement by the open doors. A waitress with high-tied very blonde hair was putting down big glasses of beer for three men at one of the tables. She gave him a quick once-over and a perfunctory smile. One of the three men, a dark-haired guy with a designer beard and showing off some bodybuilding with his T-shirt, said something close to her ear.

It took Felix a few moments to see properly indoors. He went to the bar. It was empty except for a washed-out–looking guy at the far end with hair that might as well have a signpost sticking out of it – a toupé lives here!– and a white playboy shirt open three buttons to display God knows what, beyond the gold chain.

But the barman was a cheerful enough fellow, moving down the far side of his thirties, Felix guessed. He seemed to have a twitchy manner.

"Beer," said Felix, feeling it was a shout. "Puntigamer."

"Glockl or schweigel?"

"Whatever size gives a man amnesia."

"Big glass for the big words," the barman shouted back.

Felix half sat on a stool.

"And the big wife," he said.

He looked around at the pods of seats, the raised floor, and speakers that began to the left of the bar. He returned a nod to the middle-aged playboy. Apparently, he who didn't know that he looked like a complete loser, was now thumbing something into a small mobile.

"Where is everyone?"

"Come back at nine tonight and see," said the barman. "It fairly hops."

Felix paid and made a meal of the first two draughts of the beer. He let his eyes move around the place again, looking for the exit lights and the toilets.

"Is it working?"

Felix looked back. The barman was lighting a covert cigarette now.

"The amnesia recipe?"

"It frigging better," said Felix. "Christ, that woman spends. You know?"

"I'm not married."

"Wise man: sehr klug. If you do, better get a second shift to pay for it, gell?"

The bartender kept up his smile. He'd surely been doing the pub confessional for long enough. Humouring arschlochers and grumblers was surely an art in the job.

"You could win the Lotto."

"No way, man," Felix said and shook his head. "My middle name is unglücklich."

"Well, you're not alone," said the barman, "Mr. Unlucky." He flicked his eyes once toward the playboy, who was now speaking passionately into the mobile.

"You local?"

"Uh uh," said Felix. "But I work nearby."

"Gleisdorf?"

"How'd you know?"

"The car plant? Magna?"

Felix took another swallow of beer. The bartender was amused at the reception Felix gave his apparent clairvoyance.

"Tool and die?"

"I wish," said Felix. "I'm on the line."

The bartender nodded and took a surreptitious drag from his cigarette.

"Lots of guys here," said the bartender and batted away the smoke. "But hey, it pays. Nicht war?"

"Geh scheissen," said Felix. "Take a crap. Never enough."

The bartender shrugged.

"I did it for a while," he said. "But you've got to hand it to Stronach. Goes to Canada with his arse out of his pants, and now look. Billions. You know his wife's people still live in town here, the mother and all?"

The song changed to a jittery techno that had Felix's fillings almost moving around. This was what kids in Weiz thought was so cool, even still?

"The toilets?"

The bartender pointed at a green light in the dimness beyond the pods of seats.

Felix took his time. He couldn't see any CCTV cameras. That meant nothing these days: you could fit them in a pinhead. He spotted two fire exits, so there must be alleys to both. There was a metal-clad double door at the end of the short passageway where the toilets were. Deliveries, he decided. To give the place its due, the klo was well done, well kept. There were two narrow barred and frosted windows high in the wall over the single cubicle.

He stood at the urinal, and felt the effect of the beer already. But a faint chill began to settle in his chest, and his thoughts fastened on the Himmelfarbs. It was the shock maybe, this? Maybe it was pity, or remorse or something, being ratcheted up in his subconscious to anxiety, or worse. Some part of his mind, a defence mechanism, had been holding fear at bay, ever since things had fallen apart in that cable gondola yesterday. Yesterday was a decade ago.

"Some week off," he murmured.

As though it had been waiting for this moment, an image of Speckbauer's face came to him then. It was his expression at that moment when it had finally sunk in with Felix: they don't know that the Himmelfarb kid hasn't told you something, do they? Felix felt that panic not far off now: "'They?'" he muttered. "Who–"

The door rocked open behind him. A man made a short, mocking laugh, and another voice said something in a questioning voice, like a taunt. What the hell language was it? Guys from the hilltops, so drunk that you couldn't even get beyond their accents? The vulnerable feeling overtook him. He tried to stop the flow of pee, turning a little as the two men came around the washbasins.

"Servus," he said.

One of the men had spotted him immediately he'd come

around the half-partition, and gave him a nod. End of conversation.

The quiet as they went to the urinal made the music from the pub seem even louder. Felix finished and zipped. He did not stop by the basin.

A well-turned-out man in his forties and a woman considerably younger than him were at the bar now. Felix gave them a cursory nod, and began to make up stories in his head to explain them. Daughter: no. Friend: hardly. A randsteinpflanze, a pavement hostess?

He was able to get a quick look at her when the bartender laid down their drinks with an ostentatious flourish. Her roots were dark, that much he knew about girls and their hair anyway, and there was plenty of support applied – the lashes and earrings, the makeup. Not a big-boned maiden that would top the list for desirable among farmers' sons up in the wilds of a hill village like Brandlucken. No, a dieter; a shopper.

"Another big one?"

Felix was surprised to learn he had almost finished his beer.

"Hell no. That'd be mess in a big way. A real mess. Enough problems."

"The weather is good. Can't you sleep in your car a few weeks?"

At this the blonde glanced over, but she did not smile.

"Bist närrisch?" said Felix. "Are you nuts?"

The three men were installed again under the umbrellas by the door. The sunlight hit Felix hard, and he felt the effects of the beer now. Beyond a shoe shop was a restaurant with too many arches for décor. He scuffed his shoe once, misjudging the height of the step going in.

Speckbauer closed his phone when he saw him, and got up from the table.

"Come on," he said. He slid out some coins on the table next to his cup.

"I'm ready for a snooze," Felix said.

"You don't get commendations for sleeping on the job, Gendarme. Let's go. Can you drive or not?"

"Drive?"

"Car. You. Drive."

"But I had a beer."

"So? You're not unconscious on one beer, are you? You know the area better than I do."

Felix looked to meet Speckbauer's eye, but he was already up, calling out a thanks to the waitress on his way to the door.

Felix's beery brain registered surprise now in place of his annoyance at being asked to drive. For a middle-aged guy, a desk-cop even, this dandy moved quickly. But why did he want Felix to drive, especially after a beer? He wasn't over the limit, but there had to be some calculation in Speckbauer's request. Order, more like it. Or a dare?

He noticed the newspaper curled under Speckbauer's arm. Unless he was drunk, it had Russian characters.

"You read Russian?"

"No."

"What's the newspaper?"

"Serbo-Croatian," said Speckbauer. They walked on.

The questions kept piling up in Felix's mind. Now he wanted to ask Speckbauer what the hell this meant, that he was reading a newspaper in that language. He also wanted Speckbauer to ask him about the bar he'd asked him to go into. It was hardly just to get rid of him so he could read the paper in peace, or catch up on phone calls. Now he had to drive?

"What do I do with the receipt from that place?"

"Give it to me," said Speckbauer. "I'll take care of it."

"Do you want to know how I got on in there?"

"Well, I suppose. Did you talk to the barman? Older fellow, a bit overfriendly?"

"As a matter of fact I did."

"And would you know your way around there if you went on a second visit?"

"I think so. It's loud enough now, though. There were guys speaking, I don't know, in there. They came into the klo when I was there."

Speckbauer nodded and slowed. Then he stopped abruptly at a corner.

"You drive," he said. "You know your way out? Down toward the bridge. It'll get you up to Radmangasse."

EIGHTEEN

FELIX REMEMBERED THE MAIN STREETS AND MANY OF THE lanes in the zentrum at least, from wandering here as a kid. His mother would come in for shopping on Saturdays. He could not remember his father coming into Weiz on those trips. But there had been lots of Sundays when his father had taken him up into the forest, or on a radl, where they had to wheel the bikes uphill half the time. It petered out when the adolescent thing had hit, when Felix started wanting to be with his mates, go to the movies, hang out.

Speckbauer unlocked the passenger door with a key and sat in. Odd there were no electric conveniences in this Passat, Felix thought. A crappy police model? Opening the driver's side, he saw Speckbauer closing the glove box, and locking it.

"Geh'ma," said Speckbauer. "What's it they say? 'Drobn auf da Alm?'"

Up on the mountain indeed, Felix thought. He stifled a beery belch.

"Do you mean Festring, that place with that gasthaus?"

"That's the place," said Speckbauer. "The metropolis of Festring. Population twenty-six, I believe. Blink and you'd miss it, no? A place called Gasthaus Hiebler. It is where Herr Himmelfarb used to go for his beer and card game. You know it?"

"Only to pass it. It's a couple of houses near the road only. An oasis."

"We're going to stop off at the Himmelfarb place too," said Speckbauer.

Felix noted the change in his voice when he spoke now.

"It's something we need to do."

Felix looked over.

"To jog the memory," said Speckbauer. "It won't be easy for you, I know."

Then he shifted in his seat. His voice took on a strained cheerfulness.

"But let's head through your area first. A little ramble."

"My area?"

"St. Kristoff, isn't it?"

"St. Kristoff? It's off up the hills there, not on the way."

"We'll work our way from there over the back roads. The ones maybe nobody knows about except the chosen few. Like you?"

There was a different sound from the engine than Felix expected.

"It doesn't say turbo on the back of this."

"Why should it?" said Speckbauer. "Go easy with your right foot."

Felix manoeuvred the Passat out from the narrow streets and lanes that made up the old part of Weiz and onto the Klammweg, the road that ran along the Weiz river.

"What was the objective of the visit to that bar anyway?"

"To familiarize yourself with it. Call it routine reconnaissance as well. But tell me, why are we going up to this Festring place?"

"You want to talk to the owner or whoever works there, to see who might have been there the same time Karl Himmelfarb was."

"Okay, good. And why is that necessary?"

"Because he talked to others there. And that's where people could have found out he was going to call us again."

". . . because of . . . ?"

"Hansi wanted to tell us things, maybe. I don't know."

"You're bothered," said Speckbauer. He had spoken in a slow, considerate tone that Felix could not remember hearing before.

"Annoyed I'm talking like this?" he went on.

"Who wouldn't be?"

Felix felt Speckbauer's gaze on him. He didn't look over.

"Okay," said Speckbauer, finally. "There's only one change to make to that."

"How do you mean?"

"You said we'd talk or that I would talk. Not so. It will be you." Speckbauer had his hand up even as Felix formed words.

"You are local," he said.

"But I live in Graz," Felix said.

"They will know you maybe. One less barrier, don't you see? And look – if they don't know you, they'll have known your father."

Felix took his foot off the accelerator. He looked over.

"My father? Why are you bringing him into this?"

"Is it beneath you or something? Be proud, I say. We need people to have confidence in us. To trust us. We must use everything we have."

Felix bit back the words that rose to his mind. An uneasy quiet settled in the car. Speckbauer seemed more interested than ever in the occasional car that passed them now.

Felix left it in third passing the mill, the last piece of straight road before the Weizklamm, the deep, rocky ravine full of hairpin bends and towering overhangs a couple of kilometres away.

"Itchy foot?" Speckbauer murmured, without taking his eyes off the view. So do it then. But just for a bit."

Felix's annoyance evaporated when he floored the pedal. There was no lag. He felt his seat had been shoved hard from behind. The wind began to hiss at the small opening at the top of the window.

"Genug," said Speckbauer. "You have a beer on the job, you do a Nikki Lauda. Feel better now?"

The mountains soon closed in on the road, and made it a steep, winding cut at the bottom of the gorge, its bare rockfaces hundreds of metres overhead holding back the light.

Now Felix felt a cold tension moving into his chest, something he tried to ignore. He knew it was not due to a need to push the car tight to the guardrails. Without thinking about it, he began to count backwards, a countdown to when he guessed they'd be passing the taferl to his father.

"I tell you," Speckbauer began. "I sure wouldn't want to meet one of those . . . "

He stopped then and looked over.

"Sorry," he said. "I forgot. Hereabouts . . . ?"

"No, it was near the other end."

Felix heard the river over the sound of their car's passage between the rocky walls of the klamm. It still tumbled white and fast, crashing over the rocks in its spring wildness, as they called the melt from the mountains higher up.

The first of the grassy ledges began to appear after several minutes, along with some bushes. Along with the returning brightness glowing at the edges of the precipices above, these were signs the gorge would soon open, drawing them onto the plateaus and folds that led in turn into the higher mountains.

Speckbauer opened a map that he had drawn from the door pocket.

"Remote, you might think," he murmured. "But not as the crow flies."

Felix's count was out by 20. He did not slow as he drew up to the taferl. Nor did he glance at where his father's car had gone over into the gorge. He was relieved that Speckbauer had missed it, and with sunlight returning to the car's interior again, he felt the tightness easing. He eased off the pedal at the turn-off to St. Kristoff.

Speckbauer looked up from the map.

"Festring," said Felix. "That gasthaus, right?"

"Are we at the turn-off already? Did we pass . . . ?"

"I didn't want to disturb you."

Felix let the car out of gear. He freewheeled almost to a stop while Speckbauer consulted the map.

"No," said Speckbauer. "We're going through St. Kristoff, remember?"

"That's the other way."

"Don't worry. We'll get you back to Graz in time for the train."

"I just wanted to point out something. I'm coming back up here tonight, you know."

Speckbauer gave no sign he'd noticed Felix's annoyance.

"To my grandparents' house, to sleep," Felix added. He pointed to the map. "Right here."

"A beautiful spot – if this is any indication. I'm keen to see it. Let's go."

With that, Speckbauer jammed the map down between the seat and the arm rest, and he opened his window more. Felix took the hint. He steered the Passat onto the narrow road that led toward St. Kristoff. There were few breaks in the woods that now surrounded the road that would allow any glimpses of the mountains.

"Quite a place," said Speckbauer, and let his window down a little. "Tracks, paths, wegs – everywhere."

The air was much cooler already. Felix tried to remember how many metres St. Kristoff was, 1200-something or 1800-something.

"Tell me something," Speckbauer said. "Your family goes back a long way here, huh? Both sides?"

"I don't know how many generations."

"Not interested in that sort of thing, the family story?"

"Not really."

"Why did your family leave here? If you don't mind my asking."

Felix didn't answer for several moments. Speckbauer, who had been looking up through the trees for another glimpse of the church and the houses of St. Kristoff, turned to him.

"Am I being too personal?"

"Every family has its things, I suppose."

Felix slowed when he saw the muddy tracks out onto the pavement. The sound of a chainsaw began to grow louder. He looked down the track that met with the road and caught a glimpse of a white vehicle, then another. One was an Opel Campo pickup. Maier, he guessed, or one of the men working for him.

"You're stopping?"

"No. I was just curious. It's okay, I saw who."

"In the woods there?"

"Same guy we almost bumped into a few days ago," said Felix. "We were on the way up for the anniversary."

Speckbauer craned his neck to look out Felix's side.

"You can tell from that thing, that white truck?"

"It's the guy with the licence to cut here. Maier. I was at school with him, or his family."

"Is he a friend of yours? Your family's?"

"No."

"See? You do know the people up here still then. That's nice."

Felix dropped into second again and turned up the steepest section now, barely a metre from a steep drop off. The woods began to peter out, and the high meadows took over more. The sun hit them then. Felix pulled in and came to a stop to let an older couple in a Citröen coming down. He returned a small wave.

"They are?"

"Family Fischbach. They farm two places over from my oma and opa. Well, the next one does. Stephan, I think."

"Your oma and opa on your father's side?"

"My mother's, the Nagls. I only have an opa on Dad's side."

Felix pulled out onto the pavement again.

"You know," Speckbauer said, "this is a beautiful place. One would have to be crazy to leave here."

Felix's mind was already ahead on the road out to Festring. There were 15 or 20 kilometres they'd need to drive on that corkscrew road.

"Crazier to stay," Felix said. "Believe me."

Speckbauer still seemed immune from any hint of Felix's irritation.

"Really? I can understand the attractions of town life, city life."

Felix said nothing.

"Work of course too," Speckbauer added. "And a bit of adventure. Not everyone can work a farm, or wants to, I suppose?"

"My mother worked in Graz awhile, before getting married. She liked it."

"But your dad, he liked the high country up here, I'll bet. Heimat: the homeland, even though . . . ?"

"Even though . . . ?"

"Oh oh," said Speckbauer. Then after a few moments, he added, "Well, it's just conversation."

Felix let the awkwardness curdle more.

"It's like you said yourself," Speckbauer added. "Every family has its things. Anyway. Tell me what I'm seeing up here."

Felix let the Passat freewheel by the lower wall of the graveyard before the road made its last turn up to the village.

He pointed out places: the school, the village square where the May festival, the Maifest, had been held a fortnight ago. The pine boughs that had been attached were still green. Speckbauer asked how old the church was. Felix came up with something persuasive. He wondered if Speckbauer was now going to ask to see the Kimmel family plot in the graveyard.

"Don't you want to drop by your grandparents'? Tell them you'll be by later on, perhaps?"

Felix shook his head.

"They know already. And we're going out by the other way, aren't we?"

Felix decided Speckbauer was about to say something, but had held back.

"Well," said Speckbauer after a while. "What of your father's side?"

"They don't farm anymore. I mean he doesn't, my grandfather."

"A lifetime of hard work," Speckbauer said. "No doubt?"

"It was a hard enough life up here," Felix said. "In the past, I mean."

"Until recently, would you say?"

"My grandparents could tell you, I suppose."

"Ach Mein Gött," Speckbauer said then. "You can't buy air like this in the city."

"Uh uh," said Felix. "Spend a winter up here, when you're a teenager."

"Where are teenagers happy, I ask you?"

"Claustrophobic isn't fun."

"But it's your home, still, right? Your ties are here, right?"

"Look. My parents wanted us to go to Uni, and all that."

"Your father too?"

Felix waited several moments, until he was sure Speckbauer had turned away from the window.

"Why are we talking about this?"

"Why?" Speckbauer repeated.

"Yes, 'why.' You're here investigating a murder, aren't you?"

"I am – you too. A very valuable training exercise for you too, I might add."

"But all these questions about my family?"

"I like to learn about people. Variety, human nature – all that."

"Hillbillies can be interesting, I suppose. 'G'scherter'?"

"What?" said Speckbauer. "I am a g'scherte myself."

"Well, you're not from here."

"I'm a Northerner, but a real shitkicker nonetheless. My old man still farms – well, my brother does it actually – over near Linz. Look, turnips are nothing new to me."

Felix glanced over.

"Then you'll know all about little villages, and why someone would want out."

Felix geared down to slow the Passat, but it was still picking up speed. Another two bends and they'd be back out on the road that led up higher yet into the mountains.

"Ach, you have a point," said Speckbauer. "There's always more than meets the eye."

"So they say."

"A lot of things didn't get talked about around my place. I found out only later, of course. Same for you?"

"Maybe so."

"Really? For example, I had an uncle, and he was a real believer. All the way through. You know what I'm referring to when I say 'believer'?"

"I think so."

Speckbauer's wan smile faded quickly.

"Yes," he said. "That's what I found out. He wasn't just a conscript or even a volunteer. He was the whole bit. A zealot. But he got out alive. Talk about lucky, no?"

"For him," said Felix.

"He was in the SS at age twenty. He was proud of it. I know, because I met these old guys at his funeral. I'd never seen them before, never heard of them. Strange thing, family, I began to realize. I liked him when he was alive. But after, a hard man to like."

Felix pretended to be concentrating on the ditches that ran alongside now.

"A real jäger," Speckbauer said. "He loved his hunting. I used to go with him."

He shifted the map off his lap.

"And he did the other thing too, you can be sure. They go together. You know the saying, right?"

Felix shook his head.

"Maybe it's only in the Tyrol. Wilderer und jäger sint brüder. 'The hunter and the poacher are brothers.' Hard times bring their own means, no?"

"I suppose."

Speckbauer turned in his seat to look behind.

"You see that?"

"What?"

"That clearing, a path. Forestry access, you think?"

"Probably," said Felix.

Speckbauer turned back.

"'Wildererweg' they called them back up in my place growing up. Poachers' paths. Do they call them that here?"

"I think I have heard it. Older people though."

"I wonder if that's what they call that place up by Himmelfarbs.'"

Felix kept his eyes on the bend and the shadows under the trees there. Where the bodies were, he meant.

"Ach so," said Speckbauer after a few moments, his tone changing to something almost cheerful. "No doubt we'll find that out in due course. Hardly the most important detail of this, is it now?"

Felix nodded slowly once.

"Ever do any hunting?" Speckbauer asked as Felix let the Passat straighten out after the bend.

"I've done some. Shooting rabbits is as far as I went."

"You enjoyed it?"

"Not really."

"Like deer?"

Felix nodded.

"Your father made no big deal of when you didn't want to go on?"

"No. For my dad and his mates, well it sort of was part of growing up on a farm. But my mother was never happy with that stuff. No antlers on the wall in our place."

Speckbauer began to study the map again. Felix made sure that Speckbauer would notice him checking his watch.

Speckbauer didn't look up from the map.

"Lots of time," he murmured.

NINETEEN

THE ROAD CROSSED A RIVER NOW AND BEGAN TO CURL AROUND the mountains. They were high enough for the forest to falter, but scattered clumps of smaller, tough pines had managed to root even on ridges close to the summits.

Speckbauer consulted his map again.

"We could have gone by Teichalm, I guess," he said. "What's up there? Aside from woods, bog, more woods?"

"A big inn, a gasthaus. Ski runs. A lake. A very cold lake."

There were a few cars up here, more than Felix had expected.

Speckbauer craned his neck to see a couple with two children plodding near the woods across a marshy patch. All had rosy cheeks, and wet hair. The yellow rain jackets looked like aliens amidst the green.

"Wise choice," said Speckbauer. "The yellow. Hunting season and so forth? I'm sure things have happened over the years up in these parts. Hunting accidents?"

Felix's mind lingered on how Speckbauer said "accidents."

"I suppose," he said.

"The two men up in the woods by Himmelfarbs' weren't 'accidents,'" said Speckbauer. "I don't need an autopsy to figure that one out."

"When will those results come back?"

"Some now, already. I should phone in soon. You know what toxicology is?"

"Of course."

"Than you'll know they take a long time. I have waited weeks for tests."

"Content analysis too?"

"Well, good for you. What's in the bauch, the belly, yes. Also what shape their organs are in. It helps to know. Teeth tell a lot. Hair too. Sure, the papers are full of DNA cases and all that, but all that environmental stuff has come on strong in the business the past few years. We'll need it, I tell you."

"Because they had nothing on them?"

Speckbauer frowned.

"You knew that? How?"

"I overheard."

"Good for you, I suppose."

"So you – so we – don't know much yet."

Speckbauer's frown changed to a puzzled look.

"I like the 'we' there," he said after a few moments. "But you're right. We have no idea who they are. My guess is south of the border. But they had nothing – zero, truly – on them for ID. Wallet, money, smokes, watch – nothing. Anyway. Their photos have gone out to several jurisdictions by now. So, we wait."

"Well, can you tell how long they were there?"

"A guess, again? To me, they are dead more than three days. It is high up there, cool enough. They were out of the sun."

"That's it, then? That's all?"

The frown had returned to Speckbauer's face, Felix saw.

"Well, what do you think," he said.

"You want me to make a fool of myself, four months on the job?"

"Don't worry about it," said Speckbauer. "There's a thing called 'fresh eyes.'"

"Well, they didn't fall like that, did they. They were put there."

"Genau. Did you get a look at the one with the moustache?"

Felix shook his head. He wondered if this was Speckbauer being cynical. Surely he'd heard about him vomiting.

"Well, to me, he was the runner."

"The runner?"

"He was on the move for sure when he was taken down."

"The other one, with the, you know?"

"Right," said Speckbauer. "The hole over his eye. He's the one who didn't know what hit him. There's no blood up there, did you notice? Ever see a head wound? It bleeds like a pig. You can't put a bullet neatly into a guy's kopf in the middle of a fight. It was murder, natürlich – but one was execution. That's why the second guy ran."

"So they were shot somewhere, and then brought into the woods?"

Speckbauer nodded and looked out across the stretch of open country. It was wild grass and low bushes here, growths that had been hardly enough to survive, dwarfed and delayed here in the open.

"We are of like mind, so far," he said. "But there's no law says we can't speculate, is there?"

"But if they are ausländers," Felix started to say.

Speckbauer's head jerked around, almost theatrically, to face him.

"If they are," Felix repeated. "Then . . . ?"

"Right," said Speckbauer, in a strange voice, half whisper, half sigh. "What the hell were these tschuschen doing up here in the hills? Isn't that your question?"

Using the street word for anyone from Yugoslavia was a test, Felix thought immediately, a taunt. He concentrated on driving.

"Well, Christ and His Mother," said Speckbauer in the same soft, almost bemused voice now. "Don't stop now, Gendarme Kimmel."

Felix changed for a bend that held a small pool of water by the ditch.

"Smuggling," he said. "Sorry, 'trafficking.' And that's why the Kripo is in, why you're in."

"Not bad," said Speckbauer. "Remember I said accident, how shooting two people could hardly be an accident? I wasn't being sarcastic. And I'll tell you why: it's because it was an accident in some way – a mistake, at least. 'Irregular,' let's say."

"It should not have happened, you mean? Wait – that sounds just blöd."

"There's been a slip up," Speckbauer went on. "And that is the policeman's friend. I worked many years ago with a fine fellow – actually he was an arschlocher to everyone – but he got his job done. He was my first C.O. when I went detective. I will not burden you with his name. But my point is this. As he would say, we do not need to be a genius here, Horst. We just need to find a mistake."

"Who made this mistake, then?"

"Ah, you'll give me heartburn with that one. What are they teaching guys like you about trafficking at that Gendarmerieschule these days?"

"Well, that it's a big business. Drugs, guns, anything. People, women."

"Okay. So trafficking is about articulated trucks on the autobahn, going hell for leather toward Frankfurt or Amsterdam. It's trains, it's plane cargo, five or ten kilometres up there. Depps with stuff in the frame of their car, or in their knickers. Now what?"

"Well, why would two men, ausländers, why would they be so far off the beaten track up here?"

"Congratulations," said Speckbauer. "You are saying what I say to myself. It's what I say to my fine colleagues in Graz. It's what I say to certain persons on the phone from Vienna and places even more exotic than that lovely city. The answer is . . . ?"

Felix shrugged.

"The answer is . . . we don't know. And that is why we are up here, believing that this is important, very important. The proof of that is what happened to the Himmelfarb family."

TWENTY

THE LOW THRUM OF THE ENGINE, AND THE SQUEAKS FROM THE suspension as the car wallowed and even bucked on the mountain road only made the silence of the last 10 minutes of the journey to Festring more pronounced. In that uneasy quiet Felix soon decided that Speckbauer too was marinating in his own thoughts, maybe even as much as he was in his own. The difference was that Speckbauer was showing no signs of that steady and growing foreboding that had been growing in Felix's mind. It had almost spilled over into dread at times, a dark swirl of images flaring and returning again, no matter how he tried to contain them.

It was almost a relief when the half-dozen houses of Festring came in sight, arriving abruptly after a bend, nestled in a valley whose bright green meadows had been hard-won from the hills. Gasthaus Hiebler was a modest affair in the traditional style, with ambitious flowerboxes and what looked like a recent coat of paint. Two cars were parked in a gravelled area to the side, one an Opel with fancy rims. The spring melt was not done with the land up here yet, and the soft, grassy banks of the ditches along the road outside were still saturated. Felix backed in, turned off the engine and held the keys up for Speckbauer.

"So," said Speckbauer. "Except for that shitbox Opel there, we are in a time machine up here."

Felix said nothing.

"This is going to be low key," Speckbauer went on. "We want to know who was in this place when Karl Himmelfarb was in the other night. Who he might have told about the goings on at his farm. He played cards, had a beer, like always, gell?"

Felix nodded. Speckbauer still held the door handle, and stared at the gap where the door had opened a little, and where the cold air was flowing in.

"And my bet is they'll know you, your name. Your father?"

And Speckbauer was out of the car with that fast, rolling exit that had him on his toes and stretching by the side of the car, the door shut behind him already. He nodded toward the door of the inn.

It was drawn back just as Felix prepared to push it open. A woman in her fifties with a housecoat took a step back.

"Servus," Felix said.

"Grüss, und wilkommen."

She had a business smile and grey eyes that reminded Felix of a bird. They fixed on Speckbauer, who had lingered several steps behind. She returned his greeting in the same high, musical accent she had Felix's.

"Is the gasthaus open?"

"Of course," she said, and she unclasped her hands to usher them in.

There was a heavy, brothy aroma in the air. Felix glanced at the empty dining room that was off to the left of the entrance.

"Fine day earlier," she said.

"It'll return," said Felix.

How easily it had come out, he thought; how he didn't even have to think about the reflexive reply he had heard so often from his grandparents.

"Kommen sie," she said.

The stübe even had a kachelofen, and it had been lighted. An old man was seated at a table, a walking stick beside him. He turned and smiled at Felix.

"Well, look what the day brings us," he said.

"Grüss, Herr Hartmann," said Felix. "A nice surprise to find you up here."

He saw that the woman was eyeing Speckbauer.

"Wunderbar," said Speckbauer and rubbed his hands briskly. "Did I smell soup?"

There were playing cards spread out over the gingham cloth at the booth where Willi Hartmann sat.

"You are rambling, Felix, is it? Up for the air?"

"Actually not. My friend here is new to the area. He asked if I would show him the sights."

"Marvellous," said Speckbauer to Hartmann. "Splendid countryside."

Hartmann looked from Speckbauer to Felix and back.

"It is that, sir."

"May I buy you a krügl of beer, Herr Hartmann?"

"No, no, Felix. Ach, how like your father to have said that! No, thank you. I need but the one glass of beer to get wipsi now."

Then he offered a weak smile.

"There are no prizes for old age, my friends. I should finish my game and go home for a nap."

"Home is close then?" Speckabuer asked.

"Herr Hartmann lives in the same village as my grandparents," said Felix. "St. Kristoff."

"Six hundred and twenty years," said Hartmann, with a wink. "Not all mine of course. My family."

Speckbauer trailed the woman to the bar.

"Soup and a bun would be great," Felix heard him say. "Is that possible?"

She smiled, and this time Felix saw gold to both sides of her mouth.

"I am the boss," she said. "So if it's possible, I will tell you."

Hartmann moved in on the bench and motioned to Felix.

"Sit," he said. "Sit. A nice service for your dad, wasn't it? A good turnout, eh? Respect. Some things don't change, even in this flyaway world."

He eyed Speckbauer talking to the woman at the bar.

"My niece is married, you should tell him. Liesl, who runs the place."

Felix smiled.

"I don't think he's up in the hills looking for a wife."

Hartmann moved his leg again and grimaced. Liesl called out from the bar.

"Soup and jausen for you too, sir?"

Felix shook his head. He asked for beer instead.

Speckbauer returned to the booth. He leaned in to shake hands with Hartmann and then he slid into the bench opposite. He looked at the cards, the half-empty beer glasses.

"Am I taking someone's place?"

"Macht nichts," said Hartmann, with a small wave.

"My chauffeur – he's in the klo."

Hartmann's eyes stayed on Speckbauer for several moments.

"You take your wild card-playing to teach them up here, Herr Hartmann?" Felix said.

"Little teaching they need up here," Himmelfarb replied. "No. I go on my rounds here. I am like the priest, you know? My niece married in here years ago. Her husband may own this place, but she is the boss, let me tell you. That's the Hartmanns for you."

"And what does the husband work at?" Speckbauer asked.

"This and that," said Hartmann easily, as though he had been expecting it. "Takes care of the place, he's handy. There are contracts for the woods, of course. There's always something, isn't there? Not like old times, I must say. Your opa could tell you about those, eh, Felix?"

Opa Kimmel, he meant, Felix realized. The eminence grise, was that the expression? The conversation lapsed. Felix looked around the room. It had been kept up, and it was clean, but it had a jaded feel to it. Maybe it was more a hobby, or a custom to keep it open, just to cover costs.

Footsteps and a cough came from the hall. A man appeared in the doorway, pausing when he saw the arrivals to nod.

"Servus alles."

Felix returned the greeting, followed by Speckbauer.

The man was in his thirties, with tousled red-blond hair and two days' growth of rust-coloured beard under the crinkly eyes. There was an easygoing look to him, and he was more than amply padded.

"My chauffeur," said Hartmann. "Fuchs, Anton Fuchs."

"Toni," said Fuchs shaking hands, his eye almost disappearing with his smile. He sat in slowly beside Speckbauer.

"I was telling Felix how I can't win at cards here at all, Toni. In all the years I have tried."

"No one can," said Fuchs. His eyes almost disappeared with another smile again. "Liesl can beat anyone."

"I hear my name taken in vain," she called out, as she came through a doorway with a tray. She laid a platter of cold meats, and a half-dozen buns next to a bowl of thick yellowy soup. She raised the empty beer glass.

"Mahzeit," she said. "Your health."

Hartmann shook his head. Liesl stood back from the table with her hands on her hips.

"That's not going to change," said Hartmann, and he gathered the cards. "You have all the luck meant for me, Liesl."

Fuchs chortled and had another drink from his glass. For a moment Felix thought of Hartmann's artificial leg. Had he not considered himself lucky to have survived at all?

His eyes strayed to Hartmann's wrinkled hands, shaking a little, as he packed away the cards.

"This is the best," said Speckbauer, and spooned in more soup. It only helped to make the quiet seem even stronger behind the ting of his spoon and the swallows.

"The work goes well, Felix?"

"So-so," Felix said. "There is always something."

"Oh come on now. Your dad would have been so proud of you, to see you in uniform there. So proud."

He turned to Fuchs.

"Felix's opa and I, we were kids together. I knew Felix's father too. May God be good to him, as I know He is."

"Family?" said Fuchs, his smile almost closing the heavy-lidded eyes again.

"Kimmel," said Felix. "We started out in St. Kristoff."

"The Kimmels followed us there," said Hartmann. "Us Hartmanns. They knew a good thing up here in the hills. "

Hartmann stopped shuffling the cards, and put his head back.

"'In the green wood is my home
Beside the stream no more to roam.'"

Speckbauer held his spoon away from his mouth.

"'To farm and plough, to hunt the doe.
My land to guard against the foe.'"

Hartmann smiled, put down the cards and sat back.

"It's not often these days that I meet a fan of our great poet, Peter Rossegger."

Speckbauer finished the spoonful of soup.

"What Austrian could not be?" he said.

"Well, Felix," said Hartmann, and cleared his throat. "You travel our backroads with scholars. A great blessing."

Felix noticed the beer belly now as Fuchs settled into the booth. He exchanged a thin smile with him.

Then Hartmann sighed, and shook his head once. His expression turned sombre.

"Terrible thing, the Himmelfarbs," he said. "Terrible."

He seemed to be staring, unseeing, at something across the room. He sighed again.

"I heard you were there with the boy?"

Felix sensed Speckbauer had begun listening more intently.

"You heard that?"

Hartmann nodded.

"Karl knew your name," he said. "Oh yes. You and another Gendarme, the one he phoned. A friend of his, maybe?"

"They had met over a family matter before," said Felix. "But not me."

"It was your father," said Hartmann, and paused to clear his throat. "He knew your father. Like half the province, such a fine man – may angels guard him."

"It was only by chance I was there really," he said.

"I didn't know Karl all that well," Hartmann went on, his voice barely audible. Age seemed to have returned with a vengeance to his features, Felix thought. Liesl made her way across from a door that led to a big kitchen.

"Family Himmelfarb," Hartmann said to her.

"My God," she said and clasped a dishcloth to her chest.

"Terrible," she murmured, and then blessed herself. "But 'Straight to heaven go the honest and the innocent.'"

Felix caught Speckbauer's eye as the spoon was taking the last of the soup toward his mouth. Poetry, right off the bat? Speckbauer might not be the cynic about rural piety like this, then.

"The boy – God forgive me," said Hartmann. "My brain is rusty: but what was his name . . . ?"

"Hans," said Felix. "Hansi."

"He was everything to them, that boy," said Liesl, her voice quavering. "There was a problem when he was born, they say. None followed. But on they went, with just the boy. Such a terrible thing. Tragisch."

She took out a paper hanky.

"Karl visited here," said Hartmann. A game of cards, a coffee. Never alcohol. Right, Liesl?"

She was crying quietly now. She nodded.

"Not so long ago?" said Felix.

"He was here but a day before this happened," said Hartmann. He looked around the table with a slow, baleful stare, as though to find agreement.

Fuchs, whose head was down now also, studying the glass, nodded.

"A 'friend of the house'?"

"Indeed," said Liesl between sniffs. "For years . . . And such a dignified man. I can think of no other word. Oh, but he had a cross to bear!"

Several sobs escaped her. Hartmann's veiny hand reached up. Felix looked at the patterned brocade curtains by the windows, the folk art on the walls and behind the counter.

"Did you speak with him, Frau Hiebler?"

She nodded.

"The crops," she said. "The spring. The government. But so polite!"

Felix could feel Speckbauer's questions piling up unspoken, but he waited.

"Schnappsen," Hartmann said. "He played only to be polite. But I think he enjoyed himself. The way a quiet man would. And now look."

"Indeed," said Felix, and he turned to tousle-haired Fuchs.

"Did you?"

Fuchs shook his head.

"Working," he said. "I only heard from the TV. Then a neighbour. That was after the other thing."

"The other thing?"

"I thought they'd gotten it confused," said Fuchs, "Or that I had. We all heard about what they found up there behind the farm. The two, the two ausländers."

"The poor man!" said Liesel, her eyes shining. "And his poor family!"

"He must have had a terrible shock," said Hartmann.

"Did he talk about it all, when he was here?"

"Well, it was one of us, I think brought it up," said Hartmann. "If I'm remembering. Let me see, who was by . . . "

Then Hartmann's head went up, followed by the rest of him. He stared, eyes wide at Felix.

"What am I saying, Meine Gött, I am losing my marbles! Your

opa was here! Yes! Of course he was! Speak up there, Toni! You brought him, for heaven's sake."

Fuchs nodded bashfully, and scratched at his head.

"Toni here is not one much to blow his trumpet," said Liesl. "'The chauffeur.'"

"You drive people?" Felix said to Fuchs.

"Well, only if they can't find someone," he said.

"Now Toni," said Hartmann, his voice back. "No one is accusing you of being a saint, but come on now!"

He looked to Felix again.

"Toni drives us old geezers about sometimes – yes, don't be modest now, Toni! We aren't safe behind the wheel, you see. So Toni steps in. When he can, of course."

Fuchs gave a shrug, and waved away the compliments.

"And helps out," Liesl added. "With something they can't do themselves."

"Oh yes," said Hartmann. "Fix a window – ask Toni. Move furniture – ask Toni."

Fuchs shook his head gently, and scratched it again.

"Lose at cards – ask Toni," he said quietly. He had not looked up.

The smile returned to Hartmann's face for several moments.

"Well, have you seen your opa since the memorial?"

"No," said Felix.

"I think it's a good decision, no?" Hartmann asked. Felix didn't get it.

"Moving," said Hartmann. "It's hard, but it's the right thing to do, for him."

"I daresay," said Felix.

"He's out there on his own too long," Hartmann went on. "He'll have his own room now in the village. What could be better?"

He nudged Fuchs.

"Toni will help out when the time comes, right? Moving stuff?"

Fuch's lazy smile held. He looked at Felix but nodded toward Hartmann.

"I saw that," said Hartmann.

Felix was reluctant to draw Hartmann back from the light-heartedness he seemed to be working to regain.

"Herr Himmelfarb," he said then. "And his card friends, you say, that evening?"

Sure enough, Hartmann's expression slid back. He turned toward his niece.

"There were others earlier, weren't there, Liesl?"

Liesl nodded. Felix wondered if he should ask for names. He decided to wait.

"Oh he looked worried," she said. "Rings around his eyes. Tired-looking. Of course, he knew that we'd heard what had happened. I didn't want to put talk on him about it though – if he didn't bring it up himself, of course."

"A man would have to get out," said Hartmann. "Just to get a wee break, even for an hour or two."

"But he talked about things?" Felix said. "What had gone on?"

There was a small delay before Liesl answered.

"Well, I think he was worried for his boy . . . wasn't he, Willi? He was with your players here."

"Us old farts," said Hartmann with a rueful look. "Yes. He said the boy was very . . . how can one say it, one doesn't want to say ver-rückt – crazy, like – let's say strange. Agitated. No sleep, with all the comings and goings. The boy was excited, he wanted the thing to go on, you see. He didn't understand."

"All the activity there?"

"The Gendarmerie and so forth," said Hartmann, and paused momentarily.

"Those experts, the police experts," he added.

It was a signal that Speckbauer wouldn't miss either, Felix knew. He looked over at Liesl again.

"He was not keen to discuss private matters," she said. "But he said something about how it would take ages for the boy to settle again. 'He wants the police up there all the time now.'"

"Karl did, himself?"

"No, the boy, Hansi. The police were good to him, apparently, humouring the boy. Playing the siren and that, like a toy."

"That is how they found the two," said Hartmann. "He said that Hansi liked one of the Gendarmerie so he brought him wandering up the woods, where he had his 'dolls.'"

"Dolls?"

"That's what the boy called them, he said: 'dolls.'"

No one seemed to want to keep the conversation going after Hartmann's quiet and doleful remarks. For a while everyone seemed to withdraw into themselves. Felix took another swallow from his beer. Fuchs ran his hand slowly through his hair, but the effect was only to make him look even more the bewildered elf with even more hair askew. Liesl looked away through the window toward the faraway hills, and Hartmann sighed. The quiet was broken only by the sounds of Liesl's occasional sniffle and a faint whistling that seemed to come from Fuch's nose.

Then Liesl shifted her feet.

"So geht's," she said. "And so it goes. The bad things that happen to the good people. I hope there'll be a big turnout for the funeral."

Both Hartmann and Fuchs nodded.

"I am forgetting more and more," said Hartmann then. "But now I remember. Yes! Poor Karl was clumsy, with his cup, wasn't he, Liesl? He dropped it and it broke? His hands were shaking a bit. I asked him if there was somewhere he could get a break, him and Mrs."

"Haunted, he was," said Liesl, and blew her nose in a delicate fluffing sound.

After several moments, where Liesl looked away through the window toward the faraway hills, and Hartmann sighed, the talk slowly moved to goings on in the district. The winter had been long, as always; tourism last year had not been so great, but there were more people coming up to trek now. Would the Turks finally get their way now, and get a ticket to the EU? The price of a new VW was just stupid, and the quality was down anyway.

Felix listened, saying little, and wondered what Speckbauer was making of it all here. Hayseeds, slow-in-the-heads up here in God's country? Occasionally he'd glance over at Hartmann, at the liver spots on the back of his hands, and at the lines that the wind and sun and long winter's cold had dug in from his eyes around almost to his ears. Berger Willi, yes, this ancient fellow had been mad for the hills and mountains since he was a child.

He saw Speckbauer looking at his watch.

He took out his wallet. Speckbauer's hand was on his forearm before he could open it.

"May I?" Speckbauer asked, looking around the faces. He had no takers.

Felix followed Liesl over to the counter.

"The card guys," he began. "Are there a lot of them?"

"They come in different days," she said. "But the older ones are afternooners."

"Were there many the evening Karl Himmelfarb was in?"

She stopped keying in numbers on the cash register and stared at a mirror behind the counter.

"I'd have to think," she said. "Berger Willi, of course – and Herr Kimmel, your opa. He is Peter, no? Fuchs, yes. There were others . . . Hans Prem; he's in a chair now, a wheelchair. But his daughter has a van for that, yes. . . . She stayed, but she didn't play. Let me see . . . Frank Schober, I think. He drives himself, still."

She frowned then, and turned from the mirror.

"So you are Herr Kimmel's grandson. Isn't it strange we haven't met."

"My opa is called Herr Kimmel, even here?"

She gave him a quick glance.

"Well that's the way with some people, isn't it? What odds, I say. But not like your father, I must say. Or you, I think?"

"My father? You knew him, did you?"

She looked toward the group at the booth again, but her eyes were not focused on them, Felix saw.

"Only a while," she said. "I was sorry to hear of, you know?"

He nodded.

"He used to come here?"

"If I remember it was only for a short while," she said. "Maybe a couple of years ago? But he dropped by a number of times there, in one week. That's how I remember. Yes."

"Driving my opa, was it?"

Again she frowned.

"Well I don't think so. But such a nice man to talk to. I am sorry if this is not good for you to hear this today."

Felix smiled.

"He got around, as they say."

"Oh I knew he was a Gendarme right away," she said. "Even without any uniform. But that made no difference. Great for a chat. It gets a bit isolated here after the season, you know. But he liked to know the news, no matter how small it would be from these parts. Yes. Always had time to listen. Curious about everything, yes."

She shrugged sympathetically and finished entering the numbers. The till opened as a receipt began issuing out with a scratching sound.

"Yes," she said, and began fingering some change from the leather purse. "It's hard on the older ones up here, the ones who want to stay independent. So Fuchsi there, he does them a lot of good."

She settled on the coins she had chosen as the proper change. She stopped and counted and frowned again.

"May I phone later, then?" he asked.

"Phone?"

"If you can recall who was here at the time Karl Himmelfarb made his visit?"

"In and out," she said. "Scraps. They can be quite comisch, these fellows, you know. Quite comical."

He returned her smile briefly.

"If you can recall who was here at the time Karl Himmelfarb made his visit?"

TWENTY-ONE

SPECKBAUER KEPT HIS WINDOW DOWN FOR QUITE A WHILE, ONLY closing it when his mobile went off. The connection failed as he answered it. He studied the read-out.

"Patchy up here," he said. "No signal again."

Felix let the Passat find its own way down the hills now, biting a little hard into the tighter bends.

"Well, they are true to a type," Speckbauer said. "Up these parts? The 'God help us' and the cards. But damned good soup. You know, I'm beginning to think that country people are the same the world over."

Felix saw that he continued to stare at the read-out. Waiting for a coverage signal, he decided.

"Gossipy too," Speckbauer murmured, and looked up. "But how could you not tell people if something like that happened, right?"

Felix didn't understand what Speckbauer meant.

"Two bodies turn up, you're going to want to talk about that," said Speckbauer. "Who could blame him?"

"You mean Karl Himmelfarb?"

"Well yes. I'll bet what he told those geezers was all over the area in an hour."

"Which means," Felix began, and looked over at Speckbauer.

"Yes," said Speckbauer. "A great big frigging pallawatsch for anyone trying to track who knew what, and when."

He rubbed noisily at his nose.

"Or what anyone might have decided to do with that information," he added, almost in a groan, and put down his phone.

"Whatever you said to that woman when you were talking to her, that Liesl," he said, "you sure know how to make her cry. Jesus."

"I hardly said a word to her," said Felix. "She couldn't stop crying."

"You got nothing specific from her? Beyond the names, I mean, the geezers who come by for cards?"

"No. She mentioned my father's name, and she starts crying again. Too much."

"Well your family gets about," said Speckbauer. "Was your grandfather always a card player?"

Felix braked for the junction of the road leading over toward the Himmelfarbs' farm.

"Tell you the truth, I don't really know."

"I get the impression you're not that close."

Felix pushed his foot on the accelerator. Speckbauer seemed to take the hint.

"This Hartmann," he said then. "A game old rooster, isn't he?"

"Yes and no."

"And what does that mean?"

"It's all very well to meet once in a blue moon, but he's not the most appealing fellow, I remember my dad saying."

"Is he senile or something?"

"My mother says leave him be. He's a character."

"Was that a fake leg I saw on him?"

"The war. It saved his life, I suppose."

"Sixty something years he's been bowling along on one leg? Quite an achievement. A friend of your family?"

"Not really. But he shows up for every memorial. And mass. And funeral."

Speckbauer eyed the speedometer while he felt around in his jacket pocket for something.

"Ach," he said "I think I know the type. Your grandfather and him, they're . . . ?"

"I don't know," said Felix. "Cards maybe, neighbours."

"Close enough, then."

"Living in the same area for six hundred years doesn't make you close."

"Ah," murmured Speckbauer, looking at something scribbled on a piece of paper before pocketing it again. "I hear a philosopher, do I?"

"I have to keep up with the poetry guys."

"Rossegger? Christ, every kid learned that in school in my time. Didn't you?"

Felix geared down to overtake a van before the next series of bends.

"Some. But they never told us much about his politics, did they."

"Don't spoil it," said Speckbauer. "How could a poet understand politics? How was he to know he'd be such a hit with the brownshirts a hundred years after? Him and, what's the name of that outfit, that club he founded, the one they're in still . . . ?"

"That who's in?"

"Oh come on – you're the guy did the Uni thing. You should know. The Blauers, the FPÖers, the Freedom Party – Haider and his mob."

"Sudmark, was it?"

"Stimmt. 'Only German spoken here in Styria – none of that Slovenian nonsense or the like. Out with the Yugos.' Or whatever they used to call them back then."

"Too much history," said Felix.

"Huh," said Speckbauer. "But you'll have a word with your opa then? About who was there in that Hiebler place the other night?"

"If you insist."

"Oh-oh. Is this a family issue I have stumbled in to?"

Felix shrugged.

"Tell me if you want, or not. But know that personal stuff doesn't matter to me. I am objective. Would you prefer I ask him?"

"I'll do it."

"Let's just say not everyone gets along as they might."

"Families," said Speckbauer. "They're work, sometimes. That's a fact."

Speckbauer's mobile went off again. The signal seemed to be holding here. He said a half-dozen "jas." Only one of them was even faintly interrogative, to Felix's ear. The Oberstleutnant's tone changed quickly then. He barked a "when" and a "shit, is that the best they can do?" He sounded less dispirited than disdainful about whatever he was being told.

"Franzi," he said after he ended the call, and stifled a belch.

"What's wrong?"

"'What's right?' you should ask. He's been chasing Pathology and the Ident. So far? Scheisslich: crap. But I had been hoping. I always hope."

"Still no idea who they are?"

Speckbauer shook his head.

"'Cheap shoes, from the East.' Wasn't that what Himmelfarb said?"

When Felix made no reply, Speckbauer glanced over.

"You're really not looking forward to this visit are you?"

"I don't see what purpose it'll serve."

"Okay. But police science is not always by the book. It's memory, like I told you before. Your mind plays tricks. When you retrace your steps up that track, you may remember things."

"Such as?"

"A remark. A reaction. Maybe the boy pointed at some place. Or his father, the time you all went up. Your colleague, maybe?"

"We went over our notes and statements pretty thoroughly."

"I hear you. But what I am saying is not a criticism. I'm not trying to catch anyone out. I'm working with evolution, you see? How the mind switches off certain departments, or how it notices things without the owner of the brain box realizing it. And when the lights go on again, sometimes things you did not notice, they come back."

TWENTY-TWO

FELIX WAS SURE HE COULD SMELL A SOUR TANG IN THE AIR FROM a kilometre away. Ashes from the house, he supposed, or the scent of burned material, like what lingered after smouldering rubbish was turned to burn. There was nothing visible from the road, but as he turned into the lane he saw the three wreaths hung on the fence.

There was a Gendarmerie Skoda in the farmyard. As Felix parked behind it he saw one of the Gendarmes put down the radio mouthpiece. He stepped out after Speckbauer who was already helloing them. He recognized neither man. He heard running water somewhere. He let his gaze drift around the yard and felt some spacey, acidic glow swelling in his chest. One of the policemen, a tall one who still had ferocious acne even in his thirties, shook hands.

The four men stood, awkwardly and silently, surveying the blackened rubble. It had been saturated, and pools of dark oily water shone dully up between charred rafters and the dark spindly masses that Felix supposed were remnants of furniture. The old kachelofen stood like a dark gravestone in the middle of the destruction. Felix thought of the cat he had seen snoozing there, the cake Mrs. Himmelfarb had cut up and put on plates.

"It was still smoking even this morning," said the policeman with acne. "We thought we'd have to call in the feuerwehr to hose it again."

"'Wood is a friend, wood is a foe,'" said Speckbauer.

"The families are coming this afternoon," said the other police-man, clearing his throat. "We just got word."

"Really?"

"The man had a sister, and she is coming with her husband. From Passail, I believe. She, the lady, had three – a brother and two sisters, but has only a sister left. And that one is coming in also."

"Animals?" Speckbauer murmured. "Cows?"

"Taken care of," said the acned one.

The stench began to seem almost visible to Felix, a cloud, or a fog that was permeating his clothes and even soaking his skin. The whitewashed stones that had fronted the old foundations of the house had only one or two places left that the smoke had not black-ened. It only made things look worse. He shivered.

"We're going up to the other place," said Speckbauer to the two. "Okay?"

Glad as he was to leave the farmyard behind, Felix's mind rebelled even more at the prospect of trudging up to where Hansi Himmelfarb had brought him such a short time ago.

Speckbauer's shoe slipped on a wet, grassy mound, and he swore under his breath as he put out a hand to steady himself.

"Dolls, he called them, you said. Right?"

"Yes," Felix replied. "Dolls, sleeping."

He heard Speckbauer begin to wheeze with the exertions. This pleased him.

"Did he have, maybe, little stories about these 'dolls'?"

"No. Not that I remember."

"Not a novel now, but."

Felix shook his head. Speckbauer stopped and turned to look back down over the farmyard. It was already half-hidden by the rise of ground in the field between. He turned back, breathing heavily, and looked beyond Felix.

"Now the forest begins," he said and resumed his slow trudging.

Speckbauer stopped several times, looking around, and as they stopped at the track Speckbauer spent some time looking in both directions, slowly scanning the woods. He dropped to one knee and ran his hand over the pine needles.

"Well they weren't dropped by a frigging helicopter," he said, standing. "Come on. It's close, isn't it?"

Felix nodded toward the space between trees he remembered.

"The site team had to carry their gear in here," said Speckbauer. "So as not to mess up any impressions on the road there, or the track. Turns out they needn't have bothered – there was nothing. Our old friend General Winter seems to have camped in the ground here for a long time."

The stakes and poles for the tent, along with the yellow perimeter tape, were gone. There were only tags on the trees now. Speckbauer didn't hesitate but walked over to where the bodies had been. Felix's stomach was almost lurching now. He was surprised and ashamed to feel the panic gnawing at his mind. He imagined turning, running down to the road, and not stopping the entire 30-odd kilometres back to Graz.

Speckbauer was eyeing him.

"He must have said something. The boy. Try to put yourself back there."

Felix tried not to think of his tight, aching stomach that seemed to have something moving slowly in it, and the strange taste beginning to make itself known at the back of his throat. He wanted badly to yell at Speckbauer, to tell him to stop calling Hansi Himmelfarb a boy.

"Nothing," he said instead. "Sorry."

"He was talking though?"

"He was talking to himself, words that I couldn't fit together. It made no sense."

"Words: a nursery rhyme, your notes said?"

"It was like a nursery rhyme. He kept repeating himself, over and over again. Nonsense words."

Speckbauer looked into the forest. Felix was looking at his watch when Speckbauer turned. He nodded toward the track.

"It's only ten minutes," he said to Felix. "No more."

Speckbauer slowed in places, looking around trees, and stepping between brambles. Twice he went down on his haunches to stare at the decayed leaves and pine needles.

"I know the crew was up and down here a half-dozen times," he said. "But don't be surprised at what a cop nose can still find, even afterwards."

He looked up toward the crowns of the trees.

"Planted, what, say thirty years?"

"Looks about that to me," said Felix. "Replanted, it would be, though."

Speckbauer gave him a keen glance.

"Right," he said. "Good. So this weg here, this track, it hasn't been here forever, has it?"

"Who knows? They come in every few years, and they thin out the lower branches."

"Why do you say that? Do you know this place?"

"No. But I know a bit about woodland, how it's managed."

Speckbauer slowed again, and he looked down near his feet, before walking on.

"Deer?" he said. "There's hunting still?"

"It's what people do around here."

They walked on, past the orange ribbons that had been attached to tree trunks. Felix was sure he could still smell the charred remains of the farmhouse, even up here. They rounded small clumps of bushes that already had brambles entwined in vigorous growth about them.

"Nobody drove in here," Speckbauer said. "And whoever these two turn out to be, they won't be Martians either."

A monologue intended to be overheard, Felix decided. He said nothing. His mind felt muffled, and he was beginning to believe that he couldn't hold the unease from becoming a dread that would make him want to just run back down to the car and drive like hell away from here. Every sound, even Speckbauer's careful steps through the undergrowth, and the occasional bird call, seemed amplified. The trees looked different, looming, and even the sky felt too close.

Speckbauer turned to him and raised an eyebrow. In the look Felix saw some sign that Speckbauer knew it must be hard for a new one like Felix Kimmel to be part of a grisly event and to have seen things that many Gendarmes would not see in a career.

"Sorry," Felix heard himself say, meaning: he couldn't remember anything else about that walk up here. He wasn't about to tell Speckbauer how he still felt Hansi Himmelfarb's big, soft hand grasping his at times. Nor would tell him that he saw Hansi's mother in her scarf there just as he and Gebhart had come up to the farmhouse. No: no more than he wanted to admit to himself he saw still the death grin, and the liquid slit where the eyelashes of the dead man had parted slightly.

TWENTY-THREE

Speckbauer's mobile went off after they had come in out of the hills and were closing on Weiz.

"There's shitty coverage," Speckbauer said to his caller. "That's why."

Franzi, Felix decided. That was unless Speckbauer spoke this way to everyone he worked with. It might just be possible, he decided, as he watched Speckbauer's eyes fix on the dashboard. There was that still, blankness back as he listened. It was not just that common look of concentration. There was something of an impatience close to its limits, that he was about to go off. It had been in the air too, when he had been prowling the farm and the woods alongside him.

"A what?" said Speckbauer, as though he had been called a name.

Felix caught sight of houses across the flat farmland that surrounded the town. Grass so green as to be almost luminous patched the fields across the plain, and as cool as it still remained up in the mountains, there were plenty of shoots up already from the early corn. Brindled cows moved in slow motion, their udders swinging like full sacks across a patch of field by one farmhouse.

"Not a good time to be a joker Franzi," he said. "Tell me you are being serious."

The answer he received brought a snort of disbelief.

"How by? Tell me details. Don't make me ask, you dummkopf."

"Carats," he said then almost immediately. "They measure them in carats. Any married man should know that, for the love of Christ."

A few seconds elapsed, with Speckbauer rubbing his eyes now.

"Nothing on the damned system yet? Didn't you query any diamond stuff through EKIS yet?"

Speckbauer grunted twice. Then he said, "Phone them again. Call me," and he closed the phone.

"Well," he said. "We have nothing on the two identities. The preliminary says 'Eastern Europe' the way their fillings and teeth are done. But don't mind that now: we have a peculiar item from a scan."

"A scan?"

"They took a diamond out of the guts of one of them. Wrapped up in a condom. Not so strange as one might think. Do you get it?"

"Small? Easy to carry?"

"Right," said Speckbauer. "A good way to carry a lot of money. But this guy, and his mate, they were on their way home, I say. Bringing home the loot. You think that diamond is a nice little keepsake from our own Jewelier Schulen, down at the Hauplatz there in Graz? Like hell, I say."

Felix wheeled around the outskirts of Weiz and once outside the town, he fell back to thinking about Giuliana. He tried to imagine where the Salzburg train that she was aboard was now.

"Does that change anything?" Felix asked finally.

Speckbauer had been humming the same polka-sounding tune for kilometres now.

"The diamonds? Who knows."

"I meant my situation."

Speckbauer gave him a glance.

"Well you're still going up to your grandparents' place tonight?"

"Right."

"You have your mobile, your Handi? Leave it on, and I can call you."

"You haven't answered the question though."

"Didn't I tell you I didn't know? I should have added 'yet' maybe?"

"If the fire at Himmelfarbs' was set on purpose . . . "

Speckbauer waited for the rest of Felix's sentence, but it did not come.

"Who knows where you're staying tonight?"

"You do," said Felix. "Giuliana does. I do. My grandparents do."

"No one else? What about your mother, your family?"

"I'll probably phone my mother tonight."

"And may I ask, will Giuliana be at your grandparents' place also?"

"I haven't even thought that far. I'll have enough to do trying to explain why we shouldn't be staying in the apartment tonight."

"She'll freak?"

Felix looked over at Speckbauer.

"I would think so. Just like I'm freaking."

"Are you?"

Now Felix gave Speckbauer a hard look.

"Well, okay then," said Speckbauer. "But you're doing a good job keeping it under wraps."

"What if she says, 'how long?' What do I say to her? A day, a week?"

"Hässlich – an ugly question. I don't have an answer for you. But tell her it's a precaution only. That might help?"

"Not much. I can see the reaction right now."

"Best I can do," said Speckbauer. "Or would you rather I'd said nothing to you?"

Felix's anger wasn't far off now. He studied the road ahead. In the distance the Magna plant had already appeared over the fields.

"Look," said Speckbauer. "Let's get a bit of perspective, can we? It's common to use diamonds for criminal payoff."

"To me, it says the people involved are used to this," said Felix. "Is that wrong?"

"Maybe, maybe not."

"You're holding back."

"I'm not," said Speckbauer. "But a cop has to think, well: 'Was that all?'"

"You mean more diamonds, or something?"

"Right. That's the one the guy swallowed. Are there more? Were there more?"

"So: a big organization."

"How can we know?" Speckbauer asked.

Felix had to wait until a long articulated truck had negotiated the bend ahead of them. It was hounded by two motorbikes and an impatient-looking man in a Mercedes 500-series coupe.

"Christ," said Speckbauer when the Mercedes driver floored it, only a kilometre from the entrance onto the A2. "As long as he only kills himself, I don't mind."

Felix was about to ask him why he had changed the subject, but he realized it would get him nowhere.

"Where are you parked again?" asked Speckbauer as Felix slowed for the ramp onto the A2. "I forgot."

TWENTY-FOUR

FELIX WALKED BACK TO THE TOP OF THE ESCALATORS AND looked out the plate glass to where he had parked the Polo in the yard that fronted the station on Bahnhofgürtel. Ten minutes early. There wasn't much going on at the Hauptbahnhof. Wagons were being shunted in the yards far off, but even with the local services, there were long stretches between the trains.

It wasn't going to go well, of that he was quite sure. He was sure in a hopeless, almost calm way. Already he could imagine Giuliana's face, how she sat back when she heard something ridiculous. He had tried to come up with phrases that might be an easy way to say things, or would lead into it gently. "It," he thought grimly, and let some of them stagger through his thoughts in all their wretched uselessness:

Giuliana, something like this has never happened before, and probably never will again. Giuliana, I could never have predicted this. Giuliana, I would have run the other way if I had known any of this was going to happen. But . . . ? But I feel I have to stay and help out – yes, even a new nobody-Gendarme.

He turned and walked back down the hall, the words and phrases following him and still muttering like gargoyles in his ear:

Giuliana, it is possible that the Himmelfarbs' place was – may have been – set on fire deliberately. Possible. . . ?! And yes, Giuliana, that would mean murder. And yes again, it's incredible, and it only belongs on TV shows or somewhere else. And, try to understand, my love, it's maybe possible – again, just maybe – that someone thinks I know something – which I really don't – because Hansi didn't tell me anything, anything that made sense, but he, or they, don't know that. And if he or they are so crazy or vicious or paranoid to do that to the Himmelfarbs, they might . . .

That's where it stopped.

He rubbed hard at his eyes and focused a little on his breathing. This jumpy restlessness had been gnawing at him even before he'd stepped out of Speckbauer's Passat and headed into the city proper. He had run a red light coming down Eggenbergerstrasse, and heard a shout from behind. Sometimes he was sure it was panic. Then later, when he tried to untangle it all, his thoughts dissolved in confusion.

He stared across at the traffic turning down Keplerstrasse toward the Mur, and the old city that began on its far bank, under the Schlossberg. Being used is one thing, he thought again, if it's part of your job. Wasn't that what a job was, especially if you were a cop under orders of your C.O.? But on that drive back along the A2 into Graz, Speckbauer had faltered in some way, and in spite of himself, he had revealed something. He had crossed a line, Felix was sure of it. Try as he might, he still couldn't figure what that was, much less what it meant. The fog of suspicion settled around him again.

He was hungry and he was not. His body was telling him to just get going, to release the tension somehow. He felt alert, too alert, the way you were after you woke up suddenly in the night and were on your feet before you knew it. He found himself looking around every corner of the platform and back into the gallery of shops and the broad, open space above the escalator that gave way to the plate glass and the clock.

Fine, he told himself again: it was normal to be jittery after what had been happening. That's how shock was, and you shouldn't ignore it, or make light of it. But why did everything seem so different, so suspect? There was that extra second that the shop attendant had looked at him; those CCTV cameras up over the escalators; the half-dozen teenagers with backpacks and head-phones lounging on the floor under the clock.

He hadn't been in the station more than a couple of times since it had been renovated as part of the City of Culture a few years back. There had been ski trains often enough in the high school days, and he and Lisi had been packed on to the Vienna train each winter when they were younger, to be met there by Kiti, a maiden aunt who worked in the university library.

A hatless, whistling ÖBB staff man eyed him, and as he drew close offered him a cautious "Grüss." Graz was a friendly city, no? Or more likely Gebi had been right. You could tell a cop whatever way he was dressed or acted, if you knew people at all. Felix lingered by the computer kiosk. He entered some places on the screen just to see the price of the tickets. There were three Nordic-looking backpackers at the ticket booth now, speaking bad German. A woman pushed an old man in a wheelchair. A porter was pushing a trolley half loaded with cardboard boxes. Felix watched him disap-pear around by the shops.

Speckbauer was back in his head: they'll trust one of their own, had been Speckbauer's rationale for getting him to drive around the hills. They'd know Felix Kimmel, right? And trust him, the logic went, as they'd known and trusted his father? And that stroll around the remains of the Himmelfarb home were sure as hell not part of the local scenery.

A train arrival was announced, and he looked up: Mürzzuschlag. Who cares?

Staring at the sign, however, Speckbauer was suddenly back in his mind. Him and that ogre he had as a partner, Franzi. And for a moment Felix imagined the inside of the car when it had been sprayed with the fuel. There would surely have been a millisecond before it went up in flames around him when Franzi would have known . . .

He cursed in a whisper, twice, and checked his watch again. Late? He'd count to 10, and if it wasn't announced at least, he'd skip downstairs and buy a sandwich he didn't need from the SPAR. He got to eight before the PA came on.

On his way to the platform, he took in the people who seemed to appear from nowhere, as usual when the train came, and the faint twanging sounds from the electric cables overhead as the train approached. The low burn of unease and resentment that had been around his chest like heartburn, or exhaustion, had dissolved and he felt his shoulders, or something at least, ease. He scanned the length of the train as the last metallic squeaks and ring of the coupling chains sounded and doors began to open.

TWENTY-FIVE

"It really is," Giuliana whispered, and paused, and her hands began to flail about weakly for words. She left the rest unsaid. She wouldn't even look at him. Even with the light from the overhead in the café, he saw that her face still looked kind of chalky.

"It's just . . . " she tried again, and let that go too.

"Look," he said. "Do you want a beer or something instead?"

She shook her head. She had left the biscuit on her plate. It looked like she'd be leaving most of the coffee behind too.

"I'm sorry," he said and added it to his total. He had said sorry four times now that he could recall. "I never expected this."

"It is just like, Jesus – a movie," she said, and a little gasp finished her words. "I'm waiting for, I don't know, it to be over. Just pazzo – crazy."

She fixed him with a hard look now.

"I am so numb that I'm not even scared yet. How stupid is that?"

"It'd be just a precaution," he said. "That's all."

"But Felix, listen: this is for someone else. Tell me that, can you? You're starting out, you have a job, and it's not this crazy, dangerous stuff. Right? You go into schools and talk to kids, you catch hooligans or something, get back stolen cars. Right?"

He nodded.

"Not all in one day."

"Don't try to be funny," she said. He was momentarily glad to see she was moving out of the paralyzed state she seemed to have entered.

"Just don't try to be a comedian, okay? Who is this guy you spent the day with, this big shot?"

"He's a higher-up from HQ. A detective. He's a ranking officer. He seems to run his own show."

"But I don't get it. Are you changing jobs? Were you at work today? What?"

Felix sat back and stretched. He did not want to see the dark rings around her eyes again, the ones that had seemed to erupt when the colour left her cheeks a few minutes before.

"What do they say back at your post? The one you work with, Gebhart?"

"I think he's telling me to stay back from this."

"You think?"

"It's hard to be sure what's on Gebi's mind sometimes. He doesn't expose his feelings much."

He heard her draw in a deep breath and she put her hands around the coffee cup.

"But your boss there, what's his name? Sch . . . ?"

"Schroek. He's okayed the job. Gebi went to him, because he had to okay it."

"But isn't Schroek the guy you told me, he's so low-key there that the place runs itself? Half-retired already? Does he have a clue what this is about?"

Felix didn't have an answer. Still, he felt he had to offer something.

"It's going to be fixed," he said. "It'll get settled, it'll be okay."

"How do you know this?"

"What can I tell you?"

"You can tell me we have a week together, and that we're going to get in the car and drive to Italy and do what we said we were going to do. You could tell me that you stood up to them and said, 'Look you idiots, I'm not trained in any of this, I haven't a clue what's going on, and you should leave me alone.'"

He looked down at her hands when they came to rest on the tabletop again.

"Well?"

He shook his head.

"What does that mean? 'Let's go to the beach'?"

"I've got to see the thing through," he began and raised his hand to meet hers already coming up. "Just a bit longer – but I'll tell him I'm no use, I want out."

"Christ," she said, and sagged in her chair. For a moment he thought she'd cry.

"We're stressed," he said. "At least I am, I know."

"You can say that again. Understatement of the year – I just can't take it in yet. I really can't. You're actually telling me it's a good idea to stay out of my – of our – apartment because . . . ?"

All he could manage was a nod. He reached for her hands.

"Come on," he said.

"Come on where?"

"Anywhere."

"What? Where are we going to go this evening?"

Her eyes had set into a hard look.

"My grandparents' place."

She took her fingers out of his grasp.

"No way. I wouldn't feel right. And don't even say we'll go to your mom's, or your sister's. It just wouldn't be right."

He waited a few moments.

"We could find a gasthaus somewhere then, a hotel even?"

He heard her sigh. There was more than exasperation in it now.

"Look," she said. "This isn't going to work. Are you listening to me?"

"I am. You mean this apartment thing."

She waited until she had his eyes locked on hers.

"I can't do this, Felix. Do you understand that? Do you?"

"It'll only–"

"You're not hearing me. It's more than this."

"I'm getting time off instead," he said. "And we can just hang around here, can't we? It saves money, even, you see? It's crappy but . . . "

He took her hands again. Her frown eased and he looked down at their hands.

A tiny tremor brought his gaze to her face. He saw she was near tears.

"It'll blow over," he said. "Really. Try not to worry. It'll blow over."

"It's just that things," she began but paused and drew in a fluttery breath before wiping her nose again. "We needed to talk anyway. I thought, when we were together, we'd be able to."

The foreboding flooded into his mind. He felt himself searching her face for clues.

"Talk," he said, quietly. "I never liked 'talk.' That kind, anyway."

She had a stricken look now.

"Don't try to joke now, Felix. Please."

"What else can I do? Weren't we going away for a few days?"

"Look, we've been avoiding talking about it."

"It? What's 'it'?"

"I don't want us to talk like this. It's been a long day. You probably slept lousy too."

"Maybe I'm beginning to get it," he said. "Is it about this cop life? The crappy stuff?"

She hesitated before answering.

"We talked about that already. You forgot."

The coffee was an acid snake still worming its way through his gut.

Then she sighed. He expected her to cry again, but she didn't.

"Felix. I don't want you to be like the others. But that's impossible, I see now. I've been thinking about it, trying not to think about it, running away from it, but it comes back. Now, with this horrible thing you're involved in, I am thinking this is the start of it, and it'll get worse."

"Did I make the worst mistake ever bringing you up there with those other cops? Is that what did it?"

"No, no. Peter's nice – Andreas, the one from Klagenfurt?"

"Andreas the cabbage?"

"They are nice guys," she said. "And no, nobody put the moves on me. It's just that, well, you are in the circle or you are not."

"What circle?"

"I'm not saying this right."

"You mean cops? There's a wall there?"

She returned his look but made no reply.

"For Christ's sake, Giuliana. Stuff like this never happens. Ask Gebi. It's traffic, it's domestics, or burglaries, and beer fights."

She said nothing. He felt like something had been decided already.

"I need time to think," she said.

A closing line, Felix realized. Still, he wanted to rescue something from the day.

"Jesus!" was all he managed, and he had not even intended to say it aloud.

"Please, don't get angry Felix. It's me, my problem. Can we just leave here – the banhof, I mean?"

He moved in a daze around the table and out the doors in front of the station. He didn't remember how noisy it had been here when he'd arrived.

"I started," he snapped at her when she put her hand on the straps of her carry-all. "I'll finish carrying it. Okay?"

When she put her arm in his, it felt like never before. He counted each step they walked to where he had parked.

TWENTY-SIX

BUT IT GOT A LITTLE BETTER, MUCH SOONER THAN FELIX HAD expected. They hugged in the car, and he even searched under her blouse. For a while he thought he could go all the way, right there in the street outside Giuliana's mother's building.

She murmured something to him even as he kissed her, and she pushed him away gently and when he opened his eyes he saw how flushed she had become, and the film over her eyes, that lost look. It had him aching worse.

"Phone me," she said. "When you get there."

"How about every hour."

"I'm worried about you, Felix. I am."

"I have a mom already. What I want, what I need is–"

She put a finger to his lips.

"Don't let them, whoever they are, don't do any more for those people."

For a few moments he didn't know what she meant.

He pretended to bite her finger. Her face soon turned sombre again.

"Felix, it's not just about this thing. It's been there awhile. And tell me I am not abandoning you."

"Big word, 'abandon.' How long have you been thinking about this 'talk'?"

"I feel terrible about this, you going up there by yourself."

"Don't. I spent summers there. They are easy. It'll be a mini-holiday."

"Severe, isn't that what you said? But they're older, he is, your Opa Kimmel."

She put her hand out for the door latch.

"Be careful," she said. "Driving, I mean."

Felix drove on autopilot, his head swimming, and his thoughts beginning to clot and darken again. The words that Giuliana seemed to have left behind her in the car circled endlessly even as the spring air cannoned around from the open windows. It wasn't helping, all this cool air. He couldn't trap any of those words or phrases long enough to make any sense of what she had told him. All he remembered was her eyes glistening, and the faraway look, too often near to tears. There had to be someone else. But why would she wait until their time together to tell him? Nonsense.

As if he weren't in over his head already, with what had started with a drive in the hills with Gebhart only two days ago, when he had sat in the Himmelfarb kitchen eating home-made strudel. Two days? 'A good day's work' Gebhart had called it, getting Hansi Himmelfarb out of the house at last? Off the deep end, for sure, he decided.

He yelled out the window, a long, ragged screech. When he saw there were no cars behind him still, he did it again, until his throat hurt. It sort of worked, but only in that he had a burning throat that took his attention. Within a short time, he was ready to head up into the hills from the roundabout in Weiz, beginning to wonder how the hell he had gotten all this way and not paid attention to the driving.

He earned two annoyed toots from drivers when he changed his mind at the roundabout and went the full way around, then back toward the supermarket. Oma Nagl was a sucker for blumen, any kind, but freesias most of all. Something would come of the end of this scheisslich day, with a cake, a dozen bottles of Puntigamer, and two city newspapers. Opa Nagl could laugh over them with gusto and regular quiet expressions of joyful malice that were entertaining to watch.

He found everything in the supermarket, including freesias that would have been better bought two days ago. The key in the trunk was tricky, and he stared at the reflections on the glass while he wiggled it. It wasn't working. He stopped and left the key hanging, his eyes still on the evening sky reflected on the glass. He wasn't overly surprised to feel an anger surging in him now.

So Giuliana had noticed changes in him. Sure, it was possible. Everybody did the denial thing, and he'd be the first to admit it. But somehow decided it was better to wait until their holiday to have a "talk"? Well for the love of Jesus, as Gebhart might say in pious, controlled exasperation. So she had noticed something, changes he had not. Well why hadn't she said something earlier? With the running jokes about the insensitive males, and womanly intuition, or inspiration or whatever they wanted to call it? She had given up, was why, she held out no hope. Was that fair?

He tried again and the key turned. He loaded in the beer and the cake and the newspapers and slammed the hatch shut. What had he done so wrong anyway? Before he knew it, Felix had reclined his seat and was reaching over the back seat to get at the beer. He gave the parked cars a quick once-over, opened one with the penknife he kept in the glove compartment, and took a long, long draught of warm beer. It was just fine. He held it down on the floor as a shopper pushed a trolley close by.

On his second, shorter drink from the bottle, he saw it was snobbery, Giuliana's thing that had come out of nowhere tonight. Or a day late, he had learned. She didn't want her boyfriend being a cop; she wanted the fun-loving-student-headed-for-respectability back, the one she had started with two years ago. And maybe she was right. She had graduated and was teaching already. He had worn out some shoes and lost brain cells drifting around Europe and working for the year. Pretty simple decision for her then, no?

With the bottle emptying on his fifth or sixth sip, it was all coming together. It was like one of the accordions that always showed up at a Maifest outside the church walls in St. Kristoff, when the beer started to flow finally, but the wrong notes, or no notes at all, were coming out of it. He shook the bottle to be sure it was really empty. So fast? He slid it under the seat, and wondered if this was how going mad actually started. Yes, maybe this was what if felt like to go over the edge. He stared at the top of the steering wheel, a gassy burp escaping between his lips and the giddiness starting in his head. He'd make it, he knew, up to St. Kristoff and his grandparents' place. The guilt at drinking one bottle of beer here in a car park wouldn't cripple him.

Parts of the steering wheel were worn smooth. He ran his hand along from axle to axle. Giuliana was right.

He ran his fingers around the whole wheel now, and felt the parts that had received little wear. His father had driven this car as little as possible: it dies on the hills, he had said? Yes. And, you'd nearly have to get out and push it up to the village, was another.

He had shut things out. So? Couldn't she understand that he'd had to shut things out? Hadn't he even told her once, a year afterwards, that he couldn't stop thinking what his father's last moments had been like, maybe that second or two it was still in the air, spiralling down to the rocks? Maybe it had all just brought out something maternal in her, or a pity, and he had been too dumb to spot it growing, until now, even she knew it wasn't enough to get over what he had become.

The scent of the freesias was winning out over his beery breath. He remembered what the woman wrapping them had said. Any other day it might have been funny.

"Your liebchen will love these," she had told him in accented German she had not grown up with. "After freesias comes diamonds, the engagement. Ever heard that?"

TWENTY-SEVEN

BERNDT, THE NAGLS' ANCIENT WEIMARANER, WAS NEITHER SO blind nor deaf that he did not know Felix. Little enough of the dog could wag now. He did not try to get into the car when Felix opened the door, but was content to stand there and receive attentions. The lumps on the joints of his hind legs looked bigger than Felix remembered. Berndt didn't push for more pats when Felix stopped.

There was a smell of fresh paint coming from the house. The windows were still open. Felix gathered the straps of his sports bag tighter, anxious to avoid crushing the flowers he was trying to hold aside from the straps, or the stuff from the supermarket. The dog moved on slowly and crookedly to the door without him, and then turned with a look of short-sighted curiosity and an awkward shrug of sorts.

Felix took in the deep overhanging eaves and the window boxes, and the stacked wood that ran in a line back up the vegetable garden toward the orchard. Behind the washing stirring slowly on the clothesline were the hills that lay between here and the highlands of the Teichalm.

Oma Nagl's mania for washing clothes remained as strong as ever. She particularly liked to whack carpets and rugs, and heartily too, and had initiated Felix into the rug-whacker world when he was very small. It had always been so. Other memories eddied back to him now as he closed in on the doorway: Oma Nagl with her own sisters and neighbours in the yard on benches, like some African tribe, peeling and slicing turnips. It didn't matter if it were gooseberries, apples, potatoes, turnips: she needed to be busy, to be in rhythm. She could as easily have lived the same ways of centuries ago.

In the yard was their old Opel, a vehicle that was rarely seen without a trailer or a roof-rack loaded with something. The need to replace parts only seemed to intensify Opa Nagl's stubborn attachment to it, and the brand generally. Some years ago, Opa Nagl had made a run at Vienna with it, but had given up when the traffic began to surround him more and more approaching the city.

"That car has been to Vienna," he would say. "Almost. But it knew when to stop. Better than any of those electronic things they put all over the cars now."

A cat new to Felix was prowling in the yard, but the stationary fat one, Mitzi, was in her usual spot. She had always looked malignant, perhaps because she so seldom moved but merely glared with that negligent but somehow lethal detachment Felix had always read into her expression.

He saw tools on the ground near the tractor. Opa Nagl stepped out of the shed with a hesitant step, examining something, and looked over at the dog's slowing antics.

"A senile dog," he called out. "He won't even bark. Servus Felix and how are you?"

Felix smiled and laid down his bags. His grandfather's knuckles seemed to be even more misshapen by the arthritis.

"You look worn out," said Felix's opa. "Mein Gött, what the hell kind of shitty life are you leading now?"

It had always been so with Opa Nagl's language, and Felix's mother had long tired of trying to explain it. Farm talk, she used to call it, when Felix and Lisi were small. As they grew, she said it was perhaps psychological, or maybe a need to embarrass others.

"Who knows," said Felix. "But they call it a job."

Opa Nagl narrowed his glance.

"Hmm. I could guess," he said, and winked. "A row. But don't tell me. It's great you're here – and you'll get peace and quiet up here, I can tell you that."

"You should have been a psychiatrist, Opa."

Felix looked over pieces of the power-take-off assembly that his grandfather had taken apart, and then around the yard.

"Your oma is visiting down in the village. She'll be along."

His grandfather let his glasses back down from the top of his head, and with a soft sigh went down on one knee to examine the gearing.

"Only a couple of pigs now, Felix," he said. "We rent out the fields again."

"You'll always have the speck. Nonnegotiable."

"I wonder," Opa Nagl grunted. "They'll have that coming in from Bulgaria or Romania, or China, next. And you know what? It'll be one tenth of the price, and it'll taste better. You'll see."

"Aber geh weg: get out of here, Opa. You're talking treason there."

His grandfather squinted up at him. For a few moments Felix wondered if he had actually annoyed him.

"Don't you city slickers read the paper?"

He held the wrench out straight, like a fencer, pointed at the fields and hills.

"Gerade aus," he declared. "Straight ahead, go like hell to the future. That's a train that makes no stops, Felix. Mark my words."

"Globalization, isn't that what they call it?"

Opa Nagl grunted as he put more pressure on a turn of the wrench.

"Wait for this Constitution thing," he said. "We'll show them."

Then he groaned, cursed, and let down the wrench. He massaged his hand.

"Let me."

"Leave it, Felix. I broke it, I'll fix it. Okay? It's the stupid fingers and knuckles that need a wrench."

Slowly he stood, and drew out a rag from the back pocket of his overalls. His father used to joke that Opa Nagl had arrived in the world in the same blue overalls, cursing, that it had been this way since day one.

He watched his grandfather wipe his hands, holding them out one by one, stretching them. Those are claws now, he thought, not hands.

"What've you got there?"

"Just a few things, for the kitchen."

"What? Flowers for your oma? And . . . ? You want a bite to eat, are you peckish?"

Felix shook his head. He looked around the yard.

"Just a bit of peace and quiet, right?" said Opa Nagl. "The way things used to be."

"Something like that I guess."

Opa fixed him with a mischievous eye.

"Did I hear something there maybe?"

Felix pulled out two bottles.

"Prima. It's been a long day. But stay out here, the house stinks of paint."

They strolled over to the edge of the cement area Felix had helped lay while he was still in school. The pigs heard them and began shuffling about in the pen.

Berndt flopped down beside them and soon lay his snout flat over his paws, staring too, Felix imagined, at the faraway hills to the south. There was a slight glow to the sky there, broadening as Felix turned and looked over the house toward the West.

"Your father sat here, the same as you. Damn. My big mouth."

Felix drank from the bottle again.

"I'm sorry," Opa Nagl went on. "It's probably the last thing you want to hear."

Then, after a while, he spoke again.

"Only that it reminds me of him. He never showed up empty-handed. What a man he was – and you too. You're not a complete loss – to the city I mean."

Felix smiled.

"Do you really believe that old stuff, Opa? Stadtleute and g'scherter, the city people and the country people stuff?"

"What if I do? Is that not allowed?"

Felix shrugged.

"Even if I don't believe it, plenty do. Why else do we have the Freedom Party?"

"Don't ask me. I'm a Green."

"How can you be a Green and a policeman? That I don't get."

Felix eyed him.

"Okay," Opa said. "So I have these rules in my head. But everyone does."

"But all that country versus city stuff, it's so, I don't know, so ancient."

"You think so?"

"The Internet, Opa. Osama Bin Laden. Mobile phones. Turkey, the EU."

"Jesus and Mary, you came all the way up here from Graz to educate your elders?"

"I didn't mean it that way."

"Wait until I tell our ancient Oma. She'll take a wooden spoon to you – hell, forget it, she'll take a shovel to you, kid. She's down with the Wagners there, down the hill a way. You talk about 'ancient'? She's been best friends with that Frieda since they were spots. Well kindergarten. And you know what? Their mothers were friends too. It all goes back."

Felix drained the bottle and he began to study the label.

"Maybe you went to school with that Oetzi guy, did you?"

"Oetzi? I don't know any Oetzi. Otto, I know. Otto Biedermeier?"

"Oetzi the Iceman. Remember the one they found high up, just across in Italy? Preserved, in the ice?"

A sardonic expression took over Opa Nagl's face.

"Him," he murmured. "The archaeology people? I get it now. Of course. Yes, he was on his way over the mountains to see me when he croaked."

Felix glanced over, and grinned.

Opa Nagl seemed ageless. He still had the schoolboy's vitality and mischief close to the surface. For a moment Felix imagined his opa striding over the moors in the high mountains six thousand years ago, grumbling that his friend Oetzi was late again. Then, maybe finding Oetzi curled up just as he was when a hill-walker was to find him in 1992 half encased in the ice, what would he do, or say? Maybe standing over the unresponsive, curled-up figure, Opa might berate him for losing his way: Oetzi, you clumsy clown! I'm leaving you here so someone can find you in thousands of years, a monument to the Earliest Austrian Idiot. And the figure of Opa Nagl, hill farmer, prodigious farter, mechanic and joker, would move on across the high passes, the blue overalls visible thousands of metres away to the prehistoric peoples who would deem him a god.

"What? What is so funny?"

"Just thinking old times."

Opa's face showed his skepticism.

"Ach so? Well don't do it, kid. That's not a family heirloom you should accept."

Felix watched his grandfather swallow more beer.

"By all means, keep the good stuff," he added then.

"What would that be?"

"What I said," said his grandfather, turning serious. "Your dad. He had a big heart. Never let anyone . . ."

And he turned away. After humming awhile – a sign he was restless, annoyed or wanted out, Felix knew – he turned back. He had a gentle expression now.

"Come on Felix. You are a grown man. You know me. You know more about the world already than we ever will. Don't listen to an old goat like me. It's strange how the feelings linger. It must be the anniversary, all that it brings it back."

"I never had anyone say, or suggest, anything about Dad, Opa."

The crease between his grandfather's eyebrows was anger more than bewilderment.

"Of course not. Why are you even saying that?"

"Heirloom, what does that mean?"

"I have a big mouth, that's what it means. See – this beer? You brought this on."

Felix waited but his grandfather shook his head and muttered. An uneasy silence settled between them. Felix began to feel tired, aching even. The events of the day began to roll through his mind like a silent movie, stopping at Speckbauer's face with its half-sarcastic lift of the eyebrow and that knowing look, then to his voice with the studied courtesy and fake warmth.

"Too much," he muttered.

"Too much what?"

"Too much in one day. I'm tired."

"Good. It's the mountain air. It means you are relaxed, like the weeks you used to spend with us. Christ, but we had fun! Like a couple of pranksters. Remember the tractor you nearly rolled there in the high field?"

In the distance they heard the occasional car coming up the hill. There wasn't a breath of wind. They made their way to the old bench by the wall, and soon another beer was opened. Felix no longer felt the chill of the evening air up here. They stared down the valley, the jokes and conversation now done, and Felix remembered how quiet his grandfather was when he got the few anecdotes and gossip out of the way.

"Come on," said his grandfather, we'll go in. Your oma will be home. A bit of dinner better be on the table."

Felix took his time getting up. He found his grandfather's eyes on him.

"You're going to bed early, I am thinking, no?"

"I'll pick up steam, Opa."

"You're looking broody to me. Have forty winks anyway."

Felix sighed and stretched.

"You have that one-hundred-kilometre look all right. What's going on in that head of yours?"

"It's so different here, I had almost forgotten."

"That's what the city does."

"Nothing changes up here, it feels like."

His grandfather gave him a look.

"Your mother said the exact same thing. A million times she couldn't wait, you know."

"But she came back, didn't she?"

"For your dad's sake, Felix. Not to say she was not happy here. If he was happy, that made her happy. That's what love is, Felix. Who knows, but you will find that too."

"Opa. You and Dad got along. Right?"

"Christ, natürlich, we did! And how. He was like my own son."

"Did he, well, did he talk to you about work at all?"

"Work, like the Gendarmerie? No. Why would he?"

"I just wondered."

"You need some advice about work? Ask Edelbacher. He knows everything."

"It's not that. I just wondered if you and he talked about stuff."

"Of course we did! But what stuff? Like, how to change the oil in that stupid tractor?"

"I meant, well, when he went around the place."

Opa Nagl's frown wasn't unfriendly, Felix understood.

"You have things on your mind all right," he said. "Not just that nice girl."

"How'd you know?"

"It's all over your face. But your father, it's the anniversary. Yes that's it."

"I heard how he was well liked and all, and how everyone knew him, or met him, at least."

"And isn't that good? They mean it, Felix."

Felix thought about another beer.

"Well, have you been to Slovenia and places?"

"Why are you asking?"

"Why do you answer a question with a question?"

Opa Nagl smiled.

"Because I'm from up here. Because you're a Gendarme. How do you like that?"

"I was just curious. Somebody asked me. I was thinking about it. That's all."

"Asked you what?"

"If we went to Slovenia or Croatia or those places. Our family."

"What, holidays, the beach thing?"

"I suppose. I don't know really."

"This strong beer for you, maybe?"

It was Felix's turn to smile. He felt his grandfather's hand on his shoulder.

"Why are we sitting here like two idiots? None of that brooding, like, well – let's go in."

"Like who?"

"No, nobody."

"You mean Mom."

"Did I say that? Your mother is a gentle girl, not a broody type. Quiet."

"Who then?"

"Who who! Christ am I hearing the owl here? Never mind."

Then it came to Felix.

"You mean Opa Kimmel, don't you?"

His grandfather looked at the house as though it had recently arrived here.

"That beer is turned out to be expensive for me," he said.

"Political stuff, is it?"

"You think he was the only one up here? Come on now, Felix. You grew up not two kilometres away. Ah but I forget – you and the others are wired into a different planet. The rock music, all that."

"Right. U2."

"What U2? A submarine is it? Or a name for drugs?"

"Music."

"I'll tell you about 'music,' kid – I feel some 'music' coming on here soon."

"You are too ancient, Opa. Really."

"Not as ancient as some."

"Meaning?"

His grandfather's expression was one of waiting to be dared.

"Meaning your dad's father. There, I said it. May God forgive me."

"You never got along with him, even when you and he were kids, did you?"

But now Felix's grandfather seemed to be weighing his words carefully, his head bobbing slowly and decisively as though counting out a precise number of words.

"I never went up in the wald, in the forest, with those idiots, Felix. I am proud of that."

"What idiots?"

"Those idiots – who do you think, man?"

"The Brauners?"

"Say the name, Felix. Jesus. It's sixty years ago."

"Hitler Youth?"

"Yes, Hitler Youth! When I think of it – my blood pressure . . .! Ah forget it. You and your damned beer."

"You were just a kid though."

"Enough talk. Christ on the cross, Felix, but you'll put me in a bad mood yet. Look, I don't want to speak poorly of anyone. Our Saviour had words for that."

Felix trudged across the yard after him. He heard the soft, scratching tread of the dog's paws following.

His grandfather stopped and turned to him.

"I will say one thing though. I'm only telling you this because it is advice for the next generation, for when you start your family. That crap has an effect on a family for a long, long time. Just remember that."

"What does? I don't get it."

His grandfather waved his arms about.

"Call it something, I don't know – this fanaticism. Delusions, fairy-tale rubbish that ended up with, well, war. When you think about it, Christ! Their Germanic this and their Germanic that, and all the legends and crap they came up with. Bogeymen, and Wotan for God's sake. Superstitious nonsense – and this in a country that does science and music the best in the world? You should empty your head of this stuff. It's like a snake or something, the more you look at it, the more it . . . "

Opa Nagl waved away the rest of his words, and made a sound that was more like a grunt than a sigh.

"Thank God your generation won't have this," he muttered. "And that's why I talk about your dad with such respect. He became like a son to us. I shouldn't say this out loud, I suppose. But he could relax when he came in our door. No, it wasn't just he was starry-eyed over your mom. He trusted us. A good man, coming from that . . . that, I don't have the word – wait, I do: that environment."

He looked to Felix for corroboration that his meaning was clear.

"You don't get it, do you? I'm saying he didn't pick up the, the . . . I can't say it. No."

"Bitterness?"

"A hard word, Felix. Especially for your own flesh and blood."

"We avoid too many words, I think sometimes."

"Well gossip is bad, Felix. Me, I am rough with my words. But I try to follow what Our Saviour has taught us."

Felix thought back to the anniversary and how he had caught a glimpse of his grandfather, eyes closed tight in prayer, or straining to fight off distractions, or weak thoughts. The old marterls and taferls, those roadside shrines that still dotted the mountain roads here, had been built and kept up by people like Walter Nagl. So too were many graves tended, and churches fixed. A wave of affection broke over Felix. Now wasn't the time to ask his opa how a mischievous nonconformist could still be so pious too. Maybe it was just a reflex, not a belief at all. He winked at his grandfather.

"You wink, you little noodle? You were pulling my leg after all!"

"No. I would like to know more about things like that."

His grandfather's face turned serious again.

"Well maybe you're right. It'll draw out the pus, whatever there is now after all this time."

They turned to the sound of a woman's voice from inside the house. Berndt went by then, half sideways, his stub of a tail wiggling feebly.

"You old goat," his grandmother called out. "You've got the boy drinking beer already."

"We talked," his grandfather retorted. "And that cost us nothing, eh, Felix?"

"Come," said Felix's grandmother, and he made his way to her outstretched arms, trying not to notice again how she seemed to be sinking a little into herself, or rather stooping more.

"There's something about getting a proper hug from a tall and handsome policeman," she said. "Not like that old bandit I am married to."

TWENTY-EIGHT

THEY WATCHED ZIET IM BILD AT 10. THE HEADLINES WERE about Israel again.

Felix was beyond sleepy. Berndt was dreaming still, and twitched and made little yelps. Felix was sure the dog was farting away all the while too.

"Poor Berndt," his grandfather said several times, letting his arm hang down to stroke the dog. "You're haunted, aren't you."

Oma Nagl's face was flushed from the glass of wine. She had strayed away from asking Felix questions about marriage, his or Lisi's plans. There were enough anecdotes old and new about the kids become men in the village, what they were doing now, what they were not doing.

Opa Nagl's reading glasses made him look like something in a painting of centuries past. He held out the city newspaper to read it, and cast the odd glance at the television when he picked up on something interesting.

"Look," he said, when the ads finished, and a piece about Schwarzenegger and the US presidency came on. "His old man was a cop in Graz. Look what can happen."

"He is a fool," said Oma Nagl, unraveling the sweater she had half done before realizing the needles had been wrong. "Only in America can he get this far."

"We have heard this speech before."

"If he gets anywhere near the White House, I'm going to march in the streets," she said. "He hasn't a clue. He cheats on his wife. He doesn't know acting from reality. Not that he can act."

A snort from his grandfather told Felix that the dispute would not be taken up seriously. He turned the page quickly, snapping it almost, and then dropped it on the floor.

"Wouldn't you know it," he said. "The minute Arnold turns up on the screen there, old Berndt lets a big one go."

"You're glad to blame the poor creature," said Felix's grandmother.

Felix sat forward and put his elbows on his knees, and he rubbed at his face.

"Poor boy," said his grandmother. "You should go to bed. Sleep cures."

. . . the heavy heart, went the rest of the expression, he knew. His opa must have mentioned his troubles with Giuliana.

His grandfather got up with a soft grunt, and called for the dog.

"He'll do his business and we can call it a day."

Felix watched him persuade the dog to get up and head for the door into the yard.

"Sure, he's an old goat," said his grandmother after he left. "But that stuff, that talk, is just a cover. Don't forget that."

Felix smiled.

"He never raised a hand to me, that man. Nor our children. You know that?"

"Yes, Oma."

"When old Berndt goes, well I don't know. It'll be hard. But enough about that. Can't I get you to phone your mother?"

"I will phone her tomorrow. Really."

"She was wondering why, well, why you're not on the holiday."

"You talked to her?"

"Of course I did. My daughter? After you phoned us to see about staying a while. I told her not to worry. That you had to 'get away from things' for a few days."

Annoyance flared up in Felix, but he smothered it.

"And I know there are things you're not telling your oma too. We're not dodels up here in the mountains, now."

Felix looked at the night sky on the windows behind the sofa.

"I'll phone her tomorrow, Oma."

"No secrets, not between a mother and her boy."

Felix eyed the Great Arnold waving at some fat Americans with a beach in the background.

"Oma, what went wrong between Mom's side and Dad's?"

"Wrong? What do you mean wrong?"

He gave her a wry smile.

"'No secrets'? Come on now. These are things no one talks about."

"Why are you asking me? Ask, I don't know, your mother – or him, out there."

"I tried to but he would only go so far."

She stopped pulling at the yarn and rested her hands.

"Go to bed," she said.

"After you tell me."

"You scamp! You mean your Opa Kimmel, don't you?"

He nodded.

"Well they used to say 'Kimmel – a little goes with everything.' But they only said that about your father. It's because he was so different."

She leaned forward.

"My theory is that your dad reacted to him and decided he would be different."

"But did you have a falling-out with them?"

She sat back abruptly, as though she had received a shock.

"Felix, your opa grew up near your Opa Kimmel. I knew him growing up, too. St. Kristoff is a small place. We were polite but kept a distance. It was your dad who broke the ice. We saw him growing up and what a fine boy – it was his mother, I know it, your Oma Kimmel. She made up her mind that her boy would be different from her husband. Oh, yes. I always wish I'd known her more, or better."

Her eyes moved about the room.

"Why didn't you?"

"She didn't grow up here at all. She was from the south."

For a moment Felix imagined Italy.

"Her family was one of the ones they moved out. The Danube Germans."

"Refugees?"

"After the war, yes. Her mother and her family were in a camp for years. You know about this, don't you?"

"A little."

"A little, indeed. There were thousands, tens of thousands. Camps all over the place here, and over in Carinthia too. But her father, and a lot of her family, they didn't make it. A crime to speak German then, of course. It's winner take all, isn't it? It seemed the whole world was on the move, I remember. The Tommies on the road with their strange talk – they were friendly, but the Russians? Better not to remember some things."

"I didn't know any of that part," he said. "I knew she had relatives, or we did."

"Oh, a hard life she had. And that's the kind of wife he wanted–"

She stopped suddenly and grasped Felix's arm.

"I should not say these things, much less think them! I meant 'hard' when she was a refugee."

Felix met her stare and nodded.

"But then, the cancer! Mein Gött – a few months, it was. When she was gone there was no one to care for him really."

"Political stuff between you and them, or Opa and their family at least?"

"Well natürlich. That generation, you know. Oh, everything went to hell."

"The Russians, the war, all that?"

"My God, Felix, but you bring up the strangest things. Are you going through some stress?"

"It was on my mind. The anniversary, you know."

She nodded and reached out, and squeezed his forearm again.

"It's sleep you need," she murmured. "Just like your mother. Her head would fill up with notions."

Felix's grandfather opened the door and waited for the dog.

"The poor bastard. I should give him something for it."

"Never mind," said his grandmother. "Let nature do what it can."

"He's constipated, my dear," said Felix's grandfather with a genial sarcasm. "He'll need to go outside or he'll destroy the house during the night. I'll put him in the shed then."

"So you should."

Felix's grandmother got up. It took her a moment to straighten up.

"He'll be out there tonight," she said, but smiled. "I know he will. If that dog doesn't perform, he'll get out of bed at two or three, and he'll be out there. Wait and see in the morning."

Felix brought the plates and cups to the sink. His grandmother stood by the window.

"There they go," she said. "The two old hounds."

She turned.

"I'll tell you something hard now, Felix. It's your other side, your Opa Kimmel. May God forgive me if this is not true – but your dad's dad would do away with an old crippled dog. That is their way. If they cannot use it, out it goes. The old way, you could say: 'The hill farmer must do what he must do.' But not these days. That's all gone. Or I hope it is."

The tiredness began to roll back over Felix now. His shoulders ached.

"Yes," his grandmother murmured. "We even have stuff here I'm sure, stuff that was being thrown out. From years ago. If I knew where your dad had put it."

"My dad?"

"Oh yes, he kept some things over the years. Your mother and I went through it after, well, after . . . you know. But your grandfather turned up things a while back. Out in the shed, I think, some stuff."

"Is it still here?"

She sighed.

"Oh I don't know. Ach, I should keep my trap shut. Tomorrow – ask your opa tomorrow."

TWENTY-NINE

WITH BERNDT FOR COMPANY AND A BARE LIGHT BULB DRAPED by a half-dozen strands of old cobwebs to light his way, Felix was soon elbowing his way around the rafters of what had been the vegetable store.

There was still a faint glow over the hills, but the night had come on fast. The dog was doing a lot of grunting, settling, and licking at its paws. From time to time Felix could hear the sniffling and kicks from the pigs.

The coolness soaked into his clothes and became a chill on his skin. Dust stirred, some of it falling like powder between the old boards that formed the floor of the loft. Old bicycle parts had found their way there for Opa Nagl to reuse at some date in the future, a date that had not come around and probably never would. There were even old rat poison tins that had been cleaned out.

He came upon dozens of wooden coat hangers, and then several carburetors – or so he believed they were – and at least a dozen tins that had once held cakes, but were stained with rust. There were neatly stacked pieces of Formica that Opa had used on kitchen counters. They must be 40 years old, at least. Baling twine, and rolls of wire.

The "suitcase" as Opa had called it was in fact a cheap, plasticy soft-sided bag. There were still travel tags attached where the small belt at the top had been left unbuckled. Felix slid it over, dislodging grit and dust that rained down on the dog.

"Sorry," he said as the dog laboured up and shook itself. "I appreciate the company and all that."

The tags were airline, Austrian Airways both. ATH was Athens – right: Felix's mother still mentioned how beautiful the Greek islands were. The 70s?

The other tag Felix couldn't guess, someplace ESP. Spain? The puny combination lock was set. Felix tried his mother's birthday, then his dad's, finally his and Lisi's. He started to look around for something to cut the strap, or snap the metal casing. Pincers maybe.

It was light. He might as well haul it down below and work on it there. He considered just dropping it to the hardened earthen floor but carried it down the ladder instead. A few steps from the ground he ran into the smell and he stopped, and tried to wave it away.

Berndt's tail shuddered and his ears went back at the sounds of his name. Not altogether deaf then, Felix thought, and looked into the mournful eyes as the dog let his muzzle down on his paws again.

There was nothing in the shed for the job. Felix took out his keys and levered open the Swiss penknife's blade.

"Don't tell," he muttered. "And I'll keep quiet about you and your farts, okay?"

The leatherette gave way to the blade easily when it was held tight, and Felix slid his hand into the slit. He stopped then, and tried to figure out the faint scent that was coming from the hole in the case. Musty, certainly, but there was a trace of lavender. There were papers held with rubber bands. No rats, he almost said aloud. He worked the slash more with his hands and began taking out the contents.

There were maps tied with more rubber bands, big envelopes with things sliding around in them: photos? There were copies of Gendarmerie reports too, old photostat copies that felt gritty under his fingertips.

Felix shook the case and tried again. He inserted his arm, and groped about for pockets inside. When he was sure he had all the stuff out he began to gather it. He hesitated then. He'd be here a couple of days. It was better to put the stuff back up, and then sneak the carry-all into his car and take them back to the apartment to read them again, if there was anything worth taking away.

He opened several of the maps in turn. The light bulb was almost useless. What was the point of keeping two old, identical tourist maps of Styria? They were actually from the 60s, not the 70s, he saw. There was another one of Austria: 1964? Maybe they were antiques someone was holding for some future windfall. The models on the front were worth a laugh anyway, if nothing else. The blonde hair on the girl had been lacquered into a helmet shape. Her Mann had a hairdo that aged better, a brush cut, and they seemed overjoyed with their map more than the Karmann Ghia parked conveniently in front of the mountains and the picturesque reflecting lake.

"There you go, Berndt," he whispered. "Even before your time. 'The Green Heart of Austria,' our very own Steiermark."

The dog's eyes moved but that was it. The rubber bands on the second bundle gave way when Felix lifted them, and one map fell. In the milky, dim light he saw it was different from the other. There was no colour to it, but it was well used, and strangely thick and robust, almost like a sheet.

This made no sense, he realized: it wasn't in German. It wasn't Austria. It wasn't readable. He held it up close and moved around, trying to get the light to reveal more. Serbo-Croatian, he decided, and no tourist map. He left it open and picked up some others. Of the other three, two were local district maps, Austrian ones, and Felix saw names he knew: Leibnitz, Bad Radkersburg. The language changed at the yellow stripe, the border with Slovenia. Someone had traced the course of the Mur down from Graz, to where it entered Slovenia. It was exactly at the border, where the motorway booths were. Used to be: Felix looked up from the paper when he remembered. The frontier posts had been removed when Slovenia had gotten its junior ticket into the EU.

It took effort to see more detail. Darker spots became apparent, each made with the same black marker, Felix decided. It had been fine-tipped and the lines it made showed no signs of the careless tracing of someone in a hurry. It had been used to draw small circles and symbols too, most of them were within a finger's length of the border. That was "15 km," Felix guessed. Nearly all were Ts with a stroke across the bottom, a mirrored T of some kind.

He rubbed at his eyes, and realized too late that his hands had been covered in dust. He got up from his knee and held his left eye shut. Patience, he knew; "don't rub it – it makes it worse."

"No," he said, seeing Berndt beginning to rise. "Not much longer though."

The dog's ears went up and then dropped as he bent down to pat its head. It gave a contented sigh, half snuffle, half moan.

Felix kept his watery eye shut and went back to the maps, squinting and holding it up toward the light bulb. The paper yellowed with the light behind it, but now he saw the faint marks left by a ballpoint pen higher up on the map. They had a tiny liquid glint to them even now, like a snail's track. The paper there had held the impressions left by the pen too.

It was annoying now: he just had to rub his eye. He let the map down on the ground and put the heel of his hand right on the eye, gently twisting it. He wondered but didn't care what vile germs were in the dust now scratching through his eye.

The dog gave a half-hearted yelp. Felix opened his good eye a little, and watched it raise its head and bob it slowly side to side a few times. Then it shrugged itself up to standing, and Felix watched the ears stirring. Soon its body went from the arthritic slump into something closer to the taut posture Felix remembered from a decade ago.

"What is it, Berndt? Ghosts again, you old bat?"

The dog looked up at the mention of his name, before padding with liquid-sounding, wheezy breaths to the doorway. Felix followed him, and undid the hook.

"Go then, dummy," he murmured. "Find your cat or your rat, but watch you don't run into the wall."

Whatever dirt was on his cornea was moving again. Felix closed and then opened his eyes several times. It wasn't working. He heard another bark, more a howl than a bark. He held his eyelid closed and opened his good eye. The bugger was out of sight now, beyond the gable end of the house, where the cars were parked. He heard the pigs were shuffling about, and their grunts and snuffles were almost a conversation. Felix made a low whistle, keeping his eye on the edge of the wall.

The barks were more vigorous now. Felix let his eyelid up slowly. The grit seemed to have slid off his eye. He blinked to test it, and it worked, but was still watering. He made a louder whistle and called the dog's name. So: Berndt was deaf when it suited him, apparently. But the mutt seemed to have found something

Felix headed across the yard but stopped after a few steps. Foxes, he wondered, or even a wolf down after the winter, hungry? He remembered something about a wild dog someone had told him growing up.

He returned to the storehouse and looked about for something; a pitchfork, any kind of a tool – or even a stick – would do.

There was nothing except a length of light aluminium pipe, very light, with a pinch in it. A makeshift fence post, he remembered then, from an experiment to raise rabbits. He heard the dog barking again, and gave up searching for anything with more heft.

The floodlight went on as he began to skip out into the yard. He shielded his eyes with his free hand; he wondered why the dog hadn't set it off. There was no Berndt here now. Felix heard him somewhere off in the dark close by, growling almost all the time now.

Then there was a yelp, and a second one. It was followed by a low, steady growl that broke off into a whine.

Felix rounded the gable end of the farmhouse and called out. The dark form, half skipping and half loping toward him, had better be Berndt. He lifted the pipe. It was his grandfather's dog all right. It moved low to the ground, its legs stiff and splayed.

"Felix?"

It was Opa at the door, without his dentures.

"What in the name of Christ is going on?"

"Berndt's spooked. He went after something."

He tried not to notice his grandfather's sunken mouth.

"I think he was bitten maybe," he added.

Limping a little, the dog returned to the side of Felix's car. He heard a low steady growl coming deep from its throat. Its back end wagged once or twice.

"Some light, Opa. It could track a satellite."

"It's a quartz one, they told me they're good. The Watch people – what am I saying? Your fellows, the Gendarmerie. I was wondering about burglaries a while back. They – you – said install lots of lights. With those things on them."

"Motion sensor?"

"What?"

"Do they come on if someone walks by?"

"Sure they do. That's the idea. When they're on, that is. The verdammt things go off if a goddamned bat goes by. Don't laugh. It happens up here. Sometimes I put off that thing you said. That motion thing."

He reached down to pat the dog. Beyond the whitewashed walls and the orchards' closer trees was inky black.

"Uhh," his grandfather sighed. "Something might have gotten a bite of Berndt – you know I'll bet it's that idiot Kreiner up the road. That depp who 'forgets' about his dogs. He has a couple of nasty brutes he doesn't bother to discipline, I tell you."

Felix turned the tip of the metal post on the cement.

"You poor fool," said his grandfather to the dog. "Yes, I can feel something. Where are my glasses?"

Beside the cup with your teeth in them, Felix didn't say. He walked toward the bushes. The yard light caught pieces of the trim and the windows on the cars. Felix stepped closer to be sure the interior light in his Polo was actually on.

He wasn't mistaken. He stopped, and listened, and moved his hand down the pipe, grasping it tighter. His grandfather's low chatter as he tried to soothe the dog, blended with paws scratching on the cement. There were no cars on the road this time of night up here.

The light stayed on. The door wasn't closed properly. Now he felt that pressure building in his diaphragm, the tingling and tightness at the back of his neck. Again he strained to block out the mutterings from his grandfather. There was nothing.

The lit interior of the Polo reminded him of a fish tank in the living room at night. There was a shadow following the edge of the door down where it had not been closed tight. The usual junk was still strewn about inside. There was no change, no rearranging he could discern.

He opened the door and waited a moment before leaning in to check the glove compartment. Again there was nothing different. He leaned over to lock the driver's side. He checked the trunk, and did a walk-around to both doors then to be sure he had locked them.

His grandfather was fingering Berndt's back, squinting, muttering.

"Is your car locked, Opa?"

"I never lock it."

Felix shrugged. His grandfather stood up slowly.

"Geh scheissen," he said. "You think we had a visitor here? Some gauner . . . ?"

"You said something about burglary here, and that's why you bought the lights?"

His grandfather seemed puzzled.

"Well I heard that. But your oma wanted them. We always have a crop of dummies in the area, young fellows, but–"

Felix had put up his hand without knowing it. He turned slightly to hear better. It didn't help much. The driver was not revving it much at all. The engine wasn't one of the whiny two-strokes, he was sure. Felix listened as the engine surged a little and then lessened on the bike's descent. It was a four-stroke all right. Whoever was on it was taking hilly ground, and in no apparent hurry. The sound faded quickly then.

"A motorbike."

"What motorbike?"

"You didn't hear it, Opa?"

"Hear what?"

THIRTY

FELIX HAD SAT BY THE WINDOW FOR A HALF-HOUR. HE HAD left it half open. The night air had turned cold, colder than he had expected. Every now and then he heard some fussing among the pigs, which soon returned to quiet.

It was nearly midnight now. He still felt wired. He moved around in the chair, and felt the gentle sway and then the tap on his chest as his opa's ancient binoculars settled again. He was careful not to make a racket moving the maps off his lap. Before he laid them down on the bed, he took another look over the one he had kept open.

He had seen that old Freytag & Berndt logo, the official map publisher, before. With the lousy colour and such a lame cover, he guessed it was 1950s. It qualified as an heirloom, he supposed, maybe even worth something in one of the stalls at the Saturday market off Herrengasse. It had a stale smell that reminded him of sour milk.

His eyes were itchy, prickly now. He rubbed at them before lifting the bedside lamp to hold over the map. Sure enough, the marks were still there. What had he expected, that the marks would have disappeared, or something? He followed the lines up around the contours of the hills behind the Himmelfarbs' place. These trails must have changed over the years, he thought again. Thirty, 40 years was enough to grow one of the farmed trees they had put in back then. But there was no doubt about it, no matter how many times he looked at it. He had known it right away when he had first taken this map from the bag and opened it, releasing the tart, stale smell of storage and mouldering paper into the room, his heart beating in his ears almost: the line that had been drawn there ran along where the bodies had been.

He was getting stiff now. He should get up and move around. He looked down into the farmyard below bathed in the harsh light of the quartz floodlight he'd persuaded Opa to leave on. A damned fine piece of acting to get to that point, he was sure. There had to be some award for pretending to be casual about it. He went along with his grandfather's mutterings about local teens not having enough to do. He smiled when he remembered his grandfather's expressions: a detschen, a cuff on the ear if he got hold of one of the little bastards. There'd be swat on the head, a watschen, on the way back too. And a solid kick in the arse, of course, to help them remember longer.

Felix stretched, and let his aching eyes out of focus. He should lie down and get some sleep. He was overreacting. He was overtired. He was paranoid: time spent with Speckbauer would do that though, wouldn't it? He stopped in mid-stretch and opened his eyes. No amount of talking to himself in his head would douse that feeling that something was moving around him, or by him, like the slow, almost imperceptible stirring when a landslide begins, before it gathers speed, sweeping away everything in its path He opened his phone and checked for a signal. A quarter-strength would do. He tiptoed over to the bed and pulled the duvet over his head. He already had Speckbauer's card ready. He hesitated, and he thought about just stretching out and falling asleep. A night's sleep would clear his head, and let him think straight. Speckbauer wouldn't thank him for a call at this hour of the night.

Screw Speckbauer.

Felix dialed, and pulled the duvet back up. His mind raced through the farmhouse as he heard to the first ring, and he tried to remember where Opa kept his shotgun. Maybe Oma hadn't hidden it as she had said she would even years ago, leaving him with only a pellet gun for the crows.

He almost hung up after the second ring. Then it was a low voice, Speckbauer's, flat and terse.

"Oberstleutnant?"

"Kimmel?"

"I am sorry to phone you at this hour."

"Don't be. What is it?"

"I'm not sure, but things are going a bit, weird."

Speckbauer waited. Felix heard music played faintly in the background, a piano.

"I'm up at, well, you know – well I think maybe something strange is going on."

"Strange?"

"Maybe I'm just jittery. I might have a visitor up here. Not invited."

"You need to be specific here – and where are you, in I mean, are you in your car or something? You sound like a dirty telephone call."

"I don't want to wake my grand– I don't want to scare them. But someone was snooping around here earlier tonight, I think."

"Serious? Not a farmer who lost his way home from the gasthaus, maybe?"

"Herr Oberstleutnant–"

"Give me something to go on."

"The dog heard something, it was after eleven–"

"You had something going on at eleven? Eleven was the time to call me then, gell?"

"I don't want to overreact."

Speckbauer swore softly.

"You know," Felix began to say.

"Okay," said Speckbauer, with little conviction in his voice. "You're right. Everything counts. I'm on my way."

"But maybe it is unnecessary?"

"Shut up, will you? Be quiet a moment. I need to get info off you."

Felix heard creaking, a whispered curse, rustling.

"You're in your relatives' house up there?"

"Yes – it's the far side of–"

"You drove there, right? Your car is there?"

"That's what I wanted to mention. I think someone was looking around the inside of the car."

"Eleven, you say?"

"Just after *Zeit im Bild.*"

"The late news on the TV?"

"Right. The dog was yowling. Berndt. He's an old fart but game enough. We thought maybe a loose dog got a bite out of it."

Felix paused when he heard Speckbauer's laboured breathing. There were footsteps, then the sound of a door opening. Someone made a low whistle, and called out "raus." The phone was muffled then, but Felix heard some intonations. The hand was removed after a few moments.

"I'm listening, keep talking."

"Anyway, it looks like someone or something hit the dog, or bit it, or something."

"'Hit?' 'Bit?' 'Something?'"

"He came back to us yowling. I looked around and the light was on in my car."

"Farmers don't lock their cars?"

"No."

"Any other car there?"

"My grandparents'."

"Their car too?"

"I couldn't tell. I don't think so."

He heard a man's voice, not Speckbauer's.

"That's it?" Speckbauer asked.

"Yes. That's why I didn't want to call."

"I'll be there, maybe forty minutes. It'll give me time to think."

"Is it really necessary for you to drive up here? Maybe . . . "

There were sounds of more doors, heavier ones, closing now.

"Yeah, bring it all," Speckbauer called out in an exasperated tone.

"Oberstleutnant," said Felix. "I don't want police crashing in the door here."

"I see," said Speckbauer, with a leaden tone. "We do not specialize in kicking down doors. But that's what could have happened if you had phoned the local posten, and roped in some of the Gendarmerie from there, let me tell you. So it's good: keep this to yourself, for now."

The 'for now' echoed in Felix's mind several times. He thought of Gebhart again. It only made sense to phone him in the morning, no matter what Speckbauer said.

"You need directions?"

"No. I'll find you, don't worry."

Felix scratched the top of his phone with his nail. Why had Speckbauer wanted him to drive all over the damned countryside earlier on, then?

"Here's how it's going to work," said Speckbauer. "I'm going to phone you as soon as I get there, as soon as a few minutes from your place okay? Do you have a good charge on your mobile there?"

"I do, yes."

Felix stared at the pattern on the duvet cover. The colours on the flowers were muted to dim greys in the weak light coming in from the lamp. He realized that it was Gebhart he should have phoned.

"Look," he said. "Maybe I'm not thinking straight here?"

"Straight, what?"

"It's just that, well after all, there are kids here. Maybe one of them saw my car and knows I'm a Gendarme."

"We can talk about that when we get there," said Speckbauer. "If you'd like?"

The sarcasm was plain enough.

"But right now the plan is this," Speckbauer went on. "We

won't call to the house. We just keep an eye on it, and see. When it gets light, we'll show up at the house, say hello, do a little acting job if that would suit you. Nobody freaks then. Verstehst?"

"If you say so."

"You won't see us until daylight, but we'll be there. And don't go telling anyone we're about. Really. Got all that?"

"I just don't want a false alarm, or to waste people's time."

"Okay," was Speckbauer's parting advice. "So if it turns out to be nothing, we'll take it out of your pay."

THIRTY-ONE

THE MINUTES SEEMED TO HANG THERE IN THE STILL AIR OF THE room. Felix wasn't sleepy anymore. He was even able to lean his head against the window and not feel drowsy. The occasional sound came from the old house, but never even a tiny gurgle from the pipes for the heating. The system had been turned off, he was sure, by his grandfather, a man who placed his faith in the kachelofen, the massive stone and tile fireplace. Opa was still a guarder of schillings, or cents, or Euro as they had come to be. Windows flung open to cool air, and bedcovers back until midday were still the ways here. If you couldn't see your breath in the morning over the bedcover, well that meant it must be summer, right?

Felix toured the house in his mind again, seeing the kitchen door out, then back to the hall door that no one used. Down the hall his mind moved, like an arcade game, a PlayStation shooter, he thought. Except he had no shooter.

Again, he tried to quench the worry by letting his mind out over the twisting, narrow roads that led down from the mountains. He thought of Speckbauer making his way up from the distant motorway, blasting by Weiz no doubt, and slowing only for the narrow roads that were the last parts of the journey. It was relief as much as embarrassment he was feeling. At least things were in motion, and he couldn't stop them now. Hadn't Speckbauer said it was okay? Well he'd throw it back at him if he was grumpy.

Giuliana, yes, again. He should text her, not sit there watching a farmyard in the middle of the night. With his thumb over the keypad, lust descended over him. Instead of the yard bathed in the garish light that had probably burned into his retina forever now, he was seeing her violin shape as she lay on her side. There was that stripe across her back last year where her swimsuit strap covered. He'd get her to go over to the lake at Stubensee, and lie there again by the lakeside like last summer: half asleep, half soused with the Chianti that went down so well with the snack.

Then his heart leaped. Where had that thud come from? He sat up, and tilted his head, and listened. His gaze fixed on the bedroom door.

There was a lesser, longer, fart this time. Opa was probably not even awake. Felix smiled and for a moment his grandfather's face came to him from the darkness near the door, his wink of glee lighting up the whole face of this 70-something-year-old kid. It was now 20 minutes since the phone call: 20 hours it might as well have been.

Was this what they meant in the drug-use lectures at the Gendarmerieschule, this half-crazy, half-panicky agitation that druggies got, a skin-crawling need to do something? He looked around the yard again. It was like a yellowed stage, a set for some weird movie. He began to imagine questions he'd put in the Dienstprüfung, the final exam:

Describe the effects of crack on a user who hasn't had any recently. Would it be: A) paranoid B) aggressive C) skin-crawling D) antsy E) panicking F) jumpy G) berserk . . .

He stopped at the *H*, and made it the all of the above.

He decided to head downstairs. From the kitchen widow, he might catch a glimpse of the lights of Speckbauer's car down the valley. He held the binoculars against his chest, and he tiptoed toward the door. His mind was already running to excuses for his oma or opa, if he woke them: I can't sleep, I'm reading. I'm going to the klo.

The door had a small squeak at the end of its travel. He stood in the threshold, listening for Berndt. Then he made his way to the stairs. He waited there for any sound from his grandparents. The sound of the clock from downstairs came to him, and the manifold smells of the house, something stale to do with the dog probably, his bed or food, and the ever-present soupy scent from the kitchen mixed with the smells of firewood, and dried herbs and ashes.

He stopped on the landing.

Kerosene?

His heart pounded hard enough for him to wonder if wasn't echoing through the house. He sniffed again, but it wasn't there this time. He descended a few steps and waited. Nothing. Wasn't there such a thing as smell hallucinations? He looked down the hall to the Berndt's place by the kitchen door. Half-deaf or not, the dog's head came up when Felix stepped off the stairs, a faint creak following him.

"You know me, Berndt," he whispered as loud as he dared. "Lass. Lie down."

The biscuits were in the usual place. The dog stayed in his basket and crunched on them. Felix crouched by him, looking through the doorways, trying to hear anything above the chewing and slobbering. He had a view out the kitchen window here, toward the road. There were no high beams from Speckbauer's Passat snaking through the bends and darkness up to the village.

He dropped to his knees after a while, and soon he had settled on the floor a short arm's-length from the dog, with his back against the door jamb. He kept patting and stroking the dog, but paused several times, not a little surprised that he could now simply sit there like this, waiting.

An ache began to make itself known above the tension that clawed at him steadily still. Though he couldn't pin it down, Felix began to believe that it had something to do with the fact that he was a not kid anymore, a kid just sitting with the dog. It had been Olli in those years before Berndt, a supremely stupid but good-natured dog that his grandfather hadn't the heart to get rid of, but no different from this slob here: an uncomplicated presence, a beating heart, warmth.

The ache grew in him. He remembered how his grandmother had told him so often he was truly his mother's son, when she saw him with animals. Even now this old house seemed to breed contentment. The rare visits to his Opa Kimmel made him feel he was a kid again, but a kid being sent to the office. Was it possible that happiness left something of itself in the walls of this house? His father had been drawn to this place, and so much so that he had pretty well made it his home. With his eye on their teenaged daughter, he had still been able to relax here in the company of the Nagls, that elderly pair now sleeping above.

Berndt gave a low grunt of contentment, and ran a wet tongue over Felix's knuckles.

"Enough is enough," he whispered, but his hand seemed to be independent of him, and it had returned to rubbing the dog's head. He looked at the darkness on the kitchen window again, but there were no car lights anywhere down the valley. He checked his phone again, and saw that there was still a signal. Then he went through the menu to be sure he had set it to vibrate.

Thinking about Speckbauer driving through the darkness out there, he realized that he had forgotten something. Opa Kimmel had been up in Gasthaus Maier for cards too, along with Berger Willi Hartmann when Karl Himmelfarb had come by. No, he reflected, maybe forgotten wasn't the right word. Maybe the word was hidden, hidden it from his thoughts so he wouldn't have to do it. But it was either he talk to his grandfather first, or Speckbauer would find his own way to do it. He'd bring the maps too, and see what the old man would say about the marks on them.

With that, Felix's thoughts passed across the village and out to his Opa Kimmel's farm. It was two kilometres from the Nagls' house, out on its own, at the end of the road. Pfarrenord, they called it locally, but no one else would know it even had a name. Indeed it was the North Parish, and it always seemed windy and cooler there. The place where the hailstones break, he'd heard it referred to.

Opa Kimmel would be sleeping too. Or maybe he'd lying awake

there himself though. Would he be thinking about the decision he'd made, to finally move into the village? There'd be regret no doubt, but a secret relief too, Felix guessed, something the old man would never admit to. No more than he'd admit that the solitude he always claimed he preferred had actually become loneliness. The simple facts of old age, the approach of illness and death, had thawed him out enough now. He'd let a relative persuade him that he'd be doing them a favour – no, an honour, as Lisi had heard and dryly report-ed to Felix – by coming to live in part of their house. There'd be a tidy rent, of course, but they meant well. Why shouldn't his relatives make some money out of the arrangement?

Pfarrenord, he thought. His grandfather used to go on about eagles, how they made Pfarrenord their home. Maybe it was some effort to instill something in his grandson, now that his own son had escaped to live elsewhere. Eagles were defiant and proud, no doubt, models of independence and power. But as Felix grew, he had begun to sense something else lodged in those platitudes, and it gave him pause to consider them in a new light. He began to see them now as loaded with something else.

He soon picked up hints from the spines of the old books he remembered looking at on those rare, but interminable visits. One was *The Realm of Eagles*, he recalled, with lots of photos of planes and pilots and parachutes. *Eagles on Crete*, he remembered too, a fading paperback from a company Felix had never seen elsewhere. He had looked through it several times, studied the photos of para-troops and planes, and groups of smiling young men. How different they had seemed from the studio photo that had always hung in the hall, the one with Felix's own great-grandfather in his Austrian Army uniform from the First World War.

So maybe that was where the coldness came from then, that politics thing, that knot of circumstances no one could never untan-gle, and that no one talked about. Even though families up here had known one another for generations, you seldom spoke carelessly outside your own home.

Felix tried to remember the year of Oma Kimmel's death. He remembered his father telling him that he had been 13 when his mother died. Was it just quack medicine that people believed when they said that stress brought on cancer? Surely Opa Kimmel wouldn't have been surprised that his own son soon gravitated toward the Nagls, and that he found excuses to spend his time there.

It came to Felix then that he had not fully understood at all how his own parents had shielded him, and Lisi too, from the remote person who was their grandfather. Now he wondered if Oma Kimmel had spent her own life, and probably her health, protecting her son from the same cold presence.

The dog slid onto its side with a low wheeze of contentment. Felix stopped rubbing its ears and stared instead at the faint liquid slit of its eyes. Sleeping, yes. He looked around the hall again. This house, he thought, where nothing was complicated and no one was appraising you. It was a refuge.

He was actually getting drowsy himself now. He let his eyes close, and Giuliana's face came to him. He struggled to hang onto it as other thoughts edged in, even as it became her hurt look, the reproachful one when they'd had words. The "talk" she wanted: he'd been annoyed because he'd been thinking things were actually going okay. The new police force need people like him. Lots of things would open up for him in the new police force. Even Gebi had conceded that. He might even go back to Uni for evening courses, and maybe even get paid for it too. Next thing you'd know, there'd be the applications for the Alpines, or even the Cobra, and plainclothes jobs anywhere across Austria. Why not even think about international stuff too?

The vibrations from his phone startled him, and the dog's eyes opened.

Speckbauer didn't sound one bit drowsy.

"You're doing okay?"

Felix didn't know what to say. He patted the dog's head again, but the eyes stayed open now, the ears up.

"I'm awake, for sure. Where are you?"

"Why are you whispering?"

"I don't want to wake my grandparents. Are you on the road?"

"I'm outside, beyond the light there in the yard."

"But I don't see your car – I didn't see it coming up the valley."

"You're in the house?"

"Yes. I'm downstairs. I can come out."

"Stay put," said Speckbauer. "We'll take care of things. Has there been anything since? Any noise or stuff?"

"No."

"Good. This is what we're doing, for the time being, so listen. Me and Franzi are moving about out here, eyeballing the place. We're going to keep doing that for a while. Verstehst?"

"I get it, but what do I do?"

"What? You want me to sit beside you and hold your hand?"

"It's dark, what can you see?"

"Pretty well anything I want to damned well see. Really, believe me, we've done this kind of work before."

"If I may say, Herr Oberstleutnant, I think we should try to get things clear."

"Nothing is clear," said Speckbauer sharply. "Nix. So save it. It's just the work. We're in the business of wading around in a big swamp. It's called Der schein trügt, this area we work in: the land of Nothing-Is-Clear. Shitty, isn't it, but that's life."

'All is not how it looks,' Felix thought.

Speckbauer didn't say anything for several moments.

"How am I going to explain this to them?" Felix asked.

"Deal with it later. It'll work out."

"What should I be doing, though? There has to be something."

"Know what I want from you right now? Go to bed. That's it. But here's something to think about while you're nodding off. Anyone passing down the way here, this road, can see your car parked there in the yard. That's not helpful."

THIRTY-TWO

FELIX JERKED HIS HEAD AWAY FROM THE WALL. HE COULD remember deciding to rest it there, but only for a moment. The milky half-light softened the interior of the farmhouse and made the view from where Felix had slouched both mysterious and familiar. There was a glow at the edges of the hilltops which were framed by the kitchen window, but a handful of stars held out in the pale blue above.

Five-thirty. Berndt watched him with doleful eyes, his eyebrows shooting up and down but his head never stirring from its resting place on his paws. Felix switched off the yard light and threw on an old jacket. Slowly he opened the kitchen door and stepped into the yard. The birds were busy, and the cold tang of air that met his face revived him. He heard the pigs shuffling, one of them kicking a plank, and a grunt, as he made his way across the yard to the cars. He slowed and even stopped several times on his way, but could not see traces of any visitor last night. Nothing had changed. In the distance he heard a cowbell clanking.

His phone went off.

"You're not going for a little drive now, are you?" said Speckbauer.

"Where are you?"

"I'm in a ditch. Freezing my ass off."

"I can't see you."

"Then I'm doing my job. Look, stay there. And don't walk around yet. Me and Franzi are going to do a bit of basic police work."

"You're leaving?"

"No. Now we have a bit of light, I want to give the place a look-over, from where your car is down to the road. We'll see if there are signs of any company last night, any uninvited guests. Right?"

"Yes."

"Meanwhile, wait," said Speckbauer.

Felix heard his voice change. He seemed to be getting up.

"Now remember," said Speckbauer. "Don't phone anyone. Right?"

"Who would I be phoning?"

"The local Gendarmerie, that's who. We're handling it."

Speckbauer seemed to be waiting for a reply. Felix wondered if Speckbauer had guessed he'd have been thinking of Gebhart, or even Schroek.

"I understand."

"Gut. Now can you get some coffee started or something? It's only polite."

"You're coming down to the house after?"

"Of course we are. Franzi and I have a good spiel ready – and we'll come in off the road. We'll be visiting to, let me see, 'speak with you on a very pressing matter.' If he asks, your grandfather."

"He's not stupid, you know."

"Did I say he was?"

Felix closed the connection first. He looked through bleary eyes around the fields. Speckbauer must be near the orchard. As Felix stared at it, movement to his right made him turn. It was Franzi, the spook, looking pale and very cold. As he nodded, the sky, glowing lemon where they met the hills, glanced once off his glasses. Then he said something into his collar, turned away, and stepped back behind the firs.

Felix didn't move, but pretended instead to savour the crisp air, the glory of a mountain sunrise. He was able to control his breathing, even if spots began to appear in front of his eyes. The problem he was focusing on however was that he didn't trust his knees not to buckle the minute he began to stroll about the yard. He was putting his anger into preventing Speckbauer, wherever he was, from enjoying any sign of his shock.

It wasn't the sight of Franzi – shrouded under what looked like a hooded army poncho, with the reflected dawn on his glasses giving his face the look of an insect up close – that had Felix now measuring out his breath and struggling to keep an appearance of composure. It was the glimpse of what Franzi's hand was holding down by its strap. It was a sturmgewehr, the assault rifle that every Gendarmeriepost had, which was taken out only for drills and inspection. This one with a peculiarly large sight attached.

After a minute Felix made his way back to the kitchen and began to prepare drip coffee. He cursed aloud when he dropped the lid, but he trapped it quickly with his foot to stop it skittering on the floor. He stared at it before picking it up, as though it might have a life of its own there, and tried to clear his thoughts.

Gebi would be up already. He pulled out the phone but hesitated then, and gazed back out the window and up to the slopes. A flood of sunlight built up behind the hills was about to burst. "We're taking care of it," Speckbauer had pronounced. And "we" were . . .

Someone was stirring upstairs. Now the dog was getting up himself, the lazy and contented old bag, plodding clumsily down through the kitchen. Felix closed the phone. He had enough to think about. He'd need a plan, a clear head, to sort out Speckbauer.

Felix's grandfather clumped down the stairs half-sideways.

"I thought I heard someone."

He stared at the kitchen window with a faraway look in his eyes. Then he turned to the dog.

"Have you let this old bag of bones out yet, Felix?"

"No."

"Out you hound," his grandfather growled at the dog. "You've had your charity."

"I'll take him out, Opa."

"Hell, no. Let him go wander out there. Or he'll end up like me when I don't do a day's work – locked up in the joints."

"The thing is, I'm expecting someone to drop by here."

His grandfather turned to him.

"A visitor? Up here? At this hour? And why are you looking at me like that?"

"I can't understand what you say, some of it."

A rueful look crossed his grandfather's face.

"It's too early for all this hubbub. But if it's a beautiful maiden you're expecting, I'll put my teeth in for that. Does the name start with a G?"

"I wish. It's another policeman."

Felix took in his grandfather's skeptical look.

"Here? Our house? Visiting?"

"He phoned me. He's on his way back from a job. He wants to stop by, and have a chat."

The coffee burbled as it fed down through the filter. His grandfather tilted his head slightly and squinted.

"Why not," he said. "If that's the crazy time the man works."

Felix watched him pour coffee, and place a small cookie on the saucer he'd be bringing upstairs for Oma Nagl. His grandfather yawned and headed back to the stairs. There he stopped, his foot on the first step, and looked over.

"Is this visit about last night, or something?"

Felix had prepared for the question, and even tried to rehearse an answer.

"Can I tell you later, Opa?"

⸸

Felix had a half-cup of coffee in him when he heard his grandfather's voice upstairs again, speaking to Oma, and then her reply in a voice still clotted with sleep.

His grandfather paused at the bottom of the stairs, exchanged a look with him and shuffled on to prepare some breakfast. Felix watched him pause as he stooped and craned his neck to see into the fridge. He took out some rye bread to add to the buns on the table.

"Sure enough," he said then, and stopped filling the kettle. "Here's someone now. Two men, a white VW."

Felix got up.

"Opa I'm sorry to ask you this–"

"You need to talk in private. I knew you'd ask."

"Thank you."

"Thank my arse. But I want to meet them first, look 'em in the eye. I want to give them The Look. You know what The Look is?" Felix waited.

"It says: You're in my house. These are the mountains, not some city street where putting on a suit makes you important. So mind your manners, Gendarmerie or not. And don't try to put one over on this boy here. That's what The Look says."

"You'll make them cry, Opa. Can you have that on your conscience?"

Opa Nagl was already reaching for a jacket. Felix decided not to follow him out, but to watch instead from the window.

He watched the circumspect exchange of nods and the few words out in the yard as his grandfather greeted Speckbauer. There was a wary handshake. Franzi stayed in the car, wisely enough, Felix thought, rearranging something, or pretending to. He couldn't lip-read at all, but before a minute had passed, his opa and Speckbauer had their backs to the house and were surveying the fields, each casting their arms up in the slow, appraising gestures of farmers. They nodded a lot, keeping their gaze on the view.

Franzi emerged after a few minutes. He was in nondescript outdoorsy clothes, the poncho stowed away, no doubt, and he moved like a robot with the batteries about to go out. Felix watched his grandfather's face for his reaction. It lasted an instant, the what-in-the-hell look, but it seemed to spur Opa Nagl into an overly friendly mode.

The door to the yard opened and his grandfather's resonant voice and thick accent came pouring in. The winter, cattle, how he had ploughed some fields with a horse until '67, the apple cider you could buy that would close your eyelids in five minutes flat – it all filled the hall and seemed to get louder. The Oberstleutnant Horst Speckbauer now making his way into the Nagls' kitchen spoke in the same gruff, detonating voice of the Styrian farmer. His greeting broke the spell.

"Servus, Felix."

"Give these men breakfast in God's name Felix," said his grandfather. "They had night work, they tell me. I'll go back up to the countess upstairs."

Felix put mugs on the table and waited for his grandfather to finish putting things on the tray. Speckbauer seemed keen enough to keep a conversation about corn going.

From Franzi, there was nothing. Felix could only make out occasional eye movements through the tint on his glasses. In this light, the scar tissue didn't stand out.

"Wunderbar," said Speckbauer, shaking his head slowly in admiration as he found a chair. "And the air up here? Mein Gött! It takes years off my lungs to be up here."

"If you're that keen to stay Horst," he said. "I've got plenty of jobs. I'll pay you in that mountain air."

Horst already, Felix repeated in his mind. So much for The Look. He put down a plate of bread on the table.

"Beautiful country," Speckbauer repeated, his serene look setting a little as Opa Nagl's footsteps clumping began to fade upstairs. "This is what Rossegger meant."

He turned to Felix.

"You have a motorcycle on the farm here?"

"No."

"Do the local kids go where they want on theirs?"

"Not like this," said Felix. "Why? Are there tracks out there?"

"There are indeed. They go off out to the road though."

"Well he'd hardly just drive down the lane if he was, you know?"

"Right," said Speckbauer, but in a tone that suggested to Felix that he believed the opposite. He sipped at his coffee again.

"Was there anything else out there?"

Speckbauer shook his head and took butter on his knife.

"Franzi found some dog shit, I believe."

"That's it?"

"That's it," said Speckbauer. He slid the plate with two buttered buns across toward Franzi. Felix stole a glance at Franzi's claw-like hand reaching for them. It put him in mind of a lizard that needs morning sun to wake up. He waited for Speckbauer to look up from stirring more sugar in his coffee.

"If my grandparents are in any danger, it's my fault. It's my fault because you put me up to this nonsense."

Speckbauer glanced up from the next bun he was preparing.

He continued to stare at Speckbauer.

"Okay," Speckbauer murmured. "Best you get that talk out of your system now."

"It's not just talk," said Felix.

"Well I do. I see us as Gendarmerie together here," said Speckbauer. "A team. But if you come up with that 'nonsense' talk, and that look on your face when you're working with the Polizei after the amalgamation . . . Well, you won't get much mercy then. 'Nothing's the same after the wedding.' I'd say that's an expression from up these parts too."

He leaned over the table.

"Eh Franzi?" he said.

Franzi nodded.

"You'll be using rank there, every hour of the day. The du and dich stuff from the basic decent Gendarmerie will be piss in the wind then. So keep it up while you can."

"You said you'd explain things."

Speckbauer tore off a piece of bread and began chewing.

"I bet you got a lousy sleep," he said around his chews.

"Sleep? I am supposed to be on a week's leave."

"Could be worse," said Speckbauer.

"Tell me how. A family died in a fire. It looks deliberate, and that's murder?"

"Well," said Speckbauer in the same quiet tone. "It would be that."

"On top of the ones in the forest," said Felix.

Speckbauer nodded.

"Now someone was snooping around here last night," Felix went on. "So I don't see how it could be worse."

Speckbauer nodded again, and studied the piece of bun he was holding. Franzi was chewing slowly and methodically. To Felix, it began to sound like a metronome. The clicking and gulping sounds began to nauseate him.

"Well, am I the only one who gets this?"

"Gets . . . ?"

"That they could be looking for me," said Felix. "But you say 'Don't call in the local Gendarmes, they'll just screw things up.' I'm thinking: Someone's trying to find me, or do a hell of a lot worse. Am I getting through to you?"

Speckbauer glanced at Felix, and let out a sigh. Then he looked over at Franzi.

"'Sons of bitches,' I was expecting," he said to him. "You, Franzi?"

"'Bastards,'" Felix made out through the pause in Franzi's chewing.

"Which of us is closest?" said Speckbauer to Felix. "'Sons of bitches,' or 'bastards'?"

"Not funny," said Felix. "I'm not going to be jerked around. This is not right."

"Absolutely," said Speckbauer, and nodded vigorously. "You are right, again."

That seemed to settle the matter for Speckbauer. He made a yawn and turned to his coffee again.

"So what are you proposing?" Felix asked.

Speckbauer eyed him again before sitting back and turning to Franzi.

"Any suggestions for Gendarme Kimmel here, Franzi? I'm too tired to think."

"I think Gendarme Kimmel should not panic."

"Easy for you to say," said Speckbauer. "Put yourself in his boots."

The man's lips were slashes, Felix thought, bloodless. For a moment he imagined Franzi's face on fire.

"Then he should go somewhere else."

"What's to happen to my grandparents then? I abandon them?"

"When you go, their troubles are over."

Felix stared hard at the glasses. He could not be sure that Franzi was staring back.

"Look," said Speckbauer. "We talked about this. Someone thinks the Himmelfarb boy told you something. Something that could drop someone in the shit."

"You never said to me that there's a local involvement in this," said Felix.

"Is there? Why do you say that?"

Felix waited for Speckbauer to look over again.

"If doesn't help to think I'm an idiot."

"We don't hold your university days against you. On the contrary."

Felix had a few moments to consider things but he knew he'd come around again to what he had wanted to tell Speckbauer right away.

"You've been a good help so far, Kimmel," Speckbauer went on. "Don't think that's not appreciated. It will look good on you too."

Felix put down his cup. He looked at the stain on the saucer for a moment.

"Okay," he said, and stood up. "I'm going to do what I should have done before."

"Which is?"

"Phone my C.O., or a bighead in Central Office. Ask to get you two off my back."

"Sure about that, Kimmel?" Franzi asked.

"I'd be interested to know what they think about your project being out of hand."

"'Out of hand'?" said Speckbauer. "You're being hard on us. But I understand. It's a shock to the system, all this. It's hard for you."

"I don't give a shit. I just want to protect my family."

"Your career," said Speckbauer. "You hardly want to disgrace your family."

"That doesn't work. At least I'll be able to get real police up here then."

Speckbauer pushed his cup away.

"That would not be a wise plan," he said. "It will complicate matters in ways you can't imagine."

"Are you going to phone my C.O. and get him to give me an order on that?"

Felix took the cordless phone from the wall. He thumbed through his mobile for a number he knew he had, one for Payroll. They'd switch him from there.

Speckbauer rubbed at his nose and muttered something to Franzi. 'The old ones,' Felix heard. Franzi rose, Speckbauer didn't.

"Look, Felix," said Speckbauer. "I'm looking forward to meeting your grandparents when we get through this little chat. But for the moment I'd like them to stay where they are, so they do not overhear some things I need to tell you."

Franzi had taken up a stiff-looking lean against the staircase.

"Don't make that phone call now. Make it later, if you decide then. I won't stop you."

Berndt had taken a shine to Franzi, it seemed. Felix heard his murmurs to the dog and the sighs as Franzi stroked its head.

"Really," said Speckbauer. "I'll answer your questions. Please – sit. Now, do you want to start, or will I?"

Felix sat slowly.

"Okay, I will. There are two dead men. We don't know who they are yet. It looks like they are there a couple of weeks. One of them swallowed a diamond. He wrapped it in a condom. So, we are curious: A) was he carrying it back to wherever he came from – for himself, maybe? Or . . . B) he knew he was in a tight spot. Okay so far?"

Felix nodded.

"Now. We are almost certain now that the Himmelfarb family was murdered."

He paused, eyeing Felix for a reaction.

"That is not public knowledge. It will not become so until I decide. If you want to know, someone used an accelerant – know what that is? – inside the house. People who know such things are ninety percent sure it was paraffin. The house burned hot, all that old wood. Intense, I should say. So here is deliberate, calculated murder of people who someone supposed might know something about the two dead men. Will I stop now?"

Felix glanced down the hall. He was sure that Franzi was watching him.

"The person, or the people, who knew something about this are connected with the people who know something about those two men from the forest. Got that?"

"Maybe the same people," said Felix. "Or person?"

"Exactly," said Speckbauer. He tilted his cup to move coffee around. "It is not hard to suppose they're one and the same, or that he is the one who has done everything. Verstehst?"

"So far," said Felix.

"Next, then. A more personal matter for you. And please, let your head into this more than your guts."

Speckbauer gave him a teacher's look, to see if he were paying attention.

"We are beginning to suspect," he said slowly, "that someone considers you have knowledge about the former matter. The two in the woods, what started this."

"Someone thinks Hansi Himmelfarb told me something?"

"Right. Maybe just or a hint, a clue. Something that will lead to them."

"'Them'? You seem pretty sure."

Speckbauer sat back.

"Really? And why do you say that?"

Felix nodded in Franzi's direction.

"Your job is not about any single criminal."

"Ah," said Speckbauer. "You put it so well. And you're right. We leave petty criminals to the hardworking men in uniform, the real backbone of the Gendarmerie."

"Is that what we are considered?"

"Absolutely: the backbone, the foundation."

"Not a bunch of clowns working with the dummies up here, in the hills?"

"Now really," said Speckbauer. "You know that's a myth."

Felix's irritation was cresting.

"Look," he said. "My grandparents are trusting people. They thought my dad was the greatest. They think I am half-sainted too now because I'm 'following in his footsteps,' or something."

"And you are," Speckbauer offered.

"My point is they have to be told what's going on here. They're probably up there saying to one another how nice it is that Felix's colleagues are dropping by, and how important his work is and . . . It's all crap. Something has to get done. Right now."

Speckbauer seemed to think about Felix's words. He sighed and shifted a little.

"Maria," he muttered. He stopped rubbing at his eyes and looked at Franzi.

"Didn't I tell you," he said. Franzi said nothing but made a small shrug. Felix imagined his grandparents upstairs, listening.

"Okay," said Speckbauer then. "I'll get to the point here. It'll save you all these theatrics. You wonder, don't you, why Franzi and I are up here. 'Where's everyone else?' you wonder. 'If these two coppers are the real thing, they would pull out all the stops and have police crawling all over the area.' Right?"

Felix waited for him to continue.

"Back to the dead men in the forest. Remember I said they shouldn't be there?"

Felix nodded.

"That sounds stupid, no? I mean, they're not there by choice. It wasn't just their mistake being there. No. A mistake was made by whoever shot them. Someone did something unplanned. 'Off the radar.' 'Freelance,' you could say."

"You believe a local killed them, then."

"I don't know," said Speckbauer. "What do you think?"

"I don't know how a local could get those two, two strangers, into the woods like that."

"They walked," said Speckbauer. "That's how."

"Voluntarily?"

"They trusted who they were with," said Speckbauer. "They knew him, or they knew them. My bet is that one of them was getting a bit suspicious. The one with the diamond in his guts."

"You think he just swallowed it up there on that track?"

"No. Of course not. It wouldn't have made its way to where they found it. 'An hour' is what those lab rats told me, the pathology people. But one of the two was suspicious for a while."

"It's not getting any clearer."

"How do you gain a person's trust? Answer me that."

"Trust?" said Felix. "I don't know. Help them some way?"

"Let's say you're a foreigner."

Felix's annoyance and his clouded thoughts suddenly evaporated. "Language."

"Right. You speak the language. That's a start. A few words, at least."

"Well, you know Serbo-Croatian," said Felix.

"Badly," said Speckbauer quickly. "I think I have a mental block against it."

Then his eyes settled, unfocused, on the table.

"And it has held me back, held us back, I must say, that lack of follow-up. I stopped being able to assimilate my learning in Serbo-Croatian some time ago. It was the day my colleague became a human fireball. It was on a shitty little side street in a shithole city in the former-shitty-Yugoslavia. Got that?"

His gaze went to the window. His fingers began to drum slowly on the table top.

"What were you doing in Yugoslavia? The Gendarmerie doesn't do that stuff."

"Did I say we were Gendarmerie then? Imagine for a moment that there are far-seeing people who run things in the Interior Ministry. Let's say they realize that to beat these guys, you have to be as flexible as they are – the bad guys, I mean. You'd be smart enough not to broadcast what you're doing, in a law-abiding social democracy like Austria."

"How long ago?"

"Six years in August. 'James Bond' came home. And he never went back."

"So you were some kind of, I don't know, agent then?"

Speckbauer almost grinned, but the effect was merely a grimace.

"Yes. A bad one."

"And now?"

"And now I am sitting here in the lovely mountains of my native Austria, 'never more to roam,' as our great poet of river and forest Rossegger would say. Where things should be much simpler."

Felix did not know what to say.

"Anyway. This shouldn't concern you. Back to the not-so-simple matter at hand here. Apparently you want a battalion of Gendarmerie to guard your grandparents."

"Don't make a joke out of it."

"It certainly would make a joke out of things if you had your wish. Think for a moment. Not many people know you're here. That was part of the idea, remember."

It did seem like an age ago, Felix thought.

"Well what happened? Passing along the road out there, some-one – anyone – would look over and see your car. So: that brings us back to the 'local,' doesn't it? That's why I wanted you in on this, or at least available. The extra edge: local. You."

"I didn't get any James Bond training," Felix said.

Something seemed to have given way in Speckbauer's voice now when he spoke.

"Let me tell you something," he went on. "This from a guy who did get the 'James Bond' training. It isn't foolproof. Sure, I have the badge, the hardware, and we were given room to be, shall I say 'flexible' – but you don't know what it takes away."

"Sleep?"

"Forget sleep. Think marriage. Two marriages, if you count Franzi's. But in his case it was different. His missus didn't want to be a nurse to the freak that came home from the hospital. She'd signed on for glamour, you see? Franzi was quite the performer, yes. But in my case, I was an adulterer, not the common kind. No this wasn't soap opera stuff. It was that I became obsessed with my work after, after our 'holiday' in Zagreb."

"You and him?"

"Yeah. We share a place. No, we're not gay. 'Adjusting to cir-cumstances.' It's about money, and convenience. Franzi's antics are over, I think. His grafts are getting better every year. He hasn't wrecked every stick of furniture for a year. Punching windows has definitely fallen off. That's progress."

Felix glanced over at Franzi.

"So now you chase these people, but only inside Austria? For the Gendarmerie?"

"What did you learn in training? Who do you work for?"

"'The Austrian people.'"

"The fact is you work for the Interior Ministry. So do we. Yes, Franzi and I, we still chase bad guys. Our bad guys are not the usual gallery, the low-lifes you'll find in Graz, or Vienna, say. We are allowed to be particular. But most of our housecleaning goes on in Graz. God decided on the eighth day – the day that no one knows about – to situate Graz close to the lunatics to the south, the east. Know any history? 'Balkans' . . . ?"

"A bit. A guy, a student, Gavrilo Princip shot Franz Ferdinand, Austrian bigwig."

"Twenty million died with three bullets," said Speckbauer. "Look over Hitler's shoulder and point at the same cause. War reparations, did they teach you that . . . ?"

"I can't remember being taught about it, but I know about them."

"Good. Anyway, back to Graz. Franzi and I work with a section of the Criminal Police. Yes, we're on loan to the Kripo. Actually, our original supervisors couldn't wait to ship us out when things went to hell. Imagine that trafficking, smuggling thing is a big pipe, a big sewer pipe that comes from down there. Well, if we were plumbers, our expertise is in the steady leak. A lot of the officials down there in Croatia are on the take. You know that? The smart ones are the smilers who never get their hands dirty, of course. Who's to say one of them didn't give the nod for whoever tried to torch Franzi that night? Well he didn't end up wearing his wooden pyjamas in the end, as you can see."

Speckbauer's voice trailed off then, and he returned to studying the tabletop. Franzi's breath was whistling in his nose. Maybe he was asleep after all.

When Speckbauer looked up again, Felix could not decide if it was a smile or a sneer on his face.

"I am not a betting man," Speckbauer murmured. "But I will chase any chance I can find, any chance, to find my way to the one who tipped off those people that day."

The eyes bored into Felix's now, even as Speckbauer nodded slowly, twice.

"No matter where they are."

THIRTY-THREE

To Felix, it seemed that the lull that followed lasted for many minutes. He was dimly aware of Franzi's slow movement, and re-settling, and a belief that the three men were listening to the morning sounds of distant birdsong, and the occasional creak from the beams in the old house.

It was Speckbauer who spoke first.

"Does that help, at all?"

"A little, I suppose."

"'Pull a thread, you get a coat.' So it sort of pains me to admit that I am not on top of this. It's embarrassing. And it makes me angry, as you can see. You might ask why."

"Okay. Why?"

"Because we, the great experts, are useless here. It's like starting from scratch."

"Oh this is where I come in," said Felix. "You think because I grew up around here that this gives you some kind of a head start? Better yet, get a probationer, a guy will be too awed to ask questions, a guy who'll do what he's told?"

Speckbauer continued to frown at the table. It was as if he was trying to absorb a new threat in a game of chess there, one that only he could see.

"I can tell you are impressed," he said. "But I will finish. Back to the two in the forest – hell, it's always the forest, isn't it, in the old stories? I know it's a stupid thing I keep repeating. These two men should not have been there. I have a theory, and I will tell it to you.

These two were trying to conduct business that their bosses would not have known about, and would not have been too happy about."

"A side deal."

"You're getting it. But greed is always greed. It never ends. You can never predict how far it'll go, how greedy people will get. It is the strangest thing. So these two were not ambushed, let us say, by people outside their normal course of business. They were disposed of – 'taken care of.' That's because they did something stupid. Something against the rules, this gschäftl, this little effort."

He looked up abruptly from the tabletop.

"Stanzen, as the gangsters call it," he said. "'Fired.' 'Let go.'"

Morning sunlight was carving its way high up into the woods. The deeper greens gave way to glowing patches made almost phosphorescent from the sun's slanting rays.

"These people didn't belong up here," Speckbauer went on. "I don't mean racist crap. I mean they broke some rule. They came up here for someone, or something. Now, you spoke about trust earlier on. Your grandparents are 'trusting people.'"

"They are – you see for yourself. Why bring that up?"

"Trust? Ah, your generation – what am I talking about? My generation. Nobody trusts. Look where it got us not so long ago, right? We were poisoned by our own."

Speckbauer looked around the kitchen.

"You know what I'm talking about?"

"I do," Felix said, cautiously. "I think."

"What I am blathering on about here is an open secret. About how everything went to scheisse sixty years ago. So things were bad for years after the war. All this guilt and silence, on top of all the missing men. There was rape. No one talks about that. Fires, murder. Wondering if Stalin was going to pull something. But things picked up, and moved on. Today we are polite members of the EU. Pretty good, eh? Soon we'll have our brothers, the Turks. No more Austrian nightmares then. We'll all sleep soundly."

Felix said nothing. Shafts of sunlight had broken through the treetops and were tearing into the window now, as steadily as a brightening orange glare.

"Different story here in God's country, huh. Anybody talk to you about that?"

"No."

"There's my point right there, then. You probably never asked either. Let me tell you, in those years you found whatever you could and you did whatever you did to survive. You went back in time, to what worked before. 'Don't ask, don't tell.' 'Fall back,' they say in the army."

"I don't see the point of this talk."

"My point was that this is how humans work under pressure. They go back to old ways. So when you were short of something or you wanted something, you found the ways that worked. The line between criminality and the law was gone. You knew the wegs and paths of the forest. You knew where you could stay, or rest, or wait. In fact, if you were a man, one of the lucky ones that survived the Eastern Front or labour camps, you found your way back here. And you soon got the picture. You were on your own. 'They' had won. But you had your bits of farm, maybe an animal or two. And you had your training, didn't you?"

"You mean army?"

"Natürlich. After a few years soldiering you'd be ten times better at bringing home a rabbit, or a deer."

"I suppose."

"By and by, you needed things, and you got things. You swapped, and you bartered, and you shared. And you did without too. But if you weren't an idiot, you saw how others had done it during the war while you were away getting your arse shot off for your leader. Now you wanted something better than turnips. So, what do you say?"

Felix waited until Speckbauer had finished his stretch and yawn.

"But that was fifty years ago. More. It's ancient history."

"Hah," said Speckbauer. "I won." He repeated it again, louder for Franzi. "I'll buy you a beer with my winnings, Franzi. Puntigamer or Gösser?"

"Yes," said Franzi. Had he been dozing, standing there by the kachelofen?

Speckbauer turned back to Felix.

"I bet myself five Euro you'd come up with the 'It's history' bit."

Felix heard footsteps upstairs and the tones of his grandfather resonating down to him through the floorboards. Franzi stood away from the kachelofen and slowly tilted his head up to where a door was opening.

"Ask your opa how they got gasoline then," said Speckbauer. "Medicine. Pesticide. Spare parts. Cement. Bullets even, to take down a deer. Or will I ask him?"

"Leave them alone," said Felix, rising.

"Grüss an alle," came the greeting from the head of the stairs. "Hello everyone. I am back, with news of the duchess above. She will join us shortly."

Speckbauer smiled.

"I've got to tell them something," Felix whispered. "The Gendarmerie—"

"Shut up with that," Speckbauer snapped. "I told you: we need time."

Felix's grandfather called out again. By the squeaks he knew so well, Felix could imagine him pausing halfway on the landing.

"Here we are, Herr Nagl," Speckbauer called out. His accent and tone had changed instantly again, Felix realized. "The rabbit is skinned and cooking in the pot."

"Ah a master hunter," Opa Nagl called out, chuckling. "Quick work, my friends."

Felix was stunned at how quickly Speckbauer could switch to the friendly son-of-the-soil here again. Felix waved back at the pantomime appearance of his opa peering around the end of the wall from the bottom of the stairs. Speckbauer leaned toward him.

"Before you decide; two things. Listening?"

Felix nodded.

"When did your grandfather leave the Gendarmerie?" Speckbauer whispered.

"Gendarmerie? He wasn't one."

"Your Opa Kimmel, I'm talking about, not your opa here."

"He wasn't either–"

"He certainly was. It lasted nineteen months. They let him walk, too. That's how strong it was then."

"What are you talking about?"

"The second question is this: what was your father doing the day he passed?"

THIRTY-FOUR

LATER, IN THE GIDDY GOODWILL THAT FILLED THE KITCHEN after his grandparents had arrived, Felix's thoughts dangled, spinning endlessly, only to race up to some precipice where they vanished. Several times in this sunlit kitchen where Oma Nagl bustled about he believed he was dreaming, or in a fever.

Oma was delighted with guests, keen to spoil them with more food and coffee, and even schnapps. Almost flirtatious with Speckbauer, she treated Franzi like a very old man, constantly asking if he wanted more of anything, giving him a routine smile to show he was included in spite of his silence. Felix eyed him occasionally making the slow, minute stretches that seemed to be his routine in all his waking hours.

Speckbauer's effortless transformation into a genial local only increased Felix's confusion. Speckbauer was full of gentle wit, hinting at a subtle, almost pitiful mockery of the greater world outside the farmhouse, where unfortunates could only wish for such food, in such a house, with its family bonds, its mountain views all about, and its air. He ably followed and added to a conversation about farming, the recent May festival, Chinese food, the new turbo diesel engines, car theft in the cities, proverbs that no one used anymore.

Felix looked out at the steep, jumbled meadows and hills returned to their postcard green with the sun overhead, and a blue sky to bite down on the edges all about. He imagined someone out there, watching the place, just as Speckbauer and Franzi had been doing in those hours before dawn.

As the conversation swirled around him, things around him began to take on an unfamiliar look. It was as though there had been a different light or colour spread over it. Everything was moving under him, a slow subterranean drift, but he couldn't put his finger on exactly what he wanted to do. He knew that panic wasn't far off. He stood.

His oma's smiling face turned up toward him and the talk stopped. Felix tried to smile back. He wouldn't look over in Speckbauer's direction.

"I'm falling asleep," he said. "I better get some fresh air."

He winked at his oma but it did not erase her look of concern. Behind him he heard another chair being moved. His opa launched into something about a motorbike he'd had, one that took him through snowstorms. The opening door took the rest of the conversation. Felix paused near the bench and then headed across the farmyard.

"Hey," came Speckbauer's voice behind him.

Felix didn't slow. He imagined breaking into a run.

"Don't do anything stupid," Speckbauer called out. "You can't back away now."

Felix stopped and turned.

"I have to clear my head."

Speckbauer shrugged.

"You've got to do what you've got to do," he said. "That's the job, see?"

"You mean what you've got to do. Not me."

"What does that mean?"

"I've had enough of this routine," said Felix.

Speckbauer looked back at the farmhouse.

"You want me to betray my family."

"'Betray'?"

"Now you're trying to tell me that my father was a bent cop?"

"Did I say that? Did I?"

"You don't give a shit about anyone. There you are, in my

grandparents' kitchen, eating their food, yapping. With your 'herrlich, Herr Nagl!, wunderbar, Frau Nagl!' Just because you're up in the hills here, you don't fool anyone"

"Not even your grandparents?"

"They're humouring you. They let you think you're fooling them."

"Ah, I see."

"Go back in and try more Rossegger on them. 'Oh my forest home . . .' Blah blah."

"You don't like the great Peter Rossegger?"

"He was a fascist. Him and his Brotherhood. Ancient history."

"Maybe," said Speckbauer. "But does it ruin his poetry though, this distaste he had for lesser peoples, the foreigners amongst us?"

"You probably believe that too, then. 'Send them back,' right?"

"Some, for sure. We have enough homegrown hoodlums here."

Felix was at a loss for words.

"Two more we didn't need," Speckbauer added in a groan, mid-stretch.

"This is going nowhere," said Felix. "I came out to make a telephone call."

Speckbauer didn't move off, but continued to eye Felix.

"You don't want to know," he said. "You just don't. Now that is something."

"I do know. I know I'm being used."

"You don't want to know about your grandfather. And, I guess, you won't want to know about your father."

Felix felt a surge of anger welling up again.

"Don't bring that up again. You're insulting my family. I'm phoning my C.O. They can fire me if they like."

"Who's going to sleep better tonight if you do? It doesn't fix the problem."

"You're making the damned problem," Felix retorted. "This is dangerous. This isn't some game or strategy you do in your office, sticking pins in a map or something."

"Well," said Speckbauer. "Do I look like a pin-in-a-map cop? Maybe I should be one then, so it wouldn't upset your stereotype. 'What you don't know, won't hurt you.'"

"Who knows what you'll say next, that's my take on it."

"You're not that stupid – and that's my take. And it would be a betrayal too. That doesn't sit right with me."

"But you want me to betray my own instead."

Speckbauer glared back. After a few moments his eyes lost their focus.

"Okay," he said. "I get it. I am a bit slow, but I finally get it. You win. Make your calls. And don't worry – I'll only say good things about all you've done on this. Really. We shouldn't have taken you away from your holiday, Gendarme Kimmel. I'll tell you what: I'll put up signs. 'Gendarme Kimmel doesn't know anything.' 'And Gendarme Kimmel doesn't want to find out either.'"

Felix stared at him. Speckbauer didn't turn away from his long survey of the greens and the chill, spring brightness that was showering this part of Styria.

"He doesn't want to know that his grandfather was a wannabe SS," he went on. "That he did fine, thank you very much, in the hard times after the war."

"What's that got to do with anything?"

"That his Opa Kimmel was the man to go to if you needed something, like petrol or parts or concrete, or even coffee and cigarettes?"

"Even if he did."

Speckbauer turned away from the view.

"Is it still 'ancient history'?" he snapped.

He glanced down at the phone in Felix's hand.

"That grandfather of yours did his nod-and-wink routine for longer than just survival. Maybe you don't want to know more. Maybe you just want to carry on being very modern, a Uni-dropout-poser-MP3-European type of a guy. The new copper."

Grim satisfaction leaked into Felix. He had drawn out the real Speckbauer at last.

"Been to Britain?" Speckbauer asked then, brightly. "England?"

"No."

"A strange bunch, but fair, if you can forgive their beer. My point is, the British saw how capable your grandfather was. During the occupation? They were impressed. So they offered your Opa Kimmel a job. Where? In the Gendarmerie, of course."

Speckbauer turned back toward the fields and woods. Again he seemed to be deriving satisfaction from his slow, steady survey. Felix sensed that Speckbauer was waiting for a signal from him. Still, he turned his phone over again in his hand, waited.

"Well?" Speckbauer said then.

"Go on," said Felix. "I'm listening."

"Thank you. At any rate, the British knew that there were Gendarmerie who shouldn't be put under a magnifying glass – like your grandfather Kimmel, see? The Second Republic, the New Austria, woken up from its nightmare, needed experienced men in the places where, well, where the likes of your grandfather had experience."

"Experience?"

"Smuggling. Maybe I should say trading. Okay: trading. Things were hard up here. The Russians came through here first. Christ, what didn't they take? They weren't alone in their visits. There were partisans, from up and down the Balkans. Slovenians, a lot of them. A lot of them came through from the DP camps there in Judenburg, and Graz."

Again, Felix thought of the maps he had pored over last night. For a moment he almost believed that Speckbauer knew about them, and was just baiting him here.

"Well, once the pigs and petrol business was shall we say, normal, other activities went on. Can you imagine?"

Felix nodded.

"You had Eastern Europeans who knew their way around. Sure, they'd gone home but home was what? Flattened houses? And if you were on the wrong side, the losing side . . . ? So people had connections. Sure there were borders – 'The Iron Curtain' and all that. But this coming and going was nothing new here. 'Business resumed.' Your grandfather closed shop: good for him. He told his old contacts to get lost – especially the ones up from Slovenia. Yes, he did his job. It says so right in his file."

Speckbauer waited for some reaction, but it was one that Felix would not offer.

"It also says that your oma, your Oma Kimmel, was the one who seems to have calmed your Opa Kimmel's fiery nature. She talked him down, sorted him out."

Felix stared back into his eyes. They had regained their flat, expressionless look.

"She cushioned his fall again when he was asked about some goings-on later."

"So now my grandmother was a crook?"

"Did I say that? Peter Kimmel was her husband, wasn't he? In 1953, an informer said that Gendarme Kimmel, had not quite given up all of his 'interests.' That he looked the other way at the correct time, that there were things he didn't want to know. Verstehst? A matter of not betraying those to whom he had loyalties."

"Is was hardly a crime to want to feed your family, to take care of them."

"Don't get me wrong. Those two men turned up in the forest, and part of our job is to see if it's connected with other events, present and past. Patterns, no?"

Felix took a few steps toward the side of the storehouse. What had his father known of this? Was that why he had kept those maps, with the paths marked in?

"Beautiful," he heard Speckbauer say. "What views. I far preferred Geography to History. So much more definite. You were right or you were wrong. You?"

Felix turned back to him.

"Even if this were true, it's all ancient."

"You said that already. What I'm saying is that this kind of thing still goes on. And those connections and loyalties last over time."

"You think my Opa Kimmel is wandering around the woods? Be serious. He can't even walk ten steps without a cane."

"Normally I don't dip into the sewer of pop psychology. But denial is big."

"You really think he knows something about the dead men in the forest?"

Speckbauer hesitated before answering.

"How come you don't speak Slovenian?"

"Because I'm Austrian."

"Did your parents?"

"Same answer."

"Your grandmother Kimmel's family is Slovenian."

"A hundred years ago, it was."

"There's always been Slovenian all along here. Hapsburgs, Nazis – sure they got bumped about. But not many left, really. They cleared some from DP camps in forty-six, and Tito killed them. Viktring Camp was a big one. Anyway, your grandfather can speak it."

"I never heard him speak it."

"Ask him then. It says so in his Gendarmerie records: 'Working knowledge.' You think he lied, to impress his employer?"
"What employer would care?"

"The SS might," said Speckbauer. "He was hoping, I imagine?"

Felix refused to give him any satisfaction. He said nothing.

"Ultimately unsuccessful," Speckbauer resumed. "Not to be critical now, but by forty-four there was room in the SS ranks. But faking your age, a sixteen year old?"

Speckbauer rubbed at his nose, and drew his coat around him.

"Okay," he said then. "Here is the end of this chapter. Your grandmother must have been one strong woman. Excuse me now if that sounds . . . impertinent. It was she who tried to put an end to all this 'silliness.' She made him clean up his act. He did settle down. I'm not saying she changed him or his opinions, or that. But she reintroduced him to civilian life, you could say. Normal life."

This time Felix could not resist.

"You talk about all this like it's some kind of play, or a movie or something. But your job is to lie and to con people, to get whatever you want, however you want."

Speckbauer sighed.

"I'm not saying you're wrong," he said. "But let's finish here on a good note."

"I don't see how. You are doing a number on my family."

"Really? I'm going to suggest to you things that were not handed down father to son because of your grandmother. Oh, the usual stuff came down fine, I imagine. How to plant potatoes, screw in light bulbs, fix a bike, shoot a rabbit, but from what I gather, your grandmother did her best to protect her kids from the past. Whatever else had happened, this was a new generation. They wouldn't be dragged into all that crap. Now there was a brave woman. Would to God all her generation had been like her."

Something about Speckbauer's face, his relaxed gaze and quiet tone, cooled Felix's anger a little.

"What we don't know," he added in a murmur, "is if she succeeded."

"That makes zero sense to me," Felix said.

"I don't know if you're ready for it."

"Just say it."

"Your father."

"What about my father? Now you want to spread the bullshit to him?"

A hint of humour flickered around Speckbauer's eyes only. It faded quickly.

"Franzi, that bastard, he's always right," he said. "Always. It's uncanny. He made you right from the start. 'Mark my words,' he said. 'That guy keeps a lid on things. But he could plant one on your nose too.'"

"Is that in my file?"

"Ach don't be paranoid. Of course not."

"Well you make it easy for me to decide what to do here."

There was a breeze beginning, and the cool morning air stung his nose. Speckbauer looked back toward the house, and then he turned and began a slow walk out beyond the shed and toward the fields.

"Your father had many, many acquaintances," he said. "Good policemen often do. It's their job to be able to find things out. How do you find things out? Through people. And your father was that kind of a guy, was he not? Sociable, outgoing."

Felix nodded.

"Compared to his father anyway," said Speckbauer. "He turned out the opposite, didn't he, thanks to your grandmother, if I may say. But you hardly remember her, am I right? What were you, five?"

"Yes."

"Cancer?"

"So I heard, later."

"Okay. Now, your father got about a lot. He liked the outdoors, he grew up in the hills, all that. Right? Oh, and he had a knack for cars, perhaps from your grandfather? The old VWs, the Kübelwagens? 'The thing' we used to call them growing up. Christ – the same air-cooled lump in them that the Beetles had. There were thousands dumped or abandoned after the war, did you know?"

Felix's thoughts went immediately to the snapshots of his father leaning against an overturned VW up in the woods somewhere. There he was, in his element, laughing along with his friends, big strapping guys off-duty too, out for a boys' day in the woods.

"Your father had a good knowledge of the area, I would say. Exceptionally good. I bet that your grandfather passed on a lot to him. 'The lore' I suppose you'd say."

Speckbauer tapped his forehead.

"The maps in here," he said. "Better than your satellites, I'd bet again. Can you imagine how valuable that was?"

"You're working up to some insinuation here."

"Which is?"

"That my father was in some racket. Or that he looked the other way?"

"I try to look at everything."

"That's a 'yes' then."

"It's an 'I don't know.'"

"I don't believe you."

"If I knew, I wouldn't be here. Nor would you."

"You think I'm in on something," said Felix. "That's it."

"Others may think that."

"'Others' who?"

"I'm not going to get into that. Let's conclude here. Your father was out and about even more than he usually was in those few weeks. Before his passing, I mean."

"Right," said Felix. "I think I'm beginning to get it now."

"Go on, then."

"How come a Gendarme drives an Audi? How much did he have to drink?"

"We know it was a used car. Your father was not drunk."

"Well, thank you for that. I suppose I should be grateful or something?"

"Look, we don't know where he was that afternoon. He was no stranger to a bite to eat and a krügl of beer up in Eagle's Nest or wherever, but that's where the trail ended. He was supposed to be on duty at the time, at his post in Judenburg. You knew that?"

"I found out about it later. People are polite. They didn't want him to look bad."

"Sure," said Speckbauer. "People are polite. They didn't want him to look bad. But he'd been doing this a lot."

"So he was under suspicion?"

"No. Not then. Later – and it was a bunch of unexplained things, open questions. It was not suspicion."

"But for you?"

"I'm curious, that's all. That's why I pulled the file and read it. Stuff comes across my desk. I'm like a guy with Alzheimer's.

Sometimes it makes sense, like a big jigsaw. 'Two men, apparently Slavic/Balkan background, dead in the woods up in Hohe Arschloch, Styria.' 'A junkie overdosed in an apartment in Graz with a new quality of heroin.' 'A clown gets fired from a crappy factory job in Furstenfeld. Now he gets back at his employer who caught him drinking in the klo fifty times. He phones "anonymous-ly," says illegals come in at night in the factory, cleaning up.' All that."

"How does this come up here? What does this have to do with me?"

"It depends on how you view things," said Speckbauer. He stopped and looked around. "And speaking of viewing things . . . "

He pointed toward a mountain, and glanced at Felix.

"Jacobsberg," Felix said. Speckbauer pivoted at pointed at another.

"Oberlach."

"And if I went over the top of it?"

"You're up on Sommersalm, by the river. It'd take a day."

"Trails?"

"One only. There are awkward parts."

Speckbauer kept looking about, but had no more questions.

"Did I pass?"

Speckbauer smiled tightly and resumed his walk. At the edge of the field there was a drainage cut. The ground to both sides was waterlogged and dark with the run-off.

"I was talking about coincidences," he went on. "Now to super-stitious people, or paranoids, there are no coincidences. But me, I am not like that. Well not during daylight hours anyway. What I mean is this: we – Franzi and me – see the daily 'news' we call it and note it. So, we think: two dead guys. From down south there in gangland? In the middle of nowhere? A new departure, a new group? Right by, well, within fifty kilometres anyway, of big towns like Weiz and Gleisdorf, all those new factories?"

Felix took mental note of how deftly Speckbauer stepped over the drainage cut.

"So there we are in our lair there in Strassgangerstrasse," Speckbauer went on. "And naturally we ask 'What else has gone on here in the recent past in this neck of the woods?' There is your father, his passing. And then, there is a copy of your notes as officer on scene, you and Gebhart. Kimmel One, Kimmel Two. This is a coincidence?"

Speckbauer stopped then and swore, and he shook his head. He drew out his mobile from his pocket.

"No wonder I'm feeling odd. I left it switched off. Christ and His mother."

Felix took a few steps into the field. Speckbauer had stopped and looked down at the wet soil oozing around the edges of his shoes. Felix's head was not clearing. He tried to imagine what his grandparents could be talking to Franzi about.

"There are lots of black spots up here, right?" he heard Speckbauer mutter. "And the signal you get here is piddly enough, isn't it?"

He turned when he heard Speckbauer's words trail off. Speckbauer was squinting at the screen. He tilted it against the morning sun that was still slicing the valleys into shadow and glare.

"Excuse me, a text."

Felix watched him thumb through the message again. For a moment then Speckbauer's eyes rested on the stones that had been embedded into the side of the cut.

"Well," he said. "Now that focuses the mind. Yes. Now I am awake."

"What? Is it about the situation here?"

"Perhaps. It's a message about something in the first pathology notes. They're being transcribed, but someone there was smart enough to fire an email to our office."

"Identities?"

Speckbauer shook his head, and tapped his phone gently in a slow rhythm on his chin. He was soon lost in thought and turned to rubbing his phone over the bristles.

"You know something about the two?"

Speckbauer blinked as though rudely awoken.

"No. Yes. A horseman."

He looked at the phone again.

"There is a mark," he said. "No, what am I saying? A tattoo on one. In an armpit more or less. It's sort of half ragged there, but it's something."

Felix shielded his eyes from the sun. His eyes were beginning to burn now from the flood of light and sleeplessness.

"VK," said Speckbauer. "They're out of Croatia. Well the one with the mark is. It's actually a spur, this mark. 'Vatreni Konji.' Call them Crazy Horses. It's got something to do with hunters' horses, I don't know exactly. But the exact translation doesn't work for me. 'Spirited Horses?' No: crazy is proper. You won't understand."

"Give me the short version."

"The 'runner' – the one with the four bullet holes – was mid-thirties. He had a tattoo. That puts him as a member, or a hanger-on of some degree, of a bunch of ex-soldiers, bandits, and the like. He would be no stranger to crime, I say. We have a chance of putting a name on him, with army records in Croatia. It'll take time." Speckbauer pursed his lips and then blew them loose.

"I put in a call to The Hague, to see if there's a file on him."

"The Hague? A war criminal?"

"It's possible. There were guys like that, one picked up in Vienna two years ago. Then, some arrest, or bodies, in Germany. But one of them up here? It changes things."

Speckbauer turned on his heels and concentrated on a sharp block of light thrown up by the sun on the wall of the house.

"So," he said, and nodded at Felix's mobile. "You still want to phone Gebhart, and get him to sort all this out?"

Felix shrugged.

"I'll tell you," said Speckbauer then. "These horsemen guys are big on revenge, and grudges. They make it their business to set an example. And they don't accept business losses. So, if our guy in the woods was carrying something of value, they are the type to want to get it back. And put away whoever interfered in their operation."

Felix's mind lurched, and a cold feeling descended on him again.

"The other guy has a diamond in his guts," Speckbauer murmured. "And a hole in the back of his head. A clean shot, a surprise. But Mr. Horseman guy had a chance to run or jump or try something. There's no lab test telling me he fired a gun. Say Mr. Horseman has been accompanying Mr. Diamond, but that he is no friend to him. And say he has a deal with a third party arranged for Mr. Diamond to get taken care of . . . ?"

"A third party who knew his way around the area."

"A person who had his own scheme," said Speckbauer, nodding. He seemed to be mesmerized by the stripes of hard light across the yard now. Then he wrinkled his nose and his brows lifted. He pointed his index finger to his ear, and made a popping sound.

"'Kill the two foreigners,' let's call the plan," he said. "Yes."

"He doesn't take the diamond out of the first guy's guts, though."

"Ah, Gendarme Kimmel. He doesn't know about diamonds in the guy's guts. And I think he is quite content with what he did get."

"Other diamonds," said Felix. "Cash maybe."

"I agree. And all that was supposed to be on its way to . . . ?" Felix hesitated. Then he nodded towards the hills to the north.

"Wrong direction, I say."

"I give up then. Christ, I'm a Gendarme in Stefansdorf. What do I know?"

"Traffic goes two ways. One way goes drugs, counterfeit. Human beings. Weapons. Lousy, old-fashioned, lucrative cigarettes. Other way goes payment."

"But why are they up here? Nothing goes on up here."

"It's not coincidence. There's some connection. That's all I'm guessing."

Speckbauer's eyes took on an intensity, but the sun's glare made his face sickly.

"I see three, maybe four, guys involved," he said. "The two in the woods, one a fool and the other a lesser fool. The lesser fool thought he had an arrangement. The arrangement was with a local guy, or a pair of locals. Any more than that would have made our Horseman fellow suspicious. He wouldn't have come up here."

Speckbauer seemed to have used up all his words. He stared at a distant hillside, as though the patches of light and shade there held patterns he intended to read. Behind him, in the shed, Felix heard pigs snuffling and half-heartedly kicking against something.

"Last night's visitor," Felix started to say.

"You mean 'the snooper'?" Speckbauer said without turning. "That was someone from here. Some local. Someone wants to see if Gendarme Kimmel keeps his work papers in his car. They want to know what that boy told you, the Himmelfarb kid."

Felix looked up at the window of the bedroom where he had spent the night. He imagined himself skipping upstairs to take the maps down to show Speckbauer, just to see the expression on his face. But no: this was something he had to do himself first – after he confided in Gebhart. Gebi had been around; he had the low-down on Speckbauer and Franzi, the fly-in cops with so much baggage. Gebi would understand.

"Maybe someone thinks," Speckbauer went on, pausing at each word. "That the Himmelfarb boy wandered the forests at night. Maybe he even saw the work done on the two. Who knows. But if it was someone who knows about the two dead guys, or the Himmelfarbs, there other things that are heavy on their minds, you can be sure."

When Felix didn't say anything, Speckbauer looked over at him.

"This is why I say 'local,'" said Speckbauer. "For one thing, they are concerned that Mr. Horseman's friends will be paying a call. Do they know who they're dealing with, whoever did this?

They know enough, I think. Diamonds are an easy way to take payment. The other thing . . . well another time, perhaps, after we leave this lovely place."

"What other thing?"

"Well it concerns you, Gendarme. Remember we talked about coincidences? Joked a little too? Is it coincidence that you, a son of Felix Kimmel, is involved here?"

Felix returned Speckbauer's steady gaze.

"People want to believe the best of others, I find. Colleagues, friends. Family." "Everyone except a certain type of detective."

Speckbauer shrugged.

"And someone might wonder, well, why you joined the Gendarmerie. I mean, we have guys who didn't finish high school. When we're one big happy family, the Polizei and us, you'll be a cop in that new organization. A pretty far-sighted career plan, no?" Felix bit back an answer.

"Your father, also a Gendarme, with a spotless record. Super guy. But the last few months before his accident, he's wandering all over the place. He's out of his area, on the road a lot. He's having a beer here, a coffee there – well, he's everywhere. And why? Nobody knows. Was he looking for something, someplace? An investigation? Bored? Now, Judenburg's a fine place, but was he looking at his retirement package and thinking, Maria, this is going to be less than I hoped–"

Felix's hand had come up without his thinking.

"Shut up," he said.

Speckbauer didn't shift his eyes from Felix's face. Felix let his hand down slowly. He glanced for an instant at where his hand had begun to twist Speckbauer's collar. Then he turned away, spots bursting in front of his eyes.

The greens from the new shoots and grasses were of different tints, he noticed. Dawn had moved on to morning completely now.

"Anyway," said Speckbauer. "I'll finish. If I remember some of the report, there was mention of maps. Your father had them spread out all over the place. Old ones, too, your mother remembers. Your father had an intense interest in them, according to those statements. Very intense. And now, they are not to be found apparently. Odd."

Speckbauer's words seemed to come from far off now. He waited for Felix to look his way before turning back toward the farmhouse. He made a flinty smile.

"Too much talk. It doesn't settle anything."

"That shouldn't have happened," Felix began. He let the rest of his words go.

"It didn't happen. Stress? You should see Franzi in action. Jesus: a maniac."

He looked over.

"Don't worry, it's no big secret. Franzi walloped me so hard I was seeing spaceships with little green men, not just stars. It was a medication thing. He had a lot of pain. Apparently he was sleepwalking."

"Sleepwalking," said Felix, numbly. The tiredness had suddenly landed on his shoulders like a dead weight.

"A perfect excuse. 'Re-enacting' said the shrink. 'You mean he's going to keep doing it?' I ask. 'We don't know.' 'I should tie him up? Lock him in? Wear a helmet?' They don't have the answers for post-trauma. I sleep with one eye open. Look, I need to use a land phone."

THIRTY-FIVE

FELIX FELT NO MORE AWAKE AFTER A THIRD CUP OF COFFEE, BUT at least now, with the thought of Gebhart's wary gaze, he had some kind of direction to follow.

Occasionally he heard Speckbauer's voice from the hall. Along with a tone of disbelief, or impatience, or both, but there was more often a steady metronomic 'Ja' that Speckbauer seemed to employ to speed up a conversation.

"Mein Gött but he is a different man on the phone," Felix's oma whispered. She nodded toward her husband. "I thought I'd heard them all from the count here."

"I keep reinforcements," said Felix's opa. "Don't worry. For when I am too feeble to chase you about."

"And he is speaking foreign too."

"It'll be a hell of a phone bill," said his grandfather.

"He will pay," Felix heard himself say.

"They will pay," said his grandfather. "The state."

"He writes a lot of things down," said Oma Nagl behind her hand.

"The Franzi is a character I can tell you, Felix," added Opa Nagl, also with his hand to the side of his mouth. "He went out to see the pigs. To talk to them, he said. Where do you find such people? You were a bit wild, natürlich. But these are special."

Felix made a greater effort to appear relaxed.

"An accident with chemicals," his grandfather whispered. "Lieber Gött – imagine the pain. He must be very dedicated to go on."

Felix realized he had been thinking of the pair, this odd couple of cops, in the same apartment. One, damaged and close to blowing his lid all the time, the other, an amiable pro on the outside but really, as cunning as they come, and impossible to read. But even Speckbauer could not quite cover up the signs that he was also full of some kind of a ferocity. Maybe he was just as messed up in his head as the other.

"'Kripo,'" his grandmother repeated, softly. "Kriminal Polizei. It's like those police shows on the TV."

"Shows?" his grandfather said, almost indignantly. "The American dreck that half the country watches? But Felix: this has to be good for you, no? They see you work, they see how settled you are now . . . "

Opa Nagl paused, with an awkward smile.

"When your people, our good old Gendarmerie that we know so well, our fellows – or boys – when your team gets together with the Polizei, boy, that'll be the perfect situation for you. Unbeatable, I say."

Oma Nagl put her hand over his.

"You have it good, thank God," she said to Felix.

"Do you know if you'll keep the uniform though?" asked his grandfather. "The tellerkappe? Christ, if that goes, all is lost."

"Lieber Gött," said Oma Nagl. "Why is a little beret like that important? The tradition? Ask the boy about promotions and suchlike."

"It is important. A symbol is important to ordinary people. I mean, when I see a Gendarme, and there he is under that cap, I can relax. Yes! I know I am dealing with a normal fellow. But Lord Jesus, when I see the Polizei there in Graz, I do not relax. No."

"It's just city life," whispered Oma Nagl. "Bus conductor uniforms scare you."

Felix's grandfather gave his wife a long look.

"You," he said. "You are the same. Remember on the TV the other night? The early news, the seven-thirty?"

"Those police talking in Vienna?" she asked.

"You said something about them. You did! 'Too many police uniforms in one place,' I think you said or 'too much uniform'?"

"Ach, don't be silly. With you it is your conscience, what little is left, and the naughty things of your youth. Or it's just political – you think uniforms are for the bad times, for trouble."

Opa Nagl's face took on a contented expression. He eyed Felix.

"This is Mrs. Law and Order, a woman who liked a wild one, once upon a time?"

"You were a naughty kid, Opa?"

"Of course I–"

Oma Nagl held up her hand. She tilted her head to hear Speckbauer's voice growing louder in the hall. Words were clear now.

"Jesus and Mary," Felix heard, as Speckbauer's irritation broke over something. He watched his grandparents' eyes grow bigger.

"For Christ's sake, what's the goddamned delay? This is the digital age!"

A soft smile settled on his grandfather's face now.

"Army," he whispered. "Must have been. Listen to all that bad language."

"Damn it, Martin! Step on it, will you? We need to move on this!"

Oma Nagl rolled her eyes. Her husband shook his head, half in admiration.

"Ah we were all a bit naughty then," he said. It took a moment for Felix's addled brain to pick up the thread.

"Those little Puch motorbikes we'd 'borrow.' Beer of course. Practical jokes. All fun. But those days, who knows."

"They all want cars, now, the kids," Oma Nagl added. "For you-know-what."

"Nature studies."

"You don't miss those annoying whiny two-strokes though," his grandfather added. "The Japs beat them into the ground with their motorbikes. Just like their little rice cookers beat up NSU and Audi and Merc and–"

"Rice cookers is not polite thing to say these days," said Oma Nagl.

"Rudolf Diesel is a saint," he retorted. "No rice cooked in a diesel engine, girl."

"Not so many motorbikes now?" Felix asked.

"Right. But older guys like them still I think, a few anyways. 'The old days' kind of thing perhaps. They'll come back, I tell you."

"Ach," said Oma Nagl, and brushed away his opinion. "They are still dangerous. Even with grown men on them. Not dangerous to me, no, I am in a car, but what chance do you have? Remember that crackpot there, not long back? There were still patches of snow even, and he comes out of nowhere. A madman."

"Yes," said Felix's opa. "I remember that. Like a pirate or something. It was on the bend down the far side of the church. He must have been bottled to be out in the cold like that. Big red face – no, a beard on him. A Viking or something."

"A red beard? Red hair?"

"I suppose. He had goggles. Like a Scotsman, I thought later. Like I was saying, he must have been pretty well drunk to drive like that . . . "

The conversation ebbed. Felix's mind kept backpedalling, spiralling, coming up empty. He made a long, aching stretch. Yawning, he missed half of his opa's words.

"God, that guy Speckbauer knows them all," he said.

"He will surely apologize," said Oma Nagl. "He must be under a lot of pressure but I still think he is a gentleman underneath. It's his manner. He's not a city type."

Opa Nagl groaned.

"Like he never did any mischief, this Horst? Right, Felix?"

Oma Nagl waved away her husband's observation.

"Right Felix? A man should have mischief, no?"

Felix rubbed more at his eyes.

"Every road in life should have its scenic routes. The autobahn is direct and fast of course, but it is on the byroads up in God's country that one can savour real life."

"Mein Gött, will you listen to that," said Oma Nagl.

"Rossegger has come back from the dead."

Felix eyed the shy smile his grandfather had now, the turning motion he made with his finger as though winding up a toy.

Oma Nagl began filling the sink. Felix took in the wooden table where they sat. It was hundreds of years old. His gaze wandered from chair to kacheloffen, back over the geraniums on the window sill, and then to the cats' dishes licked clean next to a pair of boots. Nothing should change here, he felt.

"Yes," his grandfather murmured, an ear cocked again to the more subdued tones of Speckbauer's voice in the hall yet. "One must make one's own map for a full life."

"Opa, I want to ask you something about this."

"Advice? Of course. You have come to the right man."

"No not joking. It's about maps."

"You need one? I think we have some. Oh, I know. It's that stuff from the shed. I forgot. Yes, your dad asked me about them, I remember."

"They were his, weren't they?"

"No. That's the thing, I remember now. I think he said he got them up at his father's place. The old house."

There was something in the way his grandfather said it, 'the old house,' that stayed with Felix.

"He dug them up, I think. Not literally. They were up there somewhere. But they're old, aren't they? They're not antiques, I don't think. Are they? No."

Felix's mind went back to the map with the marks on it.

"They were not his?"

"No. They were his father's. Or the father collected maps or something. And that's what sort of struck me then, when he left them here. He said he'd be back to look at them later, that he didn't have time. "

"Later?"

"Well, we know what that meant," said Opa Nagl. "Maybe it's

funny now, but I was thinking at the time that your grandfather, the old bas–, well I thought he might come to the house here and accuse me of stealing them or something."

"Really?"

"Oh yes. That's the way he is, the way he was. God forgive me."

Felix said nothing, and for a few moments imagined his father driving off from the farmyard here in a hurry, waving as he went out of sight.

"Your dad left them here in a big plastic bag somewhere. He said he wanted to show them to me. He said he had some questions about them for me. Sometime."

"May God and his angels be good to him," said Felix's grandmother softly, in the quiet that followed.

Speckbauer's voice was barely audible now. Felix saw that his oma seemed to be distracted in her dishwashing.

Felix heard the receiver being returned to its cradle in the hall. Pages were turned, and Speckbauer cleared his throat. Then he was in the open doorway after a polite single tap on the door.

"Many thanks," he said. "Most helpful. I have left something under the phone to cover the call."

"Not necessary," said Opa Nagl, a little too quickly.

"Still," said Speckbauer with a show of reluctance.

"Really. Graz is nothing these days."

"It is farther, I am afraid Herr Nagl. Vienna. But you will see on your bill. A mobile phone is useless here. So much for progress. But again I thank you."

"Ah, Graz is not enough for you fellows," said Opa Nagl. "See Felix? Stick with these guys and you'll go places."

Speckbauer offered a noncommittal smile. Felix wondered if he'd pretend he wasn't picking up the signal from his wily, inquisitive opa.

"Vienna," Speckbauer murmured. "Big shots my eye. They can be as slow as anywhere else."

"Coffee?" from his grandmother.

"No thank you, Frau Nagl. But how kind. We must do a little work."

He nodded at Felix.

"If I may use the klo before we leave?"

Felix waited until he heard the door close. He stood slowly.

"Opa. Was Opa Kimmel much for 'mischief,' the kind you were on about there?"

Felix's grandfather made a grimace that was half bewilderment, half suspicion.

"You have strange questions in your head today."

"A good fellow then," said Felix.

"Don't kid yourself," said his opa sharply. "We kept out of his way. Such a–"

"Walter!"

Felix looked over at his oma. How rarely she said her husband's first name, he realized. A dish poised in her hand with suds sliding down, she stared at her husband.

"I know," said Felix's opa, with a dismissive gesture of his hand. "I know."

Water running in the pipes made Felix's grandmother turn back.

"Oops," she said then. "I forgot! I must put proper towels there."

She wiped her hands as she scurried across the floor, and down the hall.

"Tell me now," said Felix. "About Opa Kimmel."

"No way! We are related, Felix. It's not proper. Your oma is right, damn her. Of course I don't mean that. God help my clumsy words."

"Political?"

"Christ no – that's easy enough in Austria, boy. No. Don't you know what he was up to, the SS thing?"

"I know they found his age. Something about a fake name."

"But he was the man of the house at sixteen. His father?"

"Stalingrad, I heard."

"Ach," said Felix's grandfather. "So they say. No one knows. He disappeared, a casualty. God only knows."

"Did you not approve of the marriage or something?"

"At first, no. But then your father came out, and bit by bit, he won us over. So much different from your granddad. Life is strange that way. It was your oma, I say."

"Farming, then his own garage too. What else did he do for a living?"

"He had other things, I think. Christ, I'm like an old woman, gossiping! Ach, it's ancient crap."

"Tell me."

"Gossip? We heard rumours he was in business of course – gasoline, coffee, cigarettes. But that was what a lot of people did. And it died out."

"I only found out he was in the Gendarmerie recently."

"Hah. They'd take any fellow then. So many men hadn't come back. There were still 'operatives,' guys up in the hills or loading trucks with things they didn't own."

"That was it? All of it?"

Felix's grandfather narrowed his eyes and stared at the door to the hallway. There were voices, Felix's oma and Speckbauer, and the intonations of polite and elaborate demurrals and assurances and appreciation.

"I heard years ago that he used to run messages for people. He had one of those motorbikes. But he was up and down a lot with it. Someone, I forgot who, told me."

"To Viktring? The DP camp there?"

"I heard Viktring too," said his opa, but with a cautious look at Felix now. "And other camps. Hey, don't kid yourself now, not all those people in the camps after the war were refugees. Believe me."

"Nobody talks about that stuff here," Felix said after a pause. "Do they?"

His opa didn't seem to hear the question. His face lit up with some recollection.

"There were DP camps right in Graz too, the city?"

His grandfather stopped as though frozen.

"Sure there were," he said quietly. His eyes settled on Felix. "Other places too. Over in Carinthia as well."

"For refugees coming in from the east? The ones who had settled up the Danube and all that? Jugoslavian Germans, Swabians?"

His grandfather nodded.

"Guys on the losing side too," he murmured. "Nothing German to them at all."

"Grandfather Kimmel was smuggling too, right?"

His grandfather darted a quick glare at him.

"Don't make my sins worse, Felix."

"Sorry. I just never heard, never knew this."

"Are you crazy? Why would a parent burden the next generation with the load of the past? Who knows what he was doing. But the DPs were Yugos, Slovenians a lot of them. I only remember that fact because I couldn't figure out what the hell Slovenes were in a 'jail' for. Okay, not a jail but it didn't make sense."

"Like Slovenes who were Austrian maybe before the war?"

His grandfather waved his hand.

"All that history and empire crap. You see? There you are: history – confusion."

"But he made his rounds, visits to these places?"

"Just a rumour, Felix. I mean no one would ever ask him. Christ! Around here? Look. He was a sour, tough fellow. People kept out of his way. 'Mustard in his arse' they used to say. But his father had been taken from him. So, who can preach? Cruel stuff, this damned history."

"But it ended, that stuff."

"Did it? It wasn't just Slovenes in those camps you know. Maybe you were thinking, it's okay to help out, say, people who are from your own side. A sausage, a crust of bread, a letter? But there were others in those places who got by the Tommys. Yes, we were really relieved when the Russkis left and the Englander took

over. Christ, yes! But they were nice men. Naïve though – but
what am I saying? I've never been beyond Munich, or that lousy
'holiday' in Italy. Italy. You're a gypsy though, the zigeune of the
family. Are they all like that in England, all nice and fair with you,
but boring?"

"Food's bad," said Felix. "Everything costs a million."

"'Dull but decent,' eh? You're in no hurry to go back there."

Felix's mind was adrift now again, cluttered and sliding, turning back on itself. He watched his oma lift a statue of Mary from
the mantel, and dust it. She crossed herself after she replaced it. His
opa rolled his eyes, and leaned in. He gestured for Felix him to
come closer.

"Did you see that? Best to keep the church at arm's-length too,
I tell you. It's part of that mess too, you know – but don't tell your
oma I said that."

"Mess?"

"Ach," he whispered. "It's years since I heard anyone talk
about those times. Even then, it was just like a story, or a fairy-tale,
like the old ones up in the forest."

"What stories."

"I'll do you a big favour and say nothing. That is what I will
do."

"Nothing, about what?"

"Ach, you are like a badger, Felix. What I'm saying is just common sense. The leopard never loses his spots. That's all."

But his opa was getting up now, making the sighs and groans
he used as a way to escape conversation. From the hall Felix heard
Speckbauer thank Oma Nagl again. There were chuckles, and he
caught most of the words: hospitable, splendid, hearty.

"Just like your dad," Opa Nagl murmured, half listening to the
talk in the hall.

"They are?"

"You are."

"He talked about this?"

"Talked? He bent my ear, how many times. But it was much later. This was only shortly before, well, you know. I think people get to an age and they look over their shoulder, and they get curious. If you ask me, that's useless. I am a farmer. I get older, slower, stupider, happier. Then comes 'freedom.' I used to worry when I was a kid, about hell and that, but I know different now. God could be a woman. And a fine one too! That fear shit they threw at us, to keep us in line . . . a crime."

He made a sharp gesture as though lopping a branch.

"When I saw what they did back then . . . It all comes back to the same thing. Them and their stupid politics."

"Around here, Opa?"

"Here? I don't know. But the priest here is a nice fellow. Still, he must do what he is told. Tell you the truth, I feel sorry for him. And you know, he probably hasn't a clue himself. If he did, he doesn't believe any of it."

"Politics?"

"No, no. You know when rats leave a sinking ship? A rat line? Rats are infernal bastards. Christ, they're smarter than a room full of Jesuits. They'll eat through anything. They can climb like frigging monkeys too. Yes, the 'ratline.'"

"Rats," said Felix. "What do rats have to do with anything there?"

"Not those rats, boy – don't be a depp. It's people I'm talking about. The 'ratline' is how a lot of the bastards got away. You know who I mean – the higher-ups."

"I don't. Who?"

"Oh come on. The bad guys."

"The war?"

"Of course! But not just here in humble little Styria. I'm talking about ones from all over, and other guys, in the DP camps. Look, is Yugo a bad word in the city?"

Felix nodded.

"Okay. Well call them what you like. I am not referring to the ordinary ones, the ordinary decent folk. No – these were the higher-ups. What did they call them, the ones down there, the ones who loved Hitler? Ustashi? Yes! That's their name. But it wasn't just them hiding in those camps. It was some of the ones from close to Berlin, the really black bastards. They had their escape plans ready for years. Some of them went to places like South America, can you believe it?"

"Where did you learn all this, Opa?"

"I forget."

"You read it?"

"I said, I forget."

"But you know a lot."

"I forget a lot too. A happy man does both equally well."

There was something sharp in the retort. Then his grandfather's face softened.

"Look," he said. "There were 'ratlines' everywhere. Switzerland, Italy, here. Some of them went right to the Vatican, they say. That's what I'm talking about. Along with loot they'd stolen off Jews, that went with them, some of it anyway. That's never going to see the light of day, now, is it?"

"Up here?"

"Why not? You ask where I heard this. It was years ago. That's why I am ashamed to tell you. I went to Grade Six, Felix, but look at you, and Lisi – Uni. Fantastic."

"You heard rumours, gossip?"

"That's it. People back then believed anything. Remember, this was after the war, when one potato was a feast. People make up stories here in the hills, it's natural: a giant deer, or a wolf with red eyes, a giant, a mountain of gold – anything."

"Who could tell me?"

His grandfather leaned against the countertop and massaged his knuckles.

"Who?"

"Niemand," his grandfather said. "No one."

The door opened and Felix's grandmother came in giggling at something Speckbauer had said in a low voice.

"Such kindness, I will not forget this. Truly."

Felix's opa nodded at Speckbauer in return for his compliment. There was a sardonic glint in his eye, Felix noticed. He remembered his opa mock-grumbling about her falling for anything in uniform after Felix had shown them his Gendarmerie uniform.

"I have asked your wife's kind indulgence, Herr Nagl," Speckbauer said. "If I might leave Franzi here a little while so that Felix and I may continue with some business that needs attending to."

As though on cue, Franzi appeared by the window and nodded.

"I hope that is not an imposition."

"He'll be put to work."

"I'm sure that will be a joy to him, Herr Nagl."

THIRTY-SIX

SPECKBAUER REPEATED FELIX'S QUESTION.

"How long, you say?"

He had closed the passenger door and was trying to find a comfortable way to fit himself in the confines of the seat of Felix's Polo.

There was a smell of soap off him. He did not look like a man who had spent half the night in a ditch watching the comings and goings in the Nagl home.

"Exactly," said Felix, shielding his eyes from the morning sun. "How long before we get real help here?"

"Franzi can do lots," said Speckbauer.

"He can barely move."

"Not so. He takes relaxants if he has to do exertions."

"So, he'll be half-drugged, being a sleeping bodyguard for my grandparents?"

"Is he a bodyguard?"

"He better be. What if those guys, or that guy decides to come back."

"This is what we are working on, you and me. Why we're going to pay a proper visit to that pub in Weiz. This time we lean on him."

"Who?"

"I didn't tell you? Mr. Friendly who serves up the drinks. Remember him? Well he does me the occasional favour. Today, it will suit him to do one. Let's go."

Again Felix thought about the maps and photocopies he had put under the bed.

"Geh'ma jetzt," said Speckbauer with an edge of impatience. "Let's go – now."

"Give me a minute," said Felix. "I forgot something."

He made it upstairs with no more than a greeting from his grandmother. When he came back into the yard, Franzi and Speckbauer were standing by the back of the Passat. Speckbauer was rummaging in the trunk. When Franzi saw Felix, he said something and held the lid down halfway. Something that Speckbauer was doing with the contents of the trunk stopped Franz closing it anymore.

"Jesus, Franzi!" Speckbauer said, emerging from under the trunk-lid.

Felix saw two grey sleeveless jackets over an open container, or case. They were Kevlar vests, the patrol-duty cut that he had trained in.

Speckbauer stood upright slowly. He held the trunk lid and looked at Felix.

"Our toy box," he said.

Felix didn't want to look surprised.

"We take things with us," said Speckbauer.

The metal box Felix had seen yesterday was open. Felix recognized the AUG 88 lying on one side, with its stock folded.

"You carry that stuff?"

"'Stuff'?"

"An assault rifle," said Felix. "The same one we trained on in the Service."

"So," said Speckbauer.

"We lock them behind two doors at the post. But you, in the trunk of a car . . . ?"

"Okay," said Speckbauer. "It looks serious, doesn't it? Don't go academic on me. Bad police, bad police state, etc. We have to move on this thing."

There were also electronics of some kind. They seemed to be bolted or attached to the bottom of the container.

"In case we get lost," said Speckbauer.

"GPS?"

"Yes."

Speckbauer let the trunk-lid up, leaned into the trunk again, and drew out the submachine gun.

"Franzi," he said, but did not turn toward either of them. "Check, safety, and then put the damned thing back on, will you? And quit arguing. The operation is ongoing. And for the love of Christ and his suffering Mother, stick your jacket over it."

"It's going to be hot," said Franzi. "It'll give me a rash. The Glock is enough."

"You are like a kid. Give me the pistol and put the damn thing on."

Slowly Franzi took off his nylon Adidas jacket. He checked the clasps for the belt of the gun, undid one, and laid the submachine gun on the floor of the boot. Speckbauer twisted the safety on it several times. He pulled out and returned the stock twice. He took a furtive look over the lid of the trunk and motioned to Franzi. Franzi lifted his right arm. The skin on his upper arm was grey and pink, and lines like a map were revealed when his shirt sleeve slid back over his wrists. Speckbauer draped the belt over Franzi's shoulder, and then held up his jacket. Felix heard Franzi grunt as he reached for the second arm of his jacket.

"Help him, will you? He is like a puppet, a stubborn puppet."

Speckbauer was speaking to him. Felix put down the bag and helped Franz guide his arm slowly down the sleeve hole.

Franzi adjusted how the gun hung under his arm. Speckbauer held up two magazines. He was muttering to himself, his upper body still bent over the lip of the trunk.

"Okay," said Franzi. "Three o'clock is the deal."

"What deal?" Felix said.

"Three it is," said Speckbauer. He fingered a keypad and then closed the lid on the box. He tested it after a small wirp came from somewhere inside.

"What deal?" Felix repeated.

Nobody answered him. Speckbauer tested the lid to the box to see it had caught on something, and was really locked. His face was flushed when he stood up.

"Look, I'm not some clown that just tags along to run errands for you."

"Nobody said you were. It was Franzi I was referring to as the idiot."

"Why are we going in my car?"

"Because it'll show you have left."

"Show who? You think the house is being watched?"

"I don't know. But anyone passing can see a car parked here. That's on purpose."

"The police car here?"

"Is it a police car? It's a car that Franzi may need. We may have to change our approach later in the day."

"My grandparents have a clue what's going on."

"They have a guest. Isn't that enough? A friend of their beloved grandson."

"If they see the AUG he's carrying–"

"Franzi will not be displaying it. Now calm down. What's with the bag anyway? Let's go. Komm."

Without any will on his part, Felix found himself following him across the yard. His anger swirled around the leaden, crushing feeling that had already settled on him. It was one of those middle-of-the-night-wake-up-for-no-reason feelings he remembered all the way back to childhood, when for a while he didn't know if he was really awake.

Speckbauer was already pulling the passenger door closed behind him. The Polo squeaked as Speckbauer wriggled about trying to get the safety belt organized.

Felix stood by the driver's side and looked back at the house. Franzi was strolling toward the kitchen door, walking in that careful stiff way, moving his right arm in small arcs. The morning sun had reached the geraniums in the window boxes now, and the stained wood looked sharp and darker in the light. Felix thought of what Giuliana would be doing now. She'd be awake, maybe brooding what to do finally with her stupid boyfriend. The last straw, this one lousy week's holiday, the precious time they'd waited a whole long winter for: screwed.

Speckbauer was tapping on the window. Felix threw the bag in the back seat and sat in behind the wheel.

"Any maps in this shitbox of yours?" said Speckbauer, craning to see some that had slid onto the floor from the bag. "Do we need them?"

THIRTY-SEVEN

THEY WERE PULLING INTO A DECENT PARKING SPOT IN WEIZ, close to the town hall at the top end of the old hauplatz, within 20 minutes. Speckbauer was out quickly. He bought a two-hour ticket from the machine.

"It'll be a nice surprise," he said, and slammed his door hard. "For Mr. Smiley."

Felix fell into step beside him. The streets were already busy. Small groups of kids were making their way along by the shops toward school. A pasty-faced assistant was sluicing the leftovers of a bucket of disinfectant along the sidewalk by the door to the butcher's. The smell from a bakery began to overcome the faint dieselly tang as they walked along. A man brushing in the doorway greeted them.

"He's not a fool," Speckbauer said. "But if I think he's spinning me one . . . "

Felix tried to remember what 'Mr. Smiley' looked like. Designer stubble, yes, and white shirt, open two buttons. An earring too?

"Here we go," said Speckbauer. "His pad."

He turned down a lane with cars parked tight to the walls of the houses. After a dozen steps he slowed and looked up at a first floor window. The blinds were drawn.

"Come here," he said to Felix and stepped into an alcove. "Watch this."

He took out his phone and began keying through a list.

Felix watched the traffic passing the mouth of the laneway while they waited for the call to go through. Then Speckbauer began speaking.

"Kurt? This is your friend from Graz. I need your expertise. I'm on the road now. Concerning that matter up in the hills recently? I'll be there in fifteen, okay?"

He closed the phone and leaned out to take a look up at the window again.

"Answering machine."

"Kurt is actually the boss in that pub?"

"Kurt, yeah. Krutzitürken Kurt, I call him. 'Mr. Smiley.' He thinks if he smiles a lot, people will trust him. He spent a lot of money on those teeth. He had to I guess after, well – he's proud of them."

"He's an informer?"

"'An informer?' I am not the Gestapo, for Christ's sake. He is a 'helper.'"

"He does it voluntarily?"

"No. Kurt's a low-life. But he'd swear otherwise. Was he nice to you yesterday?"

"As a matter of fact he was."

"Huh. He made you the minute you walked in there. He's good at that. But he's like the rest of his kind. No conscience."

Speckbauer looked at his watch.

"Three minutes, if my brain is working today. Bet me, okay?"

"What is that?"

"Kurt doesn't want trouble. Like any businessman he wants to be left alone with his interests. His housewives, and his salesmen and his coke and his operations."

"He's actually a criminal?"

"Well yes, a criminal. Log on when you get back to work, and slap in his name into an EKIS search. You could light up your house by what shows up on the screen."

"And he runs a pub?"

"Why can't he run a pub? This is a democracy."

"And carries on with criminal operations?"

"Criminal – well, textbook, yes: I suppose. You think it's just for a beer you go into his place? People get bored, you know. They want excitement. They want thrills."

"He's not arrested?"

"Why should I do that? Now what use – oh shit. What did I tell you?"

Speckbauer pressed his back against the wooden door. The footsteps were hurried, almost skipping. He waited until the footsteps came closer.

Felix couldn't help but smile. Kurt actually jumped when Speckbauer stepped out into the laneway.

"You stupid donkey," said Speckbauer. "I think you're not even awake."

Kurt stopped rolling his eyes and swearing.

"Who is this one?"

"My colleague."

"I knew it. I've seen him. Jesus!"

His chest was still heaving from the fright. His eyes kept darting around, to the traffic passing the mouth of the laneway from Speckbauer to Felix.

"Schweineri Kurt, but you're hyper. What has you out here? Jogging?"

"I have to go on a message."

"No doubt. Heading down to Piran again, maybe? Pluck a few early birds, some German hippies maybe?"

Felix tried to place Piran on a map in his head. An old town on the Adriatic, he remembered. Old buildings, nice walks, lots of stone, and not far. It was maybe four hours' drive, he guessed, and it was still in Slovenia.

"Hell no."

"Kurt likes to offer his time to ladies visiting Piran and the like. Bored women from Germany are his focus. Women of a certain age, and income, of course."

"What's the big deal, for Christ's sake," said Kurt. "We all have our thing. Have dummies in Brussels passed a law saying it's illegal to have fun now?"

"Brussels? Is that where you're heading now?"

"Are you crazy?"

"We need your advice, Kurt."

"I don't know about that."

"What do you mean, you don't know? You treat your answering machine like a grenade with the pin pulled."

"Christ man it's early! I barely got to bed. Why are you hassling me?"

"I phone you. Next thing you're out of your place like a shit off a shovel. And your eyes like saucers. Did you pee the bed too? Calm down."

Kurt took in deep breaths. He seemed momentarily lost for words.

"I can't help you," he said then. "I don't know anything."

"What's your mother's birthday then? Do you know that?"

"Look. I don't want to talk."

"You want to run."

"Look, I've got to go."

"Kurt. Don't be an arschloch. I don't want to do all the paper-work."

"Go ahead. I don't care."

Felix eyed Speckbauer for any sign of what he'd do next.

"Calm down, Kurt. How can we protect you if you get like this?"

"Protect me?" said Kurt. He turned wide-eyed to Felix.

"Do you have to work with this guy?"

"Kurt," Speckbauer said. "This isn't TV. You can't switch off the channel. These guys aren't just moving bad paper, or Ex, or coke, or whatever. So we need to talk. Really. Understand?"

Kurt's eyelid twitched.

"You know what I'm talking about," said Speckbauer. "Come

on, let's get off the street here at least. Coffee, some buns and cheese – whatever you want, around the corner. Here, I'll get you a bag to put over your head."

"That's not funny."

"What's the matter? It'll be quick — boom boom. You won't even see it coming."

"You are a sick bastard."

"You've been talking to my ex? Come, Kurt. You're awake now. Be sensible."

Kurt's tone changed.

"Jesus, Speck," he said, almost plaintively. "This is . . . This is really shitty."

"I know, I know, Kurt. I'll leave you alone after this."

Kurt shook his head slowly and said something, and did a half-turn and shook his head again. For several moments he stood frozen, staring at the cobblestones by his feet while he massaged the back of his neck.

Speckbauer nodded and Felix looked toward the traffic. Felix heard him whisper to Kurt as he headed for the street. When he got to the street, he turned. Kurt was walking with Speckbauer toward him.

Speckbauer chose a spot he seemed to know already. There was an old man reading the local newspaper near the door. Speckbauer had to duck as he made his way into a booth at the back, where one of the arches came down to the wall above the wooden partitions.

Kurt's hands were shaking, even with the coffee. He dabbed a bit of the bun into the cup and put it in his mouth like it was medicine.

"I just don't," he muttered to Speckbauer. "There's the usual bunch coming and going. They have money. They have hip clothes, watches, mobiles. I don't see them flashing car keys a lot."

"Come on," said Speckbauer, sucking foam off his moustache. "The boys out here still do that, to get the girls keen: the Beemer key ring, but a VW parked outside?"

"Who knows? These guys though, they never get pushy. Always polite. And they're not chasing girls, that I can see."

"What? The illegals come to you because they think it's a gay bar?"

"Shit, no. I'm just saying."

"You're a friendly guy, Kurt. What do they tell you?"

"Nothing," Kurt said. He eyed Felix.

"You were in the other day," he said. "It was early, wasn't it? Mr. My-Wife-Is-A-Bitch, and a crappy factory job here."

"Quit your crying Kurt. You made him right away."

"There were guys at the patio there, and I hear them talking, in their own language. And I says to myself, well they're a new bunch of illegals. It won't take long before Speck sends another one of his hounds in for a look."

"Hounds? Really."

"What else can I call them?"

"My colleague's name is Felix. So try cats, okay? Latin: Felis, cat? Got that?"

"Who speaks Latin? I don't."

"What language were they speaking, that bunch?"

"Not German, that's what. Not even farmer German from, Christ, up in the woods in . . . whatever."

"St. Kristoff am Offenegg."

"If you say so."

"So tell me what's different, Kurt."

"About what?"

"You don't usually run like a fucking greyhound when I pay a visit. Why now?"

Felix tried not to look over at Speckbauer. He wondered again how the man could hide his anger so well.

"It's a feeling, that's all I know."

"A feeling? I'll give you a feeling."

"No. Like I was saying. There's no party to those guys. They're looking around, they're not out for a good time. And I don't see the likes of them banging hammers or sweeping floors like the illegals you hear about."

"Do they hang around?"

"There's another thing. They don't. It's like they're sampling or something. But what the hell, I'm not running a psychotherapy place."

"Only a pub, with 'extras.'"

Kurt made a grimace of disdain.

"Don't freak, Kurt. I'm not here to complain about idiots who want to put stuff in their noses, or roll it up and spend the next six hours giggling and falling over."

"Really."

"Really. But tell me: Ex?"

Kurt nodded.

"A lot? More than last time we talked?"

"No. But I swear nothing goes on inside the place. Never did."

Speckbauer looked down into his cup, made a *hnhh* sound at the remains of the froth and coffee there and then shot a glance at Felix.

"You're a sophisticate. You've tried Ecstasy, haven't you?" Felix shook his head.

"Well if you haven't, here's the man to put you in the way of it."

"Oh for Christ's sake."

"Just shut up complaining, Kurt, will you? Tell me more about the new faces."

"What faces would you like?"

"New ones. What you're supposed to be noticing."

Kurt looked off into the middle distance.

"Nothing," he said. "Nothing comes to mind."

"Ausländers, Kurt. Tschuschen. Asylants. Call them what you want. But think."

"Look, why don't you bust some of the factories down there near the autobahn, down in Gleisdorf, huh? Come on, you know they have guys coming in off the books. Cleaners, night stuff, and that? I only see guys with enough money to come up here."

"A better quality of gangster?"

"Who knows. You think everyone with an accent is a crook?" Speckbauer sighed.

"A philosopher now. Really don't need that. Come on now, your sixth sense tells you something. You've never tried to make a run for it on me before."

"I get fed up with this. You put too much pressure on me. I could run myself into a lot of trouble if I tried every single thing you wanted. And you wouldn't give a shit, would you? You'd use some-one else, just move on to the next one and suck their blood."

At this he exchanged a hurried look with Felix. Speckbauer shifted slightly in his chair.

"You're worried, Kurt," he said. "Moaning more than usual, a lot more. We need to review your situation. Maybe you're trying to cover up stuff. Schleich problems?"

"The black market? I swear, now. There's no black market to speak of in this town."

"Something is different with your reaction. Hey, are you high?"

"Fuck off."

"Coming down off something? Irritable?"

Kurt looked away.

"Something specific," Speckabuer went on. "Come on. This 'feeling.' It's not just paranoia, or dope, is it?"

"Give me a break."

"I'll give you a break all right. How about I get the KD to pay you a visit? My fine colleagues there on Strassgangerstrasse, in Graz. That's what I'll do. And a premises search. The lab will come up with something."

"I don't have anything!"

"Except fear, and a 'feeling.'"

Felix was beginning to feel a faint nausea. Kurt's bloodshot eyes, his sighs of exasperation that had a whiny edge to them now, and the stale body odour that had began to emanate from him, all mixed with Felix's own feeling that he was being dirtied by just being here in part of Speckbauer's dismal world.

"Ok, it's nothing," said Kurt then. "Maybe nothing. But Stephi, she's on weekday evenings, Stephi and I were talking. Stephi's lazy, all right? But when I lay it on the line, she's good. I just have to keep going at her."

"Excuse me, but where is this going?"

"Wait," said Kurt. "I'm coming to it. She was complaining about tips and conditions. As if she's Mausi Lugner or somebody else on that stupid show. Anyway. She gets about, Stephi does. She's in a restaurant the other day gossiping with one of the trolls she hangs out with. You know the type? The bottle blonde pushing forty, the one who never got over the eighties look? The hubby's a fat bastard, the kids are brats . . . ? Plenty of them in Weiz. But Stephi sees a guy talking to the manager there. 'Heck, that guy was in the pub,' she thinks. Apparently he's quite a hunk."

"A hunk?"

"Come on," said Kurt and made a dismissive wave. "She plays the field, Stephi. She has an eye for the well-dressed guy."

"Well what about him?"

"The guy spoke with an accent – but good German. Well put together, not factory floor. More the office type, says Stephi, 'professional, dressed nice, polite.' He'd had a beer the night before. He's the guy with the pictures, she said to herself."

"Pictures?"

"I'm getting to that. Turns out the guy showed Stephi a photo of someone, asked her if she'd seen him. She knew he wasn't a copper but he had the look of one. He's doing the same routine the next day in the konditorei. Like, 'Have you seen this guy?'"

"What guy?"

"How would I know?"

"This guy, tell me more. Well dressed? Speaks German well, with an accent?"

"That's it. Talk to her – oh Christ, wait. She went up to Munich to see her stepfather or something. The bitch."

Speckbauer rolled his eyes.

"Got a number for her? Her mobile?"

"She doesn't use one, she says. I doubt that, though. Her 'step-father' probably looks different than what I'd guess an old geezer looks like. If you know what I mean."

"Nudge nudge, wink wink," Speckbauer muttered and drew out a small notepad.

"Surname?"

"Giesl. Stephi Giesl. She has a place behind the Billa there, the supermarket."

"Married, family?"

"Are you kidding? She had a steady. She has 'visitors,' I believe."

"And she's in Munich?"

"On her way, anyway."

"When did she decide that?"

"Well guess what, and thanks for asking. That's why I am so pissed here. Yesterday afternoon she tells me. I'm coming in for the evening shift. Huh. I should have just fired her, you know? Zip. And she thinks I am an idiot, that's what gets to me. First she mentions this guy, then bumping into him again, and then – suddenly she has to go visit her 'ailing stepfather' in Munich."

"She doesn't have an ailing stepfather?"

"Christ, how do I know? The rules these days, you can't ask or say a damned thing. You know that, right?"

Speckbauer looked down at the small notepad. Felix returned Kurt's guileless look.

"Stephi's from where?" Speckbauer asked.

"She's from Weiz, born and bred."

"Her family here?"

"Uh-uh. It busted up years ago. She has as sister, over in Carinthia, I think."

"She knows the area, though."

"I suppose."

"Friends, people she's in touch with?"

Kurt shrugged.

Speckbauer gave him a glare.

"Wait here will you," he said to Felix. "So Kurt doesn't go for another jog. I want to make a call."

He looked down at the display on his mobile and scowled. Then he slid out of the booth and went out the door to the street. There was a laneway to the side of the restaurant, Felix remembered.

Kurt was rubbing his bottom lip slowly with his thumbnail. Speckbauer's departure seemed to have calmed him a little. He kept staring across the table at Felix.

"Will you quit that?"

"Am I being rude? Sorry. I just waited to see what a fool looked like."

"Are you trying to be an idiot with me?"

"How long are you a copper?"

"Long enough. Shut up, why don't you."

"Well that's a change. The other wants me to talk, but you say shut up."

Felix watched a mother with a pram wait for a traffic light.

"He'll toss you on the pile eventually," said Kurt. "You know?"

When Felix made no reply, he went on.

"You'll graduate. But you'll be okay. I mean, what's he got on you, except your own – I better be careful, I suppose – your own youth."

"And you?" Felix murmured, watching the cars slowing now. "You go back to jail or something nice like that?"

"Who knows? No doubt he'll make a few phone calls. That's his specialty. Have you met his ghost?"

A van braked hard in the street outside. The woman pushing the pram hesitated. She gave the driver a hard look, and then continued pushing the pram across.

"The spook. He freaks me out. Fritz, what's his name, Hans?"

"Franz."

"So you do know him. Looks like the devil sent him back up?"

The light changed. Two elderly women came in the door. One was shaped like a question mark, and wore the green and grey loden. They were greeted and shown a table. Felix heard the hissing of the espresso machine pumping. He rubbed at his eyes.

"You know, it's about time I got out of this place anyway," said Kurt. "Sure, there's business. But the crowd is different in the last few years. Younger? Maybe I can't keep up anymore."

Felix did not turn away from the window. Outside on the pavement, the woman reached into the pram, and smiling, began to lift out her baby. An older woman who had stopped and greeted her was making those goo-goo sounds that babies seemingly liked.

"You feel sorry for me there, Mister Gendarme?"

"Shut up," said Felix, without turning from the window.

As the baby was lifted from the pram, Felix saw that it had been crying. He watched the older woman start a little pantomime to distract it. The mom undid the baby's hat. The short hair was orange and the sun caught it as the hat came off. The mother gently bobbed the redhead in her arms to soothe it.

"Oh you're going to do well," he heard Kurt mutter. "You're an arschloch to begin with."

Felix turned toward Kurt. He took into the pouchy, bleary eyes. Under his stubble the sallow skin lay like butter gone bad.

"You ever see a big red-headed fellow in your pub?"

"A red-headed guy? I don't look at their hair, especially a guy. What, am I weird or something?"

"Hair like that over there," said Felix. He watched Kurt squint through the sun filled window toward the street.

"Like that little one's? You don't see that often, do you. Maybe he'll get a job as a clown when he grows up. Is that what you mean, have I seen any clowns in the stübe?"

Felix kept up his stare.

"This is 'weird question day'?" Kurt added. "Why would I bother to remember something like that?"

"Because it's out of the ordinary. Think of a big guy, a beard to go with it."

"A beard? Like some big Kris Kringle?"

"A big fellow, like I said."

Kurt's eyes slipped out of focus. After a few moments a wry expression settled on his face. He shook his head and then began to slowly rub his eyes, and then his whole face with his hands. He stopped abruptly and let down his hands.

"Well hell," he said and smiled. "Funny how the mind works. 'Red hair.' 'Guy.' None of that means anything at first. But there was a big fellow coming in here, to the pub, every now and then. Stephi would know him, yes – she had a laugh with him. Big, yes. But a beard? I don't know about that."

"But a local guy? From the area, right?"

"Who knows? But he had a helmet – yes. He looked like one of those Hells Angels fellows that you see on the TV."

"And Stephi . . . ?"

"Oh she'd have an eye for the likes of him. Yes, talk to her. Speck is probably doing a big thing for her right now. Beats me, truly."

"Is there a name on this guy?"

"I don't know. But she called him something, if I remember. No. Wait: something to do with how he looked. Ah, shit, I forget."

"Come on. 'Giant?' 'Motorbike man'?"

"You're funny."

"Hells Angel?"

"This is like I am drunk, this game. Maybe I just dreamed you and Speck have been talking to me, asking me weird questions. And now, this guess-a-word?"

He lifted his hand to his forehead.

"Maybe I have a fever."

Then his face froze and he stared at a point just over Felix's head.

"Wait! 'Foxy,' I think. Yes? Ah Christ, Stephi talks so much I have to ignore her a lot of the time. But she was laughing about it. 'Foxy.' I think. Who knows, but . . . ?"

He put the knuckles of both hands together and winked.

"No real name? Just to do with red hair?"

Kurt sat back with a look of resigned understanding.

"Really," he said. "You guys are living on a different planet."

"What about Stephi?" Speckbauer asked as he slipped back into the booth.

"What about her?"

"Does she like 'adventures,' say? How she might leave for a couple of days with a new flame?"

"Hmm. A pavement hostess, you're trying to say?"

"Did I say prostitute? No. I said 'adventure.'"

"Well yes, if you like," said Kurt. "She is a person like that. And if she weren't so damn good with the frigging spenders who keep me in business, well I'd have let her go on a permanent 'adventure' a long time ago."

THIRTY-EIGHT

THE STREETS AND LANES OF WEIZ HAD BEEN TAKEN OVER BY the mid-morning people, as Felix had begun to think of them when he was – actually wasn't – attending his lectures back in Graz. The school would not break for lunch for an hour yet. Pensioners took their time, many of them meeting and greeting, speaking in the melodious accent that expressed politeness and a circumspect kind of humour. There were plenty of shops in Weiz, plenty of mothers and infants and babies, steady streams of cars, new most of them.

The clouds were staying away and leaving a postcard sky above the town. The winter that had lingered here until recently seemed a distant, impossible event that had passed quickly, not the dreary, endless months that had lain over the place. The blossoms were out all over the backyard orchards. From somewhere over the next street were the sounds of a pneumatic drill, and the episodic whine and gnarl of saws, followed by the taps of at least two hammers and an occasional yell. A tractor turned into the car park for the super-market.

Speckbauer was trying to get a glimpse through the window blinds on Stephi's apartment. He pushed the buzzer again, and held his head close to the door.

"It's working, all right."

Felix's thoughts kept returning to the maps that now lay in that bag on the floor of his car. His father must have talked to Opa Kimmel when he took, or borrowed, the maps at least. And what had the old man told him?

"Phone her number again," said Speckbauer.

Felix held up the piece of paper on which Speckbauer had taken Stephi's number from Kurt. Six rings, and again, nothing.

"It's a bullshit number," said Speckbauer. "'I'm sure of it.'" He mimicked Kurt.

"'I have to phone her a lot 'cause she's late.'"

"Her car maybe?" suggested Felix.

"Yeah, yeah. A Mazda 131. Look, take a stroll around there, see if it's parked, okay? I'm going to make some calls here, see if I can move this damn Stephi."

"Blue?"

"Blue-green," said Speckbauer. "Old and crappy. Maybe she parks it away from here for vandals or something? Five, ten minutes. I'll be here, okay?"

Felix began with the car park for the Billa. He threaded his way through the shoppers' cars, standing on tiptoe to see over a row, and tried to remember which lanes led off the streets nearby. Maybe the car was being repaired?

He began to imagine this Stephi, cruising around somewhere, her arm dangling out the window and the blonde hair flying about, part of her 'presentation' to snare her date. No, he thought then: Speckbauer was right. If the guy was as sharp as Kurt had said, he'd have his own wheels. They'd hardly be an old box like a Mazda 131.

His thoughts only grew stronger, and his attention on the cars kept on wavering. He had to make an effort to notice specifics. He imagined his father behind the wheel, whistling those stupid old waltzes and polkas, tapping the beat on the wheel: then the instant when he knew he couldn't avoid the truck. Again, his father, studying the maps he had gotten from his own father's house. Wondering, noting the marks on them, trying to solve some puzzle that had him covering the back roads for weeks, or even longer, before the accident.

The word echoed again in Felix's mind. He stopped even trying to spot the makes on the row of cars ahead. Instead of the car park and the door to the supermarket, now he saw the steep sides of the klamm where his father's car had been crushed, and the wooden taferl just inside the barrier wall. The Association wanted to replace it with a stone effort, a statue of St. Christopher, with the plaque under it. Felix's mother did not.

Accident. It felt like something had been spinning too fast in his mind but had now come loose, shredding his thoughts. He could sleep for a week, he realized. With Giuliana. And with all the bickering and digs past and forgotten, never to return. And somewhere far from here, far from Stefansdorf, and most of all far from anywhere Speckbauer was ever likely to turn up.

There had to be vacancies when the amalgamation happened. He could even get a spot up near Salzburg, maybe, where he and Giuliana could make a fresh start there. Into his mind now came the view from the high mountain paths over Kitzbüehl, those twisting bike trails, and the immense purple mountains across the valleys so far below. So high, your breathing was up the minute you got on the bike, even.

The doors of the Billa slid open. An old woman emerged, pushing her trolley feebly. Her head was over at an angle, and she stopped to look around for a car. Had she forgotten where she was? He should be helping the old girl, real work, instead of this cat and mouse game. But she began to move, sideways like a ship drifting, and as he watched her, his thoughts began sliding away again.

He was startled out of his blank daydream by words that suddenly formed in his head. A police matter, the maps were a police matter. What voice was in his head saying that, his police training, the so-called logical part of his brain? But there was something to that, he remembered now. It had been a joke at the Gendarmerie college right from when they had heard it used in the classes. 'A police matter' was the big, heavy phrase you had to learn to deploy if citizens got whiny, or uncooperative, or pissy. It was doubtless supposed to trigger some serious Austrian obedience reflex?

Again he looked back toward the laneway leading to where

Speckbauer was on the phone still, scheming no doubt, while he kept a vigil for this Stephi. He should go to the car and bring the maps to Speckbauer and explain.

Then Felix swore under his breath. For what, he thought: so Speckbauer could worm his way like a spreading rot further into his family?

The old woman and her trolley had changed direction. She greeted him cautiously, in a thin reedy voice. Something about the moment – the anxious look on the old woman's face, his tired, crazed mind just giving up, the thought of how simple things should be with Giuliana – something scattered Felix's confusion then.

"Grüss," he called back to her, gently, and smiled. He had decided something.

He turned his back to the lane where Speckbauer's Passat was parked, and he opened his phone. He thumbed through to Gebhart's mobile. For those few seconds before Gebhart's voice came on, Felix looked over the rooftops at the green hilltops to the north and west. His mind was up by the streams that still ran hard over the rocky beds up there, and on to where the snow still lay on the higher mountains behind, like sheets blown off a clothesline into the shade under trees where the sun could not yet reach.

THIRTY-NINE

"ZERO," SAID SPECKBAUER.

He took a last look at the door to the apartment.

"Zero. You think she'd leave a key in some obvious spot, like any other citizen."

"What now?"

Speckbauer looked at him.

"You're keen, now, are you? Well that's good. Okay, I'm expecting a call."

"Concerning Stephi Giesl?"

"She has some paper on her. I gave her a scan. EKIS shows her living an interesting life some years ago. Yes, she has her very own Strafregister."

"Fingerprints? What were her crimes?"

"Her adventures were pretty well the same as Kurt's. Isn't that a coincidence? Well, except for a few items. Mainly her interest in drugs. Forging signatures on cheques is a bit primitive, I have to say."

"How long ago?"

"Seven years. But that doesn't mean it stopped, does it."

Speckbauer let his gaze travel around the car park.

"I am hoping . . . " Felix began.

Speckbauer turned to him, with the now-familiar combination of cynicism and a cautious geniality.

". . . to get a bit of personal time," said Felix.

"You wish to absent yourself?"

Felix looked blankly back, and he nodded.

"Personal matters, I imagine?"

"Exactly. But perhaps I can be of assistance at a later time."

"Be of assistance, eh – well that would be good."

Felix was sure he was hearing sarcasm now but yet again Speckbauer's easy smile confused him. Speckbauer turned back to his survey.

"Yes," he said, "It'll take time. It always does."

"I will drop you back at my grandparents' place then?"

"You will," Speckbauer replied, slowly and reflectively. "Thank you. By the way, have we resolved this concern you had earlier? Your grandparents, their safety?"

"I think so. Yes, I've been thinking about what you said."

"You are very protective of them."

Felix said nothing. Speckbauer seemed to shake himself free of some preoccupation.

"Family indeed. Family carries us on the road of life. Isn't that the expression? The parents carry the baby, and then the baby carries the parent."

Felix nodded. Speckbauer widened his eyes. Then he shook his head, as though to clear it of nonsense.

"Too much coffee," he said. "And this beautiful corner of Austria has had an effect on me. No doubt that's obvious enough."

"Sometimes."

"Okay," said Speckbauer. "I hear you. You want some time to yourself this day."

Felix started up the Polo. He waited for Speckbauer to wrestle his way into the seat belt. While he waited, he imagined that at this same time Sepp Gebhart, a puzzled but protective Gebhart, would be halfway along the road to St. Kristoff to see what the hell his colleague Kimmel's strange request in that phone call really meant.

✠

It was a tough act back at his grandparents' house. Felix heard an irony in everything Speckbauer said now. Even Franzi's tinted glasses now seemed to mask more accusing, or more suspicious eyes.

Felix's grandmother was soon over her disappointment that Felix and his fine colleagues were not able to delay for a lunch – a proper farmer's meal. Speckbauer was at his most expansive, and his face held an expression of gentle regret and solicitude.

"Another time you must, then," Oma Nagl rallied.

As Felix expected, she had a master back-up plan. He was not surprised to see the tart appearing, and then being displayed before being covered in foil and placed in a plastic bag. The sausage was almost too much for master actor Speckbauer. There was some winking and a guffaw exchanged between Speckbauer and Opa Nagl when Felix's grandfather mentioned something about a secret ingredient in this home-made sausage that one of his neighbours made every year.

Ritual protestations followed about paying a proper price for something that in the city would be a great and treasured delicacy. Refusals were loud and firm. Speckbauer was ready with keen protests, even slipping in the accented expressions that Felix had thought were only for Styrians up here in the hills. 'The baker must at least have his flour!' 'How can there be a beautiful house without paying for good timber?!' All pertained to Speckbauer needing to know both his grandparents' favourite tipples.

It was left to Felix to intervene. He mentioned a brandy, and waited out his grandfather's protests. And then, finally, the two policemen were sitting in the Passat. With his grandparents waving and even calling out, they drove off, but not before Speckbauer mimicked a phone to his ear while nodding at Felix.

"Such an interesting fellow," said Oma Nagl. "What he knows about plants and crops, and farming. For a policeman, too."

Felix watched the Passat coast over the small rise before it gained the road proper.

"And he learned it all late enough," she said and made a final wave.

"After his injury."

"Did he tell you about it?"

"My God," said his oma and put her knuckles to her breast as though in prayer.

"That husband I have. He blunders into everything, like a child. He has no shame. 'What happened to you?' he says, right out of the blue. Franzi had been telling us about wrens, can you imagine?"

"It was obvious," his grandfather interrupted. "People are silly. Naturally I was curious. Wouldn't anyone be? So I asked."

"You should have said nothing."

"Why? People must talk. It is healthy."

Felix's grandmother leaned to one side.

"There they go, anyway."

"I will be back," said Felix.

"My God but you have a crazy life, kid. Running about . . . !"

"I will phone you."

"No need. We're not going anywhere."

"Just in case."

His grandfather made a face at him.

"But if anyone is looking for me, tell them I have gone. It doesn't matter who, even if they say they're friends."

His grandfather made a shushing sound. Then he scratched his head and said something about 'the world.'"

His grandmother held him at arm's-length. She fixed him with a keen stare.

"Are you in trouble?"

"No, Oma."

"Really?"

"Truly. I'm just tired. Really tired."

"You would tell me, eh? Your mother is faraway, so you come to me, right?"

"Of course."

"She's with that plank Edelbacher," his grandfather muttered.

"Well let's hope that 'plank' doesn't have as many knots in it as my 'plank'!"

Felix heard his grandfather tut-tut in that clicking, humorous way that had been the hallmark of this couple since he could remember. He thought again about asking his grandfather to get the hunting rifle out. He'd tell him he wanted to go after rabbits or something. But it'd never work. His opa would know something wasn't right.

He searched the fields and hedges as he made his way to his car. He opened the bonnet to check for oil, and to make sure the stupid fan belt wasn't about to shred like it had in Graz traffic last October. He scanned the bushes and the shadows where the forests began. Somehow they looked even darker now with the full sun closing on its height. Everything looked near, as though it had moved in toward the farm while no one was looking. A trick of light, or shadow, he had to decide, probably his own half-addled brain most of all.

He checked his phone for battery. He'd meet Gebhart by the church. Felix had been wondering again if he should check on Fuch's place, even a drive-by, on his way to his grandfather's. No, he decided: just go straight to the old man. After all, that was why he had gotten Gebhart into this now.

He stopped when he had reached the road and looked for any sign of the Passat. He half expected to see Franzi, gnome-like, sitting on the bank watching him from behind the two dark insect-eye lenses that protected his eyes from the light of day.

He turned off the engine for 10 seconds, and listened, but heard only the birds, and his own heart beating faster now.

FORTY

GEBHART SAID NOTHING, BUT MERELY WAITED FOR FELIX TO finish. He wore that look of vague interest that Felix had learned was a screen for something else.

"So there," he said to Gebhart when he had finished. "That's about the only way I can describe it."

Gebhart nodded his head slowly, as though something had happened as he had predicted, or didn't understand and didn't want to try. He looked out through the gap in the trees over the forestry road into where they had driven after leaving from the village. Felix had backed the Polo in at speed. It sank to the rims almost immediately. Gebhart, standing by his own car, made no comment.

"I didn't know you smoked," said Felix.

"I don't. Just some days. And today is such a day."

Felix looked down at the tracks his shoes had made in the carpet of brown pine needles.

"Well I think you're stuck," said Gebhart.

"That's why I phoned you. I swear to God I'm not making this up."

Gebhart drew on the cigarette and grimaced before exhaling. He nodded toward the Polo.

"The car, I was referring to," he said. He held out his cigarette and looked at it as though it had appeared from nowhere, and he frowned. Then he stubbed it out on the edge of his heel, before grinding it into the mushy ground underfoot.

"But it's your own doing," he said. "You look like you want to dump the car."

"I'm a bit whacked. I wasn't paying attention."

Neither man spoke for several moments. The smoke from Gebhart's cigarette was whipped away immediately by soft gusts of wind. The breeze was inconstant here amongst the trees, but it still had the trunks groaning faintly behind the louder hush of the conifers' branches high up.

"As odd a request as I've ever had," Gebhart said then. "Tell me again you're not on drugs. Or going nuts?"

"Look, I really appreciate this. Gebi?"

"What?"

"I can't believe anything from Speckbauer."

"Well I can see that. The minute I saw that guy, well, that was clear enough."

"I thought he just wanted a local guy to drive him around, maybe introduce him to the locality. But he has a different movie going on in his head."

"But of course he would," said Gebhart. "'The Big Picture' fellows."

"He must have a lot of clout to get Schroek to put me working for him."

Gebhart nodded.

"Has Schroek talked to you about him, maybe?"

Gebhart eyed him.

"Only to say that cooperating with him and his group is a priority."

"Group?"

"Well naturally I looked him up," said Gebhart. "As far as I could, before I'd get noticed. But I kept banging into unknowns. Not something that inspires confidence. All I can find out is that his section is some kind of floater, a 'task-force.' No details."

"In the BP, even?"

Gebhart flicked away the suggestion with his hand.

"Our glorious Polizei? The minute I'd try to weasel anything out of them, an old friend of mine even, they'd be looking in my keyhole."

He heard Gebhart breathe out heavily through his nose once. He took it to be exasperation more than humour.

"Okay," Gebhart said. "If this is true, half of it – some of it even – you have to report it."

He gave Felix a hard look.

"That's my advice. And furthermore, if I was you, starting out my career, and I had an eye on getting places . . . "

"Go on, Gebi. Say it."

"I'd be telling Speckbauer too. That's the real world these days. Okay?"

"About my grandfather? I can't screw over my own family."

"Wait a minute," said Gebhart and took a step away. "Don't forget what you told me on the phone. We're sticking to that. Or else, I walk."

"Of course we are."

"So we are on a timer, right? I give you two hours of my time, two hours I have manufactured as 'police work' – which is true, even if I have gone along with your fashion request here."

He paused and indicated his street clothes with a small wave of his hand.

"But if this stuff pertains to a murder investigation, or criminal activity . . . ?"

Felix nodded.

"I know," he said. "I know. We move it upstairs right away."

"No family favours," said Gebhart. "None."

"No favours," Felix repeated.

Gebhart seemed to linger on Felix's words. Then he relaxed. Felix followed him to his car and they both got in.

"And you're supposed to be on a beach somewhere," said Gebhart and turned the key. The diesel caught right away and its first wrenching revs rattled loud in the woods.

"With that nice girl?"

"That's another story," said Felix. "But not now."

"Ah," said Gebhart, and let it into reverse. He turned to see out the back window.

"Or starting out your new career, maybe looking forward to the heavenly union between us and our betters in the Bundespolizei – not running about in off-hours with those two."

Gebhart checked his mirrors, and then put it in first before the car had even stopped reversing. There was a moment's hesitation before the car changed direction when Felix thought he too had bogged down. He had not imagined Gebhart capable of blue jeans, or looking like anything but the Gendarme who showed up for work in his uniform each day.

"Those two hounds," said Gebhart. "They won't rest long."

"Speckbauer?"

"They're not idiots. It wouldn't surprise me if this was all part of their plan."

"What, us here?"

"Sure. And who is the bigger dummy here, you or me? I should know better."

Gebhart cleared his throat, and then rolled down his window full. He spat with a peculiar delicacy into the undergrowth slowly drifting by. Felix heard a truck labouring on the road outside, a clash of gears as the driver launched it at the hill with a full load.

"I may be pissing on my pension here," Gebhart murmured. "That's why I had a cigarette. Yes, two and a bit years to go, and I'm starting over. I'll be the best goddamned house painter you'll ever see."

The dark, malty smells from the thawed floor of the forest came through the car even stronger now. Dappled sunlight splashed on the window and disappeared as they rolled bumpily out toward the road.

"I didn't realize that," said Felix. "It's okay if you change your mind."

"Well now you tell me. But God has made me a magnet for scheisse, it seems. I have no doubt those two pricks will be asking me questions before the day is out."

"Gebi, look–"

"Shut up will you? You don't know. There's more here than your mess. All I'm saying is, if I had a brain, I'd be back at the post."

"I don't want you to get into scheisse. Look, I'll go on my way." Gebhart sighed.

"Don't underestimate the desire to get one back," he said.

"Okay," said Felix, uncertainly.

"'Okay'? You haven't a clue. You don't need to know. So I never told you."

"Told me what?"

Gebhart glanced over.

"I didn't trust you," he said. "To be frank."

The car rolled into a lower spot and then a big bump shook the car.

"I know how those assholes work," Gebhart went on, straining over the wheel to spot any more big dips and bumps. "I learned the hard way. They never believed me. They suspect their own mothers."

Felix stared at him. Another bump shook creaks from the shocks and Gebhart swore as he righted himself.

"What the hell are you talking about, Gebi?"

"Forget it. It's bullshit."

"You don't trust me?"

"Didn't I just tell you to forget it?"

"How can I? What's with the freak-out here?"

"You want to know? Okay. I'll tell you. You show up at the post, training for when Korschack heads off for his officer course. He won't be back, that's okay. The post is going to be closed anyway, in a year or two. It's a soft number, a good place to train. Nothing happens in Stefansdorf, right?"

"But why are you mad at me now?"

"Ach! Listen. I won't be repeating myself. You show up, I was saying. You screwed around in the Uni, making a crap job of it by the looks of things. Then you're in the Gendarmerie, the Gendarmerie that's headed for the amalgamation in a year, a new police force that you'll automatically carry your job into? And you'll move up by just turning up for duty, because you have your Matura, and a bit of Uni? Home free."

"You're like the others, Gebi. You're suspicious of anyone who doesn't talk soccer and drink Puntigamer, and trash people."

"Have I finished? No I haven't. So listen."

Felix waited.

"Well? You think you know things? Let me tell you this, then. Your father goes out and there's a whisper about him – yeah, I heard. And don't look at me like that. You know part of why they're getting rid of the Gendarmerie ? Do you?"

"Money?" said Felix. "The EU?"

"No, and it's not because they have to find jobs for the Customs guys now the Slovenians and the frigging Hungarians and the goddamned Czechs are EU. And it's not just about saving money, or some asshole in Brussels or someplace, or 9/11 crap."

"I don't get it."

"Do I have to spell it out for you? Deals – corruption, whatever the fancy word is. Nobody admits it in public. But those guys know, they know how bad it is. It's been going on awhile. There's a wave of stuff coming through, since things went nuts in Yugoslavia. It can't fit under the carpet anymore, see? So, they suspect everybody, everything. Now, imagine how you look to that pair. A background like you have."

"You're serious, I think."

"God, but you're a depp sometimes. So frigging naïve. It's why I said that I didn't trust you. And I still don't. But not the way you think. I don't think you're bent, like some plan to get you to infiltrate the new police thing or rubbish like that. You're not crook material. Believe me, I know. But I just don't trust you. I don't trust you not to land me in the crap with this stumbling around you're at. I lost both ways, see?"

"No."

"For God's sake . . . If I stay clear of you and your nonsense, and ignore those two puppet masters using you for bait or whatever they're really doing up here – well there's my stupid conscience screwed. If you get done in, how the hell can I give those brilliant lectures to my kids about doing the right thing?"

The road came in sight. Gebhart slowed his car even more. Felix felt it begin to sink a little, but Gebi kept it chugging steadily low in second gear.

"And if I get run over again . . . life has no improvement there, has it?"

"'Run over?' 'Again'?"

"Yes, 'again.' They're not going to do this again. Not to me."

"Who are you talking about?"

"Well," said Gebhart, speaking now almost through clenched teeth. "So the moment of truth here arrives. Didn't you ever wonder what the likes of me, a brilliant policeman, is doing behind the door in Stefansdorf?"

Felix saw that the anger had passed, and Gebhart's sardonic tone had returned.

"Not really."

"Well you should. I am a good policeman. It's my career."

"What do you want me to say?" Felix said. "I just thought, well Gebi, he has his security. Promotions happen. You like a quiet life maybe. 'The landing strip,' right?"

Gebhart brought the car to a slow stop near the entrance, checking for any sign of soft ground beneath. With the car idling, he rubbed at his nose and looked across at Felix.

"That's what the old guys call it, sure. No. Me, I have other things, far more important. My kids, my family. You probably think that's schmaltzy crap, don't you?"

"No."

"Bullshit. But anyway, I'll tell you. Any other day I wouldn't, but you are digging your own hole in the ground here. But when I'm done telling you, I don't want to hear any questions, observations, comment. Got that?"

Felix nodded.

"Fifteen years ago, the Yugos started up again, right? It had been brewing. They have to murder one another every few years. I don't care if that sounds bad. It's true. It's in their genes or something. But there's shooting and killing and it only gets worse. You were still in diapers probably."

"I was seven or eight, actually."

"Seven," said Gebhart, as through it were a joke. "Eight? Anyway, I'm probably never going to talk to you, or to any cop, about this again."

Felix looked up to the patches of sky between the conifers.

"Things move. Money, guns, drugs, any crime – it all goes with war – if you call that 'war.' And here we are, just in the EU. It's only been a few years, but we're next door to this crap. So a lot starts to happen. One thing leads to another. You see?"

"So far."

"Here's me then. I work with a guy, I won't even say his name. I'm friendly with him. I respect him. I socialize with him. You see the picture, what I am about to tell you?"

Felix shook his head.

"A policeman? A Gendarme? You guess the rest."

Felix returned Gebhart's gaze.

"I think I do, now."

Gebhart held his forefinger to his head, and pulled back his thumb, and let it go.

"The way out," he said. "For him. But not for me. Obviously."

"They thought . . . ?"

Speckbauer nodded several times, slowly.

"So when you show up at the post, fresh out of Gendarmerie school, I think, well, so what. It's a good post for it. But then I see your name. And I ask myself this: They're putting this kid with me? Whose father was . . . ? You don't have to be crazy, or paranoid, I should say. So: got all that? Enough of it?"

"I had no idea."

"Don't I know it," said Gebhart. "Don't I know it. I didn't either. That's what happened to me. They gave up on me after a while, the Internals, but I know damned well my file was marked that day. I mean, what was my defence when they said I must have some idea what my partner was up to, that no one can be that stupid, or naïve, or . . . ? Now: forget this. You know enough now."

Gebhart put the car in first gear. He peered over the banks that bordered this part of the road here.

"Listen," said Felix. "Just go back. I never saw you."

"Well now. You sound as out of it as I was then."

"Really. I phoned you, and you turned me down. I'll drop all this on Speckbauer, the maps, what I heard from my grandparents, all that."

"Really?" said Gebhart, from some far place behind his squint.

"I'm over my head. Everything's screwed up."

Gebhart drew in a breath, held it, and let it out noisily.

"Interesting," he murmured. "But the world has already spun on."

"What does that mean?"

"I put in the search on this Fuchs guy."

"So the system logged you."

"The system logged me. Or Korschak, or whoever was in the post. It shouldn't take them more than one half-second to figure out who."

"'Them,'" Felix muttered.

"Funny, isn't it? 'Them' 'Them' is us, right?"

"Yes," said Felix. "But are you sure you got the right Fuchs?"

"'Equipment operator – 'seasonal operator' – in the forestry, the mill?"

"Red hair, beard?"

"No beard on his driver's licence. Reddish, rusty maybe."

"Equipment operator? The only time I met him, he was driving an old man to his card games, having a beer and jausen."

"Slacker?"

"I don't know, but probably. What's his record?"

"Surprise: Herr Fuchs is not a criminal."

"You're joking."

"This is not a joking day. Zero. Like I said. I go left here, right?"

The smoother section of road that Gebhart let the Golf onto soon resumed its steep climb, the clattery sound of the engine coming back to Felix from the banks that lined it here.

"What was the passport picture like?"

"He doesn't have one. But the EU's a big place to wander now, isn't it? Anyone can get into a car and drive to, I don't know, Paris, and no one has to know."

"Married, family or anything?"

"Not married, in his thirties, does what he pleases. Sounds like a pretty good life to me. I'll bet he has a killer CD collection and a garage full of decent tools."

"And who knows," Gebhart added after a few moments. "Maybe he'll turn out to be a half-decent fellow. So he drives some local geezers about a bit? Sounds like a good thing, one would say. Families are busy these days, you know. So busy."

Felix checked his watch.

"Well I phoned my Opa Kimmel. He's not going out this afternoon, he said."

"Is he used to you calling in on him?"

Felix shook his head.

"He has all his marbles?" Gebhart asked. "Or enough of them?"

"We'll see," was all Felix could come up with. "He can be a bit . . . remote."

"You said the village," said Gebhart. He pushed against his seat belt to look around at the church and houses receding in his mirror.

"It's spread out," said Felix. "Go up the hill here, and watch for tractors. It's tight. It gets narrower further up."

Gebhart weaved his head about to get a last look at the church tower in the side mirror before the car took the summit. The road began a gradual descent into a small valley that appeared to be the last before the mountains started behind.

"Is that your family church back there, the graveyard?"

"It is."

Gebhart braked and then he geared down when the road entered a curving cut between banks. The first of the grass in the meadows here had established itself, and to Felix now seemed to almost hover above the fields in an almost luminous filament, more like baby hair than the hardy, thick grasses they'd be before the month was out.

"Well you won't often see that," Gebhart said. "Those masons know their stuff."

"The masons?"

"That wall by the graveyard. The road was made later, or it sank or something?"

"I suppose."

"You mean you don't know, and you grew up hereabouts?"

Flattened cakes of mud from tractor wheels began to spread out more across the pavement. The rumbling coming up from the tires became more constant. Winter had chewed up the edges of the road in many places. Without planning to, Felix had been rehearsing how he'd approach his grandfather, how he'd persuade him to talk about his past. He could already imagine the distant gaze and the indifference in his eyes, the slow, steady enunciation of his words, each weighed.

Gebhart slowed for two potholes.

"Maybe we should have parachuted in."

"Well you'll have something to talk to my Opa Kimmel about then."

"Parachutes? Potholes?"

"He wanted to be a paratrooper. 'To land on Crete' my dad told me once."

"And did he ?"

"He was fourteen when that was going on."

Gebhart changed into second for a steep section.

"All the wind and air up here maybe," he murmured. "Gets into you, maybe?"

The Golf chugged through the section of road that ran almost through the Klamminger's farmyard.

"What?" said Gebhart. "The one place we pass, and there's no action here?"

There was fresh mud in the yard, clothes on the line. Something about the turn in the road, or the drumming of the muddy roadway, had awakened something in Felix. He thought of his Grandfather Kimmel, that upright way he sat in the church pew, as though he were in a trance.

"Talk about out of the way," Gebhart went on. "Is he a hermit or something?"

When Felix didn't answer, Gebhart looked over.

"Second thoughts?" he asked.

"No. I'm thinking. Keep going."

Felix opened the window. There was a sharp edge to the air up here. Gebhart sighed and reached for his mobile.

"Christ," he muttered. "Nothing now. I had one bar back in the village."

Felix pointed to a line of electricity poles and the ragged clump of conifers, a windbreak, where it ended.

"You'll see the roof in a minute," he said.

"Where is everybody?" asked Gebhart. "Doesn't everyone here depend on their neighbours?"

He glanced over.

"Let me guess," he said to Felix then: "'That's another story?'"

"You said it, Gebi."

"Does this place have a name?"

"It's called Pfarrenord," Felix said, looking back down the valley.

"Is everyone here holy or something, this 'parish' thing?"

"It's a local name. Not the name on a map. It's windy here. Colder, people say. So someone came up with 'The North Parish.'"

Gebhart sighed and rubbed his nose.

"Watch, there's a bend here."

The road twisted at the spot Felix had fallen off his new bike all those years ago. He remembered having a tantrum, and his mother had soothed him. Later, when he'd brought it up in some argument as to why he had to visit his grandfather at all, she'd told him that anxiety did strange things to a kid. It was something to get over, she'd said; something to build on.

"So tell me," said Gebhart. "How are you going to get things going here? This 'little chat'?"

"We'll see how it goes, I suppose."

"Which page of the manual is that see-how-it-goes technique on?"

Felix was suddenly glad of Gebhart's breezy sarcasm.

He turned to him.

"Maybe it's changed since you last looked at it. Back in nineteen-eighty-nothing."

"Listen to you. You spend a couple of days with suits from Strassgangerstrasse, and now you're a thick-head like them. Well done, Mr. Know-It-All."

Felix studied the cloud shadows that now lay over much of the forest cover on the hills about.

"So now you know what I think about your new friends," said Gebhart.

"They didn't fool me," he said. "Completely, anyway."

"Richtig? But you're still going to unload that stuff on them, aren't you? Those maps and documents you were talking about?"

"Soon."

"'Soon'? Cheeky."

"I'll decide after I hear my opa."

Gebhart looked over.

"Well you know those two are not sitting on their hands," he said. "I'll bet they're knocking on that guy's door already, Fuchs."

"And that's why I want to be here first."

"We, Gendarme, we. Remember that, will you? I'm wearing a big bull's eye on my arsch here for these couple of hours."

"Gebi–"

"Don't tell me how you appreciate it. That only makes me worry more. The clock is ticking. Ninety minutes, and I'm back in my uniform at work, at the post."

"Watch for water on the road up ahead. Sometimes you get a pool here before the warm weather."

Gebhart left the Golf in second, pulling up the hill at a steady rate, the poles passing slowly.

"Scheisse," said Gebhart with quiet malice, placing his foot over the brake pedal. "You were right."

The pool of water seemed to run for 20 or more metres on the road.

"Deep, do you think – well look."

Gebhart brought the Golf to a stop slowly. An Opel blocked the road beyond the pool. Its back wheels were still in the water.

"There's your answer," Gebhart said. "That guy tried to plough through."

He moved the gearshift from side to side in neutral.

"Is that your opa's jalopy?"

A rally stripe with some kind of blue sparkly stuff ran across the top of the back window.

Felix heard Gebhart stroking his bottom lip.

"The alloy wheels I could forgive," Gebhart murmured. "But Maria, the Michael Schumacher stuff tacked on there? Your opa's hardly a Rock 100 FM man, is he?"

Felix couldn't be sure of another sticker, but two he recognized.

"The plate's local," said Gebhart.

"Yamaha," Felix murmured.

Gebhart stopped playing with the gearshift. He looked over, his eyebrows raised.

"Herr Red-head? Our person of interest? Mr. Fuchs up here on a visit?"

Felix shrugged.

"How very damned convenient," said Gebhart. "Ran it through here, stalled it."

He put the car in reverse.

"What are you doing?"

"You think I'm going to just park it on this cow path? I'm going to turn it around. And you're going to help me."

Felix stood by the entrance to the field.

"Make damned sure my wheels don't get stuck when I back it in there," Gebhart called out. "Or you'll pull this car out yourself."

The earth sucked at Felix's shoes as he took another step back. The diesel smoke from Gebhart's car seemed to settle around his face, like gnats. He slapped the roof when he saw the wet ridge of mud begin to form to the side of the tire.

Gebhart took his time making the 50-point turn. Felix watched his hands and arms work the wheel, but he did not make out any words in Gebhart's steady, philosophical-sounding muttering.

Gebhart stepped out of the car eventually, testing the margins of the road to both sides. Felix was listening to the breeze that was coming over the fields here, suddenly quiet after the Golf's engine was finally off.

"I'm locking it," said Gebhart. "This is the end of the road, after your opa's place, right?"

Felix nodded. He thought he had heard something on the breeze. Maybe a bird, or the faint whistle and sough from the stirring blades of new grass. He looked toward the trees that surrounded three sides of the house again, and caught a glimpse of the roof. There was no smoke from the chimney.

"Come on," said Gebhart. "Get it over with. It's going to be a mud fest anyway."

After a few steps, he put out his arm to stop Felix.

"He has a dog, right?"

"A Shepherd, yes."

"Where is it?"

"We're a bit from the house yet."

"And does this dog listen to you?"

"Usually. It knows me."

"'Usually'? Wait a minute."

Felix watched him skip back to the car and open the trunk. After a brief rummage, he drew out a rusted rebar, with a curve in it.

"I am not a dog man," said Gebhart. "But I'm not a masochist either."

The Kadett was unlocked. There were magazines on the back seat, rolled-up wrappers from McDonald's, and some pieces of machined metal covered in a fur of oil and dirt. The ashtray was used, a lot. The custom steering wheel had a wood trim.

"A boy racer," said Gebhart. "In this piece of junk?"

Felix looked at the floor mats in the front. There were moist sections on them.

"Not much of a Schumacher, is he," Gebhart muttered. "You think he'd know better."

The side of the house came into view now, its whitewashed wall looking more grey in the shadows of the trees. Felix sought out any movement that could mean the dog was about, and had at least heard them, and was coming to investigate.

"Not much farming done here," said Gebhart. "Rented out?"

"A few years now," Felix replied. He stopped and listened.

"You hear something?"

Felix couldn't be sure. They stepped down off the road by the stone pillars that marked the entrance to the farmyard.

"Cattle, before he retired?" Gebhart asked.

Felix realized that Gebhart was nervous now. The walk up from the car had him breathing loudly too.

"Yes," he said. "Look, the dog's name is Tilla. And don't worry, he's old now."

"Tilla? Big?"

"Atilla. He's a fair size, but lazy, if I remember."

Felix looked at the kitchen window. He could only make out the reflection of the trees on the surface.

"I'd sure like to know where the beast is," he heard Gebhart murmur. "I mean, how does it look I come visiting with an iron bar in my hand?"

Felix looked toward the window again. Beyond the mirrored trees and patches of sky, there was someone moving around in there.

He stopped completely when he heard the voice. It was raised, like a question, and angry, but he couldn't make out the three or four words.

"What the hell was that?"

There was no movement there now.

Then a door slammed inside the house. It was followed by a shout, and thumps that seemed to move through the house toward the side door.

"Is this how– ?"

The rest of Gebhart's sentence was cut by the sound of the side door crashing open. It was hard enough and fast enough for Felix to hear the metal grind as it hit its limit, and bounce back.

He was already moving toward the noise when he heard the rasping scrape of a shoe digging into concrete, its owner running.

A red-haired man came around the corner of the house then, his mouth wide open as much as his eyes. Felix saw that Gebhart too was manoeuvering to block Fuchs. Fuchs was breathless already, panicking. He gave a quick glance back at the house even as he came at the two policemen. He wasn't slowing.

"Fuchs!" Felix yelled, and he went into a crouch. "Stop!"

Fuchs had his arms out already. Gebhart also yelled at Fuchs to stop. Felix heard another shout too, and the sound of the door opening and rebounding again.

Felix began to weave side to side to match Fuchs efforts to sidestep him. The red face and bulging eyes of a madman, he thought, and huge eyeballs rolling around. Was it drugs, he wondered, or a fit? But this flabby bastard wasn't agile, and probably had never been. He was going to kill himself running like this.

Felix kept calculating where to meet Fuchs, and get a hold on him without risking a head-on. He kept his eyes on Fuchs' hands.

The figure that now came around the side of the house at a dash drew a quick look from Felix, but Fuchs was within a couple of metres now. He was panting, and trying to say, or shout something. Felix was aware that Gebhart had come around to his left now, and he was shouting again. But Fuchs had given up any effort to twist his overweight, flapping mass into any more dodges.

In the moments before Felix actually reached out to get hold of some passing part of Fuchs, his mind scrambled to put things together, and failed. A dog who usually met you down the road from the farm? This other man who had just run out of the house, with arms raised like wings to slow himself, had to be a policeman – one of Speckbauer's? Who else but a policeman would have a gun in his hand? Even as Fuchs filled up his view, Felix registered that Sepp Gebhart had raised the rebar and had gone into a crouch. Whatever Gebhart shouted was torn away when Fuchs barrelled into him.

Felix felt his feet leave the ground with the impact. He heard a yell on his way up, and was suddenly aware of Fuchs' smell, even the fabric of his jean jacket. His hand clung to Fuchs' jacket for a moment, but his fingers slid as he was carried on and out by the force of Fuchs' rush, and he felt himself falling. He reached out as his knee hit the ground, and grasped Fuchs' leg. He was dragged for a moment, and he had time to feel the surge of pain coming from his knee and his hip. Then Fuchs' fat legs were coming down at him, knee first.

All he knew after Fuchs landed on him was that he still had

Fuchs' leg. So it was Fuchs babbling and kicking at him then. Grit ground into his elbows and then his face as Fuchs tried to twist free, his breath ragged and wheezing in between squeals and half-shouts. Fuchs rolled over on him, and pounded on his arm with his fist. Felix tucked his head in tighter, curling himself around the leg. A floating feeling came over Felix then. He wondered how you could get such a sound out of a man, like a drum. It was Fuchs' hammering him in the ribs, while trying to kick him with his free leg. It wasn't hurting. He wondered why there was no pain yet, especially now that this huge oaf was grinding him into the cement with every twist and blow. And over it all, the absurdity of all this, out of the blue.

Then the hammering stopped, and something heavy slid over him. It was Fuchs, he knew, but a trick. His jacket smelled of petrol and cigarettes and BO. Fuchs was faking it, preparing for a sudden jerk, to get loose finally. Felix knew something was going on around him, but it seemed to be happening at a distance, in some muffled way. He called out Gebhart's name. He wanted to hear him say that things were fine, or under control, or something. He braced himself for Fuchs' big move, and he called out again. There were footsteps somewhere, and shouts.

His head felt like it was full of water now. How long had passed since he'd seen Fuchs rushing at him? This was the same as what had happened in that soccer game years ago. He had run into the goalpost for a pass, and it never came. It was that time when all his teammates seemed to go away but they had left their bodies there, and their worried faces looking down at him. But was it really concussion, when you could even think concussion? Ridiculous.

Now Fuchs was talking to him. That must be his head then, that big lump lying on his shoulders? The words were low and short and hesitant. Like talk in a dream, they made no sense.

Someone called out his name. Felix pushed up but Fuchs wasn't moving. He murmured and gave a soft lisp, like a kid in sleep.

"Gebi," Felix said, loudly.

There was a thumping sound now and Fuchs gave a jolt. Here was his move then, Felix was sure, and he pulled hard on Fuchs' jacket. Instead of the blow from Fuchs, or a sharp pull away, he only felt the oaf get heavier. Felix's mind preoccupied itself for a time with how it could be that he seemed both bigger, or at least more spread out, and heavier. Was he trying to crush him? Something had to give.

He began to push at Fuchs. His hands and knuckles sank into the belly. He heard a wheeze and a sound like Fuchs was about to clear his throat. Felix got one shoulder off the ground, and he craned his neck.

The light from the sky had changed, to a glary, milky luminescence. That was the house over there in the corner of his vision, and that policeman was there, the one that Speckbauer had sent here. He was standing a few metres back, toward the house, looking at the ground, away from him.

"Get this fat idiot off me," Felix said.

The man turned to him. His chest was heaving, and he was saying something between breaths, quietly. A frown, something like incredulity or fear twisted his whole face. He began to take slow steps toward Felix, lifting his arm as he drew closer. The man stopped and said something louder, but then made a small staggering lurch off sideways. A sharp crack sounded, and echoed across the yard. He made one swerving step, and seemed about to shout as he fell. There was a dull scraping thud. Felix realized that the policeman hadn't made any effort to check his fall.

He drew in a breath to yell out. He had to get up, to move away. He got one knee working and levered more of Fuchs' weight. He pushed again, and got his forearm into it. He had no strength. Fuchs flopped more as he pushed, and even seemed to roll back each time. His palms felt slimy grit on the cement under him as he tried to get his other shoulder free. Fuchs had knocked himself out, that was it.

With both hands free, Felix took two tries to get a roll going. Fuchs' weight began to budge.

Up on his elbows now, Felix saw red on his clothes, and sprays of red like freckles on Fuch's arms. Gebhart was lying down closer to the shed. He was not moving. Something else was: a knee waving slowly side to side. Speckbauer's man? And now he was turning on his side, groaning louder, and pushing himself up on one elbow.

A man called Felix's name now, and before he could turn around toward the house to see where the voice was coming from, the man's face flushed red and he seemed to bounce, and the noise of a gunshot echoed across the yard and into the hills.

It was still echoing faintly in the distance when Felix heard footsteps crossing the yard now, slowly, and talking. There was a metallic scrape and a loud click, as metal was pushed against metal.

Part of Felix's mind understood what the sound meant. Someone called his name again, in between his own shouts and Felix kicking free of Fuchs at last. The man with the rifle was breathing heavily and slowly, and in between breaths his voice was barely above a murmur in a slow, considered, disdainful tone that Felix recognized.

He began to hear words he could understand. He wondered if the man was dressed in his grandfather's clothes, and had a mask so exact as the slight stoop and the voice, even the dialect.

"Opa?"

"Bleib ruhig, kid. Quiet. I took care of him. Have you been shot?"

"I don't think so. I'm going to be sick, I think, or something."

There was a movement from where Gebhart lay. Felix saw a leg move, and watched Gebhart curl up slightly. He did not want to look down at Fuchs. He let his eyes move around the yard. There was a vague ripple to everything he looked at now. How small it seemed now, where it had seemed so huge when he had been a kid.

Someone was asking if he could get up. His grandfather's voice.

"I don't know," Felix said, or thought he said.

"The other one," his grandfather said. "The other tschuschen?"

"No, Opa. He came with me, he's a Gendarme–"

Something made the air quiver. Felix had a moment before his throat filled, and then he was doubled up with the spasms. The vomit burned and scraped as it burst from his throat.

Through swimming eyes he saw his grandfather lean down, stooped, over Gebhart. The spasms came slower, and he was able to call out Gebhart's name. He saw his grandfather's head turn his way before another spasm tore at him, and left him exhausted. He ignored the grit grinding into his elbow and got on all fours. He was wet, but he refused to look down as he began to scuttle slowly toward Gebhart.

"Opa," he said. "Is he okay?"

"He's saying something."

His grandfather had to pause to get his breath now. "I think he's been shot."

"Gebi?" Felix called out. "I'm here, I'm coming."

He pushed off with his hands. Rising, his leg flashed a pain that almost blinded him, and he stopped, wavering. He worked out of his jacket and threw it in front of him. Everything was rippling and folding around him now. He saw his grandfather shuffling across the yard.

"An ambulance, Opa. The police."

He let himself slowly down onto one knee. He saw that the red stain had spread and was finding its own way along the cement toward him.

"Can you hear me, Gebi?"

The reply in a calm voice that ended in a sharp intake of breath.

"Too well."

Gebhart's jean jacket was wet too.

"You're hurt. We're going to have an ambulance in here so fast . . ."

A short breath ended in a hiss. Then Gebhart's clenched eyes opened.

"What a mess," he said in voice so normal that it took Felix aback. "What a stupid, dumb mess we're in, gell?"

"They'll be here any minute," said Felix.

Gebhart's eyes strained now.

"Are there more of those guys? Are they gone?"

"They're gone. I'm okay, I think. That guy was coming over. My opa got him."

Gebhart's eyes seemed to lose their focus.

"He's phoning, Gebi, right now. They'll pull out all the stops."

He pulled up Gebhart's shirt tail and saw a darker spot amongst the wash of blood above his trouser belt. He pushed the sleeve of his jacket onto the wound.

"Gebi I have to get you over. I have to get a towel on it."

"What," said Gebhart.

Felix's hand was wet immediately as he reached around. He pushed the sleeve hard into the wettest part. Gebhart grunted, and sighed. Then he spoke in that same clear voice.

"My wife is going to be pissed."

"She can take it out on me, Gebi. I swear. We're going to get you to hospital. You can watch her beat me up there, okay?"

Gebhart frowned. His eyes regained their focus.

"That Speckbauer, one of his people?"

"No."

Gebhart winced and squeezed out a word that Felix didn't understand.

"That bastard," Gebhart whispered then. "Look what he's done. He screwed you around, and now–"

He clenched his eyes tight. When he opened them again they stayed wide, and fastened on Felix's.

"Who is that?"

"That's my opa. He's yelling at the police, I think."

Gebhart started to say something but he made a soft groan, and held his breath and closed his eyes.

Felix held the jacket tighter under Gebhart's back. He watched his chest expand and contract. His own head felt tight now, and the sourness in his mouth seemed to leak out and take over all about him. The light pulsed above the farmhouse, and he closed his eyes a second to stop it. There were footsteps in the yard again.

"They're coming," said his grandfather. "They thought I was joking."

Felix wanted to tell his grandfather to watch how he carried the hunting rifle. He saw the agitation in the face, something he couldn't remember seeing before.

He felt, more than heard, Gebi murmur under him. He looked down, and saw that the eyes were half open.

"Gebi? I'm here. Help's going to be here any minute. You hear me?"

Gebhart made a small, slow nod. Felix laid his other hand on Gebhart's ribcage and waited for each gentle rise and fall.

His grandfather held out a towel. Felix looked into his face, and saw something beyond the agitation and confusion. His grandfather shook his head once, then again, and looked away.

"I don't know," he heard him mutter, but he didn't look away from the jacket he was drawing out. Gebhart made a sigh, and said something under his breath. Felix grabbed the towel and quickly swapped it for his jacket under Gebhart.

"Talk, Gebi," he said. "I want to hear your stories. More stories, now. Okay?"

Gebhart opened one eye but didn't look at Felix.

"Oh Christ," he whispered, and grimaced, and closed his eye again.

Panic seized Felix, and the yawning space around him pulsed and quivered again.

"You listen then," he said, louder than he had intended. It was his own voice, his mind said, but it sounded like someone else's. The bile at the back of his throat hurt, and the breeze pressed his wet shirt against his skin, chilling him.

"I'm going to talk. Are you listening? I'm going to tell you what we're going to do when this is fixed. You know that stübe out near the Woods, the heurigen place . . . ?"

He paused to hear any word from Gebhart, but he was beginning to shiver.

"I'm paying, Gebi," he went on. "There's going to be everything. On me."

His grandfather was on one knee know, and his face had fallen. He looked ancient, and his eyes rested on the reddening towel in Felix's hand. He was mumbling, and for a moment Felix thought he was praying.

"Opa, phone them back, the Gendarmerie. Tell them the helicopter, a mountain rescue one. The road is blocked."

His grandfather had difficulty getting up. He hesitated before heading for the farmhouse. He looked down at Felix.

"You," he whispered and shook his head. "You and that father of yours."

FORTY-ONE

THE JULY NIGHT BEFORE FELIX WAS TO ATTEND THE Sonderkommission at Strassgangerstrasse, he slept deeply: until 2 a.m. That was when he sat up, half in sleep and half awake, with a groan. Giuliana was off the pillow almost immediately.

"What's wrong?"

He was sure she wasn't awake when she had spoken.

"It's okay," he said. "Go back to sleep. It's fine."

He had already pivoted over to the side of the bed, and had his feet on the floor. He had woken up in the middle of the running dream. Like all the other times, he was instantly awake and ready to keep running. He looked at the rectangle of yellowed light cast up from the streetlights outside. Though the windows were open to cool the apartment after the heat of the day, the room still felt stuffy. He couldn't hear any traffic. He concentrated on his breathing, and felt around his ribs to the left side. Then he tried one deep breath. There was pressure on the ribs, but it didn't hurt. Slowly he raised both arms. There had not been any real jabs of pain for weeks now, but the stiffness was staying longer than he'd expected.

The glow from the window had turned her skin to bronze. He gazed at her breasts resting in shadows, and then at her navel. The planet, they called it, for no good reason. Maybe it had something to do with rings of Saturn, or something she'd said when they had started out together and she had been self-conscious about her full figure.

"Have you got pain?"

Her eyes were closed.

"No. Really. Back to sleep."

He lay still and listened to her breathing. He had stopped being paranoid about every ache or feeling of tiredness, or even a wormy stomach. Concussion had different ways to show its effects, they kept telling him at the follow-up scans he had each Wednesday. So yet again they had detected no abnormalities, he reported to Giuliana. Except for what they had done those afternoons and nights of the week he had at home.

It seemed an age ago. Often he thought of the strange sex they'd had that night he'd gotten home from the hospital, with tensor bandages across his chest. Giuliana hadn't figured it out either, she admitted, and refused to talk about it. Pagan love, they'd agreed to call it. She was the goddess astride him, demanding. It was as if she were trying to cure him of something, to draw out poison, to exorcise something. The week was almost compensation enough for their missed holiday.

He counted back the weeks and days. He still found himself doing that even when he was at work, even when Schroek was saying something to him, or when he and Gebi's temp, a good-natured veteran named Fischbach, were on a patrol. Maybe it was the brain trying to fill in gaps by itself. But still he got that woolly feeling when he tried to remember details from the farmyard. He put it down to the concussion. There was no need for fancy theories of the unconscious, yet anyway. Even Schroek had understood that Felix wasn't holding out on him. He had stopped asking him even casual questions about it.

Try as he might, the simple fact was that he could not remember everything. There was no point in feeling guilty, or frustrated about it, that neurologist told him. He had only to do his best with the investigation, to try to answer the million questions they'd thrown at him. But understand that this is what the brain did to protect itself. And be glad you have one that still works.

She murmured something and shifted her head on the pillow. He raised his head, looked over at her. Then he reached across and put his arm around her waist, and drew her to him. Her scent began to soak into his head. He let his hand along her thigh. Her skin seemed suddenly hot.

"This is you getting well," she muttered, and drew in a breath. "Is it?"

"Medicine," he said. "Yes."

"What woke you?"

He stopped stroking. It wasn't impatience he'd heard, he told himself; it was concern.

"The usual," he said.

"The running one?"

He nodded. His hands seemed to have their own ideas. He felt them work over her hips.

"But nothing gets any clearer. There's always talk, or words, but I don't understand them."

He heard her yawn. He focused on his hands now, and traced her hip bone.

"How long do you think before . . . you know . . . "

It was what he'd hoped she wouldn't say.

Did she mean "the talk" she had postponed? The evenings at Gebhart's?

He thought about Gebhart reading the travel brochures he had his daughter gather for him. Morocco, Tunisia, Egypt. Soon then this would stop, as it had to, this sitting in Gebhart's garden reading magazines together, and interrupting their long silences with a word from Gebhart about some foolishness in a furniture plan he was studying, or the quality of Opels these days, or something the doctor had said recently about one kidney being plenty.

Gebhart's take on things had not changed: It could have been a hell of a lot worse. Right after he'd gone to see him, Gebhart had been able to make some dry crack about things. Twenty-four years of normal, too normal, and now he got his 10 minutes of excitement and fame. Gebhart had not even known about it at the time, he admitted. He pretended to feel a little cheated not to have witnessed all the fuss with the helicopter and the swarm of paramedics and police.

"How long?" he said. "As long as it takes, I suppose."

Her rested his hand, and waited for sleep, hers or his.

After several minutes, she raised her head from the pillow.

"Is that your heart?"

"Yes," he said. He felt her hand move up his leg.

"I see," she said, in a sleepy voice, and her hand moved over him now. "You have ideas, don't you."

Later he listened as her breathing became whistley. She put her hand on the pillow under her cheek, and after clearing a strand of her hair away from her mouth, her breathing became almost inaudible. He no longer expected to sleep. It was useless trying.

Thoughts continued to roll through his mind, like those slow rollers he'd seen on that beach in Spain. Gebhart's wife had glasses just like the daughter's. She sat forward without apparent effort in the chair next to her husband's bed at the hospital. On first meeting her, her eyes had seemed huge, even walleyed. It must have been the glasses.

She had known him right away the first time his visit coincided with hers. She had been there ahead of him, and sat waiting in the corridor outside for a nurse to do some procedure. It had been awkward. He had begun to believe that her steady gaze was proof of some special powers those big eyes of hers held. He felt he had to explain, to say how sorry he was. She had nodded slowly. She'd kept her gaze on the goings-on down at a nursing station.

"So wie so," was all she said that first time.

He didn't know whether it was sarcasm, or that she did not know what to say, where to begin. A doctor came along then and she began to question him about a shunt. A thing with trains, Felix thought, and realized that he should not be there, then. He heard her return his quiet goodbye, but felt her eyes on him as walked down the hallway.

But Gebhart must have gotten wind of it, and a couple of days later Felix's evening visit coincided with hers.

"It looks good for me," Gebhart said. "They put fish blood in me too so I'll never feel the cold again. And I can pee like a drunkard. What can't they do these days?"

After a pause that gave Felix a moment to see that this effort at light-heartedness had only raised a sardonic expression on Frau Gebhart's face, Gebhart eyed him.

"But you, you look worse. How is that possible?"

Felix tried to make light of it. The cracked rib and the concussion were nothing really, he tried to persuade Gebhart, but yes, he did feel achy. Gebhart did not make any jokes about how Fuchs' huge size had kept Felix alive, as well as flattened him. Nor did he ask about Dravnic, the man who had found his way to the farm that day. Felix supposed that Schroek told Gebhart all the news and the gossip, as it was the same newly energized C.O. Schroek who had daily tidbits for Felix also.

Speckbauer was apparently pushing paper in Graz, his field 'excursions' curtailed until the inquiry came up with its findings. Schroek had also heard that Speckbauer had offered to resign. Dravnic had even turned up on warrants from the European Court in The Hague. He had lived in Germany for nearly a decade before the civil war. It was not clear yet how Fuchs had first made contact with Dravnic's people. Peter Kimmel had indeed known a Dario Dravnic in years gone by, but that was as far as he went with that. Felix had heard from his mother – or was it one of Lisi's phone calls? – that Opa Kimmel had told them to figure it out themselves. And that was that.

"Well you have a good, thick Styrian head," said Gebhart. "And you're a stubborn bastard, aren't you? Runs in the family, gell? How's that old opa of yours, 'the marksman'?"

"He is enjoying the attention. But he pretends that he doesn't."

"Natürlich," said Gebhart, with a sly grin and a wink at his wife that she ignored. "I hear he told them to arrest him if they want. Quite a fellow."

Felix nodded.

"It's all Fuchs' doing, he maintains. Take it or leave it."

"You believe him – I mean I know he's your opa – but do you?"

"Actually I do. Fuchs rummaged all through his stuff."

"Some friend of the aged," said Speckbauer. "That old pistol, your opa didn't even know it was missing?"

"He says no. But now he sees why Fuchs was full of questions about old times, and what he did all those years back."

"What, he thought Fuchs was studying folklore or something? Collecting stories, or folk tales, another Peter Rossegger?"

Felix shrugged.

"I think he was glad of the company, that's all. A chance to talk. Being alone?"

Gebhart sighed and stretched out his arms.

"Christ but you can wither in here for not doing something," he groaned. "Are you back to doing your bike stuff yet?"

"Not as much as I'd like, but yes."

"Come on now. You're the kind of guy needs activity like that, for energy."

"I'll do some more maybe after this week."

"Well Schroek is Mr. Energy, let me tell you," Gebhart went on. "He wants to look good with this. He prowls the post like the captain of a ship now, I hear. But, my God, he is nosy, and a gossip, as ever."

He nodded in the direction of his wife.

"You cleared him out of here one evening, schatzi?"

"I did," she said. "He was wearing us out."

"Like another interrogation, I tell you," said Gebhart. "'Did he shoot Fuchs first?' 'Didn't he say anything?' 'How close was the old man when he put him down with the rifle?'"

Gebhart rolled his eyes and looked down at the carpentry magazines his wife had brought.

"Those two," he said then, and his face had lost its ease when he looked up from the magazines. "The two James Bonds . . . ?"

"Nix," said Felix. "The gag order – until the investigation reports."

"'Must not communicate,'" Gebhart said with a top-heavy irony. "As if they did any, when they were stringing you along. And who would want to talk to those two anyway, the mess they made?"

Felix was aware that Gebhart's wife was scrutinizing him. He looked to her with a polite smile, but her eyes darted away.

"I forgot to ask you, you know," said Gebhart. "My brain is on holiday in here. Look, did you see those two show up back at the farm?"

"No. But the place was kind of crazy, with the helicopter and the cars."

Gebhart smiled.

"That part was funny at least," he said. "Thinking about them pushing the car into the field to get by. By the way, has the garage phoned? Is it ready?"

"They did," she said. "They had to replace the handle, they said. And something that winds the window, from inside."

"That beauty better be perfect," Gebhart declared. "Or I'll sue the depp who broke the window – and I want it washed after being shoved into that field. That car was taken care of, let me tell you. No BP is going to disrespect that car, smashing a window like that. Hell, no. Maybe I'll ask Schroek to look into it. He likes that kind of thing. Then he can take credit for that too."

"Credit?" said Gebhart's wife, shifting in the chair, and regaining an even more erect posture. "Let him try. That man . . . ."

Gebhart exchanged a glance with Felix.

"You know," he said, in a different tone, "the psychology bunch found that married men live longer?"

"They take their wife's portions," she said quickly. She fixed her superpower eyes on Felix for a moment.

"Nurses like me have enough nonsense at work," she said.

"However," said Gebhart breezily. "I have a point to make here. What I'm getting at is this: Felix, this is your big chance. You understand what I'm saying?"

"Big chance for what?"

"Look: you score big when you are the wounded hero. Pop the question."

"Marriage?"

"I could use a party."

"You're a matchmaker now, Gebi?"

"Do it. Look, it's the summer. I'm on leave a few weeks for sure, maybe months. I feel good – but I'm not going to let on. You did good stuff, and you're barely out of your diapers in the job."

"Good stuff?" said Felix, and looked from Gebhart to his wife and back. "You've got to be joking."

"Do I ever joke? Look, they're going through with the Big One, have you forgotten? One big happy family, our decent, dependable, modest Gendarmerie will now share the playground with the big shots from the BP. And where will we be when the dust settles? Whatever about me, but you're detective – fast track. Believe me."

Felix said nothing. Movement on the building opposite drew his eye to the window again. Pigeons, big fat Graz pigeons, were landing on a roof.

"What did I tell you Frieda," said Gebhart. "He still thinks he screwed up."

She got up from the chair, and pushed it back to the wall.

"I must show up at some point," she said. "We're short, with all the holidays."

Felix snuck a look at how she reached around her husband's neck. She murmured something to him and kissed the top of his head. Then she gave a professional look-around to the bed and the drip, settling the bedclothes, and checking how the upper part of the bed was tilted. She tugged at her nurse's uniform under her raincoat. She glanced at Felix before turning to her husband again.

"Servus, Felix," she said, crisply. "When we get this depp home, you must visit."

Felix remembered babbling some reply. Gebhart tried to let on he hadn't noticed the awkwardness.

"Now," he said when Felix sat down again. "It just takes a bit of time, see?"

Then he winked.

"Stay away from those farmer's daughters from Carinthia. They'll whip you if you cross them."

"Really?"

"No," Gebhart retorted. "I'm making it up so you'll quit worrying."

"I'm not sure I can."

Gebhart waved some irritating thought aside.

"There you go, you see? Is it your age that makes you think nothing happens without your permission or something? Don't you get it yet? It's just a shitty thing happened. It's the way stuff happens. That's it, that's all of it. Sure, you can predict some stuff, and get out of the way of a lot of shit, but . . . ?"

Felix looked at the Gebhart's hands working the air.

"You're doing the philosophy thing, Gebi."

"Ach – I'll try to keep it simple. Ready? You put greedy people, stupid people, people who are bored, or do drugs, or drink all day, you put them near anything tempting, well you're going to get trouble. Is that too hard for you?"

Felix nodded, just to have it over for now.

"So get out of here and work on that proposal, okay?"

On the tram back down to the city centre, Felix realized that he had forgotten the Croatian guy's name. It unnerved him. Was it the concussion, he wondered, a sign that his brain still wasn't right? Getting worse, even? He could remember Fuchs' heavy weight over him, crushing him into the farmyard cement. There was something of that in his dreams, he sensed, and he had awakened several times with the dread feeling of being held, or tied, or at least being unable to move.

He rubbed hard at his eyes, as if that would help stop the replaying that was still coming to him, in sleep and at unexpected moments. Fuchs' murmurings, and that small jolt that he had thought was Fuchs trying to rise, but was a bullet that tore into his upper chest by his throat. A smell from something, a passing farm lorry on patrol last week, had brought back the nausea, and the feeling that something was flowing over the back of his hands there in the car.

D. He opened his eyes. The name started with a D. Gebi had said his name: Dal . . . Dov . . .

An old man was watching him from the seat opposite. He made no bones about his scrutiny either, taking the aged's right to pry openly. Felix glared back into the rheumy, light-blue eyes, but the gaze didn't waver. He got off two stops early, thinking of his grandfather's slack face in shock that day, aware that he had killed a man and saved others. And Fuchs, was Felix's last thought stepping down from the tram, trying to fight off the sour feeling that was surrounding him: Fuchs interred in the graveyard at St. Kristoff himself, his family plot not a hundred metres from the Kimmels' own.

Giuliana whispered something. He opened his eyes. He was still here, in bed, and he hadn't slept. She whispered something else in Italian: a table? Set the table? She swallowed slowly, and rubbed her nose and resumed her steady, slow breathing. He closed his eyes again. It was probably worse, he had decided, to try to stop the relentless orbit and roll of thoughts that crowded into his mind yet. They only came back stronger. Lisi might be right, he knew, and some day he'd admit it: go to the shrink before it gets worse. Post-trauma is real.

Soon he heard the first birds, a scooter one street over, and the beginnings of sparse traffic. Then it was bright. He stared at the ceiling: the big day, finally – 9:30 at Strassgangerstrasse, for the investigation report. But had he slept?

FORTY-TWO

FELIX FOUND PARKING ON WETZELSDORFERSTRASSE. HE WAS
20 steps along when he spotted Edelbacher's car parked in sight of
the gate into the Gendarmerie kommando that stood across the
junction ahead, where Strassgangerstrasse started its run along
under Buchkogel and the low hills that formed the western edge of
Graz.

And sure enough, it was Felix's mother sitting in the passenger
seat.

Edelbacher had seen him from a distance in his mirror. It was
his job, after all, Felix thought. Felix mustered a quasi-cheerful nod,
and even a smile, for his mother now getting out onto the footpath.

Edelbacher was in full uniform, as always, and crisp and smart
as the Gendarmes on the pamphlets Felix had been distributing all
that week in the schools. His tan from the holiday looked overdone.
He thought of asking Edelbacher how he had gotten time off for
this. What reason had he given, if any? Moral support for his friend's
son when the tribunal of inquiry released its findings today? Loyal
and fatherly concern, in place of . . . ?

Felix tried harder to stifle the aversion. He kissed his mother on
the cheek, and braced himself for Edelbacher's handshake.

"Felix," said Edelbacher. "A good day ahead of us, no?"

"I hope so."

"Hey, you look good! Those idiots in the Ministry should see
what a Gendarme uniform can do. A crime to change our uniform,
it is. A crime."

Felix's mother reached up to tuck some hair behind his ear.

"Yes," Edelbacher went on. "Today will be a great day, the day those damned cowboys will get their feet burned."

"You're sleeping better?" Felix's mother asked.

"Soon," was all Felix could offer by way of a reply.

"And how is Giuliana?"

"She sends her best. She says it's better she goes to work."

Edelbacher chuckled.

"Now there is the proper attitude," he said. "I like that girl, yes I do. Oh . . . "

Edelbacher had spotted Schroek's Nissan slowing nearby. On it went, with a wave from Schroek, in search of a parking spot.

"Good C.O.?" asked Edelbacher. "Is he? Doing right by you? Supportive?"

"Yes," said Felix.

"Atta boy."

Edelbacher turned to watch Schroek's progress. The slow trolling for a spot continued, with traffic backing up behind the Nissan.

Felix fell into slow step beside his mother.

"You'd like Rhodes," she said.

"When I get the chance," he said.

She squeezed his arm, and began to describe losing her purse in a restaurant in Rhodes, but it being handed back to her later, with nothing missing. The place had been full of tourists, she told Felix, but the drunken ones were few this time.

"You'll try where next?" he said.

"Oh, I don't know," she answered. "Maybe we'll try Cyprus."

"Absolutely," said Edelbacher, who had caught up to them now. "Great place, I hear. Super."

"I hear that Israel can be nice," she went on. "I'm not sure I could relax there."

Edelbacher turned as he strolled to watch the Nissan trolling for a spot further along the street.

"I hope he likes jogging, your Schroek."

Felix stopped and turned to watch.

"We have time," he said. "Let's wait a bit for him. He's not used to Graz parking, I imagine."

"Is anybody?" said Edelbacher.

Felix took in the quick grin and the raised eyebrows. He half-expected a whinny to erupt from the long face. His mother was studying the mass of leaves on the chestnut trees nearby. Edelbacher leaned in close to Felix, and put his hand up to the side of his mouth. Felix caught a whiff of the peppermint breath and the tangy aftershave.

"Take it from me," he whispered. "The SOKO is only good for you. I know. Not to let the cat out of the bag here, but you need have no worries. Are you worried?"

Felix managed a momentary meeting of eyes.

"Not really," he said.

"Look," Edelbacher said. "I'm passing on what I heard the other day."

Felix saw the wink, felt the pat on his upper arm.

"This is a big deal, an internal inquiry," said Edelbacher, apparently for them both. "I mean I hear people saying, well what kind of a police service will this new marriage produce if we have stuff like these things going on? This thing goes deep, oh yes. You may not know it yet, but those Croatian guys, well that gang at least, are, well, I should not say it."

Again he put his hand to his mouth.

"Virus," Felix heard in the whisper. "They are like a virus in all of Europe."

"How are Oma and Opa?" Felix asked his mother.

She smiled.

"You should phone them. They want your autograph. Opa has been buying two newspapers every day."

"They complain there's nothing on the TV news, or the radio, don't they Gretl?"

She nodded.

"They couldn't care less about the other stuff," said Felix's mother. "The goings on with Maier, and the others down at the factories. The police are checking all over."

"All the assembly plants now," said Edelbacher. "Not just the woodlots, but janitors, domestics, cooks even – everything. They were organized, you've got to hand them that."

"Lisi was shocked," Felix's mother went on. "I told her she must have had a soft spot for Maier, to be so shocked. She nearly took a fit on me."

Edelbacher scratched the back of his head and made a short guffaw.

"You know him," he said to Felix then. "That family? Maier?"

"Not really. I know he has a fancy Beemer, and stuff."

"Oh, 'and stuff' indeed," said Edelbacher, and guffawed again.

"But don't bring it up with her yet," Felix's mother said after a few moments. "She's having a time of it with her fellow lately."

She made a face and mouthed something at him, twice. A depressive.

"Well all I can say," said Edelbacher, and paused to stretched his back, "all I can say is that that fellow must have thought everyone was as stupid, or as greedy, as he was. Right, Felix?"

"Hard to say."

Edelbacher came out of his stretch and into a slight stoop. He spoke in a low, conspiratorial tone.

"Honestly. He must have seen a movie, or something, Fuchs. Hey, am I upsetting you saying that, saying his name?"

Felix shook his head. Edelbacher leaned in closer yet.

"Okay. But I mean, think about it. He drives these fellows around for Maier, and even works a bit in the woods himself when he is not feeling lazy. One of his many parts, let's say. But trying to get up the food chain like that . . . ? All the way up to the big boys, the nasty ones? What was he thinking, that he could take their stuff, their diamonds, for heaven's sake, and just go down there on Herrengasse, and sell them to some fine model behind the counter? Hah!"

Edelbacher swayed back for effect, and gave Felix the expert's wide-eyed disdain for such foolishness.

"This is drugs you're dealing with, up and down to Amsterdam and God knows where else. Did he think he could just stand in front of that and get some of it? Like: 'They take drugs up on the autobahn, and they take stolen diamonds back, so I will catch that on the way back. After all, I know these guys! I'll come up with some story that'll get their attention, they'll drop by, and that'll be that. Simple as that: I am a genius!'"

Edelbacher gave him another tap on the arm, and he stood back for Felix to nod his agreement with such superior reasoning and insight.

"I heard the 'I am a genius' part," said Felix's mother. "At least they're clean jokes you are telling there, so?"

"Oh there's no doubt," Edelbacher said, with a short, strangely polite laugh.

Felix spotted Schroek now, far off and walking fast, tugging at his uniform.

"It's just about human nature, Gretl, really. How crazy people can be. Only a policeman knows – and I don't care what they call a policeman after we merge. Gendarme, officer, 'hey you' even – it doesn't matter."

Felix's mother's mobile went off, and she stepped away to answer it.

Edelbacher had spotted Schroek now, too. He let his eyes over to Felix's mother. She was laughing about something in her phone conversation, and a small smile came over his face. Then he turned aside. The hand was up to the side of his mouth again, Felix saw.

"I know about the guys with the tattoos, you know," Edelbacher murmured.

When Felix said nothing, he leaned in again.

"The one up in the woods, the first one? Who came to meet the 'mule'?"

Felix didn't know what to say. He nodded.

"Your opa still says nothing, I hear," Edelbacher said.

"That's how he is."

"But how else would Fuchs have, you know . . . ?"

Edelbacher left Felix to fill in the rest of his question.

"Ask Opa yourself, why don't you?"

Edelbacher gave him a skeptical look.

"I don't," said Felix. "Whatever names he heard, they had pull still, didn't they? Sons, grandsons, cousins – I don't know. But they gave Fuchs enough cred for one episode anyway, didn't they."

He hoped that was enough for Edelbacher.

"Episode," Edelbacher repeated. His frown eased, and he looked up blankly to the treetops. He shook his head once. Then he looked back quickly at Felix.

"Tell you what, Felix. Whatever else, Fuchs did the world a favour, in a way. Right?"

Felix momentarily stared into Edelbacher's squid-like eyes. Two Edelbachers, he thought, neither of them bearable. One the cop with the slides into cop-talk and the casual contempt that Felix wondered if he could ever get used to. The other Edelbacher a kind of a continuing adolescent, cunning enough to try to play a boyish awkwardness as a strength to Greti Kimmel.

"What about the Himmelfarbs?" he asked Edelbacher, before he turned to greet Schroek now almost upon them.

"Of course, of course, Felix," he heard Edelbacher saying hurriedly, in a low voice nearby. "This is the worst, the absolute worst, what happened to that family."

When he glanced over, Edelbacher was shaking his big, long, jaw-dominating horse head slowly and greviously.

"Lisi says good luck," Felix's mother said. "And if it doesn't go well, she'll help you get a job down at the assembly line at Magna."

"Ha ha!"

Edelbacher gave another hearty laugh, and even slapped his knee.

"Oh sisters," he said. "They do you in every time!"

Felix stood and introduced his mother formally to Schroek.

"We can use the side door to HQ, I believe" Edelbacher declared. "The room is right there, the hearing room."

Felix looked toward the Gendarmerie kommando. The Gendarme posted by the barrier had been eyeing them since they'd arrived. Through the entrance Felix saw men jogging around the soccer fields.

A bus passed on Strassgangerstrasse, and in its wake Felix now saw three men were heading up the footpath toward the barrier. The sunglasses and the strange locomotion of one could only be Franzi. A shorter, bearded man was talking animatedly to Speckbauer, swinging a lightly packed briefcase. A lawyer, he thought, or some kind of counsel, with a hand that went continuously up to adjust his rimless glasses.

Franzi began to slow. Felix thought of a battery-operated toy winding down. Speckbauer had noticed him now, too. A truck slowed between them then. When it had passed, the three men were stationary. Speckbauer waved off something that the man with the briefcase was saying, and he leaned in to Franzi.

"Is that them?" Edelbacher asked. "Heading for the SOKO too?"

"I believe it is."

Schroek had been explaining something to Felix's mother about how he'd heard the ranks would be rearranged when the amalgamation would finally start to happen.

Speckbauer was skipping across the street now.

"Well it looks like he's headed over here," said Edelbacher in a voice intended for the others to hear. Meaning he doesn't know what to do, Felix realized.

The man with the briefcase was gesturing to Speckbauer now, and calling out.

"Oberst Schroek?" Edelbacher called out. "We have a situation here, I think."

Schroek had seen what was going on. He finished his sentence about some of the ridiculous names he'd heard being floated for the new national, unified Austrian police.

"An arranged marriage, Frau Kimmel, where both parties must change their names but to what we do not yet know."

"There's a protocol here, I'm pretty sure," said Edelbacher. "An order of the tribunal, in fact?"

Schroek came over to Felix.

"You should not talk to this guy," he murmured, and then cleared his throat. "It's a big no-no."

"Stimmt," said Edelbacher. "This is highly improper. But I hear this Speckbauer is pushy, a law unto himself? I'll have a word in his ear, set him straight, gell?"

Schroek said nothing, but continued to watch Speckbauer's approach.

"Herr Oberstleutnant?" Edelbacher called out. Speckbauer came to a stop and settled a neutral gazer on Edelbacher.

"I am here to accompany Gendarme Kimmel to the tribunal. I am a friend of the family, a colleague of the Gendarme's late father, God rest him."

Speckbauer nodded.

"Oberst Schroek, commander of the post," Edelbacher went on. "And Frau Kimmel."

Speckbauer made a small bow.

"I must say Oberstleutnant, that contact with Gendarme Kimmel here is improper. I believe the interviewers for the Sonderkommission made that clear from the start?"

Speckbauer looked around at the faces, and then at his watch.

"That'll shortly be history," he said. "So why not say I am, say, twenty minutes early with the findings. There'll be no harm done."

"Nevertheless," said Edelbacher,

"The decisions have been made," said Speckbauer.

"It was a directive, Herr Oberstleutnant," said Edelbacher.

Speckbauer looked over at Schroek.

"Would that directive prevent me from telling the Oberst here that his Gendarme has helped to do good police work?"

"We know that already, I believe," said Schroek.

Speckbauer's eyes slipped out of focus. Felix had the notion that he might be counting to 10.

"The Oberstleutnant has a point, I believe," Felix said.

Edelbacher and Schroek both changed feet at the same time. Felix did not return his mother's gaze.

"Felix?" said Edelbacher slowly.

Felix looked to Schroek who gave him a faint nod.

Felix heard Edelbacher's aggrieved tone barely held to a murmur that soon faded in the noise of the traffic behind as he and Speckbauer strolled back down the footpath.

"Who exactly is that big depp?" Speckbauer asked. "So full of himself?"

"He worked with my dad."

"Huh. I just came to tell you that you don't need to worry."

"The SOKO, you mean?"

"What else are we here for?"

Felix decided not to ask how Speckbauer could know that.

"Is anyone keeping you in the know about this stuff?" Speckbauer asked then. "Fuchs, his drug paraphernalia, for example?"

"I heard, all right."

"So it's possible – scheisse, it's likely – he was out of it, the night he went to Himmelfarbs. A fried brain."

"That doesn't help them," said Felix. "Does it?"

Speckbauer gave him a hard look.

"You think you're the only one wakes up thinking about them?"

Felix looked back at Schroek and Edelbacher.

"You go over to Gebhart's still?" Speckbauer asked.

"A couple of times a week."

"When's he coming back? The kidney . . . ?"

"It'll take time. He's not a moaner. But I don't have to worry about his wife taking a plank to me anymore."

"Ach so," said Speckbauer. He rubbed at the back of his neck as though searching for a new topic to go to.

"I mean what can you do about this whole thing," he said in a low voice. "Say it was bad luck? Or something like, you never know what a druggie will do? Or that police science goes only so far?"

Felix looked across toward the HQ. Franzi was standing motionless there, his arms hanging loosely by his side. The man with the briefcase was pacing in a short tight pattern, talking into his cell.

"So there," said Speckbauer. "Some stuff in this job, you couldn't even make it up."

"Franzi is still operational?" Felix asked.

"Franzi? Was he ever? Even before? I told him I'd been thinking of putting wheels on his shoes, like those kids you see."

And that exhausted that topic. Edelbacher was tapping at his watch and closing one eye for Felix's benefit. Felix nodded at him.

"Your mother okay?"

"She is now," said Felix. "But she freaked."

"And the lady . . . "

Giuliana he meant, Felix realized.

"It's hard to say. But we'll see."

"Ah. She wants you out of harm's way, let me guess. Back to Uni? 'Grow up'?'

"You seem to have some experience there."

"Maybe I do. But it'll come good for you, no?"

"You decide," said Felix. "It's hard to bounce back from stuff like, 'Next time you'll be the one shot, idiot.'"

"Ouch," said Speckbauer. "Does she say it in Italian? The hands going like a kung fu movie?"

Felix gave him a glance and then returned to studying Franzi. He was like a statue. The man on the phone seemed to buzz around him.

"Why did you park your car off road there that day?" Speckbauer asked. "In the woods?"

"Well I had a notion that you had some way of telling where the car was. Your gizmos in the trunk of that Passat. The GPS?"

"Did you find it?"

"Find what?"

"I get the point," said Speckbauer.

"You're forgetting that I was on your desk as a 'strange coincidence,' are you?"

"Nothing personal," said Speckbauer. "I have a job to do."

"So you assumed the worst."

"There's no polite way to say this," said Speckbauer, quietly. "But if your father had told anyone what he'd been doing, it would have been a hell of a lot different. He had copped on to something."

"You make it sound like a plot."

"You did yourself no favour by me when you ditched your car in the woods, you know. How do you think that looked to us?"

"I was just going to talk to my grandfather. I had to find out for myself first."

"Like father, like son, you go your own way first?"

"Do you think my grandfather would have talked to anyone else? You don't know him then. I brought Gebi up as witness. Isn't that enough?"

"Come on. You know by now there's nothing on your father."

"There was always a question though, in your mind."

"An accident it stays. That logging truck had nothing to do with Fuchs, or Maier. Or any of that."

Schroek was now signalling to Felix. Speckbauer pretended not to notice, but Felix turned and began walking toward the entrance to the Gendarmerie kommando.

"And you know they'd found the woman that same evening?" asked Speckbauer. "Stephi Giesl, the barmaid from the pub in Weiz, and her car? It was up at that dumpy house of Fuchs. That's how cold-blooded those guys are. And she thought she was going for a good time. Whether Fuchs knew what Dravnic had done to her or not, he surely knew he was a goner after he drove the guy up to your grandfather's. You're lucky he didn't go right through you when he tried to make his break."

"It felt like he did, I tell you."

"He saved your arsch. He'd have thrown you, thrown anyone, to that guy – even your grandfather, with that bullshit he tried. 'Where are my diamonds?' were the first words out of the guy's mouth, according to what I was heard. Is that true?"

"Yes," said Felix. "My opa thought it was a joke. But then he saw the gun, and the look on Fuchs' face."

"But he didn't screw around when he put his sights on that Dravnic, did he," said Speckbauer. "One shot. And the guy was even on the move, I heard."

Their conversation ebbed as an old woman with a small dog went by them.

"How is the old boy anyway?" Speckbauer asked then.

"They kept him overnight, for blood pressure. They expected him to be in shock or something, traumatized. He seems to be fine though. He said these doctors were annoying, standing around asking him stupid questions. My mother's been up a few times, me too. Putting stuff together for him."

"He's moved already?"

"Yes. He's famous now. 'The marksman' they call him. A lot of people talk to him about it. He says it drives him crazy. But I doubt it."

From across the street, the man with the briefcase was waving. Speckbauer watched him as though he were studying a new life form.

"You'd think it was a fire or something," he murmured.

"You know what they're going to say in there, don't you."

"The SOKO? Maybe. But it's not the end of the world."

"It doesn't bother you?"

"Should it? Did I do something wrong? If you want to know what bothers me, is that I'm missing bits of this whole thing. I just can't quite wrap up how this went from a layabout like Fuchs and his pissy little gschäftl, to multiple murders. It starts with him driving illegals up to work in the woods for that other guy . . ."

"Maier."

"Right – if it was just that, or some petty crap around his drug hobby, then he could have kept going forever and probably never been caught."

Felix nodded. Speckbauer went on in a slow, speculative tone.

"Fuchs," he said. "Big plan, small brain. There he is in the woods, and those old stories when your grandfather and Hartmann get together, those stories going around in his fat head. So it starts in the woods. And one day he thinks: here are these illegals there breaking their backs for Maier. No doubt some of them have enough words to talk to him. He gets talking. He finds out one or more of them 'know people' back home, and that there are already networks and traffic coming through the area – or near enough."

"What you've been trying to nail down," said Felix.

"And what your father might have found out something about too. But these guys in the woods want to make some serious money. Who wouldn't? And Fuchs, he thinks: they're the same people in the old stories of smuggling he hears from your grandfather or Hartmann. Everyone's on the take down there now, so why not get a piece of the action. Yes, a mastermind at work."

"You know, we didn't know anything about that stuff," said Felix. "What my grandfather did in the schleiche, or going in and out of those DP camps. We heard stories about 'the scarce times.' But him running up and down into Yugoslavia then, we hadn't a clue. It must have been dangerous."

"Christ yes," said Speckbauer. "Any DPs they sent back to Tito, he pretty well shot them all. To Tito, they were all Ustaschi, or Danube Germans, not real refugees or DPs. But your grandfather had contacts, a good bit of the language. And don't kid yourself, there was money in it for him back then. I mean those guys weren't saints, you know. It wasn't about 'the cause,' I'll bet. Not then."

"I don't know. Whatever he did, it was a cause for him, I'd say."

"What? Nazi?"

"Maybe," said Felix. "But probably not just that. He was helping people on his wife's side, on their family's side. To him they were Austrians, not Slovenians – or they should be. Plus they hated communism too."

Speckbauer returned to studying the gestures that the small man with the briefcase was making now. He made no effort to show he got the hint, even when the man began waving his watch arm at him.

"History biting us in the arsch," he said.

"Look," said Felix. "We'd better go."

"Yeah," said Speckbauer. "The bill arrives eventually. It always does. But I wish I'd had the full meal before the bill, that's all."

"The SOKO," said Felix.

"Who cares about that crap," said Speckbauer. "I probably know more than the team they put on it for the inquiry. But there are parts we'll never get to."

"I don't get what you mean."

"You don't?" said Speckbauer. "Okay, ready? We. Don't. Really. Know."

"You mean that?"

"I do."

"This is how some cases end? Like nowhere?"

"Well I don't know how Fuchs got them to go up into the forest that night. But I have my ideas."

"Fuchs had had a con going, right?"

"Are you asking me?"

"Okay, I'm asking you."

"Natürlich he had some scheme, Fuchs. But this Dravnic guy was no fool. I mean he lived the life down in Croatia. He'd done his share of that hellhound work they do to one another there. Seems to run in the family there. His own grandfather . . . ?"

Speckbauer said something under his breath that contained the word *lawyer* and he made a slow wave back to the man with the briefcase.

"As for me," he said. "Me, I think Fuchs wanted to be part of something big. Maybe he put an offer to them. Who knows – move hot cars down from Germany, credit cards, counterfeit, women, drugs. I mean, at the very least, Fuchs can drive. Let's say Fuchs is bragging. That he knows a lot about Dravnic and his people, and what they do. So Dravnic plays along, and says they'll do a try. But Fuchs wants to play his own game. And when those two don't show up back in wherever, and Dravnic sends word, well Fuchs throws up his hands, and says he hasn't a clue what's going on. When he last saw them they had all their fingers and toes. et cetera, et cetera."

"They believed him?" Felix asked. "I can't see that."

"Did it matter whether they did or not? Whether they believed him or not, those guys want to protect their operation – and their rep too. So whether he's screwing them around or not, this Fuchs character knows a bit too much about them by now anyway."

"But they had taken a pretty big chance on him," said Felix.

"Had they really?" said Speckbauer. "They were keeping a tight hold on this. That's why the other one, the runner, came to meet the mule coming down from Holland. Let's say he was told to offer Fuchs some kind of a side deal when he showed. That was just to test his loyalty. But they also wanted to see how much Fuchs might have found out about them too."

"You think they only planned to run one operation this way?"

"An experiment, probably, yes. Maybe they had found out about Fuchs' drug hobby. That was enough. Or maybe they didn't care. My bet is they never trusted him, but they knew right away when he contacted them, name-dropping from what he'd heard from the old guys, well, they knew they'd probably have to do something about him."

"You think Fuchs realized any of this?"

"Well who was conning who, that night? I don't know. I just don't. Maybe Fuchs was just greedy. Me, I say his brain was fried. But it looks like we all underestimated him that night anyway."

Speckbauer stopped strolling. He faced Felix directly.

"So there's Fuchs that night, in my mind. He just steps out of the car, leans over the roof – maybe with a flashlight to sight the guy – surprise. Poof: Mr. Diamond, the mule, gets one in the head before you know it. Then he has the second guy down, the runner, in no time. With your grandfather's Luger."

"Not his," Felix felt obliged to say. "He got it from someone's brother years ago, a war thing."

"But so very well taken care of," Speckbauer went on. "In fine condition."

"He'd forgotten about it being in the house. Fuchs just went about taking stuff."

Speckbauer's skeptical expression left his face more slowly than it had come.

"There's a charge on him for that, I know," he said. "But they'll slap that away when it comes up. On account of his, what do you want to call it, his marksmanship."

"I don't think he cares," said Felix.

Edelbacher and Felix's mother, and Schroek, had reached the entrance to the Gendarmerie kommando.

"Look," said Speckbauer. "Time's up. You're in line for a pat on the head."

"What about you and Franzi?"

"Macht nichts," he said. "Who cares. It's probably me they want, I would say."

With that he shrugged, and turned back to the others. Felix watched him for a few moments. Then he nodded at Franzi. He received no gesture in return. There was a cursory, tight-lipped nod from the man with the briefcase who was waiting for Speckbauer.

"Really," he heard Edelbacher say then, beside him. "Those guys."

Felix's mother and Schroek continued talking with deceptive earnestness about some home-made remedy for arthritis one could find up in the mountains.

Edelbacher slipped over to walk beside him.

"Felix, you've got to learn," he said. "There are rules, you know, important rules."

"Thanks," Felix said, and did nothing to conceal the acid tone. "But my father told me that many times in the past. So I know."

Felix imagined little shockwaves rippling out from his sarcasm. He didn't care that his mother had picked up on it too.

The Gendarme at the barrier was already waiting for them, but before presenting his photocard, Felix glanced back. Franzi still looked like a robot awaiting a push. The man with the briefcase was making some emphatic point to Speckbauer.

It might have had something to do with Speckbauer's vacant gaze, Felix thought. It seemed to be on something faraway, aimed perhaps at the trees so sharply defined now by the July morning's sunshine.

Felix remembered then that the weather was forecast to continue as it had for several days now, to boil the pavements here in Graz, as the saying went, and also glare down on the rest of a large area that stretched far to the south, and to the east.

GLOSSARY

Austrian German and Basic Facts about the Gendarmerie

Austrian German has its own rich store of words and expressions, of slang and idiom and accent. Regional variations are diverse. It is common to find expressions – and even accents – that are not used or understood in a neighbouring province.

The terms below are to be found in Steiermark, more often in rural areas. Part of their charm and power resides in the accent and tone in which they are uttered. As much as native Styrians may sometimes wryly deprecate their "bellen," (that characteristic baying intonation in the Styrian accent), they readily use it, and enjoy it. It may be worth noting that this same "bellen" can be heard inflecting the speech of that former Grazer and son of the former police chief of that city, Arnold Schwarzenegger.

A note on capitalization: nouns in German are capitalized, even when they are not proper nouns. To avoid confusion among readers not familiar with German, and to avoid place names being mistaken for simple nouns, only proper nouns are capitalized in the text in the story.

Abendessen: — Supper

Aber gut: — "Well, fine" or "OK." Literally "but good."

Ach so: — "Well, yes" or "Ach so wie so" – "That's how life/it goes."

Alm: — Mountains

Apfelfest: — Apple festival where visitors enjoy locally made apple cider.

Arbeiter: — Manual worker

Arsch: — Arse

Arschloch: — Arsehole

Ausländer: — A person from outside the country: negative connotation. If a foreigner's nationality is known, Austrians will use it, e.g., *Engländer.*

Bäckerei: — Bakery

Banhof: — Train station. Hauptbanhof: main station

Bauch: — Stomach

Benzin: — Gasoline, petrol

Besoffen: — Drunk

Bisschen: — A little, some

Bist närrisch: — Short form of: "Bis du narisch?! "Are you crazy?"

Blauer: — Right-wing, often secret admirers of fascism; literally "a blue one"

Blumen: — Flowers

Blöd(e): — Silly, even stupid

Bleib ruhig: — Stay quiet

Brodl: — Stomach belly (dialect)

Brauners: — Brownshirts, i.e., Nazis (often linked to "blauers")

Bruderschaft: — Brotherhood

Brummschädel: — Thick head from hangover

Bullen: — Slang for Gendarmerie or police generally; literally "bull"

Bundespolizei: — The state police force in Austria; called "Die Polizei" by the public, usually "BP" by members of the Gendarmerie

Burli (also Burschi): — Boy; fella; mate. A term of fondness between men; sometimes ironic, can be insulting

Depp: — Idiot

Detschen: — A not-too-hard slap across the face or head; "a cuff on the ear" (see Watschen)

Dodel: — Fool, but not malicious

Donauschwaben: — Ethnic Germans in Swabian region by upper River Danube

Dorf: — Village, small town

Dumkopf: — "Dumb-head"

Dickschädel: — "Thick-head"

Echte(s): — Real, genuine

Ferlangerten: — A favoured coffee in Austria

Fetzn: — Rag, piece of cloth

Fetznschädl: — Fool; literally rag-head

Feuerwehr: — Fire brigade

Fiakers: — Fixer, schemer

Föhn: — A strong, short-lived warm wind in winter; said to drive people mad

Frisch: — Literally fresh, but means new, original

Galerie: — A series of mugshots, meaning criminals (slang)

Gauner: — Petty criminal, "a loser"

Gasse: — A lane, or small street (see Weg)

Gasthaus: — Hotel or "guest house"

Geburstag: — Birthday

Geh'ma jetzt: — Here we go

Geh scheissen: — Go and shit

Geh weg: — "Get outta here"

Gell: — Unique Austrian idiom. Corresponds with: "right?"; "OK?"; "huh?"; "eh?"

Gendarmerie: — See summary of Austrian Gendarmerie at the end of this glossary

Genau: — "Just so"

Genug: — Enough

Gerade aus: — Straight ahead

Glacetrizz: — A schemer, on the shady side

Glockl: — Smaller glass of beer (see Schweigel)

Glotze: — "Die Glotze" – "The (idiot) box," i.e., TV

Gösser: — Austrian beer brand

Gott: — God

Gott sei dank: — "Thank God"

Grossen braunen: — A favoured coffee in Austria

Grüss Gott: — Hello, literally "Greet God"; often shortened to "Grüss"

Gschäftl: — A shady plan, a "con"

Gschaftlhuber: — A schemer

Gscherter: — A rural Styrian; literally "shirt"

Gut/gute/gutes: — Good

Hackn: — Plan, scheme

Halt die Pappn: — Shut up (dialect)

Handi: — A personal mobile/cell phone

Hässlich: — Ugly, unpleasant

Hauptbanhof: — Principal train station

Hauptplaz: — Main square of a town

Hausfrau: — Housewife

Heast Gschissena!: — "Well hello shit!" i.e., an unpleasant surprise

Heimat: — One's homeland. This does not necessarily correspond to the modern state, but to one's native area, or province.

Herrlich: — Lovely

Herz: — Heart

Heurigen: — An evening of wine, food, talk, visiting several gasthauses

Hochschule: — Secondary school/High school

Hof: — A house; can be a large building

Holtzpyjama: — Being killed (slang). Literally "wooden pyjamas" i.e., coffin

Hosen: — Trousers

Huber-Bauer: — Idiom for "the farmer type," "rednecks"

Hursohn: — Son of a bitch

Jäger: — A hunter

Jausen: — A light meal, often buffet style, consisting of meat, buns, cheese and a variety of add-ons

Jetzt: — Now, immediately

Junge: — Lad

Kachelofen: — Traditional masonry stove or fireplace, usually tiled, with small aperture; designed to radiate heat from its masonry mass

Kasperl: — Silly fellow (affectionate)

KD: — Kriminaldienst (see Kripo). These plainclothes Gendarmes work out of the provincial Gendarmerie HQ

Kasperl and Pezi: — Much loved and longstanding mainstays on Austrian children's TV

Kieberer: — Slang for police officer

Kleine: — Short for *Kleine Zeitung*, popular tabloid from Graz (klein/e: small)

Klo: — Toilet; short for wasser-kloset

Klopfer: — Button Du hast einen Klopfer – "You're losing it" (slang)

Klug: — Intelligent

Konditorei: — Restaurant

Kopf: — Head

Krank: — Ill

Krebs: — Cancer

Kripo: — A term used between Gendarmes for both Kriminal Polizei (police staff) and Kriminalabteilung (criminal department)

Krot: — Frog

Krügl: — A glass of beer

Kruzitürken: — A swear word suggesting what an imaginary combination of the Christian cross with the Muslim Turks would be. The Ottoman Empire long had designs on Styria, and Austria generally.

Lagers: — Camps, enclosures

Laibach: — The Austrian name for Lyubliana, capital of Slovenia. Slovenia was part of Austria, or the Austrian Empire, until the end of WWII.

Lass: — Leave (it), let it be

Leberkäse: — Meatloaf of liver, pork, and bacon

Leberknödel suppe: — Soup or broth containing liver and dumplings

Liebchen: — Sweetheart

Loden: — Woollen jackets and coats, traditional; usually green

Luder: — A trickster, mischievous

Ludeln: — To pee

Machs du: — Do you want . . .

Mädchen: — Maiden; young lady

Magenbitter: — A liquid tonic for a bilious stomach

Mahlzeit: — Enjoy (food)

Maibaumaufstellen: — A Spring festival where men of the village raise a maypole that is used as the focus for an outdoor party and meal

Mann: — Husband, also "one," i.e., a person

Mannerschnitte: — Chocolate-filled wafer biscuits

Marburg: — The German name for Mariabor, Slovenia

Marterl: — A roadside shrine of varying size and materials. Marterls were usually erected at sites of accidents. Taferls, their counterparts, are usually carved wooden statues depicting Mary, and are often found at crossroads in rural areas. They are characteristically mounted on wooden poles, under a "roof."

Matura: — High school diploma on graduation

Mutti: — Mother

National service: — Mandatory period of national service, currently eight months. Exemptions are allowed for objectors; they work as social workers or ambulance drivers for their service.

Närrisch: — Foolish, crazy

Natürlich: — Naturally, of course

Nicht war: — Is that not so?

Niemand: — Nobody

"Null Komma Josef": — See "Zero Point Joe"

Oestis: — Easterners, i.e., from Eastern Europe

Oetzi: — An ancient man found preserved in the Alps in 1991

Offenegg: — A hill

Olta!: — "Yikes!"

Oma: — Grandmother ("granny")

Opa: — Grandfather ("granddad")

Pallawatch: — (Slang) a screw-up

Pas auf: — Go away. Said with emphasis; it is hostile – get lost.

Prima: — Good, well done

Puntigamer: — A brand of beer popular in Styria, named after a suburb of Graz

Platz: — A (town, village, city) square – Hauplatz: main square

Prolete: — Boorish

Posten: (post) — Gendarmerie station

Radl: — Bicycling

Randsteinpflanze: — Slang for a prostitute. Literally "a sidewalk flower"

Rathaus: — Town hall

Raus: — "Let's go"

Reiskocher: — Japanese car (slang). Literally "rice cooker"

Riegel: — Troll (slang). Literally "a lock"

Rossegger, Peter: — Rossegger, a Styrian, was nativist poet and writer who collected local lore and observations of rural Steiermark in the 19th century

Rote: — "Red." Used to describe left wingers; also ironic use (see Sozi)

Rotkopf: — "Redhead"

Ruhig: — Quiet. "Bleib ruhig" – "Be quiet"

Schandi: — Slang for Gendarmerie

Schass: — Fart (slang)

Scheisse: — Shit

Schleiche: — Black market

Schmutzig: — Sooty, also implies embers

Schnapps: — Spirits (alcohol)

Schnappsen: — card game

Schatzi: — Sweetheart. Literally "little cat"

Schnabel: — Nose (dialect)

Schau: — "Look"

Schön: — Lovely

Schrecklich: — Terrible

Schule: — School

Schwartz: — Literally "black"; used ironically to refer to supporters of the right-wing Freedom Party; suggests "conservatives" are in fact fascists

Schwartzarbeiters: — Workers in the underground economy, without legal status

Schweigel: — Larger glass of beer (see glockel)

Schweinerei: — Pig-like; used to express disapproval of situation, place

Semmel: — A bun (baked bread)

Servus: — Greeting – "hello"

Schwuchtel: — Homosexual (slang)

Shreklich: — Terrible

So geht's: — So it goes – "That's the way of the world"

Sonderkommission: — Police investigation, a "SOKO" is called for a case that goes badly

"Sozi": — A supporter of Austria's Social Democratic Party (see "Rote")

Spatzieren: — Going out, travelling about

Speck: — Home-cured bacon, ham

Stadleute: — City people

Stadt: — City

Stanzen: — Fired, but slang for murdered

Strafregister: — Fingerprint/Police file

Strassgänger: — Strassgänger strasse: Styrian Gendarmerie HQ, in Graz West

Steiermark: — Styria

Stübe: — A pub

Teufel: — The devil

Tischlerei: — Carpenter or joiner's shop; also furniture shop

Tragisch: — Tragic

Trottel: — A fool, but a conniving and malicious one

Tschuschen: — A highly derogatory term for peoples of the former Yugoslavia

Unglucklich: — Unlucky

Ungerade: — Unusual

Vati: — Short form of Vater – father

Verlauer: — Outspoken, indiscreet

Verrückt: — Crazy

Verstehst: — Short form of *Verstanden sie* – Do you understand? i.e., "Get it?"

Verstunkene: — Stinky, lousy

Vielleicht: — Perhaps

Volksdeutsch(en): — Ethnic Germans who had settled in other parts of Europe, often for generations. Most became refugees after WWII.

Wald: — Forest

Watschen: — Slap delivered with back of the hand ("backhander") (see Detschen)

Weg: — Literally "a way." Weg is usually a path, paved or unpaved

Wehrdienst: — National military service (compulsory)

Wilkommen: — Welcome

Weib(i): — Derogatory term for wife – shrewish

Wipsi: — Groggy, tipsy, giddy

Wirt: — Host/waiter

Wissenchaft: — Organized knowledge, e.g., science

Wunderbar: — Wonderful

Wunderschön: — Truly lovely

Wurst: — Sausage

Zahlen: — Bill

Zentrum: — The centre of town

Zero Point Joe: — Viennese slang equivalent to US/Canadian "diddly squat" or UK "bugger all," i.e., nothing. It is even less than nothing, because it implies an ironic or cynical realization. This term originated in Vienna during the years of Allied occupation after WWII. Zero Point Joe, a beer made in Vienna, contains no alcohol.

Zigeune: — Derogatory slang for Roma/Gypsies

Zoll: — Customs and border post

The Austrian Gendarmerie originated over 150 years ago as a locally recruited militia to police Austria's countryside and towns. Its counterpart, the Bundespolizei – "Polizei" – police cities and key areas around the country. Though the Gendarmerie has lost most of its original military character and has long been under the sole command of the Interior Ministry, it still retains military ranks, along with aspects of its training and some of its weaponry and facilities.

Each Austrian province has its own provincial Gendarmerie command under the command of its own Gendarmerie Brigadier. These Brigadiers answer to the Minister of the Interior. The *Landesgendarmeriekommando* (provincial HQ) for Styria is on Strassgangerstrasse, in Wetzelsdorf, a western suburb of Graz, adjacent to the army's provincial headquarters.

In many respects the Gendarmerie and Polizei reflect a city/country divide in Austria. Gendarmes are known to be more informal than their state police counterparts, and their appearance in their green and grey uniforms and traditional *tellerkappe* (beret) is a common sight in rural Austria. Officers of any rank in the Gendarmerie go by the informal *Du* and their colleague's Christian name. The Polizei use the formal *Sie* along with their ranks, even in day-to-day conversation.

Both police forces concede that the Gendarmerie is looked down upon by the Polizei. Gendarmes will point out that their pay does not compare well to the other police service. The Polizei may offer in return that the Gendarmerie will "take anyone," and may even mention how in former times a reward was given for the recruitment of a new Gendarme. Though they are not taken as seriously as their city counterparts, the Gendarmerie record is acknowledged to be one of very effective policing. Their specialist units in mountain rescue and counterterrorism are highly regarded internationally.

Ranking, status and promotion in the Gendarmerie are unusual. On completing their training and duty exam (*Dienstprüfung*), recruits are given the junior rank of Inspektor but they are on probation for no less than six years. Then an Inspektor becomes a "Pragmatisierte" Gendarme – holder of a tenured job. Promotion is then automatic after given years of service, to Revierinspektor (district inspector). The next rank, Bezirkinspektor, however, requires a training course of eight months in Vienna. Ranks beyond that require that the candidate has a Matura, and also undergoes training for each successive post of more responsibility.

With changes to institutional structures all over the EU, perhaps it was only a matter of time before the Ministry of the Interior considered that amalgamation of the two police forces was necessary. Many officers in both services were not happy about this. There was considerable conflict in a trial run of some Gendarmerie and Polizei departments in Vienna recently. Indeed, the union was widely regarded as so improbable that the former Interior Minister dismissed the idea as "about as likely as the Catholics joining the Protestants." The amalgamation has nonetheless gone ahead, backed by a court decision, even though the process is accompanied by a confusion that is very uncharacteristic of Austrians. Skepticism and suspicion remain.